"[...]
F[...]
a[...]
memorable [...]"
—*Harlequin Junkie*

"*Fatal Reckoning* is the perfect blending of scandals, lies, detective skills, and deep passionate romance."
—*The Dixon Independent Voice*

"[*Fatal Threat*] has all the right elements to keep the reader turning pages, whether engaged in the seamy details of the case or the steamy elements of Sam's relationship with her hot green-eyed husband."
—*BookPage*

"Marie Force is an awesome storyteller and her Fatal series is one that will just suck you right in. It doesn't matter if you start at the first book or the latest, each has a unique story that you can enjoy."
—*Night Owl Reviews* (Top Pick)

"This novel is *The O.C.* does D.C., and you just can't get enough."
—*RT Book Reviews* on *Fatal Affair*

"Marie Force always seems to keep this series on the pulse of the current political and social climate. Her writing and these characters make it impossible to put the book down until the very end."
—*Cocktails and Books*

"The suspense is thick, the passion between Nick and Sam just keeps getting hotter and hotter."
—*Guilty Pleasures Book Reviews* on *Fatal Deception*

Praise for Marie Force

Poignant. Heartbreaking. Redemptive. Inspiring.
of Reckoning

**The Fatal Series
by *New York Times* bestselling author
Marie Force**

Suggested reading order

One Night with You (the Fatal Series prequel novella)

Fatal Affair

Fatal Justice

Fatal Consequences

Fatal Destiny

Fatal Flaw

Fatal Deception

Fatal Mistake

Fatal Jeopardy

Fatal Scandal

Fatal Frenzy

Fatal Identity

Fatal Threat

Fatal Chaos

Fatal Invasion

Fatal Reckoning

Fatal Accusation

MARIE FORCE

Fatal ACCUSATION

HQN™

ISBN-13: 978-1-335-04151-7

Fatal Accusation

Copyright © 2019 by HTJB, Inc.

Fatal
ACCUSATION

CHAPTER ONE

NICK HAD LOOKED forward to this evening all week. Their friends Harry and Lilia had rescheduled the dinner party so Nick and his wife, Sam, could attend. He had no doubt their family had been heavily on the minds of the people who loved them since the sudden death of Sam's beloved father. Everyone was concerned about her and how she was holding up after losing one of the most important people in her life. Nick had found himself watching over her even more closely than usual, looking for signs of trouble.

She'd been remarkably composed since she helped solve the four-year-old mystery of who had shot her father and left him a quadriplegic. Too composed, if you asked him. Other than one breakdown in the immediate aftermath of closing the case, she'd held it together as the media went wild over the story of the Metro Police Department deputy chief who'd kept vital information about the shooting of Skip Holland to himself while pretending to be a friend to Skip and his family.

There'd been round-the-clock coverage of the gambling ring and the involvement of the longtime city councilman, Roy Gallagher, and his associates, Mick Santoro and Dermott Ryan, as well as the lengths they'd gone to in order to protect their illegal enterprise. Other prominent city residents and political players had been caught up in the dragnet of arrests related to the gambling operation. The arrests were ongoing a week later. People were shocked by the news that Skip's shooting was connected to the murder of his first partner, Steven Coyne, whose case had gone cold in the ensuing decades.

And through it all, Sam had kept her chin up and her eyes on the ultimate prize of seeing the men who'd shortened her father's life—and Steven's—brought to justice.

Nick had never been prouder of the woman he'd married than he'd been in the last two weeks. Sitting beside his wife at Lilia's beautifully appointed dining room table, with Sam's hand tucked into his as they chatted with their closest friends, Nick was filled with a sense of foreboding, a fear that her composure couldn't possibly last. Eventually she would break, and he could only hope he'd be close by when she did.

"It's really not funny," Lilia was saying when Nick tuned back into the spirited conversation. "And we do *not* need to tell that story."

"It *is* funny," his friend Dr. Harry Flynn replied, "and we absolutely *do* need to tell it."

Lilia Van Nostrand, Sam's chief of staff at the White House, had met Nick's longtime friend Harry through them, and they were madly in love. That was obvious to anyone who knew them. On the recent trip Harry had taken with Nick to Europe, Harry had confided that he planned to marry Lilia as soon as he possibly could.

Harry's beloved dropped her head into her hands, resigned to telling the story despite her objections.

"We were in Chincoteague," Harry said, grinning gleefully, "at a bed-and-breakfast. Lilia woke up early and went down to get coffee wearing only her robe."

"I figured it was safe at six in the morning." Her face

had gone bright red with embarrassment. "Who else is going to be up at that ungodly hour?"

"Did you or did you not have your pearls on too?" Sam asked.

Lilia shot her an offended look. "Of course I did. I'm not a savage."

Everyone at the table lost it laughing.

While the others focused on Lilia, Nick found himself watching Harry. The way his friend looked at Lilia had to be the way Nick gazed at Sam, as if he'd found the other half of his soul. There was, Nick thought, nothing like knowing for certain you were exactly and finally where you belonged, with the person you were meant to find since the day you took your first breath. Nick couldn't be happier that Harry had found his own Sam.

"Anyway," Harry continued. "There she is in the breakfast room of the B and B in nothing more than a sexy robe—and the pearls, of course—when the senate majority leader walks in wearing only his boxers."

Derek Kavanaugh, deputy chief of staff to President Nelson, choked on his wine. *"No way."*

"Yes, way." Lilia's blush overtook her entire face. "And he started talking to me as if he wasn't standing there in nothing more than his underwear."

"Did he know who you were?" Nick's lawyer friend Andy Simone asked.

"Yes! He asked me how Mrs. Cappuano is doing since she lost her dad and if I think the vice president is going to run in the next election."

Andy's wife, Elsa, covered her mouth with her hand, her eyes gone wide with laughter. "Oh my God."

"See?" Harry said gleefully. "Funny, right?"

"This may be the funniest thing that's ever happened to anyone," Sam said, earning a glare from Lilia.

"No, babe, your Brazilian wax story is better," Nick said.

"Uh," Chief Medical Examiner Dr. Lindsey McNamara said. "I think we need to hear that."

Her fiancé, Terry O'Connor, who was also Nick's chief of staff, groaned. "Is there no decorum at this dinner party?"

"We most definitely do *not* need to hear that," Detective Freddie Cruz said. "In fact, if that story is getting told, I'm out."

"Relax," Sam said to her partner. "Nick would never tell that story because he lives in fear of my rusty steak knife."

Nick nodded, keeping his expression grave. "Mortal fear."

"Back to the majority leader and his underwear," Sam said, rolling her hand. "What happened next?"

"He told me I was a very pretty girl and asked if I was seeing anyone."

"Come on," Freddie's wife, Elin, said. "Isn't he like ninety?"

"He's eighty-two," Lilia said. "And thinks he's still got game."

Harry sat back, grinning widely. "You haven't heard the best part yet."

"It gets *better*?" Sam asked.

"Oh yeah," Harry said. "Tell them, babe."

Lilia dropped her face into her hands again. "I *can't*."

"Allow me, then," Harry said. "The leader leaned in and said, 'I'm here by myself too, and if you want to join me in my room, I could show you a good time.' And then he added, 'I got some of them little blue pills.'"

A collective groan came from the group.

"And he winked," Lilia said, "in case I didn't get the message."

"He did not!" Lindsey said.

"Oh yes, he did," Harry confirmed.

"What did you say?" Sam asked, wiping away laughter tears.

Lilia raised her head from her hands, her face blazing with color. "I told him I was with my boyfriend, and he probably wouldn't appreciate me joining the leader in his room. And then I leaned in and said, 'My boyfriend doesn't need any pills, if you know what I mean.'"

"Stop it!" Sam said. "I can't picture you saying that!"

"She did," Harry proudly confirmed. "My little hellcat."

Lilia sat up straighter and squared her shoulders. "I am *not* a hellcat."

"Oh yes, you are," Harry said.

"I'm not one to take sides." Derek blotted tears from his eyes. "But I gotta agree with my boy Harry. That story needed to be told."

"The first mistake I made was telling *him* about it," Lilia said.

"Baby, there is no way you could've kept that from me. I took one look at you when you came back with the coffee, and I knew something big had happened. Your color was *high*, like it is now."

Lilia placed her hands over her flaming cheeks. "I hate how that happens."

Harry waggled his brows at her. "But it's so damned cute."

"Is that our cue to get out?" Nick hoped the evening wasn't going to end yet. It had taken an act of God to get everyone there, not to mention the prep work the Secret Service had done ahead of time to get him there.

"Absolutely not." Lilia shot a stern look at Harry that only made his smile bigger. "We haven't even had dessert yet."

"About the Brazilian story," Lindsey said over tiramisu.

"No, no and *no*," Sam said.

"What she said," Freddie added. "*Hell* no."

Nick was about to say something that would get him in big trouble with his beloved when his phone and the phones of several others started ringing. "What the hell?" He pulled his phone from his pants pocket and noted the number of his communications director Trevor Donnolly.

Nick released Sam's hand, excused himself and stood to take the call away from the table. "What's up, Trev?"

"Sorry to interrupt your evening, Mr. Vice President, but a story just broke online that I thought you should be made aware of."

"What fresh hell has befallen us now?"

"A story has gone live online claiming a staffer had an affair with President Nelson during the most recent campaign and that it lasted into the new administration. Apparently, the woman has recently given birth to a child that may or may not be the president's."

The news rendered Nick momentarily speechless.

Across the room, he caught the gaze of Derek Kavanaugh, who'd apparently just received the same news.

"Are you there, sir?" Trevor asked.

"I'm here."

"I'll send you a link to the story."

"And we're sure this is legit?"

"I've had several sources confirm that the story is legit in that the woman did work on the campaign. Whether the affair happened or the kid is his remains to be proven."

"He barely survived the last scandal."

"That was my first thought too. I think you ought to be prepared, sir, you know, for anything…"

"Don't go there."

"Okay, I won't, but everyone else will."

"Right, well, thanks for letting me know."

"Of course. I'll keep you posted."

As Trevor ended the call, Nick wanted to tell him not to bother, but Trevor was nothing if not thorough when it came to his job.

Sam joined him away from the group. "What's up?"

"Oh nothing much, just a possible presidential affair and love child." He noted that Derek was updating the others, and everyone was looking at Nick. The entire world would be looking to him for reaction, and he needed to start right now in schooling his features to give nothing away.

Sam's eyes bugged. *"What?"*

"Here we go again."

"Nick… When was Gloria treated for ovarian cancer?"

"Last October."

"Would the affair coincide?"

"God, I hope not." Few people knew the first lady had undergone cancer surgery and treatment during the campaign, as the Nelsons had chosen to keep her condition private. The president had told Nick about it after the first lady was in remission.

With Sam looking on, Nick took a quick look at the story Trevor had sent, scrolling through the details of the alleged affair with Tara Weber, who had been a senior policy adviser to the president during the campaign.

"I remember her. People wondered why he'd brought in someone new to that role when he certainly had plenty of other advisers he could've brought into the campaign."

"Did I meet her?"

"If you did, you'd remember her. She's the full package—smart, beautiful and savvy as all hell. She's tall with curly dark hair."

"I did meet her at the inaugural ball."

"Oh right, I remember that. Wasn't she with Nelson when you met her?"

"She was. I recall being very impressed by her."

They exchanged glances.

"This is going to be a big deal, isn't it?" Sam rested a hand over her stomach, which bothered her during times of stress.

She'd had enough stress lately.

"Not for us. Nelson's team will handle it."

Derek approached them. "I have to go." He pulled on his coat and zipped it. "Thankfully my parents are in town and can stay with Maeve," he said, referring to his two-year-old daughter. "It's gonna be a long night."

"What're you hearing?"

"That the story is credible and their 'friendship' raised brows during the campaign, the transition and into the new administration. I knew they were close, but it never occurred to me that there was more to it. She was abruptly let go in the spring, but Nelson handled that himself, and we never heard why. He just said her services were no longer needed."

Terry joined them. "What can I do?"

"There's nothing to do," Nick said. "Not yet anyway."

"We're the ones with the big problem," Derek said, "and I'm off to help solve it."

"Better you than me," Nick said.

"Ah yes," Derek said, grinning, "and people think it's so cool to work in the White House. We know better, don't we?"

"We certainly do." At times like this—hell, most of the time, actually—Nick deeply regretted accepting Nelson's invitation to replace Vice President Gooding after he was diagnosed with a brain tumor and had to resign. "Check in with me in the morning. Let me know what level of concern I need to have about my own future."

"Will do."

After Derek left, Nick was determined to get this evening back on track. He refused to think about what *might* happen until he had to.

"Are you okay?" Sam gazed up at him with concern etched into her gorgeous face.

He couldn't have that, so he wrapped an arm around her waist and kissed her. "I'm out on a hot date with my best girl. I'm great." Lowering his voice, he added, "And even though I can't wait to get my best girl home so I can be alone with her, I'm really enjoying the time with our friends."

"I am too. Tonight is all about you. Whatever you want."

Hearing that, he wanted to say to hell with the friends he rarely got to see. "Is it my birthday and no one told me?"

Sam laughed and kissed his neck, taking a little bite

that made him instantly hard. "No, but we can celebrate like it is when we get home."

"Let's go now." The Nelson news might've happened a year ago for all he cared when his wife was handing out birthday-level favors.

"Easy, big guy. It'll still be your not-birthday when we get home. It took an act of God to get you here, now let's go enjoy our friends for a little while longer."

Sam took his hand and led him back to the table, and he let her, because he'd follow her anywhere she chose to take him.

CHAPTER TWO

THE NELSON NEWS had spiked Sam's anxiety, but she went out of her way not to let Nick see that as they rode home from Lilia's in the Secret Service motorcade. He didn't need to know that the idea of him becoming president freaked her out to the point of panic, not when he had enough of his own worries. The insomnia that plagued him during the best of times was exacerbated by stress, and she was determined to make sure he was relaxed so he would get some badly needed rest.

Whatever was going to happen with the latest presidential scandal didn't have to touch them. At least not tonight.

Sam's niece Brooke had stayed with the kids while they were out. At almost nineteen, she had grown into a gorgeous young woman with long dark hair, blue eyes and flawless skin that Sam would kill for. Brooke was now in college, but home for the weekend and had jumped at the chance to make some extra money.

Nick handed her a hundred-dollar bill.

Brooke tried to give it back. "That's too much."

"You have no idea how much date night with my wife meant to me. You made it possible. That's not enough."

"Thank you." Brooke went up on tiptoe to kiss his cheek. "I had fun hanging with Scotty and the twins. They're so adorable, and he's great with them."

"He really is," Sam said. "He loves being a big brother."

"It's terrible what happened to them." Alden and Aubrey had lost their parents in a home invasion. "But I'm so happy they landed with you guys."

"They've changed our lives for the better," Nick said.

Sam put an arm around her niece. "We didn't get to talk earlier. How're you holding up since Gramps passed away?"

"I find myself in tears at the weirdest times," Brooke confessed. "I still can't believe he's gone."

"I know."

"It must be so hard for you. Everyone knew you were his favorite."

"We were all his favorites."

"You were his BFF, Sam."

Sam shrugged. "And he was mine." She tugged playfully on a strand of Brooke's hair. "Your mom tells me there's a boy…"

Brooke rolled her eyes, which reminded Sam of the girl's tumultuous teenage years. "My mom has a big mouth."

"And this is news to you? Spill it, sister."

"His name is Ryan, and it's new, so don't freak out."

Sam had to force herself not to laugh. "Wouldn't dream of it. I'll just say that I'm happy you're happy. That's all that matters to me—and your mom."

"Thanks." Brooke hugged and kissed her. "I'll see you soon."

"Hope so."

"Thanks for the C-note, Nick."

"You're more than welcome. Thanks for babysitting."

"Anytime."

Sam walked her to the door that Nate, the Secret Service agent on duty, opened for them. "Text me when you get home."

"You're just like my mom."

"Gee, wonder how that happened? Love you, kid."

"Love you too, you pain in the butt."

Sam laughed and watched Brooke take the ramp they no longer needed down to the sidewalk. At some point, they would take down the ramps that'd been erected here and at her father's house down the street to accommodate his wheelchair. That didn't need to happen yet. Sam waited until Brooke was in her car and waved as she drove off, flashing her lights as she went by the house, heading for the Secret Service checkpoint.

"'Night, Nate," Sam said to the agent when she went back inside.

"Good night, Mrs. Cappuano, and if I may add… Your niece is an impressive young woman."

"Yes, she certainly is," Sam said, intrigued by the handsome agent's comment. She wondered if he knew the half of just how impressive Brooke was after having survived and thrived following a gang rape her senior year of high school.

"You have a good night, ma'am."

"You too."

Sam went upstairs and noted that the agent usually stationed in the hallway when Scotty and the twins were home wasn't there. She ducked her head in to check on the twins, who were wrapped up in each other and fast asleep in the big bed that they shared. Sam pulled the comforter over them and ran her fingers through their soft hair. They were so damned cute, and it had taken about four seconds for her and the rest of their family to fall madly in love with the children Nick called "the Littles." She glanced at the photo of their parents on the bedside table before bending to kiss them both.

When she looked in on Scotty, she found he'd once again fallen asleep with the TV and light on. Sam shut off the TV and adjusted his blanket before kissing his forehead. Their little boy was growing into a handsome young man who bore a startling resemblance to Nick, which was an amazing coincidence, as they were technically not related.

Technically not related... She hated those words. They were as related as any father and son could be, and she loved that Scotty looked like his dad. She shut off the bedside light and left his room, closing the door behind her and heading into her own room, where she found a note on the bed written in her husband's distinctive scrawl.

Date night continues upstairs. Hurry up.

She smiled. So that's where the Secret Service agent had gone. Nick had told the agent to take a break because he was well aware she hated that the agents knew they were headed upstairs for a booty call. In her dresser, she found the nightgown she'd recently ordered online that she'd been saving for a special occasion. Although every occasion with her sexy husband was special.

In the bathroom, she applied the vanilla-and-jasmine-scented lotion that Nick went crazy over and put on the nearly see-through nightgown. He would expect her to be naked under the decidedly unsexy robe she wore to walk upstairs, so she hoped he enjoyed her little surprise.

When she thought about the Nelson news, her stomach ached as she wondered how it would affect her and Nick. The president had barely survived the scandal his son Christopher had caused by trying to discredit Nick and Sam. Christopher hated that the young, handsome vice president had become the most popular politician in America. They'd learned that Christopher Nelson had presidential aspirations of his own and wanted Nick out of the way. Now he was in prison awaiting trial for murdering Sam's ex-husband, Peter, among other crimes.

After holding their breath for weeks while waiting to see if Nelson would be forced to resign, Sam and Nick had begun to relax. And now this.

As she brushed her hair and teeth, Sam thought of Gloria Nelson, whom she'd gotten to know fairly well since Nick became vice president, and especially since Christopher's crimes came to light. Her heart ached for the woman who'd already been through so much—and now this humiliating betrayal by her husband.

And what had he been thinking, having an affair as the most closely scrutinized human being on the planet?

Sam left her bedroom and headed toward the stairs to the loft Nick had created as their place to escape from the realities of everyday life. Halfway up the stairs, she caught the distinctive scent of coconut from the candles he'd lit and heard the Polynesian music that reminded them of their honeymoon and anniversary trips to Bora Bora.

At the top of the stairs, she stopped short at the sight of Nick curled onto his side, wearing only a pair of cotton pajama pants, and sleeping soundly. It was so rare for her to see him sleeping that she found herself staring at him for a few minutes, noting the smooth olive-toned skin, the defined chest and abdomen that came from regular workouts, the dark hair that she loved to run her fingers through and the lips that kissed her with everything from tenderness to fiery passion.

She removed her robe and settled next to him on her side, facing him.

"Took you long enough," he muttered, keeping his eyes closed.

Sam placed her hand on his face. "Shhh, you're actually sleeping."

"I wasn't sleeping."

"Yes, you were."

He took the hand from his face and placed it on top of his hard cock. "I'm very much awake because I knew my beautiful wife was on her way."

"Nick, you need the rest more than you need me."

He opened hazel eyes that burned with desire for her. You would think that after all this time she would cease to be amazed by how fiercely he wanted her. You would be wrong.

"I need nothing more than I need you, Samantha." He blinked, seeming to realize she was wearing something he hadn't seen before. "What have we here?"

"This old thing?"

"Come closer. I can't see you all the way over there."

Less than a foot of space separated them, but Sam slid into his waiting embrace and breathed in the scent of home.

"Much better." He ran his hand over her back and down over her ass. "Where did this sexy little number come from?"

"The internet. Where else?" They joked about being prisoners in their own home since he became vice president. Sam couldn't recall the last time she'd shopped in an actual store. They had so little time together. If he couldn't go with her, she didn't want to go.

He ran his index finger from her throat to her chest to the deep valley between her breasts, the place he'd once told her he'd like to be when he took his last breath. "What did we ever do without the internet?"

"It does come in handy when there's no time to shop or do anything other than work and take care of kids."

"You're an awesome multitasker, my love."

"I suppose."

He propped himself up on his elbow. "You suppose? Everyone who knows you marvels at what you get done in a day."

She looked up at him. "I worry that I'm not giving the twins enough of myself and my time."

"Sam... They may be little, but they know who stepped up for them and who got justice for their parents. They adore you."

"I just think about their mom, how she did everything with them and I can't do that. She was the crafty mom. That'll never be me."

"It doesn't have to be you, babe. They just need you to love and protect them, which you do every single day."

"I love them so much, which is just amazing to me. We didn't even know them a month ago, and now..."

"Now they're part of us."

"Yes, exactly."

"And they know it, Sam. They know we love them and that we're here for them, even when we're not physically in this house. We've gotten them into therapy and made sure they feel loved all the time. The most important things are covered."

"Are you sure?"

He unleashed the smile that had left her powerless to resist him from the first second she met him. "I grew up with none of the things we give them every day. So I'm very sure that they're getting what they need, even if it's not exactly what they had before."

"I hate to think of you being so lonely as a kid. It makes me crazy."

"My adulthood has more than made up for my childhood."

"Sometimes I want to find your mother and throat punch her for what she did to you—what she continues to do to you."

"She's not worth the bother."

"No, she isn't, but you should know that I fantasize about throat punching her."

Chuckling, he kissed her. "What else do you fantasize about?"

"All kinds of things."

He unleashed a wolfish grin. "Oh, do tell."

"I dream about us having a month off to spend every day together."

"That'd be a dream come true for sure."

"A month probably wouldn't be enough."

"It definitely wouldn't be enough. What else do you fantasize about?" As he nuzzled her neck, he slid his hand down to cup her ass, bringing her in tight against his erection.

"I fantasize about going back to Bora Bora."

"We can go for our anniversary."

"What about our three children?"

"We can go when Elijah is on spring break, and he can be here with the kids." Elijah, a student at Princeton, was the twins' older brother and legal guardian.

"Ohhh, I do like the way you think."

"I like the way you smell and the way you feel and the way you look and the way you do everything."

"Really?" she asked, amused. *"Everything?"*

"Every. Single. Thing."

"You must really love me."

"I really, *really* do."

Kissing him ranked among her favorite things in life. Anything with him topped her favorite things list, but when they were able to be together this way, in this place he had created for them to escape from the difficult reality of their daily lives, this was the best of the best. For the longest time, they only kissed. Hours and days could've passed for all she knew or cared as everything else fell away leaving only the undisputed love of her life.

His hands moved over her body, arousing her to the point of madness, but still he did nothing but kiss her. "I could do this every minute for the rest of my life and never get bored."

"You'd get bored eventually."

He shook his head. "Never."

Sam put her hands above her head, surrendering completely to him.

"Samantha." His lips were soft and persuasive as they moved to her breasts, the silk of her gown abrading her tight nipples. "You're so incredibly beautiful. Tonight I was thinking how it never gets old that I get to go home with the incomparable Samantha Holland Cappuano. My dream girl."

He aroused her as much with his words as his hands and lips and the light drag of his tongue over her silk-covered nipples. Moving down, he continued to worship her until she was writhing beneath him.

Sam spread her legs to make room for him where she wanted him most. "Nick…"

"Hmmm?"

She raised her hips to tell him what she wanted.

"Is my baby being impatient?"

"Me? Impatient? *Never.*"

His snort of laughter made her smile too. "No, you're just the epitome of patience. And by now you know that the more you try to rush me, the slower I'll go."

Her growl of frustration was greeted by laughter from her beloved. It was a good thing he always made it worth the wait, she thought, as he propped her legs on his shoulders and opened her to his tongue. And *God*, he was good at that. She, who'd had such trouble finding sexual pleasure in other relationships, could get there almost effortlessly with him. He played her like a maestro. Her maestro.

His tongue and fingers were right where she needed them, and as the sensations grew and multiplied, she rode the wave that swelled with every stroke of his tongue and deep thrust of his fingers inside her. Waves of bliss arrived in an explosive storm that touched every part of her, leaving her boneless and wrecked and yet somehow energized too. How he managed to make her feel this way was one of life's greatest mysteries, and the only one she had no desire to solve.

When he moved up, she wrapped her arms around him and held on tight to the feeling that could only be described as magical.

He entered her with a slow, smooth glide that took her breath away, like it always did.

She had to remind herself that she wasn't allowed to scream. Not here with their children sleeping downstairs and the Secret Service nearby. But she wanted to scream from the powerful desire they generated together. She bit his shoulder, which seemed to make him crazy as he picked up the pace, driving into her until they were both straining for the peak.

Like they'd charged up the side of a mountain and then leaped from the top, they soared, in total harmony as their bodies came together in a moment that felt almost holy.

Much of her life was a red-hot mess, but this…

This was perfection. *They* were perfection.

CHAPTER THREE

SAM AND NICK spent all day Sunday with their three kids, while ignoring the incessant ringing of Nick's personal cell phone. After a trip to the twins' favorite playground in their old neighborhood, they went to the movies, played video games at the movie theater for an hour and then headed home for pizza. It had been a perfect family day that the Secret Service had helped them pull off with a minimum of fuss. The Nelson affair story dominated the news cycle, but by focusing on their family, the second couple had been able to avoid the unfolding drama for one more day.

Overnight, storm clouds rolled into the District, and rumbles of thunder shook the house in the morning as Sam and Nick tried to get three kids up and moving.

Aubrey was scared of the thunder and clung to Sam, who felt guilty that she had to get to work and had to send the little girl to school. She'd much rather stay home and snuggle with her all day the way Aubrey's mother probably would've done. While investigating the murders of Jameson and Cleo Armstrong, she'd learned that Cleo had been the kind of fully engaged mother that Sam could never be—crafts and baking and playdates and elaborate birthday parties.

While she had nothing but admiration and awe for

the kind of mother Cleo had been, Sam considered it a good day for her family if everyone was fed and bathed.

Nick took over with Aubrey when he saw that the little girl's anxiety was upsetting Sam.

"Is she okay?" Sam asked when he came in from seeing off the Secret Service details taking Aubrey and Alden to kindergarten and Scotty to middle school.

"She was giggling by the time they left. Alden told her the thunder was Mommy and Daddy bowling in heaven, and she shouldn't be upset. That it was their way of saying hello."

Sam placed her hand over her heart. "Dear God, I'm going to sob."

"I know. I had a lump the size of an orange in my throat and so did the agents."

"He's very wise for someone so young."

"He reminds me of Scotty when I first knew him."

"Like Scotty, he's seen far too much." Alden had witnessed part of the assault his parents had endured.

Nick hugged her and dropped a kiss on her forehead. "Yes, he has. Are you okay?"

"I will be, but it kills me to see Aubrey upset and not be able to comfort her."

"She's okay, so try to shake it off so it doesn't ruin your day."

He released her and dropped the morning papers on the table.

They eyed them with trepidation.

"I'm almost afraid to look," she said.

"I'm completely afraid to look." Nick flipped open the *Washington Star*, which boasted the banner headline Nelson Acknowledges Affair, Denies Fathering Child.

"Ugh," Sam said.

"That about sums it up."

Sam stood over his shoulder as they read the salacious details about the president's affair with the campaign staffer.

"Sources tell the *Star* that the affair began during the campaign, during which time the president and Ms. Weber were near-constant companions."

Reading the words out loud, Sam felt her stomach start to ache again as the ramifications compounded. Nelson had barely hung on after his son was charged in a series of politically motivated murders, and now this…

"The affair is bad enough," Nick said, "but when word gets out that it happened while his wife had cancer? People will never forgive him for that."

"They don't have to forgive him. They just need to keep him around for three more years."

"Which is a big ask after this."

That didn't help Sam's stomach. "What're your people saying?"

"I haven't looked yet."

"Are you in denial?"

He looked up at her. "Aren't you?"

"Hell, yes. I can't believe this is happening so soon after the other thing. I mean, how much scandal can one administration handle? Not to mention the fuel he's giving the opposition for the next election cycle. *Look at them,* they'll say, *they elected a president—twice—whose son was a murderer and who cheated on his wife at her lowest moment.*"

Sam liked to think that the next election cycle wouldn't be their problem, but with Nick as the heir apparent, it was still very much their concern. Or his concern, she should say. She tried to stay detached from the realities of his role as vice president. Not that she didn't fully support him. She did, but she supported him from inside a comfortable bubble that kept her insulated from the possibility that he might have to become president at any moment.

Despite his promotion to vice president, they'd managed to eke out a fairly normal existence. Other than the ever-present Secret Service that surrounded him and the three children, and Nick's inability to move freely, life was still relatively similar to what it had been before. Well, it was for her anyway.

They'd declined Secret Service protection for her so she could continue to do her job as the lieutenant in charge of the Metropolitan Police Department's Homicide division. For the most part, people left her alone, even if they were endlessly fascinated by her dual roles as a cop and second lady. But if he became president, they were under no illusions that she'd be able to continue running the streets the way she did now.

The possibility of losing her freedom made Sam a little panicky, which was ridiculous. So the president had had an affair and possibly produced a love child at sixty-something years old. People did stupid shit all the time and got away with it. If only it hadn't happened while his wife was being treated for cancer. That detail could be the deal breaker for everyone who mattered.

Sam's phone rang with a call from Darren Tabor, a reporter with the *Washington Star* who'd become a friend of sorts over the years.

She took the call. "Morning."

"Morning. Have you seen the paper?"

"Looking at it now."

"You could make my day, my life *and* my career with a comment from yourself and/or the vice president about your feelings on the latest Nelson scandal."

"It makes me sad, Darren."

"What does?"

"That after all this time, it seems you don't know me at all." Sam had to force herself not to crack up at her own joke.

"Sam! Come on! It's the story of the year, and you guys certainly have a stake in it."

She met Nick's gaze and held it. "That may be true, but I can assure you that I speak for the vice president when I tell you we'll have no comment about it now or ever."

Her husband gave a subtle nod of approval.

"How can you say that? If Nelson has to resign—"

"Darren, listen to me. We're well aware of what *could* happen, but we're not going to speculate publicly. And that's not for attribution."

"You're killing me, Sam."

"No, I'm not, because I wouldn't want to have to deal with the paperwork that would involve."

His frustrated growl came through the phone loud and clear.

"Have a good day, Darren."

"Yeah, you too."

Sam closed her phone with the satisfying slap that kept her firmly in the 3G while the rest of the world had long ago moved on. "That went rather well, if I do say so myself."

Nick laughed. "You missed your calling as a political spokesperson, my love."

Sam rolled her eyes. "That is the last job I could ever do. I don't possess an ounce of diplomacy or restraint."

"And that's why I love you so much."

Raising a brow in his direction, she said, "*That's* why?"

"One of so many reasons, I can't count them all."

"And that, right there, is why you're the politician. You always have the perfect line at the ready."

"Only when I'm discussing my gorgeous, sexy, non-politically-correct wife."

"You're good, Mr. Vice President. I gotta give you that."

His shit-eating grin made him sexier than he already was, if that was possible.

"And now I must leave you, to continue cleaning up the absolute mess that my father's case has made of my life at work. The paperwork never ends."

"What's the latest?"

"The three defendants are appearing in court this morning to enter pleas."

"Are you planning to go?"

"Probably not."

"If you go, you shouldn't go alone. I can move some things around—"

She placed a finger over his lips. "No need. If I go, Freddie will be with me, and there's going to be a lot of court crap over the next few years. You're not going to be able to go every time."

"I would if I could. You know that, I hope."

"Of course I do, and I appreciate it. But it's going to be a marathon, not a sprint, and we need to pace ourselves."

"Does that mean you'll be pacing yourself too?"

"As much as I can. The arrests were part one. Making sure they're convicted is part two, and it's every bit as critical as part one."

He took her hand and brought it to his lips. "I know it's hard for you to be patient while the system takes its own sweet time, but you all have put together an airtight case. You've done all you can to make sure the U.S. Attorney has what he needs to make them pay."

"That may be true, but until I hear the words *guilty*, *guilty* and *guilty*, it won't truly be over for me."

"I know, babe, but please tell me you'll be careful with my wife in the meantime. She's my whole world, and when she hurts, I hurt."

She smiled down at him. "I'll be careful. I promise. And you, my friend, need to schedule some time with the boss today to get a handle on what we're looking at with this affair situation."

"I know," Nick said glumly. "I already texted Terry to tell him to get me on the schedule."

Sam leaned in to kiss him goodbye, dreading the long, arduous day ahead until she could be with him again. "Let me know how that goes."

"You'll be the first to know."

WHEN SAM ARRIVED at HQ a short time later, she noted the massive scrum of reporters outside the main door and drove around to the morgue entrance to avoid them. Whenever scandal struck the administration, they stalked her workplace, hoping to get a comment from her. She never gave them anything, deferring questions about her husband to the White House, but still they came. They were going to leave disappointed again today.

She popped into the morgue to say hello to Lindsey, who was at her computer nursing a tall cup of the tea she said she couldn't function without.

"Morning."

"Hey, I was just thinking of you. Any word on what the hell is happening at the White House?"

"Nothing official, but I suspect the president isn't having a good day."

"I feel so bad for Gloria. She's such an amazing person, who's dedicated her life to people less fortunate."

Sam hesitated, but only for a second, deciding she could trust Lindsey with the rest of the story. "There's more to it that no one knows yet."

"Can you tell?"

"If you keep a lid on it."

"My lips are sealed."

"Gloria was being treated for stage two ovarian cancer around the time the affair supposedly started."

"Ugh, you've got to be kidding me. That makes it extra revolting."

"I know. That's the part I can't get over either. I mean, the infidelity is bad enough, but the timing of her illness takes it to a whole other level of disgusting."

"Seriously." Lindsey shuddered. "If Terry ever did something like that to me..."

"He never would. He's fully aware that he's marrying up, and he'll continue to treat you like the goddess you are, or I'll stab him with my rusty steak knife."

Lindsey tried not to smile. "May I quote you on that?"

"By all means. Put him on notice."

"It's not something I worry about where he's concerned, but when the president does it, you start to wonder if it's something they all do."

"It's not," Sam said. "If there is one thing in my life I'm absolutely sure of, it's that my husband has no interest in anyone but me."

"The whole world is sure of that with you two. The man is thoroughly besotted."

"So is yours, Linds. You got nothing to worry about."

"I know." As usual when she spoke of Terry O'Connor, Lindsey's entire demeanor softened.

"How's the wedding planning coming?" Sam honestly didn't want to hear about the wedding, but she tried to be a good friend, and being a good friend to Lindsey right now meant asking about the wedding.

"Shelby is a godsend, as you know," Lindsey said of Sam and Nick's personal assistant, whom they met when she planned their wedding. She kept a hand in her wedding planning business even as she worked for them full-time.

"I'm well aware," Sam said. "I'd be lost without her, and my wedding would've been a disaster if she hadn't handled every detail."

"She told me yesterday that I need to get my wedding party in order, and as such, I was hoping it would be okay if I asked you to be one of my attendants even though I know you hate such things with the passion of a thousand bloody hemorrhoids."

Sam sputtered. "I'm not *that* bad."

"Um, yes, you are, but I'd still be honored to have you. Terry is going to ask Nick to be his best man."

"He'll be honored and so am I—with one caveat. There'd better not be any of those stupid fucking shower games. You need to promise me there won't be any of that crap. I absolutely refuse to participate in wrapping you in toilet paper."

Lindsey cracked up. "I'll let my sister, the matron of honor, know that there are to be no shower games under any circumstances."

"Great, then I'm all yours. Oh, and the dress can't be fugly either."

Lindsey continued to laugh helplessly. "I'm giving you guys a color and letting you pick what you want. Believe me, I've worn enough fugly dresses in my time. I'd never do that to my girls. The benefit of being an older bride is knowing what you don't want."

"Older," Sam scoffed. "What're you, thirty-three?"

"Six and hearing the tick, tick, tick of my biological clock." As soon as she said that, she grimaced. "I'm sorry. I shouldn't have—"

"Stop. Please don't do that. Just because I seem to be infertile doesn't mean I begrudge others their ability to procreate. The world is probably better off without another Sam Holland running around out there."

"The world would be lucky to have another Sam Holland."

"Aww, you're sweet, but I'm honestly okay with it. Don't get me wrong—I'd still love nothing more than to have a baby with Nick, but ever since Scotty came to live with us, the burning need for it isn't quite the same as it was. Now it's more like it would be nice if it happens, but if it doesn't, that's okay too."

"I'm glad to hear you say that."

"Believe me, my plate is more than full with the twins and Scotty and this job that never lets up. If I had a baby, I'd have to make some big changes I'm probably not prepared to make right now." She shrugged, as if having a baby hadn't once been the most important thing in her life. "Things change, and people evolve. I couldn't be happier with the family I have or feel more fortunate to have three beautiful kids to love as well as the twins' older brother in our lives."

"You are fortunate, and it's nice that you can see that."

"We don't always get what we want, but sometimes we get what we need."

"I seem to recall a song that said something like that…"

Sam laughed. "One of my favorites."

"You like a song by someone other than Bon Jovi?" Lindsey asked, scandalized.

"Only like six songs by others, so don't make a thing of it."

"Hate to ask, but any word on Stahl's trial?"

"The defense is putting on their shit show this week and then it goes to the jury. His attorneys actually got a few people to say what an upstanding public servant he was. Whatever. When you wrap someone in razor wire and try to set them on fire, it sort of negates your service to the homeless, you know?"

"Ah, yeah, I agree. Everyone here is hoping for a conviction."

"Everyone?" Sam asked, brow raised.

"Well, almost everyone."

"I'm sure Ramsey would love to see him get off so they can continue to torture me in their own special way." Sam had tangled frequently with the sergeant from Special Victims, who hated her for reasons known only to him. "What's life without a few good enemies?"

"Peaceful?"

"What fun would that be?" Sam's phone rang and she took the call from her partner, Detective Freddie Cruz. "What's up?"

"Malone is looking for you."

"I'll be right there." She slapped the phone closed. "Gotta run. The captain is looking for me."

"What'd you do now?"

"Could be so many things. Have a good day, Doc."

"You too." Sam left the morgue and navigated the winding corridors that led to the pit where her detectives were hard at work—or at least they'd better be. The paperwork surrounding the investigation into her father's shooting had been voluminous, and they'd been meticulous to make sure every thread was firmly sewn up. With their deputy chief implicated in the crime, they'd gone the extra mile of working with the FBI to ensure the investigation was unimpeachable.

Captain Malone was waiting for her, leaning against Freddie's cubicle, chatting about the Capitals and their chances for another Stanley Cup.

"There you are. I saw your car and wondered where you were."

"I was in the morgue with Lindsey."

"Ah, gotcha. Can we talk?"

Sam glanced at her mentor and friend, who sounded off. "Sure. Come in." As she followed him to her office, she looked back at Freddie, who shrugged.

CHAPTER FOUR

SAM UNLOCKED THE office door and gestured for the captain to go in ahead of her as she flipped on the lights and closed the door behind her, thinking, *What fresh hell awaits me today?* "Everything okay?" She walked around the desk to sit while he took her visitor chair.

"I just keep going over it and over it in my mind, and I can't get it to make sense."

"What's that?"

"Conklin."

"That may never make sense to us."

"It's unfathomable to me that he sat on this info for all this time. Skip was one of ours. He was Conklin's *friend.* Skip took him in when Conklin was at his lowest point and saved his career. How could he do this to Skip? To *us?*"

"We may never know the answer to that, Cap."

"Maybe we will."

Sam tipped her head.

"He wants to see you."

Her immediate, visceral response was *no fucking way.* She shook her head. "I don't think that's a good idea. I'm not sure I could resist the urge to spit in his face."

"No one would blame you if you did."

"I don't need the publicity of the second lady behaving badly—again."

He leaned forward, elbows on knees, eyes imploring. "Don't you want to know, Sam?"

She slapped her hand on the desktop. "*Hell, yes*, I want to know, but I'm not sure I can sit in a room with the man who knew all along what happened to my dad and kept it to himself. I might actually be tempted to murder him."

Malone sat back, his shoulders sagging with uncharacteristic defeat. "Believe me, I get it."

"I'm trying to survive this, you know?"

"Yeah, I get that too."

"I'll think about seeing him. That's all I've got right now. It's a big deal for me to get out of bed."

"It's new. It'll get easier."

"So they say. At the moment? Not so good."

"I don't mean to make it harder on you than it already is."

"You're not the one doing that. He is. He's been doing that for years now."

"His arrest has created an opening. The chief asked me if I'm interested in being promoted, but I don't know. Part of me doesn't want it."

"How come?"

"I like what I'm doing now, supervising the detectives. Being deputy chief is all about schmoozing at City Hall and overseeing the budget and admin shit that'd drive me mad."

"You're the ranking captain, so you get first right of refusal. Who's next in line?" She paid zero attention to such things because she didn't give a rat's ass about anything other than her own cases and her own squad and the colleagues she worked with regularly. Getting caught up in department politics had never been her jam.

"Nickleson from SWAT."

"He'd be a good deputy chief."

"The mayor wants a woman."

"Does the mayor understand that these things are done by rank and seniority?"

"The chief explained how it works to her, and she insisted that it's time for a woman—and a woman of color at that—to be considered."

"I agree with that. We need more women in general in the upper ranks since we already run the world."

He grunted out a laugh. "I'm all for that, and so is the chief. But there's a protocol in place, for better or worse, and we can't ignore the people who've put in the time on the job. All the current captains are men, which is a damned shame, but let's face it, the mayor could decide to put you in the job if she wanted to, and it would be hard for us to tell her no."

"Dear God, let's hope she doesn't get an idea like that."

"From your lips to God's ears."

Sam scowled at him. "We've got a few female lieutenants who're going to run the place in a couple of years, but we need to do better in advancing women, especially women of color, in this department."

"I couldn't agree more."

"Officer Charles," Sam said, referring to the young black officer who'd assisted in the planning of her father's police funeral.

"What about her?"

"She impressed the shit out of me with her organization skills and attention to detail during my dad's funeral."

"It's not easy to impress you."

"No, it isn't. She's going to be the chief someday. Mark my words. I'd love to have her as my assistant, if she'd like the job, that is."

"She reports to the chief. You'd have to fight him for her, and besides, you have an entire squad to assist you."

"You guys are always after me to get the reports done faster, and with my dyslexia, that's not easy for me."

"You're actually playing the dyslexia card?"

"Yes, because it's convenient for me."

Malone barked out a laugh that was a welcome relief from his earlier morose demeanor. Even in the worst of times, Sam counted on her mentor, boss and friend to be upbeat and positive. He helped to keep her spirits up when they took a beating like they had lately.

"I'll talk to the chief about your interest in working with Officer Charles."

"Thank you. Any updates on the Stahl trial?"

"I heard the defense will rest today or tomorrow, and then it'll go to the jury. Almost there."

"If they don't convict him…"

"How can they not convict him? He wrapped you in razor wire and threatened to set you on fire."

"He would've succeeded in setting me on fire if you guys hadn't shown up when you did. Took you long enough, by the way."

He scowled. "It took us a while to figure out where you were—alone—and without a cell phone that could be tracked."

"Mistakes were made. I'll give you that."

"Good of you to acknowledge that."

"I want to dig in further on that anonymous note we got that info about my father's shooter was closer than we thought and we needed to look inside our own house."

"We had the letter thoroughly analyzed."

"I know, but someone knew about Conklin. I want to know who."

"What're you thinking?"

"I'd like to talk to his wife, for starters."

"She's apt to lawyer up when she hears you're coming."

"Let her. All I can do is ask the questions. I don't know her at all though." For whatever reason, Conklin's second wife had never socialized with their group or been with him when he visited Skip. At times, Sam had forgotten Conklin was actually married.

"I'll go with you. I know her a little. I'll set it up." He stood, seeming infused with purpose now that he had a mission.

"Hey, Cap?"

Malone turned back to her, raised a brow.

"I know it's hard, but we all have to find a way to survive this or we won't be able to do the job or anything else, for that matter. I refuse to give these people any more than they've already taken from me, and you shouldn't either."

"That's good advice, and I'll keep it in mind as I work to keep the cauldron of rage inside me from boiling over."

"It helps to know that I'm not the only one contending with the cauldron of rage."

"You're far from alone with this. A lot of people around here loved Skip and can't make sense of what Conklin did—or didn't do. It defies belief for those of us who wear the badge with pride. I'll be back to you about the Mrs."

"Sounds good, thanks."

After he left, she picked up the photocopy of the anonymous note she had received after her father died, which had been nagging at her since they closed the case.

Look inside your own "house" and City Hall. The answers are closer than you think.

The note had been hastily scrawled in handwriting someone would recognize. "Cruz!"

Freddie popped up from his cubicle and scowled at her. "What?"

She returned his scowl. "Come here."

He came. "You bellowed?"

"I did." She held up the copy of the note. "We're going to dig into this and figure out where it came from."

"Okay…"

"I was just letting you know. Talk to the others about ideas of how we might approach this."

"Anything else, Your Majesty?"

Sam smiled. "I like that nickname. You can call me that instead of lieutenant going forward."

"In your dreams."

"That'll be all for now, young grasshopper." For the rest of her life, she'd never forget how he'd cut short the honeymoon in Italy he'd looked forward to for months so he could be with her in the aftermath of her father's death.

Detective Cameron Green came to the door, stopping Freddie from leaving. As usual, Cameron wore a shirt and tie that made the rest of them look sloppy in comparison. To Sam, he said, "I just saw that the president is planning to speak at the daily press briefing. Thought you might want to see that."

She didn't, really, but she got up to follow them into the conference room where Detective Jeannie McBride and her new partner, Detective Matt O'Brien, were already parked in front of the TV. Sam realized they were as concerned as she was about what would happen to her job and career if Nick were to become president.

Her stomach began to ache when she saw the press secretary turn the podium over to President David Nelson. Tall with silver hair and blue eyes, Nelson was usually the picture of decorum and presidential demeanor. Today, he was visibly agitated and off his game.

"Thank you for allowing me a minute of your time." He kept his gaze down to avoid eye contact with the reporters. "I'm here today to confirm the reports of an extramarital affair with Tara Weber. Ms. Weber served as a policy analyst on my reelection team, and we became close while traveling together." He looked up, and the emotions she saw swirling in his troubled eyes didn't do much to calm her nerves. "The affair continued until shortly after the inauguration. Ms. Weber conceived a child, a son, who was born last week. I do not believe the child is mine."

Sam wondered how he could be so certain. Would the president have to take a paternity test? It was all so sordid.

The press corps erupted with shouted questions.

Nelson ignored them all. "I made a mistake having an affair," he said, his voice breaking. "I made several of them, actually. I dishonored the promises I made to my wonderful, beautiful, supportive wife, Gloria, and disappointed her at a time when she needed me most. I've let down my family, Ms. Weber and the American people. For that, all I can do is apologize and promise to do better in the future."

As he stepped back from the podium, one of the reporters asked why Gloria had needed him most while another asked if he planned to resign, but he left the room without answering either question.

"God, I hope he doesn't resign," Sam said, shuddering at the thought.

The others laughed nervously.

"Have you guys heard anything?" Jeannie asked.

"Nothing official, but we're holding our breath like everyone else."

"You just wonder how much scandal one administration can withstand before it becomes too much," Cameron said.

"True, but he took a big mea culpa just now, and that ought to help," Freddie said. "At least he owned it rather than denying it the way so many of them do."

"His wife was undergoing treatment for ovarian cancer when he had the affair," Sam said as the others gasped. "She'd chosen to keep the diagnosis private. That's what he meant about the timing. I wonder how long it'll take for her illness to become public now that he's alluded to there being something to find."

"Damn," O'Brien said. "What a scumbag."

"When that gets out, it could be game over for him," Freddie said, looking stricken.

"Let's hope they're able to keep a lid on that info," Sam said. "In the meantime, we've got work to do. How's it coming with finishing the reports on the Conklin, Gallagher, Santoro and Ryan arrests?"

"Slowly." Freddie answered for all of them. "We're working with Vice, which is conducting the gambling portion of the investigation, and that's what's taking so long. They had thirty years' worth of crap to sift through. Our part is mostly done. Just waiting on them."

"Send me what you have, and I'll take a look." Sam's phone rang and she took the call from Nick, signaling to her team to get back to work. "Hey."

"How's it going?"

"I was just going to ask you the same thing."

"The West Wing is in chaos. I just saw Derek and he mentioned he's thinking about resigning. He doesn't want to work for Nelson anymore, and he's not alone in that. People like Gloria, and they hate that he did this to her, especially when she was sick."

"That does make it that much more disgusting."

"Indeed."

"Please tell me you think he's going to be able to hold on."

"I don't know, Sam. If it gets out that Gloria was being treated for cancer while he was carrying on an affair with a staffer... I just don't know."

"They're not going to be able to keep a lid on that. Someone will leak it."

"That's my fear as well."

His use of the word *fear* sent her anxiety spiking into the red zone.

"Other than that, Mrs. Lincoln, how was the theater?" Sam asked.

Nick's husky laugh echoed through the phone, reminding her that no matter what happened, she still had him, and he would always have her. "What was I thinking accepting this job from hell?"

"That's a very good question."

"I'm sorry to have done this to us."

"Don't say that. We both knew what we were getting into." They'd had no idea, but he didn't need to hear that. Not from her. "No matter what happens, we got this."

"You won't leave me if I have to become president?"

The question was asked in a teasing tone, but under the humor she sensed deeper concerns. "Are you for real right now? I recently spent one week without you while you were traveling, and I thought I was going to lose my shit. Do you honestly think there's anything that could happen that would make me *leave* you?"

"Just making sure."

"Nick…" That he could still wonder made her ache. "We're going to discuss this further later."

"I'll look forward to that."

"Until then, don't worry about me. You've got enough to think about without stressing about things that're never going to happen."

"Never?"

Where was this coming from? *"Never."* After a pause, she said, "Are we good now?"

"We're good."

"Call me if you need me, and hang in there. He survived a murdering son. Odds are good that he'll get through this too."

"From your lips to God's ears."

"Love you."

"Love you too, babe."

As Sam slapped her phone closed, unease trickled down her backbone. A sense of foreboding had her wondering just how dire the situation was for Nelson and his presidency. Nick didn't use the word *fear* lightly.

She placed a hand over her aching stomach. Before him, the thought of her fate being tied to any man's would've made her laugh. Even when she was married to Peter, she did her own thing, which only added to the discontent in their marriage.

But with Nick, his fate was hers, and whatever happened, they were in it together. When she got home tonight, she'd make sure he fully understood her commitment to him.

If he became president, she'd have to give up her job. There'd be no way she could continue to run the streets chasing down murderers as first lady. The exposure was bad enough as second lady. Though the first lady wasn't required to have Secret Service protection, the stakes would be even higher than they were now. Her lack of a detail as second lady had been a minor scandal that would turn into a circus if they were "promoted."

No, she'd have to step aside because the distractions would make it impossible to do the job her way. And while the thought of giving up the job she loved broke her heart, she'd do it to make life easier for him. Maybe it was time to tell him that, to make sure he knew that there was nothing she wouldn't do for him, even give up the job that had defined her adult life.

A job was just that—a job.

But he… He was her whole world, and she couldn't have him wondering if she'd leave him if he became president.

That wouldn't do at all.

"HOW BAD IS IT?" Nick asked Terry when he returned from a briefing with Nelson's staff.

"Bad."

"Ugh, do I want to hear this?"

"No, you don't."

Terry was one of the few people who knew that Nick had no real desire to be president, despite taking the vice president's job when it was offered to him. Most politicians would've viewed it as a stepping stone to the most powerful job on earth, but Nick wasn't most politicians. To be president, you needed a fire in the belly for the job that Nick didn't have. Not now anyway. And the more he saw from his vantage point close to the presidency, the less he wanted it.

"The *Post* is going to run a story within the hour detailing Gloria's ongoing battle with ovarian cancer."

"Fuck," Nick hissed under his breath.

"I thought you might say that."

For a long moment, the two of them stared at each other as the implications settled on them like a thousand-pound weight.

"My dad is on his way in with Halliwell," Terry said, referring to the Democratic National Committee chairman.

Nick shook his head. "Tell them not to come. I don't want to talk about it."

"Don't shoot the messenger, but when I told Halliwell you wouldn't want to meet with him, his response was, 'Too bad. This isn't just about him.' We need to take the meeting, and let them have their say. After that, we can do what we want."

"We're not doing anything. I can't believe we're already back in this boat so soon after the last time." When the scandal had erupted around Nelson's son, Christopher, who'd gone so far as to torture Sam's ex-husband to death looking for dirt on them, Nick thought he'd seen the precipice of disaster.

But this…

"This feels different than Christopher," Nick said.

"Because it is. This one belongs squarely to Nelson himself whereas that was on his son, and while the argument could be made that the father was guilty by association, the fact was that he wasn't the one who killed people. This time, it's on him, and it's going to look really bad when the American public finds out their beloved first lady was battling ovarian cancer while her husband was having an affair with a much-younger staffer on the campaign trail—and in the White House after the election."

Nick winced at Terry's blunt words. "How did this happen without anyone catching wind of it?"

"I'm sure the Secret Service knew, but it's not their job to stop or report it."

"Did his staff know?"

"I don't think they did. Hanigan is on fire," Terry said of the president's chief of staff, "and Derek didn't have much of anything to say in our meeting."

"Derek said he's thinking about resigning, and who could blame him? No one signs on to clean up the kind of messes they've been dealing with lately."

The extension on Nick's desk buzzed. He picked up the receiver.

"Pardon the interruption, Mr. Vice President, but Senator O'Connor and Mr. Halliwell are here to see you."

"Send them in." He glanced at Terry. "Here we go."

Senator Graham O'Connor, father to Terry, and mentor and father figure to Nick, came busting through the door, smiling from ear to ear. Though he'd been retired from the Senate for most of a decade, he still relished being in the mix, especially when it came to his burning desire to see Nick occupying the Oval Office.

Nick hated to disappoint one of the most influential men in his life, but he didn't share that burning desire, and sooner or later, he was going to have to come right out and say so. Judging by the glee on Graham's sunbrowned face, it was probably going to have to be sooner.

"Well, boys." Graham made an attempt to tame his mop of untamed white hair but only succeeded in making it messier. "What we have here is known as a three-alarm fire."

"And you don't know the half of it," Terry muttered, earning a glare from Nick. "They're going to hear about it within the hour anyway."

Nick waved a hand to tell Terry to fill them in.

"Nelson's affair happened when Gloria was undergoing treatment for ovarian cancer."

As if the legs had been knocked out from under him, Graham sat in one of Nick's visitor chairs, his mouth hanging open in shock.

"Jesus," Halliwell said. "As if it wasn't bad enough." He took a seat, his shoulders sagging. "What're the odds that's not going to get out?"

"Nonexistent," Terry said. "The *Post* has it."

"Fuck!"

"My thoughts exactly," Nick said in response to Halliwell.

"What the hell was he thinking?" Graham asked.

"If I'm guessing," Nick said, "there wasn't a lot of thinking involved."

"He's president of the United States," Halliwell said. "And it started in the midst of a hotly contested reelection campaign. How could he take a chance like that, especially when his wife was battling cancer?"

"Maybe it was *because* his wife was sick." Graham held up a hand to stop the others from pouncing. "I can't imagine anything would be more stressful than my Laine being sick with cancer and me being separated from her for weeks at a time during a presidential campaign. I'm not excusing him in any way, but it could've been the stress."

"All the stress in the world wouldn't have me jumping into bed with another woman, especially if my wife was sick." Nick didn't want to even think about Sam being anything but perfectly healthy.

"You and I agree on that," Graham said, "but not all marriages are built like ours."

Halliwell stood and began to pace. He was known for his passion for the job, but days like this would test even the most dedicated of party loyalists. "How does he survive this after what just went down with his son?"

"He'd be better off resigning to care for his ailing wife," Graham said with barely restrained glee.

"Easy, cowboy," Nick said, equal parts amused and horrified. "No one in this room is going to suggest that Nelson resign. Do you hear me?"

"The suggestion won't come from us," Halliwell said grimly. "But it *will* be coming. I heard Stenhouse on the radio on the way in suggesting that the only ethical thing for Nelson to do would be to resign the presidency so he can tend to his chaotic personal life."

"Goddamned Stenhouse." Graham's disdain for the minority leader—and vice versa—was well known in Washington. "Already running his mouth. Why am I not surprised?"

"We'd be doing the same thing if a Republican president got caught with his pants down," Halliwell said.

Nick liked that about Halliwell—he understood how the game was played, played it fairly and kept his head about him even when engulfed in a political calamity. "Why're you meeting with me rather than Nelson's team?"

Halliwell gave him a withering look. "You really have to ask?"

"He's not going to resign." He *couldn't* resign.

"He may have no choice, and if he does, we need to be ready."

Nick held up his hand. "Like I said when the mess with Christopher exploded, I'm not talking about that until I have to."

Halliwell stared him down, his expression grave. "With all due respect, Mr. Vice President, you have to talk about it. This could go down very quickly after word gets out that Gloria was undergoing cancer treatment while he was banging a staffer."

"I think you should meet with his team to see what can be done to preserve his presidency rather than planning mine." Nick hoped to leave no room for negotiation. "Your time is better spent over there."

Halliwell didn't like that, but to his credit, he chose not to argue the point. "I'll be in touch, Mr. Vice President."

"I'll look forward to that, Mr. Halliwell."

"Sure you will," Halliwell said on the way out.

Terry followed Halliwell to the door, probably because he knew his father wanted a minute alone with Nick.

"What the hell is wrong with you?" Graham asked

after the door closed behind Terry. "He's handing you the presidency on a silver platter, and you're declining?"

"I don't want it this way. Who would?"

"Um, *everyone*?"

Elbows on his desk, Nick leaned forward, addressing his mentor directly. "I know you want this for me, Graham, and I love you for that and so many other things. But I don't want it. Not now and not like this. Maybe not ever, but definitely not like this."

"You may not have a choice if this blows up into a bigger scandal than the last one. People are scandal weary with this administration. This could go very bad for him quickly, and you need to be ready."

Nick sat back in his chair, amused as always by Graham's unrelenting agenda for his career. "What would you suggest I do to 'get ready' as you put it?"

"You need a vice president on standby and a statement ready to go, if he resigns, to reassure the American people that the Republic is strong and that Democracy is working the way the framers intended."

"If he decides to resign, I feel fairly confident he'd at least notify me before it happens."

"And if he doesn't?"

"I know my approach to these things drives you crazy—"

"That's one word for what it does to me," Graham said dryly. "It also sends my blood pressure into the danger zone."

"I'm sorry about that, but I'm not doing anything until I have to. If he resigns, I'll react then. If I do *anything* now, it'll be misinterpreted as me trying to push him out, when that is the *last* thing I want to do."

"Do you honestly believe this guy deserves to be president after all this?"

"I'm not going to be his judge and jury. That's up to the voters and Congress to decide, and with the Democrats owning the Senate, there's no chance of him being impeached."

"The House Republicans can vote to impeach."

"Why? Because he cheated on his wife? Is he the first president to do that? Nope, and he won't be the last. Do I condone what he did? Not at all. It's disgusting, especially since his wife was ill when it happened. If my wife were ill like that, you can bet I wouldn't be out campaigning for reelection. I'd be wherever she was."

"This country needs you in the Oval Office, Nick."

Nick's bark of laughter obviously annoyed Graham.

"It's not funny."

"No, it isn't, but if I don't laugh, I might cry, and that wouldn't be good for the American people."

"I don't understand you. Anyone else in this town would be dancing a jig today, but you're Mr. Calm, Cool and Collected, as always."

"Believe me, I'm not unaffected by this—at all. Quite to the contrary. I just need to take it one step at a time and not get ahead of myself."

"I want you to be president so freaking badly."

"No, *really*? I had no idea!"

Graham grunted out a laugh. "You'd be legendary."

"Your faith in me never fails to amaze and humble me. I hope you know that."

"I do." Graham eyed Nick with the shrewd blue eyes that'd seen something in him as a college freshman. Only thanks to him had Nick made a career of politics. On days like this, he wasn't sure if he should thank or curse the man who'd made him. "You know what I respect most about you?"

"What's that?"

"You march to the beat of your own drummer and don't let blowhards like me or Halliwell or anyone else dictate your path."

"Thank you," Nick said, touched by Graham's observation. "That means everything coming from you, and PS, you're not a blowhard. You want big things for me, and I would've been disappointed if you hadn't come in hot today after this news broke."

"I did come in rather hot, didn't I?"

"Yeah," Nick said, smiling, "but I wouldn't expect anything less. And I'll promise you this—if and when the time comes for me to be president, you'll be the second one to know and the first one I'll want by my side telling me what to do."

Graham returned his smile. "Thank you for that, but you, my friend, won't need anyone telling you what to do."

CHAPTER FIVE

CONKLIN'S WIFE AGREED to see them at four o'clock. Sam drove Malone to Conklin's home in Alexandria. As they crossed the Potomac on the 14th Street Bridge, they listened to the news on the radio, which is how they heard that the *Post* had dropped the other half of the story in the latest scandal enveloping the Nelson administration— Gloria Nelson had been undergoing treatment for ovarian cancer when her husband had the affair with the campaign staffer.

Malone looked over at her. "Did you know that?"

Sam kept her eyes on the road even as her heart leaped into her throat. "Yep."

"Jesus, Sam."

"Yep."

"That's all you got?"

"Yep."

Laughing, he shook his head. "Is Nick freaking out?"

"I don't think so, at least not that he's said to me. We're in a deep state of denial that this is happening again."

"People are going to be infuriated by this. Everyone loves her."

"I know. She's a lovely lady who deserved better from her husband of forty-something years."

"Indeed she did. What possesses a guy in his position to take such a gamble?"

"I'd imagine the power goes to their head, and they think they won't get caught."

"The power goes to their head all right, just not the one on their neck."

Sam sputtered with laughter. "Captain!"

"Oh, sorry. Should I not have put it that way?"

"Nah, you're fine. It was just funny coming from you."

"I'm not always the prim and proper professional you encounter at work, you know."

"I had no idea!" Of course she knew the off-duty side of him, as he'd been one of her father's closest friends.

"Sure, you didn't. I just can't get over this thing with Nelson. He's the most scrutinized human being on the planet, and he can't keep it in his pants while his wife is being treated for cancer?"

"Apparently not." Sam's stomach had turned when he referred to "the most scrutinized human being on the planet." Dear God, that could be her husband before long if this went bad for Nelson. And it was already pretty damned bad.

"Did he think he'd get away with it?"

"He might've if the affair hadn't become public."

Malone sighed. "What a sordid mess."

"I'd like to know *how* it became public."

"You and me both."

Following Malone's directions, Sam pulled into Conklin's condo and parked her black BMW in one of the designated visitor spots. "So tell me what to expect with Mrs. Conklin. I take it she wasn't thrilled to hear we wanted to see her?"

"Correct. I had to talk her into seeing us. She said she's already told us everything she knows."

Sam looked over at him and found him staring at Conklin's front door as a muscle in his cheek pulsed with tension. "You believe her?"

"I don't know what to believe anymore."

Sam reached for the door handle. "Let's go see what she has to say."

"Sam."

She paused and looked back at him.

"She particularly didn't want to see you."

"Gee, could it be because her husband held back info and evidence that could've helped me solve my father's case years ago?"

"Something like that."

"How's that my fault?"

"It's not."

"If she's uncomfortable about seeing me, that's too damned bad. She's lucky she's not locked up with her scumbag husband." Conklin had given up his coconspirators in exchange for his wife not being charged as an accessory. Sam's phone rang, and when she saw Darren Tabor's name on the screen, she ignored the call. "Let's get this over with."

They got out of the car and walked to Conklin's unit, which was one of four three-story townhouses in one of several similar buildings. His was white with black shutters and a black front door. Sam had never been there before and hadn't known what to expect. The place was nice, if you liked living in a complex where every house looked more or less the same.

While Sam hung back, Malone went ahead of her up the stairs and rang the bell.

A woman with blond shoulder-length hair came to the door. She was younger than Sam would've expected and only the dark circles under her eyes gave away the ordeal she'd been through in recent weeks. As far as Sam was concerned, she deserved those dark circles and every other negative thing that came her way. She'd had Skip's missing messenger bag in her possession and never thought to ask her husband what was in the bag or who it belonged to.

Why hadn't she asked?

That was one of many questions Sam had for her.

"Come in." The woman held the door for Malone and then led him and Sam inside a beautifully decorated space.

Sam wanted to hate everything about this house, but she couldn't help but admire it. Had they hired a professional decorator with the money Conklin had made gambling while he was protecting her father's killers? Another question to add to the growing list.

"Kaitlyn Conklin, this is Sam Holland," Malone said.

"I'd say it was a pleasure to meet you," Sam said, "but under the circumstances that'd be inappropriate."

Kaitlyn glanced at Malone, probably hoping he would do something about Sam.

To his credit, he only said, "Can we sit?"

She nodded and took the seat located the farthest from where Sam sat. *Coward.* Sam wished she'd brought her rusty steak knife to work today. She hadn't known she might need it when she left the house that morning. The foolish thoughts kept her from howling with outrage at the display of police department awards and citations that lined the wall behind Kaitlyn. As far as Sam was concerned, Conklin should have to give back every award, citation and promotion he'd ever received. She also planned to make it her mission to ensure he never got a dime of his pension after the way his career had ended. Pensions were for cops who'd served with honor and distinction. They weren't for criminals.

Kaitlyn cleared her throat. "Um, what can I do for you?"

Sam decided to go for the jugular. "How long did you know your husband was hiding information relevant to my father's case?"

"I didn't know! I knew nothing about it until he was arrested."

"Yet you had my father's messenger bag in your possession and never bothered to ask who it belonged to or why your husband wanted it hidden?"

"I didn't know what it was. It was in a box with some other stuff he asked me to keep at my office."

"You didn't question why he suddenly wanted to keep things at your office?" Malone asked.

"I know now that I should have, but at the time, I just did what he asked me to do. I was busy. Work had been crazy... I didn't look at what he gave me or ask him why he wanted me to take it."

"Were you always so agreeable when your husband asked you to hide evidence in a murder investigation?"

Kaitlyn blanched.

"Sam. Stop."

Ignoring the captain, Sam said, "Are my questions about my father's murder making you uncomfortable?"

"I'm so sorry." Her voice was soft as she blinked back tears. "I had no idea that he was involved. He always talked about your father in such glowing terms."

"I don't need to hear that. Especially not now that I

know how little regard he actually had for my father or our family. Did you know my dad took him in after his first marriage ended and he went on a drinking bender that threatened to ruin his career? He slept in my room. I didn't know that until my mom told me recently. My dad saved his career and possibly his life. Don't you think he deserved better from your husband than what he got?"

A sob erupted from Kaitlyn. "He deserved much better. I'm as disgusted as you are by all of this."

"I doubt that."

"What do you want from me?" Kaitlyn's chin quivered and her big doe eyes glistened with tears.

"I want to know every single thing you know about your husband, his career, his friends inside the department." Sam produced a copy of the anonymous note they'd received, tucked into a sympathy card. "I want to know who would've sent this to me after my father died."

As Kaitlyn reached for the paper, Sam noticed the other woman's hand was trembling and took satisfaction in her nervousness. She ought to be nervous. Her husband had covered up an attempted murder of a police officer who'd been his friend for thirty years and the murder of another officer who'd been killed years earlier.

Sam watched intently as Kaitlyn read the message.

"I have no idea who could've sent this. Paul hardly ever talked to me about his work. He would say he needed to leave it at the office and get a break from it when he was home."

"Someone knew that he and Councilman Gallagher were involved. I want to know who that is." Gallagher and two other prominent city businessmen had run a secret gambling ring for years that Conklin had gotten sucked into. The three coconspirators had resorted to the murders of two police officers to keep their cash cow from being discovered, and Conklin had known that the entire time Sam was desperately trying to figure out who'd shot her father.

"I don't know! I never met Gallagher, Santoro or Ryan or had any idea he was involved in anything with them. I didn't know until the rest of the world knew." She broke down into sobs. "Do you *know* what it's like to realize you didn't know the man you were married to for years? Do you have any idea what that's like?"

"No, I don't." Maybe that made her a heartless bitch, but so be it. She had no patience for this woman or her rat fink husband.

"You're so smug. Do you honestly think you know everything there is to know about your husband?"

"Probably not, but one thing I know for certain is that he's never been an accessory to murder."

"I didn't know that about Paul!"

"So you said. Tell me this—when he asked you to take my father's messenger bag and do something with it, what did you think of that request?"

"That was a particularly busy week for me at work, so I tossed it in my car and never gave it another thought."

"It didn't strike you as at all odd that he was asking you to basically hide something for him?"

Kaitlyn met Sam's gaze with defiance that only further irritated Sam. "No, it didn't."

"That's kind of funny, don't you think, Captain? I mean, if my husband asked me to basically dispose of something outside of our house, I'd at least stop to ask him what it was I was disposing of."

Kaitlyn smirked and shook her head. "Paul always said you were a cocky bitch."

"Did he?" Sam smiled widely at Malone. "I bet he thought that was an insult, right?"

"He said you were allowed to do what you want because your dad was good friends with the top brass."

"He said that, did he?"

Kaitlyn leaned in, her expression filled with hatred. "*Everyone* says that."

Sam rubbed her hands over her eyes, affecting a childlike pout. "Oh, my feelings are so hurt! Captain, *how will I go on*?"

Malone's subtle eye roll amused her, even if the things Kaitlyn said left a sting in her gut. She knew perfectly well that not *everyone* within the department thought she got special treatment due to her father's long friendship with Farnsworth, Conklin and Malone. But certainly some people thought that, and even though she knew how hard she'd worked to get justice for her victims, the idea that people thought she only succeeded due to favoritism rankled.

"I think it's time for you to leave my house."

"And I think it's time for you to think long and hard about who might've sent that note. If we find out you had information material to this investigation, we won't hesitate to charge you."

"You can't charge me. Paul made a deal."

"If you're holding out on us, the deal is null and void for him—and for you. So do some soul-searching. Think about who else might've known about this and let me know." Sam placed her business card on the coffee table. "If we discover later that you held out on us, we *will* charge you, deal or no deal."

Sam got up and headed for the front door, eager to get out of the house where the answers to her father's case had been for four of the longest years of her life. If she lived forever, that would never make sense to her.

"I want to see Conklin," Sam said to Malone when they were back in the cold air that washed over her like a balm after being inside that stifling house. "I need to know who sent that note, and I bet he knows who it was."

"What makes you think he'll tell you?"

"Maybe he's feeling guilty for what he kept from me for all that time. It's worth a shot, isn't it?"

Malone leaned against the car, arms crossed, expression serious. "I don't know if it is."

"What do you mean?"

After a long pause, he removed the aviator sunglasses that covered his gray eyes. "I've thought a lot about this after we talked earlier. You've done an admirable job of powering through this, of losing your father suddenly and then solving the case. But this—you seeing Conklin—that might be too much, you know?"

"I get what you're saying, but if other people knew, I want to *nail* them. Don't you?"

"You know I do."

"Then what choice do we have but to confront him with this?"

"Well, we could confront him, but it doesn't have to be you who does it."

Sam thought about that for a second, trying to take her emotions out of the equation, but that was nearly impossible in this case. "I feel so betrayed by him, as a daughter, a friend, a fellow law enforcement officer. It's worse, in some ways, than what Stahl did. At least I always knew Stahl hated my guts, but Conklin... He pretended to be a friend to me and my father while keeping a secret that blew my dad's case wide-open. He *knew*

who did it. All that time… Maybe it's not in my best interest to see him, but I want to anyway."

Malone pondered what she'd said. "All right then,
we'll do it in the morning. But if it goes bad, I reserve
the right to end it. That's nonnegotiable."

"I can live with that." As they got back into the car,
Sam was determined to make sure she got what she
needed from Conklin before it went bad.

CHAPTER SIX

LATER THAT NIGHT, after they had dinner with the kids and got them off to bed, Sam and Nick watched a cable news panel dissect the story about President Nelson's affair. Medical experts described the sort of treatment Gloria Nelson would've undergone to combat stage two ovarian cancer.

"What does it mean to the American people that Nelson would have an affair while his wife was having cancer treatment?" the host asked the panel.

"It certainly makes what was already a sordid story that much more so," one of the female panelists said.

After thoroughly discussing Gloria Nelson's private medical condition, the host moved on to an even more exacting recitation of what was known about Tara Weber, the woman at the center of the scandal. Video footage showed her being chased down a DC side street by reporters as she tried to leave her home.

"They need to get security for her ASAP," Sam said.

"Brant said the Secret Service is hoping to coordinate something with her. Since her child could be the president's son, he could warrant protection and thus she does too. They're just awaiting approval from headquarters to make it happen, which could take a few days. Apparently, they're demanding a paternity test before they'll approve the request."

"Wonder what the opposition will have to say about even more family members getting protection." She was still furious that members of the other party had questioned whether the taxpayers should have to foot the bill to protect Aubrey and Alden after she and Nick took them in.

As the coverage continued, they learned that Tara Weber was thirty-five years old and a graduate of Cornell University and UPenn school of Law, that her newborn child was her first.

"Poor kid to be born into such a circus." The dull, flat tone of Nick's voice had her glancing at him in concern.

"Are you okay?"

"I've never been better."

"What're you hearing about all of this?"

"Well, Graham is thrilled, of course. He can't wait for me to be president—and it doesn't matter to him how it happens. Tomorrow, I have a breakfast meeting with Nelson that was already on the schedule when the shit hit the fan. He couldn't see me today and hasn't canceled the breakfast, so I assume that's still on."

"Ugh, what will you say to him?"

"What can I say? Gee, it was probably a dick move to have an affair in the first place, but especially while your wife of more than forty years was having cancer treatment?"

"You might not want to say that."

"Right, but it's what I *want* to say. I mean, who does that? I get that people cheat, and while I'll never understand that choice, how do you do it while your wife is fighting cancer? It's just disgusting."

"It really is. I feel so badly for her, being dragged into this storm when things are already hard enough for her." Sam swallowed before she asked the question she'd been wanting to pose all evening but hadn't been able to bring herself to ask. "Do you think he'll have to resign?"

"I don't know." Nick sighed deeply. "I was surprised he managed to survive what Christopher did, and he only held on because we gave him a pass. But this? It's anyone's guess. I saw Derek on the way out tonight, and he took me aside to tell me he's still seriously thinking about resigning from Nelson's team. From what he said, the entire staff is just revolted by this."

"I can't blame them. How do you continue to support him if you're revolted by him?"

"That's the very question I've been asking myself all day."

Sam turned so she could see his face. "What do you mean?"

"Nothing says I have to continue to be his vice president."

"You… You're thinking about resigning?"

"Thought's crossed my mind. Why should we twist in the wind waiting to hear whether he's going to survive. I don't want to be president right now, and you have zero desire to be first lady ever, so why stick around to wait for the whole thing to come down on me and us?"

"I never said I wouldn't want to be first lady *ever*."

He rolled his eyes. "Please. You would hate that. And you'd have to give up your job, which would make you hate me."

"Nick… Seriously? You honestly think it's possible for me to hate you?"

"If my job upends your entire life, then yeah, I think it's possible."

Sam sat back, astounded and more than a little hurt,

especially after what he'd said earlier about her leaving him. "If that's what you think, then you don't know me at all. (A) I could *never* hate you. Ever. (B) When you signed on to be vice president, we both knew what we were taking on, that at any time you could be tapped to take the president's place. I mean, that's the primary role of the vice president. (C) I've always known that if you were promoted, I'd have to take a leave of absence from my job."

"I don't want you to have to do that."

"I'd do it for you. How can you not know that?"

"You'd hate it."

"Maybe I would, but I wouldn't hate *you*. How can you say that? How can you even *think* that?"

"I'm sorry. Poor choice of words."

"Extremely poor choice of words, which isn't like you." He almost always got it right, so when he didn't, it was jarring, to say the least.

"I'm just so pissed with him. When I agreed to take this job, I had no idea we were going to have to deal with his murdering son and then his philandering. It's bad enough contemplating all the things outside our control that could happen. But this… This is on him, and I'm fucking furious that he put himself—and me, by extension—in this position."

"I don't blame you for being furious. It's a betrayal of his wife, his family, you and the rest of his team, the American people. But I don't think you should quit."

"Why not?"

"Because if he's forced out, the country will need someone like you to step in and take over—someone strong and competent and worthy of the role."

He shook his head. "I don't want it to be me. I can't

even believe we're back here again, holding our collective breath to see if he'll be able to hang on. The last time wasn't his fault, but this…"

"I know. As a man who believes in faithfulness and loyalty, this is hard for you to understand."

"It's impossible for me to understand. Gloria stood by him through everything. Hell, she's more popular than he is. And this is how he thanks her for her unwavering support?"

Sam picked up the remote and shut off the TV. Anxiety only made his chronic insomnia worse, and more news wasn't helping anything.

"I was watching that."

"You've seen enough." She curled up to him, wishing she had a magic wand that could take his mind off the scandal that threatened to engulf them both. "What can I do?"

He ran his fingers through her hair. "Snuggling with my beautiful wife helps."

"Do you believe me when I tell you there's *nothing* that could happen that would make me hate or leave you?"

"Nothing at all?" he asked with a hint of humor in his tone.

"Nothing that you would ever do."

"I'm sorry I said that."

"I'm sorry if I gave you reason to think it."

"You didn't. I'm not thinking clearly at the moment."

"I hate that you're so stressed out." She raised herself up on one arm and peppered his chest with kisses. "I wish there was *something* I could do to take your mind off it." She flashed her best vixen smile and drew a laugh from him as she kissed her way down the front of him, outlining each of his well-defined abdominal muscles with the tip of her tongue. "Oh, wait... I'm having an idea of something I could do that might help."

His gorgeous eyes danced with amusement. "Do tell."

"I'd rather show than tell."

He twirled lengths of her hair around his fingers. "Don't let me stop you."

Smiling at him, she took his hard cock into her mouth and went for broke, taking him as far as she could and drawing a deep groan from him that pleased her greatly. For this moment, anyway, he wasn't worried about becoming president.

DRIVING TO WORK in the morning, Sam stewed over the dark circles under Nick's eyes that were indicative of another sleepless night, despite her best efforts to relax him. He'd promised to call after his meeting with the president, at which he planned to tell Nelson he was thinking of resigning. He might not follow through, but the president needed to know how revolted he was by what the man had done.

How the most scrutinized human being on the planet thought he'd get away with an affair was beyond her ability to comprehend. And what if the baby turned out to be his? Had he not given a thought to possible pregnancy? Although, how exactly would the president go about acquiring condoms?

The whole thing was so sordid, and at the heart of it was an innocent child whose birth would forever be tied to scandal.

While she waited at a stoplight, it occurred to her that they'd been so caught up in the Nelson business last night that she'd never mentioned to Nick that she planned to see Conklin today. It was probably just as well. The poor guy had enough on his mind without having to worry about her too.

She pulled into HQ and parked in the back, as she did so often these days, to avoid the media that camped out at the main entrance. Mostly they wanted to talk to her, but she gave them as little as possible. One of these days, she hoped they'd realize she would never speak to them about Nick's job or her role as second lady. She was here to do her other job, and that's where her focus would remain.

Before she went in, she took a minute to text Terry.

Nick is wound up over all this crap. Keep an eye on him. Let me know if I'm needed over there.

Like Nick did so often for her, she'd drop everything and run to him if he needed her.

Terry responded quickly.

Thanks for letting me know. I'm on it and will let you know if you should come by.

Thanks, Terry.

Wanting to cover all bases, she also placed a call to Lilia. Other than Nick, Lilia was the smartest Washington insider Sam knew, and she wanted her chief of staff's take on the latest situation.

"Good morning," Lilia said, chipper as always, even first thing.

"Morning."

"I was going to call you to let you know we've re-

ceived a request for you to keynote at the National Association of Police Organizations' Top Cops award
ceremony next May."

"Ugh, what do they want with me?"

"Gee, I wonder. Could it be that you're the second
lady and a high-profile Homicide detective in the na-
tion's capital? They didn't come right out and say so,
but I got the sense that they're also planning to nomi-
nate you as a Top Cop."

"Seriously?" Of course she knew of NAPO and had
been a member since the beginning of her career but
had never been active in the organization.

Lilia laughed. "Yes, seriously. Why are you so surprised? Your career is very deserving of recognition."

"If you say so."

"I say so and so do they. I'll email the info they sent
over and you can decide about the keynote. It's not until
May, so you have time to prepare, but they'd like an answer in the next few weeks."

"Fine, I'll look at it."

"I assume you had another reason for calling."

"You assume correctly. I wanted your take on this
insanity with Nelson and how it's going to affect me
and my husband."

"I really wish I knew. Everyone in this place is on pins
and needles waiting to see what will happen."

"Nick is a stressed-out mess." Sam had come to trust
Lilia and felt she could say that without fear of it being
repeated to anyone.

"I'm sure he is. I hate that this is happening again."

"And I hate making it about me and us when Gloria
has to be so hurt by this. She's such an awesome first
lady."

"She is, and my heart goes out to her."

"My stomach aches from not knowing how it will play out."

"I know it's hard to put it out of your mind, but try not to think about it until you have to. That's the best advice I can give you."

"We're trying." Sam glanced at the clock, which inched closer to eight and the start of her tour. "I've got to get to work, but thanks for the advice."

"If I can do anything—anything at all—you know where I am."

"I do, thanks. Just let me know if you hear anything new."

"Of course I will."

"Thank you for a great time the other night. You throw one hell of a dinner party."

"It was fun. I'm only sorry it ended with more stress for everyone."

"Me too. Talk soon." Sam ended the call and thought about what Lilia had said, wishing it was possible to not think about *it* for the next eight hours. She went inside and made a beeline for her office in the pit. Minutes after she arrived, Dr. Trulo, the department's resident shrink, appeared in her doorway.

"Got a minute?"

"For you, Doc? Always. Come in." At one time, she'd resisted his attempts to shrink her, but she couldn't deny that he'd put her back together after Stahl attacked her. He had become a trusted friend and colleague. With kind gray eyes and thinning hair, he projected an aura of competence and calm in the maelstrom that was her life.

He stepped into the office and shut the door.

"What's up?"

He sat in her visitor chair. "I wanted to check in with you about a couple of things. First, I heard back from the chief about our idea to start the support group for victims of violent crime. He loved the idea but had some questions that I've taken the liberty of answering for both of us."

"Thank you for that. Happy to avoid paperwork whenever I can."

"Had a feeling you'd approve," he said, smiling. "The other thing I wanted to talk to you about involves the trial."

"Stahl's trial?"

He nodded. "It's looking good for conviction, but I think we need to be prepared for the possibility—"

Sam held up a hand to stop him. "If you're preparing me for the possibility of him walking, don't go there. If that happens, they're going to have to lock me up."

"It's a slim possibility, Sam, but there's always a chance the jury won't be swayed."

"The man wrapped me in razor wire and threatened to set me on fire. How does he not get convicted after that?"

"You've been doing this long enough to know how these things go sometimes."

She sat back, crossed her arms and gave him her best defiant look. "I refuse to believe the jury won't do the right thing in this case. It's a slam dunk."

"Humor me… Let's talk about worst-case scenario."

"I can't, Doc," she said softly. "I've held it together all this time since the attack because I believe in the justice system. I believe that the twelve citizens on that jury will hear what he did and put him away for the rest of his life. If that doesn't happen, if I don't get justice in this case, I don't know what I'll do or how I'll continue to fight for justice for others. He *needs* to be convicted."

"I agree with you, and I don't bring this up to upset you. I always want the people I work with to be prepared for what-if."

"I appreciate the concern, but I can't entertain the possibility of him walking. I just can't. Not after he tried to kill me twice."

"I understand, but always remember I'm here for you no matter how it goes down."

"I know, and I appreciate it even if I don't show that." She paused, considered and decided, all in the scope of a few seconds. "Can I talk to you about something else?"

"Anything."

"I'm going to see Conklin today."

His frown overtook his entire face. "Why?"

She handed him a copy of the anonymous note they'd received after her father died.

Trulo quickly scanned it.

"I want to know who sent that."

"You think he knows?"

"If other people inside this department were involved or had knowledge they failed to share for four years, he would know that."

"Does it have to be you who asks the question?"

"Probably not, but part of me wants to force him to look me in the eye and own what he did to me, my dad and our family all while pretending to be our friend."

"I understand that desire. I truly do. But I'm not sure it's in your best interest."

"Maybe it isn't, but I'm still going to do it. And besides, he asked to see me anyway."

"What do you hope to gain?"

"Other than finding out who might've sent this note?"

"Yes, other than that."

"I want to understand how he could've done this to us, to all of us. Not just to my dad and our family, but to the department. You've seen what people are saying about the chief and how this happened on his watch—that his deputy chief was withholding info critical to the shooting of two fellow officers."

"I have. It's unfortunate that Joe is bearing the brunt of something he had nothing to do with."

"It's completely unfair. No one wanted to know what happened to my dad more than the chief, and for him to be blamed for what Conklin did just adds insult to injury."

"It really does, but that's how leadership works. The guy—or gal—at the top gets the blame for everything that happens beneath them, regardless of whether they were involved. But I wouldn't worry too much about Joe Farnsworth. If anyone can weather the storm, he can. I'm far more concerned about you."

"You don't need to be."

"Don't I? You're about to face off with a former colleague who knew all along who shot your dad and why, and you don't think that's cause for concern?"

"I'm trying to think of him the way I would any other perp."

"And how's that working for you?"

"So far so good."

"Until you're in the room with him for the first time since learning he was involved."

"I've had some time to wrap my head around it."

"I'm glad you have, because I'm still struggling with how he could've done this to Skip, to you, to all of us."

"Of course I'm still struggling with that too. But more than anything, I want to know if other people were involved. I want everyone who knew about this and didn't do the right thing out of this department and off the pension rolls." She wanted that with a ferocity that couldn't be measured.

"Come see me after you meet with him?"

"If I need to."

"I mean it, Sam. Don't shrug this off like it's no big deal. This man, who you considered a friend and colleague, was involved in your father's death. Come see me after if you need me."

"I will. Thank you for talking it out with me."

"That's what I'm here for." He stood to leave. "It's important that you be kind to yourself after a loss like this. I understand the burning desire for answers, as long as you understand the risk for further injury to a healing wound. And with that, I'll leave you to carry on."

He opened the office door to reveal Captain Malone, his hand raised to knock. "Tag. You're it."

"Oh joy," Malone said with a wry grin.

Amused by their banter, Sam was grateful for the normalcy of being there, for being on the receiving end of their jokes, for working a case. It helped to keep her mind off the scandal engulfing the White House and allowed her to forget, even for a few minutes, that her dad was no longer waiting for her to get home from a long day on the job. He'd loved to hear all about her cases and to contribute his wisdom wherever he could. She would miss that more than anything. It was the thing they'd shared that no one else in their family could understand the way he could.

"Conklin is being brought up to interview two,"

Malone said. "We think he's still hoping for an opportunity to deal for lesser charges."

"Ha. That'll be the day."

"You know that, and I know that…"

Sam's stomach twisted with nerves, which was rare when she was about to interrogate a witness. Most of the time, she got an incredible high out of confronting murdering sons of bitches. Not this time.

This time was personal.

CHAPTER SEVEN

THE WEEK IN jail had left the former deputy chief looking worn, exhausted and rattled.

Good, Sam thought. *That's the least of what he deserves.*

His wispy blond hair had started to turn gray, and there were bags under his blue eyes that hadn't been there before his arrest. He wore an orange jumpsuit, handcuffs and leg chains that gave Sam tremendous satisfaction. The officers who'd brought him up could've removed the cuffs and shackles but had chosen not to, something Conklin would surely realize. That he was receiving no special treatment gave her special pleasure.

In this room, he was just like any other scumbag with his attorney seated next to him. Sam found it interesting that the lawyer was a public defender and not one of the high-dollar attorneys who usually defended the scumbags.

"Mr. Conklin." Sam took a page from the playbook of FBI Special Agent Avery Hill. He'd refused to use Conklin's rank during an earlier interrogation. "Fancy meeting you here."

"I asked for the chance to see you because I want to say how sorry I am—"

Good thing she didn't have her rusty steak knife

handy. "Save it. Your apologies mean nothing to me now. That's not what I came to talk to you about."

Conklin cast a glance at Malone, seeking help that Malone clearly wasn't inclined to give him.

Sam had to fight the urge to crack up. She had never loved the captain more than she did in that moment, and that was saying something. Sam turned on the recorder and noted who was in the room.

With the recorder running, she sat across from Conklin and for the longest time did nothing but stare at the face of the man who'd been part of her life for longer than she could remember. She'd been too young to recall giving up her room to him after his first marriage ended and her father brought him home to sober him up, effectively saving his career. She didn't remember that, but he certainly did.

"Remember the time you lived in my room for a couple of months?"

Judging by the shocked expression on his pale face, Conklin hadn't expected that question.

"I don't remember it, because I was too young, but my sisters do. They remember you living with us while my dad helped to dry you out so you wouldn't lose your job along with your marriage. Bring back any memories?"

Conklin looked to Malone for rescue.

Malone ignored the silent request, sending the message that Sam had the floor.

"Mr. Dunning," Sam said to the attorney without taking her gaze off Conklin. "Would you please remind your client that it's a good idea to answer the questions he's asked in this room? We'd be happy to review interrogation etiquette for him if he's forgotten how it works along with the other things he learned on the job about withholding evidence in a felony investigation, witness tampering, lying—"

"I remember it," Conklin snapped.

"Oh good." Sam shifted into her zone and felt the buzz of nuts on the block that made this dreadful job so rewarding. "My family will be so glad to know that you *do* recall what my dad did for you during that difficult time in your life. Didn't you also often say that you never would've been deputy chief without him? Hell, I think it's safe to say you never would've made lieutenant or captain without him, isn't it?"

"Yes," Conklin said through gritted teeth.

Sam stared at him, without blinking, for two or three minutes. In that time, she hoped he was thinking about her father and the way he'd let him down.

"I told him to leave the Coyne case alone." Conklin sputtered and tripped over words he couldn't seem to say fast enough. "I tried to warn him."

"What exactly did you warn him about? Did you say, for instance, the same men who murdered Steven Coyne will come for you if you dig into what happened to your dead partner? Were those the words you used?"

"No. I told him a case that cold was a waste of time."

Sam sat back in her chair, folding her arms. "And what was his response?"

Conklin took a deep breath and looked down at his hands on the table. "He said it was never too late to get justice for a fellow officer."

"Isn't that rich?" Sam ached from head to toe with grief for her dad. Of course that's what he'd said. He'd never gotten over the brutal murder of his beloved first partner, who'd been gunned down feet from him in a drive-by shooting that'd remained unsolved until recently. They'd gotten two for the price of one by solving Skip's case—and Steven's. "Don't you think that's rich, Captain?"

"Indeed, I do. But then, Skip was the cop we all wanted to be, and it would be just like him to use his final months on the job to finally get justice for his late partner."

"Yes," Sam said softly, "it would be just like him to do that. When Arnold was killed, he was right there for me, sharing the grief. He got it because he'd been there himself after Steven was killed. He never got over that. I mean, how would anyone get over something like that?"

"Is there a point to this conversation?" Dunning asked. "Or are we simply here to reminisce about old times?"

If looks could kill, he'd have a rusty steak knife sticking out of his heart. "You got somewhere to be, Mr. Dunning? Because I'm pretty sure your client has nowhere to be but back in a cell. He might actually prefer it in here. I hear the lighting is better up here than it is downstairs."

While Conklin and his attorney visibly fumed, Sam settled into the groove of the moment, determined to take her own sweet time. In the meantime, she kept her gaze fixed on Conklin because it rattled him, and rattling him satisfied her greatly. *This is for you, Dad*, she thought, making sure to keep her expression flat so Conklin would never see the emotion she fought so hard to keep out of this room.

"Who else knew?"

Conklin glanced at his attorney and then at Sam. "What do you mean?"

She sat up straight, elbows on the table. "I mean,

who else knew who was behind the shootings of Officer Coyne and Deputy Chief Holland?"

"I, ah, I don't know of anyone, other than Gallagher, Santoro and Ryan."

"This would be a really good time to tell the truth, Mr. Conklin," Sam said.

His face got very red. "I *am* telling the truth!"

"Someone else knew that you and Gallagher were involved—and I'm guessing Ryan and Santoro would have no inclination to help us. So who would that someone else be?"

"How do you know someone else knew?" Dunning asked.

Sam slid the photocopy of the anonymous note across the table and gave them a minute to look at it. "Any other questions?"

"I don't know who could've sent this," Conklin said.

Had she ever noticed before that his lip twitched when he lied? "You're sure about that? Since all your dirty secrets have come to light, I'd think you'd be bending over backward to make things right for the people you harmed, including the man who stepped up for you at your lowest moment. Didn't he deserve better than what he got from you?"

Sam was gratified to see tears in Conklin's eyes.

"I loved him," he said imploringly. "You know I did."

Sam slapped her hand on the table, making the two men jolt. Apparently, Malone had anticipated it, because he remained stoically still. "Don't you *dare* insult his memory by pretending you understood what it meant to love him."

Conklin dropped his head into his hands, sobs shaking him. "I'm so sorry, Sam."

"Stop talking, Paul," Dunning said.

"No, I need to say this." Conklin raised his head and wiped the tears from his face. "I am so sorry about all of this. It was never my intention…"

"What? To hide the fact that you knew who shot my dad for nearly four years?"

"None of it," he said softly. "I didn't intend for any of this to happen."

"Why don't you tell me how it *did* happen."

"Paul," Dunning said, the warning clear.

Conklin shook off Dunning's hand from his shoulder. "I replaced one addiction with another. I got in so deep with the gambling that I couldn't find my way out. Gallagher and Ryan… They owned me."

"How did they find out that Skip was taking another look at Steven's shooting before he retired?" Malone asked.

"I have to stop this right here," Dunning said. "It's not in my client's best interest to have this conversation."

"I need to have it," Conklin said. "I need people to understand that I never would've…"

"What wouldn't you have done? Hidden the truth from your colleagues, your friend's family, the city that's paid your salary for thirty years? You wouldn't have done that?"

"No," he said softly. "Under normal circumstances, I never would've done that. But they *owned* me."

"Who else knew that?" Sam asked again, staring at him without blinking.

"I told you. I don't know."

She leaned in. "Guess what? I don't believe you. So you know what happens now? We rip apart your life and your wife's life, and we find out who else knew."

"Leave Kaitlyn out of it. She knew nothing about any of this."

"So you say."

"It's the truth!"

Sam laughed and glanced at Malone, who seemed equally disgusted. "He wants us to believe him now." She stood. "Let's go, Captain. We've got work to do."

On legs that felt wooden, Sam walked out of the room. She made it halfway down the hallway that led out of the interrogation area before leaning against a wall to collect herself as the adrenaline from the interview drained from her system, leaving her shaky.

"You okay?" Malone asked.

"I need a minute."

"Take as much time as you need."

"I'll catch up to you in a few."

Nodding, he left her and headed toward his office.

Sam made her way to the pit and went straight to her office, closing the door behind her. She sat in the chair behind her desk and tried to get herself together. Even more than a week after the truth had been revealed, it was still surreal to sit in a room with Conklin, with the awareness that while she'd spent years hunting down her father's shooter, he'd had the truth and kept it to himself.

He'd let her chase her tail like a crazy person while continuing to regularly visit her dad as the longtime friend he'd been to all of them. That was the worst part, in her mind. That he'd dared to cross Skip Holland's threshold, pretending to be a friend to him in his time of need, when he'd been partially responsible for putting him in that chair to begin with.

The thought of that man in her father's house made

her feel sick, so much so that she feared she might vomit into the trash can next to her desk.

How could he live with himself, she wondered, seeing Skip in a wheelchair, confined to the first floor of his home, his once-vibrant life reduced so greatly? Had it haunted Conklin's days and kept him awake at night? She would never be able to keep that kind of secret, no matter the consequences for herself. If someone was threatening her life to keep something like that quiet, she'd rather be killed than sit on information that would bring peace and closure to a victim's family—especially if that victim was a longtime friend.

Unfathomable.

A knock on the door jolted her out of her thoughts. "Come in."

Freddie stepped into the office, closing the door. Her partner was tall, dark, handsome and ridiculously in love with his new wife. Thinking about Freddie and Elin was much better than wondering how Conklin could've done what he did to all of them.

He leaned against the door. "Heard you saw Conklin."

"Yeah."

"How'd that go?"

"As you might imagine. He's sorry, didn't mean for this to happen… Yada, yada."

"Whatever." Freddie's normally kind brown eyes were hard. He'd loved and respected Skip, and her dad's death had been difficult for him too. "Did he give you anything?"

She shook her head. "He has no idea who could've sent the anonymous note."

"He knows exactly where it came from."

"I think so too."

"So what's the plan?"

She loved that he knew she'd have a plan and wanted in on it. That was one of many reasons why he was the best partner she'd ever had. "We're going to dig into him—and his wife. I want to know every officer he interacted with outside of work, to start with. If the wife was friends with any of their wives, I want to know."

"We'll get on that." His hard-eyed gaze softened as he studied her. "Are you okay?"

"I will be. Eventually."

"You don't have to be the one to confront these guys, you know. You have people who'd be more than happy to take care of that for you."

"I know, and I appreciate that, but I needed to do this one myself."

"I understand."

"I was just sitting here wondering how he could live with himself, especially after seeing my dad so diminished."

"I wouldn't have been able to do it."

"Me either. What else is he sitting on?"

"You think there's more?"

"If he'd sit on something like this, the shooting of one of his closest friends, how much you want to bet that wasn't all he was keeping to himself?"

"Jeez," Freddie said, sagging a bit. "It's already bad enough. I can't imagine it getting any worse."

"I know," she said, sighing. They might never know the full extent of how Conklin had betrayed them all, but if Sam ever caught an inkling of anything else, she'd fully pursue it. She hoped he spent the rest of his life in prison for what he'd done to all of them.

"Have you seen the papers today?"

"Just the front-page crap about Nelson. Why?"

"There's all kinds of stuff about the department, the dual scandals surrounding Stahl's trial and the charges against Conklin, and what kind of shop Joe Farnsworth is running over here at HQ."

"As if it's his fault that they turned out to be criminals."

"We know it's not his fault, but try telling the mayor that. She's on fire over it and possibly gunning for his job."

Hearing that didn't do much to help the sick feeling in Sam's stomach. She couldn't imagine doing this job without Joe Farnsworth's support. If he got pushed out, maybe the timing would coincide with Nick becoming president, and it would be a good time for her to retire her badge. The thought made her want to break into hysterical laughter.

"My dad is being honored after the holidays by the city's Little League for his years of support for the program. I included you and Elin in the ticket count. No pressure though."

"Of course we want to go. Thanks for including us."

"You were like a son to him." Sam glanced up in time to see his emotional reaction to her comment. "You have to know that."

Freddie nodded. "I did, and it was one of the greatest honors of my life to get to spend time with him and learn from him. Every day I wake up and have to remind myself that he's actually gone. I can't imagine how hard that must be for you."

"It's hard for all of us who loved him. People say that going quick the way he did is better for him, but

for those of us left behind… It's going to take a while
for it to really sink in."

"I guess so. Cleaning up the case is helping me. I hope
it does the same for you."

"I really, *really* want to know who sent that note. I
want to know who else had this info for four years and
didn't see fit to share it."

"We'll get on it."

"Hey, so how's O'Brien working out so far?"

"So far so good. He fits right in, which we knew he
would."

"Good. Glad to hear it. Keep an eye on him and let
me know if he needs anything."

"I will."

The extension on Sam's desk rang, and she took the
call.

"Lieutenant."

She sat up straighter at the sound of the chief's voice.
"Yes, sir. What can I do for you?"

"Come by the office when you get a minute?"

Did he sound weird? And why was he calling her
himself when his admin, Helen, usually made calls for
him. "Of course. I'll be right there."

"Thank you."

The line went dead, and she replaced the receiver on
the desktop unit.

"What's up?" Freddie asked.

"The chief wants to see me."

"He called you himself?"

"Yeah, and he sounded weird." She dropped her head
into her hands. "What's this going to be now?"

"I hope to God he's not going to resign."

She forced herself to rally, standing as she sighed. "You and me both."

Her greatest hope was that neither her boss nor Nick's would resign anytime soon. Or ever, for that matter.

CHAPTER EIGHT

SAM WALKED FROM the pit to the main lobby, where she ran into Malone, who seemed to be heading in her direction.

"What's up?" he asked.

"The chief called and asked me to come by."

"He called you himself?"

Sam nodded. "And he sounded weird."

Malone's deep sigh did nothing to settle her nerves. "He's sounded weird the last few days as the firestorm swirled around him."

"I absolutely hate that people are blaming him for shit he had nothing to do with."

"I know, but that's how it goes, unfortunately."

"Do you think it would matter if I went on the record saying no one in my family blames him for what Conklin or Stahl did? I could say that we never could've gotten through the last four years without his support and that of the department."

"Couldn't hurt, but see what he has to say before you do anything."

"I'd do it if it would make a difference."

"And we all know how much you love talking to the press."

Sam forced a smile even as her heart lodged in her

throat. The chief could *not* resign. He absolutely couldn't. "You want to come with me to see him?"

"He didn't invite me."

"I'll tell him I did."

"Sure, I'll tag along, but only because I'm nosy."

Sam was irrationally relieved to have the captain with her as she walked toward the chief's suite of offices and nodded to Helen.

"Go ahead in," Helen said. "He's expecting you."

Did she sound weird too, or was Sam imagining that?

She knocked on the door, and when the chief called out for her to come in, she opened the door and ducked her head in. "Is it okay that I brought the captain?"

"Yeah," Chief Farnsworth said. "It's fine."

The two of them walked in, and the captain closed the door behind him.

"What's up?" Sam asked.

"Heard you met with Conklin. I was wondering what that was about."

"He asked to see me because he wanted to apologize. You can imagine how that went. I'm trying to figure out who sent the anonymous note during the investigation, the one that told us to look inside our own house and City Hall. Someone else knew that people inside the department had information pertaining to my dad's case, and I want to know who."

"I'd like to know that too, although once we find out, the press will have even more arrows to aim at me and my lackluster leadership of the department."

He didn't sound weird in person, Sam decided, but he did sound depressed, disheartened, demoralized. Not that she could blame him for any of those things. She felt the same way knowing the answers they'd needed for so long had been right under their noses. Taking a seat in front of his desk, she considered her words carefully. "The people who matter know the truth, Chief."

"For all the good that does me in the court of public opinion." As he spoke, he fiddled with a pen in an aimless way that was contrary to his normal sharp, focused demeanor. "I've got a lieutenant about to be convicted of attempted murder, among other felonies—or at least he'd better be—and a deputy chief charged with multiple felonies. It's not a good look on me or any of us."

"In a department of this size, these things will happen," Malone said.

The chief raised a brow. "In the top leadership?"

"Would it help if I released a statement making it clear that no one in my family blames you for what Conklin did and that we never would've gotten through the four years of my father's injury without your support and that of the department?"

Farnsworth appeared to give that consideration. "It might be better coming from Celia rather than you."

"I'm sure she'd be happy to do it. I'll take care of it."

"Thanks for the sentiment. Even if it doesn't put out the firestorm, it helps me cope with it to know you feel that way."

"We *all* feel that way, Chief. You were my dad's best friend. You wanted his case solved as badly as we did."

"I really did. If I'd had any idea…"

"You don't have to say it. We know. I'm worried you're letting them get to you, and that's not usually your style."

"It's hard not to take the criticism to heart in this case. Conklin was my deputy chief, my close friend. I deserve the crap coming at me."

"How do you deserve it?" Malone asked. "You didn't know what he was hiding."

"I misjudged him for all these years."

"We *all* did," Malone said. "*Skip* did. He welcomed him into his home, almost weekly after the shooting. Would he have done that if he'd had the slightest inkling that Conklin held the key to the entire thing?"

"No, but—"

"No buts. Sir. You had no way to know your deputy was hiding information that would lead to him being charged as an accessory to murder." Malone's forceful statement seemed to get the chief's attention. "This is *not* your fault, and if you quit, you'll be handing the haters an easy victory."

"I think I've had enough."

"No," Sam said. "No, you haven't. You're grief-stricken from the loss of Dad, and you're shocked by what Conklin did. People say you shouldn't do anything rash after a big loss. Don't make any big decisions, they say. That applies to you too. If you go out like this, it'll haunt you when the grief fades and the anger recedes. You'll regret it."

"She's right," Malone said. "This isn't the time to make any big decisions."

"When did our young lieutenant get so wise?" Farnsworth asked Malone, as if Sam wasn't sitting right there.

"Around the time she married up," Malone said.

Farnsworth laughed—hard—and Sam exhaled for the first time since she entered his office.

"Now that's more like it," Sam said.

"I hear what you guys are saying," the chief said, "and I appreciate the wisdom as well as the counsel."

"So you're not going to quit?" Sam asked. That was

the only thing he hadn't said for sure and the one thing she needed to know so she'd be able to sleep that night.

"Not today."

"You'll talk to us before you do anything?" Malone asked.

"I will."

"I know you'd normally talk to Dad about something like this," Sam said, hoping she wasn't out of line for what she was about to suggest. "I know I'm no substitute, but I'm here if you need me."

He shot her a wry look full of amusement and affection. "Why do you think I called you?"

She was unreasonably touched by the sentiment. "Oh, um, well, I'm glad you thought of me when you needed a friend."

"You're not alone in this office, Joe," Malone said, "despite how it might seem at times. A lot of people around here have got your back."

"That's good to know, and this helped."

"Anytime," Malone said. "We're always here for you."

Sam stood. "I'll talk to Celia about issuing a statement."

"Thanks. And by the way, I hear you're trying to poach my amazing Officer Charles, and you can't have her."

"I *need* her, Uncle Joe."

He rolled his eyes at her shameless use of the name she'd called him as a child. "I need her more."

Sam flashed her most charming grin. "Will you think about *sharing her* with a friend?"

The chief's brows furrowed as he scowled. "Maybe. We'll see."

Sam clapped her hands and glanced at Malone. "Maybe means yes."

Farnsworth wasn't having it. "Maybe means *maybe*. Now get back to work and keep me posted on what you find out about the anonymous note."

"I will," Sam said.

She walked out with Malone, past Helen's inquiring gaze, and waited until they were out of earshot of her or anyone before she spoke. "Did we just talk him off the cliff?"

"I think we did. You were spot-on in there. What you said about not making any rash decisions was good advice."

"He *would* regret it when the dust settles. The *Post* article threw gas on a simmering fire." The newspaper had published an article detailing the department's recent troubles, recapping the case against former Lieutenant Stahl and the new charges against former Deputy Chief Conklin, among other high-profile personnel matters that had occurred on the chief's watch.

"I agree, and when he has a chance to think about it, he will too. No one wants to go out of a job like this in the midst of a firestorm of criticism."

"We need to keep an eye on this, check in with him. Frequently."

"I'll stay on it," Malone said. "Losing your dad puts a big hole in his support system. Hell, losing Conklin does too. Joe thought Conklin was on his team, and to find out otherwise is a shock to his system."

"It's a tough thing for everyone involved. It has us questioning everything. Wondering who we can trust on this job isn't a question any of us want to be asking. I'm going to call Celia. Getting that statement out ought to help."

"Let's hope so."

Sam left him in the lobby and headed for the pit, keeping her head down to discourage people from talking to her. She went into her office and shut the door to place the call to her stepmother.

"Hi there," she said when Celia answered the call to her cell.

"This is a nice surprise. Aren't you at work?"

"I am. Do you have a second?"

"For you? Always."

Her stepmother's kindness was one of the things Sam loved best about her. "I'm sure you've seen the stuff in the papers and on the news about the chief."

"I have and I'm disgusted by it. As if he knew what his deputy was up to. He would've been the first one to throw the book at Conklin if he'd known."

"I'm glad you feel that way. We were wondering if you might issue a statement in support of the chief."

"Absolutely. Tell me what you want it to say, and I'll do it today."

"Speak from your heart about what Joe Farnsworth meant to you and Dad during the years following his shooting."

"That's easy enough. We wouldn't have gotten through it without his friendship and the unwavering support of the department."

"Say that too."

"Should I email it to you?"

"That'd be great."

"I'll text you when I send it."

"Thank you so much for this. It'll mean a lot to the chief."

"It's the least I can do after all he did for us. I'll get to it. Watch for my text."

"Thanks, Celia."

"You got it."

She sounded feisty and empowered, which was much preferred to the pervasive sadness that had clung to her since her husband's sudden death.

A knock sounded at the door.

"Enter!"

Freddie came in, his eyes wide with shock. "Tara Weber has been found dead in her home."

As his words registered, Sam felt as if someone had pulled the chair out from under her.

"Sam."

She looked at him, her mind racing with the possible implications.

"We need to go."

Operating on autopilot, Sam stood, grabbed her keys, radio and cell phone and walked toward the door, going through the motions even while feeling as if she were underwater, unable to take a breath or do anything other than fight her way to the surface.

Nick. She had to tell him before he heard it from someone else. Was she allowed to tell him? She wasn't sure and didn't care. Not this time.

She flipped open her phone and placed the call to the top person on her list of contacts.

He answered on the second ring. "Hey, babe. How's your day going?"

"Nick."

"What? What's wrong?"

"Tara Weber was found dead in her home."

His sharp exhale echoed through the phone. "Oh my God. What about the baby?"

"Haven't heard anything yet, but there was no report of him being there."

For a long moment, neither of them said anything as they both tried to wrap their heads around what this would mean for them.

"What do you know?" he asked.

"Only that so far."

"I feel like I'm going to be sick."

"You and me both."

"You don't think Nelson had anything to do with this, do you?"

"I honestly have no idea what to think," Sam said. "Obviously, there's no way he could've done it himself, not with the Secret Service shadowing his every move. But could he have gotten someone else to do it? I suppose that's possible. That begs the question of why would he though, with the whole world watching him—and her—at the moment."

"Sam… You're going to have a matter of *days* to figure this out before he's forced out. People in both parties wanted him out before this. Now…"

"I hear you. I'm on it."

"Keep me posted?"

"I will, but you can't tell anyone. Let them hear about it through their channels. I'm out on a limb telling you."

"I hear you."

"You going to be okay?"

"I will once you figure out who did this and prove that my boss had nothing to do with it."

"I'll call you as soon as I know anything."

"Assume you'll be working late tonight."

"Probably. You're on kid duty?"

"Yep. I got it covered. See you when you get home. Wake me up if I'm asleep."

She never would but said what he wanted to hear. "I will. Love you."

"Love you too. Be careful out there with my wife. She means the whole world to me."

"I'm always careful. See you."

Talking to him helped her feel more grounded, more focused, prepared to go to battle once again for someone who'd been murdered in her city. Regardless of how Tara Weber's murder impacted her life and her husband's, Sam would give everything she had to get justice for Tara—and her family.

FREDDIE DROVE THEM to Georgetown while Sam pondered the implications. Who had killed Tara days after her affair with the president had gone public, and so soon after the birth of her son, who may or may not be Nelson's? Would the investigation she was about to launch lead to her own husband becoming president?

Dear God, the implications... It was enough to make her want to run and hide. After only recently closing her father's case, did she have it in her to fight this new battle?

When they were stopped at a red light, Freddie looked over at her. "I can hear your brain frying."

"You can't hear a brain fry."

"I can hear yours. It makes a very particular sizzling sound. What're you thinking?"

"That this can't be happening. It was bad enough that he had the affair. Now the woman is dead?"

"What did Nick say?"

"He can't believe it either."

"Does he think Nelson was involved?"

"Neither of us knows what to think where he's concerned. Did he go to her house and murder her himself? Highly unlikely. He couldn't have done that with Secret Service all around him. But could he have gotten someone else to do it? Sure. Anything is possible."

"I can't get my head around the president of the United States arranging a murder."

"Maybe someone close to him did it without his involvement, hoping to solve a big problem for him."

"Instead, they created a whole new one."

And whoever killed Tara had created a whole new problem for her to solve too. Normally, Sam felt a rush of adrenaline as she headed to the scene of a new homicide that would require her full attention. This time she felt… Numb, exhausted, drained, oddly detached from what was happening right in front of her.

Dr. Trulo had warned her about this, the inevitable "come down" after the frantic activity that followed her father's death and the renewed focus on his case. Not to mention, four years of pursuing leads and asking questions that had led nowhere. And now they had answers—answers they didn't like, but answers, nonetheless. A hollow pit had formed inside her, taking the place of the potent, boiling rage she'd carried with her since the day their lives had been changed forever by a bullet that hadn't killed her father but might as well have.

The hollowness made her ache—for her dad, for the suffering he'd endured, for the years they'd never have together, for the betrayal at the hands of a man they'd considered a friend. She'd done her best to be stoic and strong for the people around her who were also in pain, but inside… Inside, she ached.

"Meant to tell you that Gonzo called me last night," Freddie said, breaking a long silence.

"How's he doing?"

"Really well. He sounded better than he has in a long time."

"I'm glad to hear that. Any news about a release date?"

"Not yet. He said he'll know more in a week or two, but he's planning to stay for as long as they'll have him so he doesn't have to go back ever again."

"That's good news." Hearing her sergeant was on the road to recovery from the pain medication addiction he'd developed after the murder of his partner was the best news she'd heard in ages.

"He was asking about you, how you're handling everything with Conklin."

"I'm handling it, just like everyone else." The last thing she wanted to do was *talk* about it any more than she had to. She was so sick of *talking* about it.

"Except you're not everyone else. You're Skip's daughter, and no one else in the department was as close to him as you were, so that makes it very different for you."

She wanted to scream at him, to thank him for stating the obvious, but she didn't do either of those things because he was trying to help and didn't deserve to be attacked.

"People are concerned, Sam, because they care. We care. I hope you know that."

Sam forced a small smile for his benefit. "I do know, and I appreciate it. I'm just not sure what else to say."

Right now, her biggest concern was the fucking traffic that was impeding their progress. "Flip on the lights."

Freddie did as directed and cars started to slowly—far too slowly for her liking—get the hell out of their way. Twelve minutes later, they arrived at the address in Georgetown that they'd been given by Dispatch.

"Third floor." Freddie led the way past the scrum of reporters who screamed questions about Nick becoming president and her becoming first lady and would she have to give up her job and would she have a Secret Service detail and what did she think of the president's affair and did he kill his mistress and—

The main door closed, sealing them off from the ravenous shouts.

"They're out of control," Freddie said.

"Let's get Patrol over here to get them under control."

He used his handheld radio to make the call.

They took the elevator to the third floor, where they were met by Patrolman Clare, who Sam hadn't met before. He was young and fresh faced with the pale complexion and wide eyes of someone who'd just seen murder for the first time.

"What've we got?"

Clare consulted his notebook, his hands trembling ever so slightly. "Tara Weber, age thirty-five, found dead in her bed by her assistant, Delany Russo, a Georgetown University graduate student, who has worked for Ms. Weber for two years."

"Where's Russo now?"

"Inside."

"Assume the ME is on the way?"

"Yes, she's en route."

"Is Ms. Weber's baby here?"

"No."

"Ask the assistant where he is," Sam said to Officer Clare as they entered an apartment painted bright white with gorgeous, gleaming hardwood floors. Big windows allowed in so much light that the glare brought tears to Sam's eyes. How did anyone stand that? She'd need sunglasses to live here.

On a white leather sofa, a young blonde woman sat with a female Patrol officer whom Sam did not recognize. Officer Clare went over to consult with the blonde woman and then came back to report to Sam and Freddie.

"The baby is with Ms. Weber's parents in Herndon."

That was a relief. "Thank you. Take me to the victim."

"This way." Officer Clare's reluctance to see the crime scene again was obvious, but to his credit he did the job and held up.

Sam wasn't sure what she'd been expecting, but the reminder that Tara Weber had been shockingly beautiful only added to the pervasive sadness percolating inside her. Not that less-than-beautiful people didn't stir her emotions at times like these, but Sam's immediate, visceral reaction to seeing Tara naked in her bed, her perfect face still perfect even in death, her skin unmarked except for the violent bruises on her neck, rattled her. Long, dark, wildly curly hair fanned out on the white pillow. Without the bruises, one might mistake her for a woman asleep rather than dead.

Sam stepped in for a closer look at the bruises that had turned the woman's neck a vibrant shade of dark purple.

"Were you able to locate her cell phone?"

"I haven't seen it, but I haven't done a full search."

"Let's get a warrant to search the apartment," she said to Freddie.

"On it." He went off to call Malone, who'd put forth the request. They had to dot the i's and cross the t's to make sure any evidence uncovered was done so legally.

"Any sign of forced entry?" she asked Clare.

"No, ma'am."

"So whoever it was, she let them in. Can you please get with building security to obtain video from the building entrance and the third-floor hallway?"

"Yes, ma'am." Clare beat feet out of there, no doubt anxious to put distance between himself and the dead woman.

Working Homicide was, in some ways, like any other job once you got used to the things you saw on a daily basis, Sam thought. You built up calluses on your soul that protected you from the reality of what you were experiencing. Most days they did, anyway. Some days, like this one, when you were already raw, the calluses provided little protection and the pain sneaked by them, lodging itself in the places normally kept sealed off so you could function on the job.

Deep thoughts by Lieutenant Sam Holland.

She would've laughed if it weren't for the dead woman on the bed and the investigation that required her to put aside her own emotions to focus on the task at hand.

"You okay?" Freddie asked, his brows knitted with the concern that had been directed her way far too often lately.

"How about we make a deal, you and I?"

"Um, if we must…"

Her little grasshopper had learned to be wary. She'd

taught him well. "If I'm not okay, I'll let you know. Otherwise, you don't need to check on me."

"I'm sorry. I'm not trying to smother you. I can't help but be concerned after…well, everything."

"I understand, and if the roles were reversed, I'd feel the same way. It's just that I can't talk about it every minute of the day and still do what I'm supposed to do, you know?"

He immediately looked stricken. "Yeah, I get it."

"Don't do that either."

"What?"

"Worry about saying the wrong thing. Let's keep it real. That's what I need more than anything right now."

"I'll do my best to keep it real while not worrying too much about how you really are."

"Thank you." He was the best partner she'd ever had, and she knew how much he cared about her, not just as a boss and colleague but as a treasured friend and the ball-busting older sister he'd never had. She felt the same way about him, so much so that she probably shouldn't still partner with him. But that was an applecart she had no desire to upset. Not now anyway.

"I'll stop asking if you actually promise to tell me if or when you're not okay. No bullshit, no evasions. Just the truth."

"Ummm," she said in a scandalized whisper, "you said a swearword."

"Sam." Displeasure radiated off him. "Be serious."

"I promise." She looked him in the eye as she said the words, knowing that would matter to him.

His terse nod was his only reply. "Have you ever seen so much white in anyone's house?"

"It was definitely her favorite color."

The conversation, the sparring, the inanity kept them sane while they waited for the ME, standing watch over their latest victim until she could be turned over to Lindsey's team.

"This should be fairly slam dunk, right? A place like this will have the best security footage money can buy."

Sam glared at him. "You didn't really use the words 'slam dunk,' did you?"

His brows furrowed with confusion. "Why?"

"Way to put a hex on us. If it *was* going to be an SD, it won't be now."

"Whatever." He rolled his eyes as he did so often during a shift with her that she wondered how he didn't manage to sprain his eye sockets.

They were in that room with Tara Weber's body for a long time before Lindsey arrived with her deputy, Dr. Byron Tomlinson.

"The president's mistress?" Byron all but salivated from the salaciousness of it.

Sam shot a look to Lindsey.

"Shut up, Byron, and have some respect. That's certainly not all she was."

Sam would've given Lindsey a high five if she'd been close enough. She couldn't have said it better herself. There was much more to Tara Weber than the headlines she'd starred in over the last few days, and Sam was determined to make sure she didn't become a caricature in death.

"Apologies." Byron sounded more like his usual professional self. "I just can't believe everything that's come out about her and Nelson and the kid." He looked to Sam. "Is the baby here?"

"Nope." Sam stepped back to give Lindsey and Byron

access to Tara. "That's one of many things we need to figure out. Now that you're here with her, we're going to get to it."

"I've got her." Lindsey gazed at their victim with the compassion that made her the best at her grim job. "What a beautiful woman she was."

"I thought the same thing. It's awful."

"She was very dynamic in person," Byron said, gaining the attention of both women.

"How do you know that?" Sam asked.

"I've been following the story about her and Nelson online. I watched some YouTube videos that showed her working on the campaign. She had that special something that gets people to pay attention to her. What do they call it? *Je ne sais quoi?*"

"Look at you, all bilingual, Dr. Tomlinson," Sam said, amused even as her mind raced with next steps in the investigation.

Byron scoffed. "Hardly. But whatever you want to call the *it* factor, she had it in spades. The woman was going to be a rock star long after Nelson was out of office."

"Thanks for the insight, Byron. It helps." If nothing else, Byron had given her some threads to pull. Who else, besides Nelson, would have reason to want a so-called rock star like Tara dead?

CHAPTER NINE

SAM GESTURED FOR Freddie to follow her into the living room. Sam sat on the sofa across from the Patrol officer and the distraught young woman who'd discovered her employer dead in her bed. Sam focused on the witness. "Delany, I'm Lieutenant Sam Holland. This is my partner, Detective Cruz."

"I know who you are," she said between sobs.

Sam heard that a lot these days. Everyone knew who she was since her husband became vice president, which caused her heartburn on the job that she hadn't had to contend with before his big promotion, not that she'd ever tell him that. He had more than enough on his mind where she was concerned.

Delany's face was red and blotchy, her eyes swollen.

"Talk to me about Tara."

"She was the best person I've ever known. She's helped me so much."

"How so?"

"I was working as a barista in a coffee shop off campus my senior year at Georgetown."

The Patrol officer, a young black woman named Youncy, handed Delany another tissue.

"Thank you." Delany wiped her eyes and nose. "We got to know each other because she came in at the same time every day. I...I was a scholarship student paying my own expenses, and she commented on my work ethic. I told her I had big dreams. The next day she asked if she could hear about them. We met for coffee after my shift, and she became my mentor. After I graduated, she hired me to be her personal assistant."

Sam took notes as Delany spoke. This woman had the goods on Weber and would be their most valuable asset in this investigation. Her first order of business would be to arrange protection for Delany. An officer would be positioned outside her door until an arrest was made. "Did you travel with her during the campaign?"

Delany nodded. "A couple of times. It was the most exciting thing I was ever part of."

"Were you aware of her affair with the president?"

"Not until everyone else was."

"How's that possible if you were her personal assistant?"

"I wasn't with her twenty-four hours a day. I was her professional assistant, not her babysitter."

Okay, Sam thought. *She's loyal to the woman, and understandably so. Tara plucked her out of a coffee shop and gave her a dream career.*

"Did you observe her interacting with the president?"

Delany nodded. "She was a critical member of his campaign team, in charge of market research and polling. He was always coming to her for information. *Gimme the numbers, T,* he would say."

"But you had no inkling that there was more to their relationship than business?"

"No one did. Everyone I've talked to from the campaign is shocked by the news they were involved on a personal level."

"Can you think of anyone who'd want her dead?"

"No! Everyone loved her. She was just… She was amazing," she said in a soft whisper. "I can't believe she's gone, and her little boy…" Delany's eyes filled. "She loves him so much."

"Where will I find her parents and the baby?"

Delany consulted her phone and gave Sam the parents' address in Herndon. "She wanted him out of here for a few days until the story about her affair with the president died down."

"And she thought that would happen in a few days?"

"I think she was hoping it would." Delany dabbed at her eyes again. "People are saying the most awful things about her, and it's so unfair. She was such a great person. Maybe she made a mistake, but that shouldn't define her entire life."

Sam tried not to judge other women for the choices they made. God knows, she didn't want anyone judging her. But this was a tough one. Tara had slept with the most high-profile man in the world, a man who'd been married for forty years to the most beloved woman in the country. As someone who worked in the political field, she had to know what she was in for if the affair ever became public. And *how* had it become public? That was something else she needed to figure out.

"I'm going to need her schedule for the last couple of days—let's make it the last week."

Delany nodded, picked up her iPad from the table and began typing. "What's your email?"

Sam gave it to her.

"Sent."

That was easier than usual. Often assistants and receptionists made a blood sport out of stonewalling her, but Sam always won those battles. It was nice to get what she needed without having to fight for it. "Thank you. We're going to arrange to have an officer outside your door until we make an arrest."

She stared at Sam, seeming stricken by the thought of cops underfoot. "Why?"

"Because whoever killed Tara will know that you're cooperating with us. We'd like to keep you alive. I assume you'd prefer that as well."

"Y-yes, but I have a life and…"

"Ms. Russo, this is a Homicide investigation. I want justice for Tara Weber, and I'd like to think you want that too."

"I do! Of course I do. How anyone could hurt her…" She broke down into sobs again. "She didn't deserve this."

"No one deserves to be murdered."

"Especially Tara. She was so good to all the people in her life. I can give you five other stories of people like me who she 'elevated,' as she put it. She liked to say she could spot a winner, and she liked to give people a chance to shine. I loved that about her." She gave Sam a hesitant look. "You don't think the president had anything to do with this, do you?"

Sam's stomach ached at the thought of that possibility. "I really hope not."

SAM CALLED IN the rest of the squad, and they knocked on every door in the building hoping to find someone who had heard a disturbance in Tara's unit, but their canvass turned up nothing useful.

"What's next?" Freddie asked when they were outside in the cold again.

Sam zipped up her parka and pulled on gloves. Winter was coming in fast and furious, along with shorter days and long, dark nights. "I want to see the parents."

"Have they been notified?"

"Yes, Herndon police took care of that, thank goodness."

"No kidding. I hate having to do that."

"You and me both."

The rest of the squad joined them on the sidewalk.

"What can we do?" Detective Green asked.

"I'm going to forward Tara's schedule for the last week to you. Get with Carlucci and Dominguez," she said of her third-shift detectives. "Have them arrange protection for Delany Russo and put together a list of people we need to talk to. Have them work with IT to see what the security film yielded. When Crime Scene gets here, tell them we're looking for her cell phone."

"I'll wait for Crime Scene," Detective Green said.

"Thanks. We'll regroup in the a.m. Good work today, everyone."

The others said their goodbyes and headed for their cars while Sam and Freddie got into hers, this time with her at the wheel. "I need to check in with Nick."

"Same with Elin. Lucky me that I get to work late."

"I can reassign you if being my partner is too arduous for you."

"No need, Lieutenant. You know I'm delighted to work with you."

She snorted out a laugh at his predictable reply. He was nothing if not entertaining.

They sent texts to their spouses and then hit the road, battling westbound rush hour traffic leaving the District on Route 66.

"Had to be freaking Herndon," she muttered. "Way the fuck out there."

"I know, and this traffic is hideous."

"How do people do this every day?"

"No idea. I couldn't stand it."

"How many years of their lives do they lose to commuting, do you suppose?"

"I'm sure someone has done the math." He tinkered with the radio and put on WTOP to get traffic updates.

Sam would've preferred to blast Bon Jovi, but she could do that on the way back. Her phone chimed with a text. She handed it to Freddie. "Read that to me?"

"I'm scared to look. If it's a sext from your husband, I quit."

Sam laughed. "Just read it!"

"Oh thank God. It's from Celia." He read aloud.

"Sam, how does this sound? On behalf of the entire Holland family, I wish to express my thanks to Chief Joe Farnsworth and the distinguished members of the Metropolitan Police Department for their friendship and loyalty to my late husband, Deputy Chief Skip Holland, and for the beautiful send-off they recently gave him. There is no way Skip would've survived the aftermath of the shooting that left him a quadriplegic without the friendship and support of Joe Farnsworth. It breaks my heart to see the press savaging Joe, who stood resolutely by my husband for the four long years that followed his devastating injury. While we're saddened by the involvement of a man we considered a close friend, we're heartened by the love we've received from Joe, as well as the men and women of the MPD who serve our city every day with distinction and honor. I ask that the media and other concerned citizens keep their focus on the men responsible for this heinous act as they are brought to justice. Sincerely, Celia Holland."

Sam blinked back a flood of tears. "It's perfect. Will you respond and tell her that and then forward it to Malone to be released?"

"Yep."

The gruff tone of his voice as he said the single word told her he was equally affected by Celia's heartfelt words.

Sam cleared her throat and forced herself to refocus on the job at hand. "What's your thought on Weber?"

"Don't really have one yet, but from Delany's description of her, she seems like a top-notch kind of person."

"I thought so too. I like the way she met Delany, saw something in her and offered her an opportunity—and that it wasn't a one-off. She did it for others too."

"It's too bad that the sum of her story is going to be her affair with the president though."

"Not if I have anything to say about it." Sam would make sure that the rest of Tara's story got as much airtime as the salacious stuff. "Tell me this… It's not a coincidence, is it, that the story about her and Nelson hits and two days later she's dead?"

"I was thinking the same thing. It has to be connected somehow."

Sam released a deep sigh. "I was afraid you were going to say that." Her phone rang and she took the call from Nick on the Bluetooth. "Hey, I'm driving so you get me and Freddie."

"Hi, Freddie."

"Hi there."

"What's the latest?"

"We're on our way to Herndon to see Tara Weber's parents. They've got her son with them."

"Oh good. I'm glad he was located."

"Yeah, we got lucky. Her assistant was the one who found her and had the four-one-one on where the kid was, her schedule for the last week and other info that would've taken us days to get without her."

"That's something anyway. Did she know about the affair with Nelson?"

"She says no, but I find that hard to believe. She traveled some with the campaign and knew everything else that Weber was doing. How did she not know that? I also want to know if his Secret Service detail knew what was going on. They had to know."

"Even if they did, it's not their job to interfere with the president's personal life."

"Maybe not, but how does something like that stay secret in the midst of a campaign in which people are always around and watching everything?"

"I can't imagine something like that staying secret in the fishbowl of a national campaign."

"Hopefully, the parents can give us some insight into who knew what and when."

"God, I hope so." He sounded far more stressed than usual. "The White House is on fire over this. Brandon Halliwell has called me three times since the news broke about Tara being murdered."

That news spiked Sam's anxiety. "What does he want?"

"Mostly he's making sure I haven't skipped town."

"Are you thinking about doing that? Skipping town?"

"Not without you and the kids."

"This might be the perfect time for a family trip to Bora Bora. We always said we wanted to take Scotty there someday. If they can't find us…"

Nick's low chuckle echoed through the car. "They'd find us. We'd have to take the Secret Service with us and they'd snitch."

"They totally would," she said, sighing.

"The best thing you can do for all of us right now is to quickly figure out who killed Tara, preferably someone who has no connection whatsoever to Nelson."

"Is that all you need from me?"

"Well, that's all I can say in front of young Freddie." His sexy, suggestive tone would've made her swoon had she not been driving in bumper-to-bumper traffic.

"Thank you, Jesus," Freddie muttered, making them both laugh.

Sam was always grateful for the two of them and the levity they brought to her life, but never more so than at times like this, when her stress level would be in the radioactive zone without them around to keep it real.

"Let me know when you're on the way home," Nick said. "I'll make sure there's food waiting."

"Will you be home soon? Someone needs to relieve Shelby." Their assistant would be eager to get her baby son, Noah, home to bed, but was always willing to stay if need be. She kept a portable crib in their laundry room for emergencies.

"I'm on the way now."

"Okay, thanks. See you soon."

"Love you. Bye, Freddie."

"See ya," Freddie said.

"Love you too," Sam said.

When the connection ended, the radio blared back to life with news of an accident on Route 66 in Falls Church.

Sam groaned. *"Shit, fuck, damn, hell."*

"Tell me how you really feel, Lieutenant," he said dryly.

"I just did! Why can't people *fucking learn to drive*?"

"Is that a rhetorical question or one that requires an answer?"

She glared at him.

"What?"

"Rhetorical," she growled. They battled traffic for more than an hour before taking the exit to Herndon and following GPS directions to the address Delany had given them. The road to the subdivision where Weber's parents lived was lined with satellite trucks. "We've got ourselves a full-on media campout," Sam said.

"Looks that way."

"Never takes long for the jackals to arrive on the scent of a hot story."

They were stopped by local police. "Sorry, road's closed," the officer said. "Detour that way."

Sam showed him her badge. "Lieutenant Holland, Metro PD. I need to get through as part of a Homicide investigation."

"No one is getting through."

Young, cocky, stupid. Sam had his number in two seconds.

"Did you hear me say I'm working a Homicide investigation?"

"I heard you, and I don't care who you are or what you're doing, you're not getting in here."

"Wow, so much for professional courtesy."

"Move along."

Sam put the car in Park and reached for her cell phone, putting through a call to Captain Malone. "We're running into an issue with Herndon police. An Officer Chavez is telling me I can't get in to see my victim's parents. Anything you can do?"

"Yep. Hang on." The line went dead, and she knew he'd be calling his counterparts in the Herndon Police Department.

"You can't just park here," Chavez said.

"Oh, sorry, am I hanging things up? You should probably call a tow because I'm not going anywhere until I speak to the people I came to see."

"You're exactly what people say you are," he said, snarling.

"Listen up, Detective Cruz. You won't want to miss hearing what people say I am."

"I'm rapt with fascination," Freddie said.

"Well?" Sam said, looking up at Chavez. "I'm waiting."

His ferocious scowl did nothing to intimidate her. He was about to say something when his radio crackled to life with orders from his superior officer to allow Sam through the roadblock.

All she heard was "let them through." She grinned widely at Chavez, whose scowl became even more fierce.

"Not sure who you're sleeping with."

"You're not? That's something the rest of the world is pretty clear on."

Chavez signaled to another officer to move the cruiser that was blocking the road.

"Have a nice day, Officer, and thank you for the interdepartmental cooperation."

"Fuck you."

Laughing, Sam hit the gas and took off, honking the horn as she went by him. "God, that was fun."

"Look at you. Making friends everywhere we go."

"I know! I'm like little Miss Mary Sunshine."

Freddie laughed and then coughed, trying to hide the laugh.

"You find that funny, Detective?"

"Not at all, Lieutenant. I think it's the perfect nickname for you."

"Glad you agree. I'm not sure what I do to stir the ire of people I've never even met."

"You're good at your job. That irritates the old boys' club."

"He was a young boy."

"Probably raised by one of the dinosaurs who thinks women belong in the kitchen and not on the job."

"I like that explanation better than him taking an immediate and intense dislike to me simply because I was trying to do my job."

"You're also high profile, married to the VP, running around without a detail and generally the kind of badass they all want to be when their nuts let down."

Sam parked two doors down from the Weber home, shut off the engine and then looked over at her partner, somewhat stunned by his unusually forceful language.

"What?" he asked. "It's the truth. They hate the fact that you're the kind of rock star they could only dream of being someday."

"Thank you."

He shrugged. "I didn't say anything you don't already know."

"It just means a lot to know you have my back."

"Always."

CHAPTER TEN

THEY GOT OUT of the car and walked toward the house, where the driveway was full of cars.

"The nuts letting down was a nice touch."

He laughed. "You liked that, huh?"

"Yep. I mean, the guy still had acne, and he was busting *my* balls?"

"When will they ever learn that it's pointless to argue with you?"

Sam pretended to be *verklempt*, dabbing at her eyes. "I'm just so proud of my little grasshopper. I need to give you a certificate or something to indicate that your training is complete, and you are fluent in the language known as Sam Holland."

"I thought you said my training would never be complete?"

"That was before I realized you were gifted and talented."

They stopped walking at the foot of the sidewalk that led to the front door of a large white colonial with black shutters. Sam took in the leafy neighborhood full of big houses and expensive cars. "Looks like a nice place to grow up."

"Is it okay to say I hate this? That we have to go in there and bother these people at a time like this?"

"It's okay to say because I hate it too. Let's get it over with so we can finish this endless day."

"I'm with you, LT."

Sam led the way to the door and rang the doorbell.

A young man with Tara's coloring answered it.

Sam flashed her badge through the storm door.

His eyes widened with recognition that he quickly schooled as he opened the door a crack. "This isn't a good time."

"I apologize for intruding, but we need to speak to Mr. and Mrs. Weber."

"They aren't seeing anyone right now."

In the kindest possible tone, Sam said, "Don't make me say this is a Homicide investigation and if need be, we'll take them in to be questioned downtown. I don't want to have to say that."

They engaged in a stare down that Sam won when he blinked.

"Wait here." The inside door slammed shut.

"Was it something I said?" Sam asked.

"It usually is."

"What the hell time is it anyway?"

"Almost six thirty."

"Ugh, at this rate the twins will be in bed before I get home. I hate when I don't get to see them."

"It's working out well with them?"

"So far, so good. They seem to like being with us, and we sure as hell love them."

"Has Elijah said what his plans are?" Freddie asked of the twins' older brother, who was their legal guardian.

"He told Nick that he has no plans to take them from us, even after he graduates from college. He's hoping to get a job in DC so he can have them on weekends and spend holidays with us."

"That must've been a relief."

"Yeah, we were glad to hear that he's not going to uproot them in eighteen months."

"He'll be a twenty-two-year-old recent college grad. What's he going to do with two seven-year-olds?"

"Exactly. We're just relieved that he gets it."

"He's lucky to have you guys, and he knows it."

"What the hell are they doing in there?" Sam was about to ring the doorbell again when the inside door opened.

The same guy pushed open the storm door. "Come in."

Sam and Freddie stepped into the foyer.

"I'm Lieutenant Holland. This is my partner, Detective Cruz. And you are?"

"Tara's cousin Ben. Her parents are Charles and Diana—and yes, we know that's funny. They're in rough shape, as you can imagine. I can only ask that you be gentle with them. We're all in shock."

"I understand. Does Tara have other siblings?"

He shook his head. "She was their only child."

Ugh, Sam thought. *Extra devastating.* "I'm sorry for your loss."

"Thank you. I'll take you to them." Ben led them down a hallway to a family room in the back of the house where a good-looking older couple, both with gray hair, sat together on a sofa, surrounded by people.

"Ben." Sam stopped him before they stepped into the room.

He turned to her.

"Can you please clear the room for us?"

"Yeah, okay." He went ahead of them. "Excuse me, everyone, but could you please give my aunt and uncle a moment to speak to the officers?"

The people filed past them, each taking a good long look at Sam as they went by. She thought of how Nick often said that being vice president—and second lady—must be what it was like to be a goldfish swimming around in a bowl where everyone can see you.

"Uncle Charlie, Aunt Di, this is Lieutenant Holland and Detective Cruz."

"Thank you so much for seeing us." Sam tried to be as polite and caring as possible toward the secondary victims of murder, but her goal was always getting justice for the primary victim. "We're so sorry for your loss."

"Thank you," Mrs. Weber said. "Do you know yet what happened to our daughter?"

"We know she was strangled in her bed. We're working the case and following the leads. It's early yet."

"It's not a coincidence, is it," Mr. Weber asked, "that the news of her affair with the president came out and days later she's dead?"

"We don't know that yet, sir."

He scoffed. "Please. Don't insult my intelligence. How can it not be related?"

"Naturally, our thinking matches yours, but in my years of working homicides, I've learned not to jump to conclusions until the evidence supports them. Right now, we have nothing tying her murder to the president or anyone in his circle."

"It's only a matter of time," Mr. Weber said, his tone rife with bitterness.

"Were you aware of the affair before it was made public?" Sam asked.

"She finally told us about it two days before the rest of the world found out," Mrs. Weber said. "Needless to say, we were as shocked as everyone else."

"She didn't tell us because she knew we wouldn't approve of her carrying on with a married man, not to mention someone like him," Mr. Weber said.

"I take it you aren't a fan of the president?" Sam asked.

"I used to be, until his son was charged with murder. After that, I thought he was a scumbag like the rest of them."

Sam wanted to remind him that their investigation had concluded that the president and first lady had had no knowledge of their son's activities, but Mr. Weber certainly had that information and had made up his mind accordingly. "Did Tara indicate any fear or concern for her life?"

"Not to us," Mrs. Weber said. "Mostly she seemed ashamed to have her good name and ours dragged through the mud that's been flying since the news of the affair went public. She was mortified to be at the center of a scandal."

Sam wanted to ask what Tara thought would happen when she had an affair with the president that possibly led to a baby, but she bit her tongue.

"She was a star," Mrs. Weber said softly. "From the time she was a little girl, she excelled at everything she did. She went to Cornell and UPenn Law on full scholarships, ran her own consulting practice. And when her company was hired by the Nelson campaign..." Mrs. Weber dabbed at her eyes with a tissue. "We were so proud. Our daughter was working for the *president* of the United States."

"Needless to say, we were disappointed to hear of her involvement with Nelson, but we supported and loved our daughter without reservation," Mr. Weber added.

"So she hadn't told you who the baby's father was?"

"She said the baby had resulted from a brief relationship that was now over," Mrs. Weber said.

"And her son is with you?"

"He is," she said. "And he will remain with us."

Sam wondered if they were in for a fight with the baby's father if he turned out not to be the president. That would add fuel to the media frenzy. "Was there anyone in Tara's life who might've been put out by the news that she'd had an affair and possibly a child with the president?"

The couple exchanged glances before Mr. Weber shook his head.

Sam's lie radar registered a hit. "It would be far easier for all of us, yourselves included, if you tell me what I need to know now, rather than forcing me to come back when I uncover what you're not telling me."

"It's her personal business," Mrs. Weber said.

"This is a Homicide investigation, ma'am. Her personal business is now my personal business. I assume your goals and mine are the same—to get justice for Tara."

"Of course that's our goal," Mr. Weber snapped. "But we don't want our daughter's reputation besmirched any further than it's already been."

"I'm afraid it's going to probably get worse before it gets better," Sam said gently. "This is a huge story, and it got even bigger when she was found murdered. If you know something, tell me now so we can move forward in the investigation. The sooner we can close the case, the sooner we can allow Tara to rest in peace."

They looked at each other again.

"Her ex-boyfriend, Bryce Massey, would've been upset by the affair," Mrs. Weber said.

"How long were they together?"

"Six years, on and off. They finally called it quits right before she joined the Nelson campaign."

"Who called it off?"

"He did. She wanted to get married. He didn't. They were in different places, and Tara was getting impatient waiting for him to catch up. She wanted children, and he didn't. He told her she needed to move on because she wanted things from him he wasn't willing to give." Her mom's eyes filled with tears. "From the time she was a young girl, she always wanted to be a mother." She shook her head. "She was so happy since the baby arrived. In the midst of all the controversy, she saw only him."

"Her assistant said they came to stay with you after the story broke?" Freddie asked.

Mrs. Weber nodded. "She said she had to run home to get more clothes, and when she never came back and wasn't answering her phone, we called Delany to check on her. She was close by and had a key to the apartment."

"I see," Freddie said. "What time did she leave here?"

"Around noon," Mrs. Weber said. "She planned to be back for Jackson's next feeding at two."

"Did anyone else have a key to her apartment?" Sam asked.

"We did, and her next-door neighbor did. Tara had a key to his place too."

"And what's his name?"

Mrs. Weber shook her head. "Brian is out of the country for work. Has been for a month now. They were good friends, so I sent him a text to let him know what happened. He's devastated and trying to get home."

"Where would we find Bryce?"

"He didn't kill her," Mr. Weber said. "He loved her. Their relationship didn't work out, but he would never harm her."

"And where would we find him?" Sam asked, meeting his glare with her own.

"He lives in the District," Mrs. Weber said. "Not far from Tara."

"Any other keys out there that you know of?" Sam asked.

"Bryce had one when they were together," Mrs. Weber said. "I'm sure Tara got it back when they split."

"Do you know that for certain?"

"I don't," she said, "but Tara was a stickler for safety. She would've asked for her key back."

Sam wondered if he'd made a copy.

"Can you think of anyone else who might've had a beef with your daughter? Even something small… You'd be surprised at the unbelievably petty motives for murder we've seen."

"When she was first in business, she had a partner," Mr. Weber said. "Paige Thompson. She later left the company and we never heard why. Tara refused to talk about it, and after a while, we stopped asking."

"Where would we find her?" Sam asked.

"We have no idea where she is now," Mrs. Weber said. "We haven't seen her in years."

It was a long shot, but they would track down Ms. Thompson and find out where she'd been when Tara was murdered.

"Is there anything else you can think of that might be relevant?"

"Only that she'd been distracted in the last few months," Mrs. Weber said. "We chalked it up to pregnancy, but now I wonder if it wasn't something else."

"Can you give us her cell number?" Sam asked, writing it down as Tara's mother recited it. "You weren't tracking her by any chance, were you?"

"No, we weren't."

That would've been too simple, Sam thought. "Her cell phone wasn't located in a surface search of her apartment, so we're looking for it." Sam asked for a number where they could be reached and handed her card to Mrs. Weber. "If you think of anything else, please let me know. My cell number is on there, and you should feel free to call me at any time."

Sam glanced at Freddie and then returned her gaze to the Webers. "We're going to need a sample of the baby's DNA."

"Why?" Mr. Weber asked, immediately on guard.

"The baby's paternity could factor into the investigation."

He looked to his wife. "I'm not sure we should do that. What if the president tries to take him from us?"

"I'm sorry that I have to make a difficult situation more so for you, but I'll get a warrant if need be."

Both Webers seemed to sag when she mentioned the warrant.

"Fine," he said, his teeth gritted with outrage.

"I'll send someone out to get it tomorrow."

She stood to leave, and Freddie followed her lead. "We appreciate your cooperation at this difficult time."

"Will you keep us informed of what you learn?" Mr. Weber asked.

"To the best of our ability."

He didn't like that answer, but it was all she had.

When they were outside, Sam turned to Freddie. "Call in Tara's phone number to Archie." Sam wasn't sure what the IT detectives could do to track down the phone, but Lieutenant Archelotta and his team would do what they could.

"Already texted it to him."

"I want to see the ex-boyfriend tonight."

"Had a feeling you might say that." He held up his phone. "Found his address."

"Have I mentioned you're the best partner I ever had?"

"A few times, but feel free to repeat yourself anytime. It never gets old."

They got into the car, with Sam driving. "I'm sure it gets old when everyone else gets to go home on time, and you're stuck with me."

"I don't mind."

"I'm sure your wife does."

"She knew who she was marrying. She gets it."

Thankfully, the traffic returning to the city wasn't as bad as it had been on the way out to Herndon, and they made good time, arriving at Bryce's address just after seven thirty.

"Let's make this quick," Sam said. "I'm ready to call it a day."

"You and me both, LT."

CHAPTER ELEVEN

BRYCE LIVED IN a townhome near Rock Creek Park. Sam went up the stairs and rang the doorbell. After being recently shot at through a closed door, she was warier than she'd been in the past and kept an eye on the beveled glass door, watching for movement from within before she rang the bell again.

She peered through the window and saw nothing but darkness. "It would've been too easy if he'd been home."

"Help you with something?" a male voice called from the sidewalk.

Sam turned to see a good-looking, dark-haired man wearing an overcoat over a suit. His eyes went wide when he recognized her.

"Are you Bryce Massey?"

"I am."

Sam and Freddie went down the stairs and showed their badges.

"Lieutenant Holland, Detective Cruz, Metro PD."

"Is this about Tara?"

"It is. Do you have a few minutes to talk?"

"Sure," he said, sighing. "Come on in."

They followed him back up the stairs, where he used a key to open the door. Inside, he turned on lights and showed them to a formal front living room that people kept for guests—and cops. They did a lot of interviews in those formal living rooms.

"How did you hear that Tara had been killed?" Sam asked.

"Delany called me. She said Tara would've wanted me to know. She called a couple of hours ago. I left work, and I've been walking ever since. I just can't believe she's gone."

"When was the last time you saw her?"

"It's got to be six or seven months ago. Before she was showing. I had no idea she was pregnant until I heard the news about Nelson and the baby."

"So you didn't know she'd had an affair with him?"

"Ah, no, I didn't know that, but it's not like she would've called to tell me. We texted from time to time, but we weren't in close contact after we broke up."

"And when did that happen?"

"Last year, around the time she joined the Nelson campaign."

"Her parents told us you and she were on again, off again. Is that an accurate description?"

"They don't think I had anything to do with this, do they?" He seemed stricken by the possibility.

"Her father was quite adamant that you wouldn't have had anything to do with it. We explained to them that we're required to dot the i's and cross the t's, which is what we're doing."

"I could never have hurt her. I loved her. She was the love of my life, but she wanted to move things along faster than I did. She wanted kids. I wasn't there yet. My career…" He dropped his head into his hands. "It all seems so stupid now."

"What do you do for a living?" Sam asked.

"I'm a lawyer for the World Bank."

"Do you still have a key to her place?"

"Nope. She took it back when we broke up."

"Did you make a copy of it?"

"Absolutely not. I'd never do something like that."

She wasn't sure she believed him. "Where were you today?"

"At work all day. I got there at seven, and I left after I got the call about Tara. You can confirm that with my assistant."

"We'll need his or her name and contact info."

He seemed startled that she intended to confirm it. Of course she would confirm it. People lied to their faces all the time. "Um, yeah, sure." He rattled off the woman's name and number, which Freddie wrote down.

"Can you think of anyone else in Tara's life who might've had a beef with her?"

"I imagine the president isn't having a good week now that the whole world knows they were together."

"Anyone else?"

"Not that I can think of, but like I said, I wasn't in close touch with her recently."

Sam handed her card to him. "If you think of anything else, my cell number is on there."

"Tara, she was… She was a sweetheart. People liked her. I can't imagine anyone hurting her this way." His eyes glittered with unshed tears. "How can she be gone forever?"

"We're sorry for your loss, Mr. Massey. Please let us know if you think of anything else that might be relevant to our investigation."

They went outside where the temperature had dropped

considerably. Sam zipped her coat up and pulled gloves from her pockets. "Impressions?"

"One in particular."

"Let's hear it."

"If she was the love of his life, how did he let her get away?"

"From the sound of it, she wanted kids right away and he didn't."

"Think about it, Sam. If it was a choice between having Nick and losing Nick, wouldn't you compromise so everyone got what they wanted? I would've done that for Elin because living without her isn't an option for me."

"You make a good point," Sam said.

"I know I do."

"Stop being smug and tell me what it means that he let her get away, and now she's dead after having an affair with the president and giving birth to a baby who may or may not be the offspring of the president."

"That I don't know, but all I do know is that if Elin had given me that kind of ultimatum, I would've said, okay, babe, whatever you want."

"Even if you weren't ready for kids?"

"I would've done whatever it took to make her happy. If she was truly the love of his life, he would've done the same. That's all I'm saying."

Sam thought about that, recalling the six long years she'd wondered about Nick after the first night they met. "You're right. If he was able to let her go, she wasn't the one for him."

"I know I'm right."

She rolled her eyes at him. "Does that take him off our list of suspects who could've killed her?"

"I think it does, because if he didn't care enough

about her to keep her from getting away, would he care enough to kill her when she had a baby with someone else?"

"Probably not. I still want to dig into him and make sure we're not missing something. Pass that on to Carlucci and Dominguez to take care of tonight as well as reaching out to his assistant to confirm he was at work all day. In the morning, we need to pull Tara's financials and check with Archie to see if he's found Tara's cell and what the security footage showed."

"Got it and will do it. Are we done?"

"For now." Back in the day, she would've spent all night working a new case. Now she had a husband and family to get home to and two third-shift detectives who could move the ball down the field overnight. "Am I dropping you at HQ?"

"Nah, I'll take the Metro. It'll get me home sooner."

"Give my best to Mrs. Cruz."

He grinned like a loon. "That, too, never gets old."

She wanted to groan or gag or roll her eyes again, but she managed to restrain herself. "Don't sprain something, Romeo."

"I'll try not to." And then he was gone with a grin and a wave as he jogged toward the Metro, eager to get home to his gorgeous wife. The two of them were ridiculously happy, which made her happy, not that she could tell him that. He was already on the verge of becoming completely unmanageable, but she wouldn't have him any other way.

As she turned to walk to her car, she nearly crashed into Bryce Massey, who'd emerged from his home in running clothes. He had buds hanging from his ears and reached out to steady her after their collision.

He pulled one of the buds out of his ear. "Sorry about that. Didn't realize you were still out here."

"I was talking to my partner." A tinge of unease traveled down her backbone. "I'll, ah, let you get going on your run." If the love of her life had been murdered that day, the last thing she'd be doing would be going for a run, but different strokes for different folks.

He reached for her arm and the tinge became actual alarm.

Sam glared at his hand on her, and he wisely dropped it before she was forced to break it.

"I was going to ask you earlier... Why don't you have a Secret Service detail?"

She forced herself to make eye contact. "Because I don't need one. I'm perfectly capable of taking care of myself. You should take off before I have no choice but to arrest you for being weird."

Hands up, he took a step back. "I'm sorry."

"Here's a piece of advice for you. When cops have just interviewed you about the murder of your ex-girlfriend, it's a good idea to keep your hands to yourself if you encounter one of those cops on the sidewalk. It's also a good idea not to ask why said cop doesn't have a Secret Service detail because that leads the cop to wonder why you'd want to know such things."

"I didn't mean anything by it."

"Take off, Mr. Massey. And go that way." She pointed in the opposite direction of where her car was parked.

Thankfully, he did as he was told and jogged off in the other direction. She watched until he'd rounded the corner of the next block before she turned and headed for her car, her steps quicker than usual, her heart pounding a little harder than it normally would. The second she was in her car, she hit the locks and called Freddie.

"Didn't I just leave you?"

"Yeah, and right after you did I had a weird encounter with Massey."

"Define 'weird,'" he said, his tone serious.

She told him what'd happened.

"Did you get the feeling he was trying to intimidate you?"

"Not particularly, but it had that effect anyway. Tell Carlucci and Dominguez to take a hard look at him. I want to know what size tighty-whities he wears."

"Will do. Are you okay?"

"Of course I am." He didn't need to know her hands were shaking or that her heart was beating crazy fast.

"I apologize for asking."

"As you should."

"I'll call Carlucci now. We'll get you a tighty-whities size by morning."

"Thanks."

"Sam—"

"Don't make it into a thing. It wasn't a thing."

"If you say so."

"I say so, and I'm the boss."

"As if I could ever forget that. Call me if you need anything."

"I will. Have a good night."

"You too." She slapped the phone closed, ending another long day on the job. Or so she thought. The phone rang two seconds after the satisfying slap. "Holland."

"It's me." Malone. "Conklin wants to talk to us again."

"About what?"

"The defense attorney, Dunning, didn't say."

"Well, since we just caught a new homicide, maybe Mr. Conklin should have to chill for a bit until we have time for him."

Malone snorted. "I had a feeling you might say that."

"As much as I want to know what he knows, I refuse to treat him like some kind of VIP prisoner."

"Agreed. We'll get to it when we get to it."

"But we'll get to it sometime tomorrow."

"Sounds good. What's up with the Weber investigation?"

"Nothing much yet. Following the leads, pulling the threads, doing what I do." She decided not to mention the creepy encounter with Massey. It would be enough that Freddie knew. She didn't need everyone up in her grill about it. She'd handled it the way she always did, by taking care of herself. "I'm heading home now, but Carlucci and Dominguez have been given a long list of marching orders."

"Let's meet in the morning to go over what we have so far."

"I'll be there." Sam slapped the phone closed again, hoping that was it for today. She pushed the gas pedal down, eager to see the twins before they went to bed. Arriving at the Ninth Street Secret Service checkpoint twelve minutes later, she let out a groan when she saw the street lined with media trucks. She laid on the horn to let the crowd of reporters know she was prepared to mow them down to get past them.

The agents working the checkpoint came out of the little building they had erected to protect them from the elements and began clearing a path for her.

Give her Homicide over what reporters did any day and twice on Sunday. How could they waste their lives hanging outside someone's home hoping for a comment they weren't going to get?

Sam inched forward until she cleared the checkpoint, sighing with exasperation when she saw it had taken seven valuable minutes to pull onto her own damned street. That was seven minutes she could've spent with her family. She parked and got out of the car, ignoring the shouts from the jackals who wanted to know where the investigation stood, if the president had killed his mistress, if she and Nick were prepared to move to the White House.

Utter madness.

As she took the ramp to her house, she looked up to find her gorgeous husband waiting in the doorway for her. That was all it took, the sight of him, to erase the aggravation, frustration and generally bitchy mood she'd brought home with her.

"Sorry about that, babe." He drew her into his embrace as she came through the door, mindless of the agent standing nearby.

Sam didn't even get a chance to see which agent it was or to say hello.

Nick whisked her away, into the sanctuary that was their home, their refuge from the insanity of their lives. "Are you okay?"

She took a deep breath and wallowed in the scent of home—cologne, starch and the unmistakable fragrance that was his alone. Her love, her life, her everything. "I am now."

CHAPTER TWELVE

NICK HELD HER for a long time, long enough to clear her mind and switch gears from out there to in here. "I want to see the twins and Scotty before bed."

"I was just going to read the twins a story. You want to come up?"

She was starving, but she wouldn't miss story time for anything. "Let's do it."

Alden and Aubrey were tucked into bed with books they were "reading" to each other when Sam and Nick appeared at the doorway.

He held her back for a second, not wanting to interrupt the adorableness of their little voices coming from behind one of the picture books that had come from their home.

Her heart melted at the sound of Alden attempting to read to his sister, using inflections and voices that she suspected had come from hearing their parents read the book, which was a favorite of theirs.

Only because it was getting late did Nick clear his throat to let them know they were there.

"May we join you?"

"Sam!" As usual, Aubrey's face lit up with pleasure at the sight of Sam. "You're home!"

Sam adored them both, and almost couldn't recall

what it had been like before they were part of her life and deeply imprinted upon her heart. "I'm so sorry I'm late."

"That's okay." Aubrey moved closer to Alden to make room for Sam.

Children, she had found, were endlessly forgiving toward the people they loved, and thank God for that.

Nick scooted in next to Alden. "You were doing a great job," he said to the little guy. "You want to keep going?"

"Okay." Alden turned the page and continued the story.

Sam wondered if he was reading or reciting it from memory. Either way, he got it just about right.

His sister hung on his every word while Sam ran her fingers through the little girl's silky blond hair.

Nick caught her eye over their heads, a smile stretching across his handsome face. This was what he'd always wanted, a family of his own, and now they had that with the twins and Scotty. Nothing made her happier than having had a hand in giving him something he'd never had before.

They'd taken a lot of flak for bringing the twins into their family—from the children's extended family, who hadn't wanted anything to do with them until after their parents' murderers had been apprehended, to the politicians who'd tried to make an issue out of providing two innocent children with Secret Service protection. It had been worth the drama to make the adorable children and their older brother, Elijah, a part of their family.

For the longest time, Sam had thought she had to give birth in order to have a family. Now she knew better. Not everyone was meant to have children the traditional way. *Sometimes the best families are the ones we choose for ourselves.* She and Nick had chosen to adopt Scotty and they had chosen to provide a home for Alden and Aubrey when they needed a place to be after their parents were murdered. Sam had no doubt that those two choices would be among the best ones she ever made, along with the choice to marry Nick—as if that had been an actual choice. Since she couldn't live without him, she'd done the only thing she could and made sure he could never get away.

Not that he wanted to. Neither of them wanted to be anywhere but right here with the three children who were now their family.

Aubrey popped her thumb in her mouth, which meant she would be asleep in minutes.

Sam continued to stroke her hair, all the while hoping she was giving the children a fraction of the love and attention they'd gotten from their late parents.

Alden yawned twice in rapid succession.

"Let's call it a night, bud," Nick said.

Alden turned on his side, cuddled up to Aubrey and closed his eyes.

Sam and Nick kissed both of them, shut off the bedside light, made sure the night-light was on and sneaked out of the room.

"I can't handle the cuteness," Nick whispered.

"I'm on overload. They're so sweet."

"Thank God we get to keep them."

"Right? Let's go see our teenager."

Darcy, the agent on duty in the hallway, nodded to them.

Sam knocked on Scotty's door, and when he said to come in, she opened the door and stuck her head in. "Are parents welcome at the moment?"

"Visiting hours are over, but we'll make an exception for you."

Smiling at his witty reply, she stepped inside and Nick followed, closing the door behind him. Privacy was a tough thing to come by in their house these days, but they worked around the constant presence of the Secret Service.

"How was your day?" Sam sat on the edge of his bed. He had the Redskins game muted on his TV while he worked on some homework in bed.

"Long and boring. How many years until I can take classes that actually interest me?"

"Ahhh…" Sam glanced at Nick. She'd learned to let him answer school-related inquiries since her comments undercut their goal of seeing their son through college. But first he had to conquer eighth grade.

"About six," Nick said, always truthful, even when the truth hurt.

Scotty groaned. "I'll never make it until then."

"What would you like to be studying?" Sam asked.

"Sports management. I think I'd like to be an agent. They make *bank*, and they get to hang out with all the coolest athletes. What could be a better job than that?"

"I can't think of anything cooler," Nick said.

"It's way cooler than being vice president," Scotty said, his eyes brimming with amusement.

"Dude," Nick said, "being the dog catcher is cooler than being VP."

Scotty lost it laughing. "And you don't have to have Secret Service if you're the dog catcher. And hello? *Dogs*."

"That's the job I want next," Nick said.

"We need a dog around here," Scotty said. "Kids shouldn't grow up without a dog."

"Says who?" Sam asked. The last thing they needed was someone else to take care of.

"I saw it on Instagram."

"Change the Wi-Fi password," Sam said to Nick, who grunted out a laugh. "The kid has access to too many ideas."

"Stop trying to change the subject and the Wi-Fi password. We *need* a dog."

Sam shook her head. "We do not need a dog. We can barely remember to feed you and the twins every day. A dog would starve to death in this house."

"It would not. I'd take care of it."

Sam hooted with laughter. "Famous last words uttered by kids everywhere before the dog shows up. Once the dog is in residence, no one wants to take care of it."

"I would," Scotty said, completely serious now. "I'd never let my dog go hungry or not take care of it. *Ever*."

Sam believed him. He wasn't your average thirteen-year-old. He'd been through a lot, seen too much, and would probably be the best kind of dog owner. "The management will take it under advisement." When his eyes lit up with excitement, she quickly added, "That is *not* a yes. It's a we'll-think-about-it."

"That's better than a no."

"Another half hour and then lights out," Sam said when she leaned in to kiss his forehead.

"Yeah, yeah."

"Night, pal," Nick said.

"Night."

"We love you," Sam said on her way out the door.

"Love you too."

In the hallway, they headed for their own room.

"Did you just tell him we'll think about getting a dog?" Nick asked.

"I think I did."

"What're you smoking?"

"Wouldn't you like to know?"

He cracked up laughing. "Be careful. My wife is a cop. If she catches you, she'll bust your ass."

"She's got to catch me first." Sam pulled off her clothes and changed into the sweats that were hanging on a hook on the back of the bathroom door. "Ah, much better. What did Shelby leave for dinner? I'm *starving*."

"Roast beef and potatoes."

"Yum. Feed me."

"Right this way." He led her downstairs to the kitchen and got her plate out of the oven, uncovered it and served it to her with a bow and a flourish.

"Sexiest waiter in town." She never got tired of looking at his handsome face, chiseled body and sexy ass.

"Stop objectifying me and eat your dinner."

He poured two glasses of red wine and brought them to the table, sitting across from her while she devoured the tasty dinner. Thank God for Shelby Faircloth, who made sure none of them starved to death.

"So, how bad is it?"

Sam knew exactly what he was asking and noticed the torment he'd managed to keep hidden until they were alone. "It's early days yet, but I can tell you she was manually strangled in her bed. There was no sign of forced entry, so we're running with the theory that she knew the perp and let him—or her—in."

With his elbows propped on the table, Nick ran his

fingers through his hair repeatedly until it was standing on end. "Are you seeing any link to Nelson?"

"Nothing yet. I'm hoping something pops from the building security video and/or the autopsy. Hopefully, we'll know more tomorrow."

"As you could see when you came home, the press is going wild over this story. The speculation alone is going to drive Nelson from office. 'How could it not be him' one of the pundits said. People are asking what he'd have to gain by killing her, which is a good point. The damage was done when news of the affair came out."

"I need to dig into how that leaked. I doubt that either of them would've told anyone. Who would want to bring this kind of attention down on themselves, especially him. What would be his motive in killing her after the whole world found out about them and the possibility that the affair had led to a baby?"

"It wouldn't make any sense."

"Which is why I like the jealous lover possibility better."

"You mean she had someone else?"

"I haven't seen any sign of another man yet, but we're still looking into her movements over the last few weeks. Her cell phone is missing, so that's making everything more difficult. Archie has her laptop in the lab, and now it's just a waiting game to see what he and Lindsey find."

"The pressure on Nelson to resign is nuclear level. It's all people were talking about in the West Wing today. Hanigan and Derek want to resign," he said of Nelson's chief and deputy chief of staff. "They're disgusted by the whole thing. People like Gloria. They hate that he did this to her, especially when she was sick. The media has also been relentless in their criticism of her choosing to keep her illness private."

Sam shook her head as she sighed. "What right do they think they had to that info?"

"She's a public figure, and as such, the public has a right to know."

"No, they don't. She didn't run for anything. She's not on the taxpayer payroll. She plays a huge role and doesn't get paid a dime for her time or her talents."

"I totally agree and said as much to Derek when we talked earlier. He's beside himself over this. Wants nothing to do with Nelson or the White House or any of this nonsense."

"This would hit him hard after losing his own wife," Sam said.

"It hits every guy who loves his wife and can't imagine ever betraying her the way Nelson did Gloria. It's revolting."

"It really is. The thing I can't get over is, did he honestly think he'd get away with it?"

"He did get away with it for a long time."

"True. I'm afraid I'm going to end up having to interview him for the investigation."

Nick winced. "That'd be awkward."

"Right? What I want to know is how did the word leak out about the affair? Who else knew about it?"

"You should definitely dig into that. It might yield some threads you can pull."

"I will. Tomorrow." She drained the last of her wine. "Is there more?"

"Yep." He got up and brought the bottle back to the table, refilling both their glasses.

"How are you holding up?" She noted the furrowed

brows and the tick of tension in his cheek that gave away his current stress level.

"Just ducky. Never been better."

She smiled at his predictable effort to deflect so she wouldn't worry about him on top of everything else. "You know what you need?"

"Um, is that a multiple-choice question?"

Sam dissolved into helpless laughter. He was so damned cute. "It can be. But what I was going to suggest was a massage. You're looking awfully tense, Mr. Vice President."

He raised a brow, a look that took him from handsome to devastatingly sexy in one subtle move. "And you think your hands all over me will *reduce* my tension?"

"It might increase your tension at first, but we think we have the secret to achieving an overall reduction in the gross national tension."

Nick choked on a sip of wine, coughing as he laughed. "Your analysis of the situation is spot-on. We may have a job for you at OMB."

"Oh dear God. Can you see me working at the Office of Management and Budget?"

"Not even kinda," he said, deadpan. "I think they do a *lot* of algebra there."

"I'd stab someone with my rusty steak knife on the first day."

"It's probably better if you continue to hunt down killers rather than becoming one. You'd look hot in prison orange, but I'd miss you."

"We'd have conjugal visits though." She waggled her brows. "We need to play that game again."

"Yes, please." He panted dramatically. "That was so hot."

She reached for his hand. "Thanks for this."

"For what?"

"This. You, me, wine, flirting, laughing. It's just what I needed."

He brought her hand to his lips and kissed the back of it. "You don't ever need to thank me for doing my favorite thing in the whole world."

"It's my favorite thing too. How about that massage?"

"Yes, please." They cleaned up the kitchen, started the dishwasher and went upstairs together, peeking in on the twins, who were out cold, and Scotty, who was watching the end of the game.

"Lights out the minute it's over," Nick said.

"'K," Scotty said, sounding sleepy.

"He might not make it to the end of the game," Sam said, after Nick had closed the door to their room, sealing them off from the rest of the world for the night. They had a monitor on the bedside table that would alert them if either of the twins awoke, which was rare. The first few weeks had been tough, but they had settled into their new home and routine and were sleeping better now.

Which meant *she* was sleeping better too. Nick's insomnia was made worse by stress. Being vice president hadn't been good for that situation, and sometimes she wondered how he functioned at such a high level when he got so little sleep. Hopefully, she could help him relax a bit so he could rest. "Get naked."

"And this is supposed to *help* with the tension? Just clarifying."

Sam laughed as she went into the bathroom to get changed into one of the sexy nightgowns that he loved so much, brush her teeth and retrieve the massage oil. "Are you naked?"

"Yes, dear."

Thank God for him and their family and the respite she found here after spending her days dwelling in murder and mayhem, she thought as she smoothed on the vanilla-and-jasmine-scented lotion he loved. Sometimes she wondered if she'd still be doing the job if she hadn't reconnected with him when she did. After a crack house shooting had left a child dead on her watch, she'd questioned whether she could go on. Shortly after that, she'd run into her unforgettable one-night stand from six years earlier at a murder scene. In their relationship, she'd found a source of strength that allowed her to deal with the insanity in the rest of her life.

Her dad used to tell her not to bring the job home with her. That was often difficult in light of the nature of what she did, but Nick made it easier to draw that line between work and home because when she was with him, it was almost impossible to think of anything but him.

She tucked a towel under her arm. "Are you ready for me?"

"If I were any more ready, it would already be over."

She ventured to the doorway, striking a pose.

He lay facedown on the bed, his head turned toward her and his eyes brightening at the sight of her.

"What would be over?"

"What's about to transpire here."

"I offered a massage. Not sure what kind of massage parlor you think I'm running here, sailor…"

"I paid for the happy-ending package."

She lost it laughing. "That's *so* gross."

"Nothing gross about it, baby. Come on over. I'll show you."

Sam sauntered toward him, going for maximum effect, and watched his hazel eyes go hot with lust. She loved the way he looked at her. No one had ever looked at her the way he did. "If your constituents could see you now, Mr. Vice President, bare-ass naked and propositioning a masseuse for the happy-ending package… It'd be a scandal, I tell you."

"I'm willing to buy your silence."

Sam got on the bed, straddled his back and squeezed her thighs against his sides, drawing a deep groan from him. "I'm listening."

"I'd like to set up regular appointments. I'll pay top dollar."

"You have my attention."

"The only thing is, my wife, she's the jealous type, carries a gun and rusty steak knife. We'll need to be careful. I'd hate to see anything happen to you."

"I've heard your wife can be a nasty bitch when someone looks at her man."

"She's quite unmanageable. That's why I need you, a nice docile woman to lube me up and finish me off."

Sam laughed hard. "I'm not sure whether to be amused or alarmed by these fantasies of yours."

"Only amused. All in good fun."

She rubbed the oil into his muscular back, kneading the knots from his shoulders and neck, and taking note of just how many knots there were. The poor guy was riddled with them. "You can't take all of this to heart, Nick," she said, dropping the act. "It's not good for you."

"Hard not to when you're a heartbeat away from the Oval Office and the current occupant keeps fucking up. I know I've said it before, but I wish I'd stayed in the Senate where at least I could make an impact that matters."

"You *are* making an impact that matters. Knowing you're there, waiting in the wings if need be, is the steadying presence we need right now. That matters to people. If the worst should happen, we'll be in good hands with you at the helm."

"How do we know that? I'd be one of the youngest presidents to ever hold the office. Who's to say I wouldn't make a bigger mess of it than Nelson did?"

"Me. I say. You'd be magnificent at it. You care so much about people and making things better for them. You know what it's like to come from humble beginnings and the struggles of regular people. You'd be the best president we ever had. I have no doubt whatsoever about that."

"You're making me want to leave my wife for you."

Sam snorted with laughter and gave him a playful spank. "Watch your mouth, sailor."

"Let me turn over."

She sat up and placed the towel so the oil wouldn't ruin the sheets she'd splurged on, not that she had any idea what the hell a thread count was. All she knew was that the number was high, as was the price, so she wasn't looking to ruin them. When he was settled, she resumed her spot on top of him.

He ran his hands up her legs, under the gown to cup her ass. "Hi there."

"How's it going?"

"So much better now."

"I'm worried about how stressed out you are. I don't need you keeling over with a heart attack or something equally dreadful."

"I'm fine. I swear. Harry keeps a close eye on me."

"He'd better." Sam made a mental note to check in with the good doctor tomorrow to share her concerns about the VP's stress.

"There's this other thing you could do that would really help my blood pressure." He lifted his hips ever so slightly, pressing his hard cock against her while waggling his brows suggestively.

"I'm new to this happy-endings thing, but won't that raise your blood pressure?"

"Temporarily. The end result is well worth the risk."

"If you're sure there won't be any negative effects... I wouldn't want to have to face your wife if you die in my bed."

"Are you really so good that I'd be risking my life?"

"Wouldn't you like to know?"

"Yes, I really would."

"Alrighty then. It's your life." She raised herself up and took him in, sliding down slowly and going for maximum effect. Judging by the way his eyes rolled back in his head, maximum effect was achieved.

"God, Samantha... How does this get better all the time? How is that even possible?"

"I have no idea, but you're right. It does."

They moved together effortlessly, like two actors who'd practiced the blocking of this scene so many times they could perform the moves by heart. But every time they played the roles, there was something different from the time before.

He ran his hands up her back and brought her down for a kiss. "I can't get enough of you."

"Same."

"I always want more."

"Mmm, we're ridiculous that way."

"I love our kind of ridiculous."

"Me too."

"Now, about that happy ending I was promised..."

She broke free of his hold and sat up. "Coming right up, sir."

CHAPTER THIRTEEN

IN THE MORNING, Sam had breakfast with the kids and was on her way out the door when Nick came downstairs, fresh from a workout and a shower and dressed for work. He had his phone in hand and a frown on his face.

"What fresh hell are you coming to deliver?"

"I was texting with the guys about a possible poker night in the next few weeks. Imagine my surprise when Freddie asked me how you were after seeing Conklin yesterday."

He was pissed and a little hurt, if her guess was correct. "Sorry that I didn't mention it, but it was really no big deal."

"Seriously, Sam? It was no big deal to confront the man who sat on the info about who shot your dad for *four years*? That was just another day at the office?"

"Okay, so it was a thing, and I dealt with it. Then Tara was found dead, and that took over my day. It's called compartmentalizing. It's my special gift."

"You should've told me."

"Yes, I should have, and I'm sorry you had to hear it from Freddie. He needs to learn to keep his big mouth shut."

"Don't make this about him. He was concerned about you, as I would've been had I known."

"I'm sorry. It was the last thing I wanted to talk about

when I got home last night. You were so stressed out. I didn't want to add to it."

That seemed to pacify him somewhat. "We've come a million miles from the days when you kept shit from me."

"Yes, we have, and this wasn't me keeping it from you. This was me not wanting to relive it even with you."

He slipped an arm around her. "I hate that you have to deal with that guy in any capacity."

Sam wanted to wallow in the fresh, clean smell of him. If only she had time to wallow. "So do I, but he has information that I want."

"What information does he have?"

"I'm trying to figure out where the anonymous tip came from, the one that said the answers were closer than they seemed, to look inside our own house and City Hall."

"Someone else in the department knew."

"Yes, and concealing evidence in an attempted murder is a felony. If I'm working with another felon, I want to know who it is."

"I understand that you need to know, but you also need to protect yourself, Sam. The wound of your father's loss is new and raw, and I'd hate to see it reopened when it's beginning to scab over."

She grimaced. "Thank you for that colorful metaphor."

"I'm serious."

"I know you are." Looking up at him she said, "Is it weird that I just want to stand here and smell you for a few more minutes before I go to work?"

"Yes, it's very weird."

She burrowed into him. "Okay then. You're married to a weirdo."

"You say that like it's news to me."

Smiling, she took deep breaths of the scent of home. "Don't be mad at me. You'll ruin my whole day."

"I'm not mad, and don't you be mad at Freddie. He's just looking out for you like always."

"I know."

"Are you done smelling me yet, weirdo?"

"Not quite."

That's where Shelby found them when she came bustling through the front door, her baby son, Noah, strapped to her chest in a sling that he would soon outgrow.

"What's going on?" she asked Nate, the agent working the door.

"Mom is smelling Dad. He says she's weird."

"Ah," Shelby said. "Business as usual around here, I see."

"Indeed," Nate replied.

Sam shook with silent laughter. Someday the agents would write a book about their tenure with the Cappuanos. They would have plenty of material to work with. "I think I'm done now."

Before he released her, Nick kissed her and whispered in her ear. "Be careful with my wife. She may be a weirdo, but she's my weirdo."

"Will do. Have Harry take your BP today and send me a report."

"That's not happening."

"That's what you think." Sam gave Noah a smooch on the forehead. "Your charges are in the kitchen—washed, dressed and fed."

"Excellent," Shelby said.

"You all have a nice day," Sam said.

"You do the same, ma'am," Nate said when he opened the door for her.

Sam went down the ramp and got into her car, fortified by the time with her family and ready to face whatever this day had in store for her. At the checkpoint, she was dismayed to find that the jackals had multiplied overnight, and the Secret Service had added additional agents to the usual group.

The need for enhanced security spiked her anxiety. All those people wanting something from her family made her crazy. And again, what did they think they were going to get staking out their home? Was Nick going to suddenly get chatty with them about the murder of the president's mistress? *Hardly.*

It took much longer than it should have for her to get through the checkpoint and accelerate out of there, leaving the screaming reporters behind. And people thought her job was fucked-up. *That* was fucked-up.

Her phone rang with a call from Darren Tabor.

"What's up, Darren?"

"You asked me to let you know the details for Roni's husband's service."

Patrick Connolly, an up-and-coming DEA agent, had been killed by a stray bullet. His wife, Roni, worked with Darren, and Sam had recently had the dreadful task of telling her that her new husband had been killed.

"Sam? Are you there?"

"I'm here."

"The service is on Thursday. The DEA administrator pulled some strings and it's going to be at the National Cathedral."

"That's great. By all accounts, he certainly deserves the honor. I was hoping to be there for the service, but now that we've caught the Weber case, I can't get away from work. Will you tell her I'd planned to attend and I'm sorry I can't?"

"Sure. It's not like you to get so personally involved."

"You think you know me well enough to say that?"

"Yep."

"I feel for her. How could anyone not feel for her?"

"She's a special person, and they were a special couple. It's still so hard to believe it happened. Everyone who knows them is in total shock."

"I can only imagine." Roni was living Sam's worst nightmare. Maybe that was why Sam felt so deeply for her.

"While I have you, you got anything for me on the Weber murder or how you and the VP are handling this latest insanity in the White House?"

"I'll do a briefing on Weber at some point today, and I got nada on the other thing."

"Come on, Sam. You must have something. People are saying Nelson isn't going to survive this."

"They also said that when his son committed murder."

"The only reason he survived that was because you and Nick gave him a pass."

"And we did that because we believed him and his wife when they told us they had no idea what their nefarious son was up to."

"People are disgusted that he cheated on Gloria when she was sick."

"It's a pretty disgusting thing to do, but that's not for attribution."

"What do we know about the baby? Is it his?"

"We won't know for certain until we get a paternity test."

"Is that happening?"

"It's on my list for today, but that's off-the-record. Where did the reports about the affair come from? Do you know?"

"I'm not sure."

"Can you do some digging and see if you can uncover the source for me?"

"I can do that, in exchange for a comment from the second couple on the current scandal engulfing the Nelson administration?" he asked hopefully.

"Dream on, Darren."

"Do you have *any* understanding of the concept of quid pro quo?"

"Yep, but in this case I want the *quid* without the *pro quo*." Sam laughed at her own joke. That was a pretty good one, if she said so herself.

"You think you're so funny."

"I am kinda funny. Ask anyone."

He huffed out a laugh. "Whatever you say. I'll see what I can find out and pass it along. And when I do, I'll have a *pro quo* in my account that I will cash in at a date to be determined in the future."

"Yeah, yeah, whatever. I give you more exclusives than anyone else. Next thing I know, people will say I'm banging you on the side."

"Sam, I never knew you liked me that way."

"Go to work, Darren." She ended the call to the sound of his laughter. Cheeky bastard. Theirs was an odd friendship that consisted mostly of him trying to get her to tell him things she didn't want to talk about. But he did her a solid from time to time, and she would never forget his kindness the day her dad died or the hell they'd faced together when they had to tell Roni about her husband's death.

Sam pulled into the parking lot at HQ, which was full of those damned satellite trucks. Didn't they have anything else to cover? Wasn't the government doing something that needed their attention? Apparently not, if the trucks parked on Ninth Street and at HQ were any indication.

When they saw her drive in, they gave chase.

"Shit!" She pressed the accelerator and gunned it toward the morgue entrance, pulling into the first parking spot she found and then bolting for the door. As she came flying through the door, she nearly crashed into Lindsey.

"Good morning to you too, Lieutenant."

"Hey."

"What's up?"

Sam gestured over her shoulder, where one of her worst nightmares was unfolding. The jackals had discovered the morgue entrance that she regularly used to dodge them.

"Are you being pursued?"

"You could call it that. They're camped out at my house and here. Not sure what they think they're going to get from me. I'm not exactly known for my verbosity where they're concerned."

Lindsey laughed. "True. How're you guys holding up? Terry said last night that he's not sure what's going to happen this time. Nelson's made a bad mess for himself."

"We're holding up fine, but we'd be better if the media would leave us alone. We aren't going to talk about it now or ever."

"I hate to say it, but if the worst happens, you'll have to talk about it."

Sam scowled at her. "That's not going to happen, do you hear me?"

Lindsey did a terrible job of trying to hide her smile. "If you say so, Lieutenant."

"I say so, and what I say goes."

"Gotcha. Is Nick okay?"

"He's stressed, and I hate that. He has awful insomnia on a good day. This just makes a bad situation worse."

"I really feel for him. When he agreed to take Gooding's place, who could've seen all this coming?"

"Not him and not us, that's for sure. What've you got for me on the Weber autopsy?"

"Come on in, and we'll talk."

Sam followed Lindsey into the cold, antiseptic-smelling lab. She hated this place more than anywhere else on the planet. Even after years of working in Homicide, she never got used to the things she saw in here.

Lindsey pulled the sheet down to reveal Tara's face and neck, which bore the signs of manual strangulation.

"Tell me you were able to get some prints off her neck?"

"I was, but they're not in the system."

"Great, so we're looking for a possible first-time offender."

"Or someone who's never been caught before."

"Who *starts* with murder?" Sam took a closer look at Tara's injuries. "Any sign of sexual assault?"

"No, and for that I'm very thankful since she recently gave birth."

Sam winced at the thought of the poor woman being sexually assaulted right after giving birth. "What I want to know is how did she end up naked? She went home to get a few things and was planning to return to her parents' home right away. Why was she naked?"

"I wish I could tell you more. I put her time of death right around one o'clock yesterday afternoon. Sorry I don't have more for you."

"Thanks for trying. Send me the full report when you have it."

"Will do. Have a good day and let me know if I can do anything for you or Nick."

"I will. Thanks."

CHAPTER FOURTEEN

SAM LEFT THE MORGUE, grateful for Lindsey and the rest of the friends and family who would support her and Nick through whatever came next. She was strangely calm about the possibility of their world being turned upside down if Nick was forced to assume the presidency. If that happened, they'd deal with it like they dealt with everything else. Together.

In the pit, she found her team gathered around the speakerphone in Freddie's cubicle.

"What's going on?" Sam asked.

"Hey, boss," Sergeant Tommy "Gonzo" Gonzales said.

"Hey! How are you?"

"I'm good. I earned an extra phone call and decided to waste it on you losers."

A low hum of laughter went through the group.

"Nice to hear your voice." Sam was encouraged by how good he sounded and to hear him cracking jokes for the first time in nearly a year. "How's it going?"

"It's going. Three more weeks, and I should be able to get out of here. Not sure when I'll be cleared to work, but I'm jonesing to get back."

That, too, was an improvement over the months after his partner was gunned down in front of him, when he hadn't seemed to give a shit about the job, his family or anything else.

"We're looking forward to having you back," Detective Jeannie McBride said. "It's not the same without you."

"Aw, thanks. I miss you guys. What the hell is going on with Nelson and the mistress?"

"That's what we'd like to know too," Freddie said.

"You guys aren't looking at him for her murder, are you?"

"Not yet, but it's early days," Sam said. "Lindsey got some prints off her neck, but they aren't in the system."

"Of course they aren't," Gonzo said, sharing their frustration.

"We interviewed her ex last night." Freddie handed Sam a printout. "He has an airtight alibi at work for all day yesterday, according to his assistant, Janice, but he was kinda creepy so we took a deeper look at him. The guy is in debt up to his eyeballs." He handed Sam another piece of paper. "Looks like he's heavily into online gambling."

Sam scanned the report that showed Massey's bank accounts were all but drained. "I assume he makes a decent salary as a lawyer at the World Bank."

"He must, but he's clearly got an issue," Cameron Green said.

"That has nothing to do with his ex-girlfriend, unfortunately for us," Sam said.

Malone came into the pit, looking stressed. "Lieutenant? A moment, please."

"Good to talk to you, Sergeant," Sam said. "Keep us posted on how you're doing."

"Will do. Good luck with the case, everyone. Wish I was there to help."

"We do too." Sam followed Malone into her office and closed the door. "What's up?"

"Conklin is making a stink. Wants to see you right now."

"Too bad. I'm busy right now, and I no longer have to jump at his command. He can wait."

"All right then." Malone propped his hands on his hips. "What's the latest on the Weber case?"

"Lindsey got some prints off her neck, but they're not in the system. I need a few minutes to get briefed on what Carlucci and Dominguez found out overnight."

"And then we need you to brief the media."

"Ugh, do I have to?"

"I'm afraid so. They're going wild speculating about how the president would go about arranging a murder."

"All right. Just give me thirty to get up to speed."

"You got it."

Sam put her hair up in the clip that kept it out of her way for work and went out to the pit. "Conference room, everyone."

The rest of her team followed her into the room.

"Get the door, Green." When everyone was settled around the room, Sam turned to her third-shift detectives. "What've we got?"

"The most interesting thing is an entirely blank security video," Carlucci said. "We doubled back with building management, and they have no explanation for why it's blank."

"Was it wiped or did someone cover the camera?" Freddie asked.

"Archie couldn't say for certain."

Sam bit back a groan. "We need to get the video from the surrounding area."

"Archie and his team are on that, but it's a busy area. It'll take a while."

Of course it would. "What else?"

"We pulled the financials for Weber and Massey. He's completely tapped out, but his assistant confirmed he was in meetings at the office all day yesterday. He never left."

"I want to circle back to him today and ask about the financial situation," Sam said. "He never mentioned that to us."

"The campaign was profitable for Tara," Dominguez said. "She was paid more than two hundred and fifty thousand for her work."

"Cruz and I will dig in deeper to her personal life and figure out how the story connecting her to the president got out. Who else knew? Besides Nelson, that is."

"Are you going to interview him?" McBride asked.

"God, I hope not."

A low rumble of laughter went through the group.

"I'm not going to lie to you guys. Nick and I are under the gun here to figure out who did this before Nelson gets run out of office. Every minute counts."

"We're on it, LT," McBride said. She and O'Brien got up to leave the room.

"I'll keep you posted on what I find," Green said as he followed them out.

"Good work, ladies," Sam said to Carlucci and Dominguez. "We'll update you before your tour tonight."

"We can stay if you need us to," Dominguez said.

"Nah, go get some sleep while you can. But thanks for offering."

"Call if anything comes up or if you need us," Carlucci said.

"Will do."

After they took off, Sam glanced at Freddie. "How do you feel about a field trip to the World Bank to see the creepy ex?"

"I'm with you, LT."

"Let's do it." Sam headed out of the conference room and stopped short when she remembered the media briefing she'd agreed to do. "Ugh, I gotta brief the jackals first. That oughta be fun today."

Freddie winced. "Better you than me."

"Actually, better anyone than me. You know they're going to make it all about Nick being VP and in the hot seat if Nelson is forced to resign."

"Yep. Good luck."

"Go talk to Archie while I'm gone to see if he's gotten anywhere on the video and check with Crime Scene to see if they have anything for us or any leads on her cell phone."

"I'm on it."

Sam proceeded to the lobby area where the chief and Malone were conferring. She approached them while taking a close look at the chief. His expression gave nothing away, but that didn't surprise her. He played his cards close to the vest most of the time. Yesterday was a definite exception to his normal routine. "How's it going?" she asked him.

"Just another day in paradise."

"No fresh hells?"

"Not yet, but the day is new. Give it time to turn to shit."

She smiled, happy to hear him joking. "You coming out with me?"

"Yep."

"You don't have to if it would be better not to."

"I'm not going to turn you over to them without backup."

"I could do it," Malone said.

"Thank you both, but I'm the one who needs to do it. Celia's statement helped a lot. That was a good call, Lieutenant."

"Glad to hear it."

"The firestorm hasn't exactly passed, but it's definitely better than it was this time yesterday. Ready?"

"As I'll ever be." Sam's stomach twisted with nerves. She hated these briefings on a good day. This was most definitely not a good day. In addition to the usual challenges of dealing with the always-voracious media, today they would make it personal for her, Nick and the chief.

They pushed through the double doors to where the reporters camped out waiting for updates. There were easily triple the usual number of people gathered. She even recognized a few faces from the networks, which was unusual, and they had her anxiety spiking even more.

Before she could say a word, they started shouting questions. Sam didn't see Darren in the crowd. She hoped that meant he was getting her the info she'd requested.

"Did Nelson kill his mistress?"

"Are you going to arrest him?"

"Is your husband ready to be president?"

Sam waited for them to shut up before she began speaking. "Shortly before three p.m. yesterday, Tara Weber's assistant found her dead in her Georgetown home from manual strangulation. Her newborn son was not in the home at the time of the murder. He was with her parents in Herndon and has been accounted for. We're working a number of leads and asking the public to reach out to our tip line with any information you may have about the murder of Tara Weber." Sam recited the number twice, hoping it would yield some leads. "I understand the high level of interest in this case and the obvious reasons for it, but I would caution you and the public not to jump to conclusions. As always, we will fully investigate the case and follow the leads wherever they take us."

"If they take you to the White House, will you arrest the president?"

"That's all I have at this time. We'll provide another briefing as new information becomes available."

"Chief, are you going to resign?"

Sam and the chief turned their backs on the reporters and went inside. She breathed a sigh of relief when the doors closed behind them, silencing the barrage of questions. "That went well, all things considered."

"You did good."

"I'll never understand why they think I'm suddenly going to start giving them info they should be getting from the White House. They need to abandon all hope when it comes to that line of questioning. It ain't gonna happen." She took a closer look at him, saw the signs of sleepless nights in the dark circles under his eyes. "You sure you're okay?"

"I've been better, but I'm hanging in there. I've decided that if the city council wants my job, they're going to have to come for me. I'm not going to roll over and cede to pressure to resign. I don't want it to end that way."

"Good for you. I was hoping you'd find your fighting spirit."

"It's been tough without your dad to kick my ass. He had a way of doing that even when he couldn't move."

"I know what you mean. He got a lot done with that eyebrow."

"Yeah." Joe offered a small, sad smile. "He sure did. I miss the hell out of him. I actually started to go see him yesterday and was halfway there when I remembered…"

"I have to remind myself every day that he's gone. I suppose we'll have to do that for a while."

"Probably. Are you holding up okay?"

Sam didn't have time to chat, but she gave him time she didn't have because she wanted to be there for him the way he always was for her. "As well as can be expected. I'm very well supported. That helps."

"It's just going to take time to process and learn to navigate the new normal. I remember going through that after losing my parents."

"I feel like there ought to be a law that parents should have to stick around for as long as they're needed."

"Parents and pets."

"Ugh, speaking of… Scotty wants a dog."

"Of course he does. All kids do. And they all swear they'll take care of it. Remember when your dad brought that mangy stray home for you girls? What was his name?"

"Ranger."

"Right! He was a hot mess, and you girls promised you'd take such good care of him. Which lasted how long?"

"Not even a week. My mom was *not* happy that she ended up taking care of him. He was faithfully devoted to her because she was the one who fed him."

"Is Scotty swearing he'll take care of it?"

"He is. I think maybe in his case he actually would since he knows what it's like to not be well cared for."

"True. He may be up to the task."

"We can barely handle three kids—and we have a ton of help. I can't believe I'm even thinking about adding another mouth to feed."

"You may be surprised by the joy a dog can bring to your lives. Don't rule it out."

"Hmmm, if you say so. Well, I'd better get to it. The clock is ticking on this one. If I don't close this case soon, I may find myself living at 1600 Pennsylvania Avenue." She added a grimace so he'd know exactly how she really felt about that possibility.

"I didn't want to ask how you guys are holding up…"

"It's stressful. Nick's insomnia is awful. Who could've seen all this shit coming when he agreed to be Nelson's VP? Not us, that's for sure."

"No kidding. He was the most boring president we've had in a long time, and I mean that as a compliment. No scandals or anything overly interesting. I actually used to like him."

"I think a lot of people would say that. He was re-elected convincingly. And now…"

"I can't believe he cheated on his wife when she was sick. That's so unbelievable."

"It really is."

"We aren't liking him for the Weber murder, are we?"

"God, I hope not."

"Keep me in that loop, will you?"

"You got it."

They parted company, and she returned to the pit just as Freddie was coming in from the other corridor. "Anything?"

"Archie and company are working their way through footage from the area, as well as trying to figure out how the security film got wiped, and Crime Scene is still trying to track down Tara's phone."

"So in other words, they've got dick."

"What you said."

"This case is pissing me off."

"Most of them do."

FBI Special Agent in Charge Avery Hill came into the pit. "Good morning."

"Agent Hill," Sam said, immediately on guard. "To what do we owe the honor?" The man was sinfully handsome, with golden-brown hair that he wore combed straight back, matching golden-brown eyes and prominent cheekbones. He was blissfully in love with and engaged to Shelby Faircloth, which was a huge relief from the days when he'd crushed on Sam.

"I stopped by to see if I can offer any assistance on the Weber investigation."

"Is it possible that you really just want to know if the president is implicated?"

"Is he?"

"We have no info on that." Sam almost said "yet," but caught herself. She didn't want to imply that they suspected him when they didn't have any reason to. At the moment. This case was fraught, no matter how she looked at it.

"Is there anything we can do to help?"

"Check in with Lieutenant Archelotta about the fact

that the building's security tape was wiped. We also can't find the victim's cell phone. He might welcome your assistance."

"I'll see if we can help."

"Thank you. Detective Cruz, let's hit it."

CHAPTER FIFTEEN

THEY LEFT HQ in Sam's car for the drive to the 18th Street headquarters of the World Bank. "I should know this, but what do they do there?"

Freddie got busy on his phone. "Reading from their website, 'The World Bank Group is one of the world's largest sources of funding and knowledge for developing countries. Its five institutions share a commitment to reducing poverty, increasing shared prosperity and promoting sustainable development.'"

"Huh, well, that sounds like a noble cause."

"Indeed."

"It's funny, isn't it, that we hear about things all our lives but never have any real idea what they're about."

"I read this article recently about how much most people will never know and how the things we *do* know are a microcosmic sample of all things we could possibly know."

"That's interesting. For example, I will never be a brain surgeon."

"And for that, everyone with a brain is thankful."

Sam laughed. "Yes, they are. I'll never understand engineering, most things about science and math. Ugh, math is my nemesis."

"We'll never know any language other than our own

and some Spanish in my case, how manned space travel works or anything useful about engines."

"I can't build anything, draw anything and I can't read music to save my life. I tried when I was in sixth grade and played the flute."

"You played the flute?"

"Briefly. Add that to the list of things I'll never be able to do."

"I played the trumpet—badly—for a year. This exercise is actually rather demoralizing."

Sam snorted. "Because we've basically discovered that at the end of the day, we're a couple of dumb shits."

"Speak for yourself. I'm known for being quite brilliant."

"Sure you are."

"We're quite brilliant at what we do, a job most people couldn't do if they tried."

She nodded. "True."

"The article talked about how everyone brings something unique to the table and each of those special skills form the fabric that brings us together as a society. What I can't do, that guy over there can, and so on. Society works because we all have different talents."

"This is a very deep conversation to have before lunch."

"It all started because you asked what they do at the World Bank."

"I guess we should expect some bureaucracy and roadblocks in a place like that."

"Probably."

The thought of obstacles exhausted her. She deeply resented the inevitable bullshit that got in the way of investigating homicides. Shouldn't murder victims take precedence over just about anything? One would think so. One would be wrong.

"I heard Conklin wants to talk to you again," Freddie said after a long silence.

"Yeah."

"You want me to take that for you? No need for you to have to be in a room with him if it's too much for you."

"It's fine."

"Sam—"

"I said it's fine. I refuse to give him any more power over my life than he's already had. He's just another scumbag to me now."

"If you're sure."

"I am. Let's get this done."

They parked in the visitor lot and walked to the main doors, where they were immediately confronted with robust security.

Even though the guard recognized Sam, he put them through the paces anyway, which is exactly what he should've done. She didn't have a beef with that kind of roadblock. Security was a necessary evil in today's world, so she followed directions, surrendered her firearm—albeit reluctantly—walked through the metal detector and signed in to receive a visitor's badge.

Fifteen minutes later they were in an elevator being escorted to Massey's office by a young woman named Isabel, who'd been introduced to them as an intern.

She cast side-eyed glances at Sam the whole time they were in the slow-moving elevator.

"Something on your mind, Isabel?"

The young woman's face turned bright red. "I'm so sorry. I'm just in awe of you, and it's such an honor to meet you. I'm studying criminal justice at the University of Virginia. I want to *be* you when I grow up."

Freddie choked on a laugh and then coughed, trying to mask his laughter.

"That's very nice of you. Thank you."

Isabel escorted them to the legal department and gestured toward the receptionist who stood between them and the man they'd come to see. Sam's disdain for flying and needles was topped only by her dislike of receptionists, who often tried to stop her from doing her job. That never went well. For them.

"Thank you." She handed Isabel her card. "Get in touch if I can do anything to help you."

Isabel took her card and held it as reverently as a newborn baby. *"Seriously?"*

"Sure. I remember what it was like to be just starting out. Everyone needs a mentor. Text me so I have your number, and I'll get in touch when things calm down."

Isabel's eyes sparkled with the starting of tears. "This means so much to me. Thank you so much."

"No problem."

After the young woman had walked away, Freddie glanced at Sam. "You never cease to amaze me."

"My goal in life."

"That was nice."

"I'm actually a nice person." Her phone chimed with a message from Isabel, gushing about her excitement to have met Sam. She held it up for Freddie to see, grinning.

He rolled his lips in, as if wisely trying to hold back whatever he was dying to say.

Sam approached the receptionist, a young woman identified as Ashley by the nameplate on the desk. She flashed her badge. "I'm Lieutenant Holland, DC Metro

Police. This is my partner, Detective Cruz. We're here to see Mr. Massey."

"Do you have an appointment?"

That was one of Sam's favorite receptionist questions. "Nope."

"I'm afraid he's in meetings and can't be disturbed."

Sam took a seat on the corner of Ashley's desk. "You know what I love about that answer?"

Ashley's gaze darted to Freddie, as if he might save her. He wouldn't. "Um, no?"

"It totally discounts the fact that someone has to be dead for me to show up here wanting to talk to your colleague. Do you understand that *someone is dead*? Someone has been *murdered*, and my job is to figure out who did it?"

Ashley swallowed hard. "I, um, let me check to see if he can make himself available."

"You do that."

She got up and scurried away.

"Magnanimous and scary all in the same two-minute period." Freddie shook his head. "I stand in awe of your never-ending range."

Sam was endlessly amused by him, not that he could ever know that. "I may be seen as a one-trick pony, but I'm a pony of many facets."

"Indeed you are, Lieutenant."

"Props on your use of *magnanimous*. That's a big word for a young grasshopper like you."

"Aw, gee. Thanks, Mom."

Ashley returned a few minutes later, noticeably paler than she'd been before Sam arrived to make her day.

"H-he'll see you in his office in five minutes."

"Tell him to make it two minutes. We're busy people."

"O-okay." She took off again.

Still perched on the corner of Ashley's desk, Sam folded her arms and got comfortable for the two minutes she was giving these people to get their shit together. "Sometimes this job is just fun."

"Most of the time it sucks donkey balls."

"That's my line, and it's trademarked. You're not allowed to use my stuff without permission."

"So sue me."

"I may do that."

As long as they had their ability to spar and joke, they were able to get through the worst days on the job.

Some might find it disrespectful. Those people could kiss her ass. Until they'd walked a mile in her shoes or Freddie's or any of the people who hunted murderers for a living, they would never know how incredibly difficult and heartbreaking it could be.

"I wish I could go to Patrick Connolly's funeral."

Freddie seemed surprised to hear that. "How come?"

"I'm not sure exactly. Something about Roni has really stayed with me."

"It's such an awful thing, but are you sure it's in your best interest to take that on when you're in the midst of your own awful thing?"

Sam shrugged. "I wish I could be there to support her." She glanced at the clock on the far wall. "I think their two minutes are up." She started walking in the direction Ashley had gone, scanning the nameplates outside each office until she found Massey's.

An older woman with a stern face and sturdy body sat at a desk outside.

Sam walked right by her.

Most people would knock before opening a closed

door. Sam wasn't most people. She opened the door to find Massey in an embrace with Ashley.

Very interesting. After their encounter on the street last night, the sight of him made Sam's skin crawl. She was still getting a weird vibe from him. Whether that vibe was related to Tara's death or not remained to be seen.

"Leave," she said to Ashley.

Her green eyes flashed with outrage. "You can't just come in here—"

"Detective Cruz, would you mind setting our friend Ashley straight on what I can do?"

"Um, she can arrest you if you don't shut up and get out of here."

God, he was good.

Thankfully, Ashley took his advice, casting one last lovelorn look over her shoulder at Massey on her way out.

Freddie closed the door behind her.

"Is all of this necessary?" Massey asked. "Coming to my workplace and flashing your badges around?"

"Is it necessary, Detective Cruz?"

"Clearly it is or we wouldn't be here. Does your boss know you're fooling around with your assistant?"

His eyes narrowed into a look of pure fury. "What do you need? I have very important meetings today."

"We could always do this at our place, if you'd prefer," Sam said.

He blanched. "Do *what*? I had nothing to do with Tara's death. I told you that."

"Talk to me about your financial situation," Sam said.

At that, he lost some of his rigidity. "What does that have to do with anything?"

"Not sure yet. That's what we're trying to find out. How does a guy like you with a fancy law degree from—" She leaned in for a closer look at the diploma on his wall. "Yale and a big job at the World Bank end up on the verge of bankruptcy."

"I got into some trouble with gambling." His teeth were gritted with outrage. "Not that it's any of your business."

"Murder makes everything my business."

"I think you secretly enjoy the little power trip you get from throwing that badge around."

"Sure, I love seeing a woman who recently gave birth to a child she's wanted all her life, according to her parents, naked and strangled in her bed when she'd planned to be home for her child's next feeding. The power of that just goes straight to my head."

He paled somewhat at hearing the details of Tara's death, which was actually good news for him. That he hadn't seemed to know those things could support his claim that he'd had nothing to do with it.

"She didn't deserve that," he said softly. "She was a good person, even if she made a mistake getting involved with Nelson."

"Why do you see it as a mistake?"

He looked at her like she was crazy. She got that look a lot. "The guy is *married*, he's the freaking *president* and he's *old*. What the hell did she want with him?"

"When she could've had you, you mean?"

"She could've had *anyone*. What did she want with *him*?"

"Who knows? Maybe she was seduced by the power."

"Whatever. She made a lot of questionable decisions after we broke up."

"Funny, you didn't mention those questionable decisions yesterday."

"I wanted to protect her reputation."

"She's dead, Mr. Massey. The most important thing now is finding the person who took her life, not preserving her reputation. What questionable decisions did she make?"

"She went out with a lot of guys."

"How do you know that?"

"I kept tabs on her. I was concerned."

"Did she know you kept tabs on her?"

"I don't think she did."

"And how exactly did you keep these so-called tabs?"

"I kept in touch with her friends, who were also concerned."

"Did you keep the tabs because she was dating again and you were jealous or because you honestly felt concerned for her safety?"

"I said I was concerned."

"It sounds to me like you didn't want her, but you didn't want anyone else to have her either."

"That's not true! I wanted her to be happy." His shoulders slumped. "The money situation was the main reason I ended it with her. I didn't want to drag her into my mess right when her business was starting to really take off. It wouldn't have been fair."

"Why didn't you mention that last night when we asked why your relationship with her ended?"

"It's embarrassing. A guy my age with my education and a good job shouldn't be struggling financially. It's not something I talk about."

"Here's a tip for you—when cops ask you questions, it's a good idea to tell the truth, even if it's embarrassing."

He glared at her. "I don't have a lot of experience with cops."

"I'll give you a pass this time. But I'd encourage you to be honest with us going forward. Who were her closest friends?"

"Carly Sargant and Suzanne King. They go back to high school."

"Where would I find them?"

Massey withdrew his phone from his pocket and wrote down phone numbers he found in his contacts.

"Put your number on there too."

After glancing at her, he wrote it down and handed her the piece of paper. "Carly owns a flower shop in Georgetown. Suzanne is a stay-at-home mom in Alexandria. If you've talked to one, you've pretty much talked to them both. The three of them were tight."

"Stay available."

"That's it?"

"Unless you have something else to add, which if you do, now is the time. If I find out you're stonewalling us, I'll come for you, and I won't be as friendly next time."

"I have nothing else except I hope you find whoever did this to Tara."

"We'll show ourselves out." Sam headed for the door, stopping at the desk of the older woman outside, who glared at her.

"Are you his assistant, Janice?"

"I am."

"You told our officers that he never left the office yesterday?"

"That's correct. He was in meetings all day until he got the news about his former girlfriend and left."

"Were you here all day?"

"I never left the building."

Sam handed her notebook over to the woman. "Write down your full name and phone number."

She took the notebook, her hostility toward Sam coming through loud and clear, which told Sam that Janice was protective of her boss.

Sam took the notebook back from Janice. "Thank you." She took off toward the exit, and as she went past Ashley's desk, she stopped to address her. "I just gave your boss a tip, so now I've got one for you too. When cops show up wanting to talk to someone you work with, get the person. Don't go have a romantic snuggle with them, because that wastes our time. We don't like having our time wasted, got me?"

The woman's big eyes got bigger, which left Sam feeling satisfied she'd put a scare into her. Good. People who wasted her time infuriated her. "Our work here is finished, Detective Cruz. Let's go."

In the elevator, he glanced at her. "Mean and scary."

"Thank you for the review. I hate people."

"Often with good reason."

"Tara is lucky that guy dumped her. He's a scumbag pretending to be a successful professional."

"And he's a cliché, fooling around with his much-younger assistant."

"Right?"

"What's next?"

"We're going to find her friend Carly in Georgetown. When we get outside, call Carly to get the address of her shop and let her know we're coming by. Also get Suzanne's address in Alexandria." She hoped they didn't have to make a trip to Northern Virginia. In addition to hating people, she also hated having to leave the District for any reason.

They retrieved their weapons at the security checkpoint. Sam returned hers to the holster she wore on her hip with a feeling of relief. She hated being unarmed on the job.

Freddie made the call to Carly as they walked to the car and wrapped up the conversation as they got in.

"Petals on M Street."

Sam directed the car toward Georgetown. "That Massey guy seriously gives me the creeps."

"I can see why."

"I want to like him for this, but as creepy as he is, I believe him when he says he wanted the best for her. I think he really did love her, and he's been a disaster since he lost her."

"Maybe so. The friends will know the deal."

"I hope so."

"Parking in Georgetown ought to be an Olympic sport," Sam said as they arrived in one of the swankier parts of town.

"Seriously. Just double-park over there." He pointed. "The flower shop is in the next block."

Sam pulled up to the spot he'd identified and put on her hazards. They got out of the car and walked the short distance to their destination. Everyone she passed on the sidewalk did a double take when they realized who she was. Sam hated that almost as much as she hated people who wasted her time. But she kept that to herself since the reason for her higher profile was her much-beloved husband, the vice president.

For him, she'd put up with just about anything.

CHAPTER SIXTEEN

THEY ENTERED THE fragrant flower shop, which even Sam had to admit was flat-out adorable, with colorful displays and a wide assortment of gifts in addition to the main attraction. The woman working behind the counter had her back to them. "Be right with you."

"Lieutenant Holland and Detective Cruz, Metro PD. We're sorry for the loss of your friend."

The woman who turned to face them was tall, blonde, pretty in a patrician sort of way with fine features and blue eyes. "I'm devastated, sick to my stomach."

On a closer look, Sam noticed deep, dark circles under her eyes. "We're hoping you can help us figure out who might've wanted her dead."

"Other than the president?" The woman did nothing to hide her fury. "Why haven't you arrested him?"

"Well, it'd be awfully difficult for a man surrounded by world-class security to commit murder."

"That doesn't mean he couldn't hire it done. He probably asked his degenerate son to recommend one of his disgusting friends to get rid of her before she ruined everything for him."

"Did you know about the affair with Nelson?"

"No." Carly sighed and her shoulders sagged. "I found out when everyone else did. I knew she enjoyed working with Nelson and thought he was an impressive person. But an affair? I had no clue."

"And normally you'd be in the know on something like that?"

"Always. That's how we rolled."

"We talked to Bryce."

Carly's eyes hardened at the mention of his name. "And what did he have to say?"

"That he loved her and hoped we find whoever did this to her."

She scoffed. "He loved her so much he dumped her and broke her heart."

"We're looking for someone who would've wanted her dead. Does he fit that bill?"

"I can't imagine that. I don't like the guy, but he did love her. Or at least he acted like he did until he dumped her."

"Can you think of anyone else who might want her dead?"

"Not really. For a while after they broke up, she went a little crazy on that DateMe app that everyone's so in love with, but that stopped when she joined the campaign. And then, after she left the Nelson administration, she was pregnant but wouldn't tell us who the baby's father was, so we assumed he was probably married. But we never could've imagined that the president was the father."

"That hasn't been confirmed."

"But it's assumed by everyone after the news of her affair broke."

"Who would've known about her affair with the president?"

"If she didn't tell Suzanne and me, she didn't tell *any-*

one. We weren't able to reach her after the story broke, which was worrisome."

So, had the leak come from Nelson's camp, then? The thought of having to pursue that angle gave Sam heartburn. "What about the ex–business partner? Paige Thompson?"

"They weren't in touch as far as I know. They went their separate ways after Paige left the business."

"Do you know why Paige left?"

"I never did hear the details about why Paige left when she did. Tara was bummed because the business was really taking off around that time, and it was a lot for her to handle on her own. She promoted Delany from part-time to full-time, and that worked out well as far as I could tell."

"Can you think of anyone else who would've had insight into the affair with Nelson or any of the other men she dated recently?"

"Check the app if you want to know who she was spending time with."

"We're still trying to locate her phone."

Carly gasped. "Hang on. I was tracking her. I insisted on it because she was dating so much." She went into the back room and returned with her phone, tapping the screen and then frowning. "It's not on, so I can't get a location."

It would've been too easy for the phone's location to show up. They never got that lucky.

"I'll keep checking to see if it shows up," Carly said.

Sam handed her a business card. "Call me if it does or if you think of anything else we should know."

"I will. Ever since she broke up with Bryce, she'd been kind of lost. Her career was booming, but her personal life was messy. I had no idea how messy until the news about Nelson came out."

"What did you think when you heard that?"

"Like everyone else, I was stunned. Tara dated a lot of men, but she had rules about married guys. It would've been wildly out of character for her to have an affair with a married man."

"That's very helpful to know. Thank you for your time and the insight."

"I hope you can find the person who did this. It's so sad that she finally had the child she'd craved and was taken from us right when she had finally gotten the one thing she wanted the most. I'm heartbroken over it."

"We're so sorry for your loss. Please call me if you get a bead on her phone."

"I will."

When they left the flower shop, Sam took a deep cleansing breath of the cold air outside. Approaching the car, Sam noticed a well-dressed man on a cell phone, pacing the sidewalk near where she'd parked.

"Some asshole blocked me in. I've called the police, but they're taking their own sweet time, as usual."

Sam flashed her badge along with a smile. "I'm your asshole. Sorry for the inconvenience."

"Uh, I have to go." The guy ended the call. "You can't just block people in. I'm late for a very important meeting because of you."

"I'd apologize, but I'm not sorry. Murder trumps whatever you've got going on."

His brows narrowed into an expression he probably practiced in front of the mirror for when he wanted to be fierce and intimidating. It had zero effect on her. "I know who you are."

"Did you hear that, Detective Cruz? He *knows* who I am!"

"That never happens." The dry, acerbic tone made him the best wingman ever.

"You think you're so special, the second lady running around with a gun and a badge, but you're not special, and you have no right to break the law."

"Feel free to report me to my superiors. They love getting complaints about me." Having better things to do, she headed for the driver's side of her car and got in. When Freddie was in the passenger seat, she reached for her phone. "This would be a good time to take a call, don't you think?"

He snorted with laughter. "He's gonna blow a gasket."

"I can't talk and drive. That's not safe."

Freddie shook his head as he chuckled. "You're in rare form today, Lieutenant."

With an eye toward the guy on the sidewalk, Sam pretended to talk on the phone, and sure enough, the man's anger level spiked into the nuclear zone. Maybe if he hadn't been such a dick, she might've cut him a break. "I think I might have anger issues."

"Really? That's just now occurring to you?"

"I'm serious."

"So am I. Of course you have anger issues. So do I. With the crap we see on a daily basis, who could blame us?"

Sam "talked" on the phone for a full five minutes before starting the car and pulling away from the curb, waving to her new friend on the curb, who looked like he might be having an actual stroke. "He needs to take a chill pill."

"You enjoyed that a little too much."

"I have to find joy where I can."

"What's our next move?"

"I want to talk to Archie about getting us into her account on DateMe."

"That's not going to be easy."

"He'll know how to do it."

"I hate to mention the elephant in the room, but the one person who has the most significant motive isn't on our list."

"No, he isn't."

"Why not?"

"What reason would the president have to kill her when the story was already out? The damage was done. What does killing her do for him but add to the shitstorm?"

"True. Would he have insight into her life that would be helpful to us?"

"I doubt it, but you know who might?"

"Who?"

"His Secret Service detail."

"Would they tell us?"

"It's a Homicide investigation. They're obligated to tell us if they know anything material to the investigation." The first opportunity she got, Sam hooked a left and headed toward Pennsylvania Avenue.

"Um, where're we going?"

"To the White House."

"Alrighty then."

THERE WOULD NEVER come a time when it would be "routine" for Sam to swing by the White House, where her husband worked and where she had her own parking space.

Freddie glanced over his shoulder at the security checkpoint. "That was pretty fresh."

"What was?"

"The way they waved you through to your own parking space."

"I know people here."

He laughed. "Yes, you do."

"They'll still need you to bend over and spread 'em before they'll let you in."

"Ew. Thanks for that visual."

Inside, the Secret Service examined Freddie's badge and waved him through with a minimum of fuss, probably because he was with her.

"Damn it. I was looking forward to you getting probed."

"Sorry you're disappointed."

"I'll get over it." Sam made her way to Nick's office, where she intended to ask John Brantley Jr., the head of Nick's detail, to get her the people she needed to see from the president's detail. And if she got five minutes with her husband during the workday? Bonus.

An entire team of receptionists was positioned outside of Nick's office. Thankfully, these receptionists had been trained to suck up to her.

"Mrs. Cappuano," one of them said. "This is a nice surprise. Does he know you're coming?"

"No, he doesn't, but if he's free, I'd love to see him."

"Let me check." She rang Nick's extension, told him his wife was there to see him and nodded, returning the extension to the unit on the desk. "He said—"

The door to his office swung open, and there he was, tall, handsome, beautiful in a gray suit with a light blue dress shirt and navy tie.

"Samantha."

"Nicholas."

He smiled. "Come in."

To Freddie, she said, "Be right back."

"No nooners allowed at the White House," he muttered.

"Bite me." Aware of several sets of eyes on them, she breezed past Nick into the office.

He shut the door and leaned back against it. "To what do I owe the honor of a midday visit from my gorgeous wife?"

She turned to face him. "I need information." Taking two steps to close the distance between them, she added, "But first I need this." With her hand on the back of his neck, she drew him into a kiss that she'd intended to be quick, but damn, the man could kiss.

Many minutes later, he said, "This rather shitty day just got a whole lot better."

"Why is it shitty?"

"Oh, you know, the usual stuff, such as the Democratic National Committee chair once again pressuring me to have my ducks in a row just in case the president is forced to resign. That kind of thing."

"I hate that you're under so much pressure."

"We also got two media inquiries this morning about why we aren't moving to the Naval Observatory now that your father has passed away."

Sam stared up at him. "For real?"

"Yep."

"Please tell me we don't have to move."

"We don't have to move. It's another one of those manufactured stories that come up from time to time because I don't give them anything else to use against me. I'm ignoring it, so don't sweat it."

"At least they gave us almost two weeks after he died before they came at us."

"Decent of them."

"Did Harry check your BP?"

"He was here earlier. When I told him you were concerned he did a check of it, and it's completely normal."

Sam gave him her best perp stare. "You're not lying to me, are you?"

He huffed out a laugh. "Never. I'd like to think I know better than to try to lie to you." He gazed down at her, taking a visual inventory of her features. "How's your day going?"

"Not bad, not good. I've only gotten into a couple of fights so far."

"A slow day then."

She smiled. She did that a lot around him, the most perfect human to ever cross her path. "At times like this, right here, I wonder how I would've survived if you hadn't been at my crime scene that day at the Watergate."

"Me too. That day was the best and worst day of my life." Sam knew that the murder of his former boss and best friend, Senator John O'Connor, was never far from his mind, nor was the fact that his career had taken off in the wake of John's death. He wrestled with how it all had happened.

Reluctantly, Sam stepped back from him. "So I was wondering if I could talk to Brant about the Weber investigation."

"What do you need from him?"

"Info about the president's detail and what they might know about Nelson and Weber."

Nick blew out a low whistle. "That's a big ask. They're trained to be circumspect about the things they see on the job. Protecting the privacy of their subjects is almost as important as their safety."

"I understand that, and I'm not asking them to spill state secrets. I'd just like to know if they saw anything that might be cause for further investigation. This is a Homicide investigation. If they saw something, they're obligated to share it. I'd also like to talk to Nelson's top advisers from the campaign."

"That'd be Derek and Tom Hanigan. They were the campaign managers for the reelection effort."

"Thanks for that info. I'm going to use my office for these interviews."

"Will you come by for another kiss before you leave?"

"I can do that." She went up on tiptoe to kiss him. "There's one to hold you over."

He moaned. "I want to call in sick for the rest of this day and go home with you."

"Not today, cowboy. But we should do that some-day soon."

"Yes, please."

"Elijah is coming next weekend. Maybe we could talk him into hanging with all the kids for a night while we escape the madhouse."

"Let's make that happen. I'll talk to him."

"Something to look forward to." She nudged him to get him to move so she could leave. "Ask Brant to come see me?"

"I will."

She left him with a smile and returned to Freddie, cooling his heels in reception.

"All done with your booty call?"

"That was not a booty call."

"Whatever you say, Lieutenant."

Sam led him through the hallways to her office in the East Wing.

Lilia was coming out of Sam's suite of offices as she approached the door. "What're you doing here?"

"Hello to you too." Lilia always amused Sam. They had become friends under the most unlikely of circumstances.

"I meant to say, hello, Mrs. Cappuano. It's a pleasure to see you."

Sam laughed. "Sure, it is. I need to use my office for a couple of meetings relating to my *other* job."

"Oh." Even though no one else was nearby, Lilia glanced around to make sure they wouldn't be overheard. "The Weber investigation?"

"Yes."

Lilia lowered her voice. "People here are outraged by what he did."

"People everywhere seem to be outraged by it. Gloria is very well liked."

"She certainly is, especially inside this building." After another look around, Lilia lowered her voice to a whisper. "You don't suspect *him*, do you?"

"Not at the moment."

"Oh, okay. I guess that's good, right?"

"Ah yeah, it's good." She continued to believe that Nelson had nothing to gain by killing the woman after the story of the affair had already leaked. That reminded her that she needed to circle back to Darren about whether he'd figured out the origin of the story.

Brant approached them. "You wanted to see me, Mrs. Cappuano?"

"I did, Brant. Come in. Excuse us, Lilia." Sam led Brant and Freddie into her office and closed the door. "I wondered if you could help me get in touch with the agents who were on the president's detail during the campaign."

"I can do that, but they won't talk to you about his personal business."

"I'm not going to ask them to, but I will ask them if they have any information about who might've wanted Tara dead."

"Fair enough. Let me make a call."

Sam gestured to the extension on her desk and then walked across the room to the seating area where Freddie had made himself comfortable.

"This is *sick*. I still can't believe you have an office in the White House."

"Believe me, neither can I. Not that it gets much use." She often felt guilty about the small amount of time she gave to being second lady, but Nick had no qualms. At least not that he'd shared with her. "I should spend more time here."

"You don't have time to spend anywhere but at work and at home."

"I know, and that's why I suck at being second lady."

"You show up when it matters. People are still talking about your infertility speech. That meant so much to so many."

"I guess."

Brant ended his call and came over to them. "They'll be here in a few minutes. We got lucky. Most of the people you need to see are in the building today."

"That's great," Sam said. "We never get lucky on this job."

CHAPTER SEVENTEEN

A FEW MINUTES LATER, Brant admitted Agents Robert Mercer, Olivia Jenson and Hank Reynolds, and introduced them to Sam and Freddie.

"Thanks for making the time to meet with us." Sam gestured for them to have a seat on the sofa. "I understand that you were three of the agents on President Nelson's detail during the campaign."

"We were," Jenson said.

"Were you aware that he was involved in an affair with Tara Weber?"

"We aren't at liberty to speak about the president's personal business," Mercer said.

"I understand and respect your position, but what I'm looking for is a sense of whether this was a well-kept secret or something everyone was aware of."

"We aren't at liberty to discuss the president's personal business," Reynolds said.

Sam realized they weren't going to budge on that, so she changed tactics. "What can you tell me about Ms. Weber and the role she played on the campaign?"

"She was a pollster and strategist," Mercer said. "She was a central figure in the campaign."

"Do you know of anyone related to the campaign who might've had a beef with her?"

"She tangled with Hanigan a lot," Jenson said. "They

often disagreed about the strategy. But it was all professional disagreement as far as I saw."

"I concur," Reynolds said. "They frequently disagreed, but it was always regarding the campaign. It wasn't personal."

"That's very helpful," Sam said. "Is there anything else you can tell me about her that might be helpful in determining who killed her?"

"I can't think of anything," Jenson said. "It wasn't our job to pay attention to her as anything other than someone who was around the president during the campaign."

Sam handed each of them a business card. "If you think of anything else that might be relevant, please get in touch. No detail is too small." After they took the cards from her, she thanked them for their time.

They got up and left the room.

"Did I detect a chill in the air?" Sam asked Brant when the three of them were alone again.

"Not that I'm aware of," Brant said.

"Could it be they think I should have a detail and are annoyed that I don't?"

"That's possible," Brant said, "but I've never heard any of them come right out and say that."

"Would they say it to you as Nick's lead agent?"

"I honestly don't know that, ma'am."

Sam realized she was putting the agent on the spot and backed off. "Thank you for your help."

"Anytime."

After he left, she asked Lilia to ask Derek Kavanaugh to come see her. After the insight provided by the agents regarding Tara's tumultuous relationship with Hanigan, Sam decided to see the two men separately.

Derek Kavanaugh arrived at her door ten minutes later. "You wanted to see me?"

"Hi there. Come in. Thanks for making the time."

"Sure. What's up?" He had light brown hair, warm brown eyes and a wiry but muscular build.

"We're investigating Tara Weber's murder."

"Oh. Right." His eyes held the haunted gaze of a man whose own life had been touched by murder.

"I know this strikes close to home for you," Sam said gently to the man who was a close friend of Nick's and thus hers as well. "But we're looking for any insight you can give us about the relationship between Tara and the president during the campaign."

"I didn't travel with the campaign because I have Maeve and couldn't leave her for that long." His daughter had been just over a year old when his wife, Victoria, was murdered. They'd recently celebrated Maeve's second birthday. "So I wasn't there for whatever went on."

"Did you hear about it from others who were there?"

He shrugged. "There were rumblings."

"What sort of rumblings?"

"That they seemed cozy. That was the word Tom Hanigan used to describe it to me."

"Was he concerned? Were you?"

"Yeah, we both were. We were concerned about the optics of him appearing cozy with one of his staffers and what would happen if the press noticed they were spending a lot of time together."

"Were you aware that Mrs. Nelson was undergoing cancer treatment at that time?"

"We knew something was up with her, because she wasn't available to campaign with him the way she'd been the first time. We didn't know what exactly until after the inauguration when he confided in us that she'd received good news. He was elated, telling us she was cancer free. Tom and I were stunned to hear that she'd had cancer in the first place. We commented later that we were surprised they'd been able to keep something like that from us, but they'd pulled it off."

"How did they pull it off?"

"She sought treatment at MD Anderson in Houston. The hospital staff worked with the Secret Service to ensure her privacy was maintained. When she basically disappeared from public life for six months, it was explained as a family situation that no one questioned. All eyes were focused on the campaign at that time, so she was able to quietly disappear."

"If you and Tom noticed the president and Ms. Weber were cozy, as you put it, surely others did too. Is that the case?"

"People were definitely talking. Tom had a conversation with Tara. He told her she was being cut from the traveling staff."

"What did she say?"

"You'd have to ask him for the specifics, but the president intervened and said she would continue to travel with the team. Basically, Tom was overruled."

"And how did Tom take that?"

"He wasn't happy. He felt the president's behavior was foolish and risky and so far out of character as to be worrisome."

"How so?"

"David Nelson isn't a man who takes unnecessary risks, especially in his political career. He's always played by the book, but in this case, he seemed to lose all perspective at the worst possible time."

"Was he in love with her?"

"I guess he probably was since he risked everything to be with her." Derek leaned in, his expression intense. "I want to be clear—I didn't approve of what he was doing and not just as his employee. It disgusted me as a man and a husband. Or, well, a former husband. Gloria deserved better than to be humiliated in this way. It was infuriating to me that he would take chances not only with his political reputation but with his personal life too. A lot of people depend on him, and I felt like he was letting us all down." He sat back in his chair, slumping as if the fight had gone out of him. "I almost quit during the campaign."

"Why didn't you?"

"For the same reason I haven't quit since the affair became public. I need the job. I have a daughter to support. During the campaign, I was still getting used to being a single parent. The thought of starting over was more than I cared to take on at that time. So I stayed, even though I was appalled."

"Did the relationship continue after the campaign?"

"I believe it did."

"How?" Sam struggled to figure out the logistics of an affair with one of the most well-protected men on earth.

"One-on-one 'strategy' sessions." Derek made air quotes around the word "strategy." "The sessions continued well into the new administration."

Sam wrinkled her nose. "They were fooling around in the Oval Office?"

"Obviously, I don't know that for sure, but that's the theory."

"Ugh, this is so seedy."

"Believe me, I know. The thing I never understood is why someone who had everything he does would risk his reputation, his legacy, his family, his marriage… I just don't get it."

"It does seem rather insane for someone who has the eyes of the world on him to take such a chance." Sam knew she had to ask, even if the possibility felt preposterous. But a week ago, she would've said the idea of Nelson having an affair with a campaign staffer was equally preposterous. "Let me ask you this… Is there any possibility he had something to do with her murder?"

"You know, I've asked myself that, and while I can't picture him arranging a hit on his mistress, two years ago I couldn't imagine him having an affair in the first place. But I keep coming back to what would he have to gain? The news was already out about the affair and the baby. How would killing her fix anything? It's only made everything worse. The media is crucifying him."

"Who would benefit from seeing him crucified?"

"His political enemies, for one."

"Anyone in particular?"

"It's no secret that there's no love lost between him and Senator Stenhouse."

"Ah, our old friend Senator Stenhouse. Remember him, Detective Cruz?"

"All too well," Freddie said.

They had interviewed the senate minority leader during the O'Connor investigation. Suffice it to say the man had not appreciated their visit. He was a pompous ass, and she'd love nothing more than to have cause to question him in another Homicide investigation. "Anyone else?"

"The list of people who hate Nelson is endless. You

know how this town works. If you're the one in power, people hate you. A lot of people are celebrating the fact that his dead mistress is causing trouble for him."

Add that to the long list of reasons Sam hoped that Nick never ascended to the top job. It was bad enough that people hated him simply because he was vice president. That hatred would grow exponentially if he became president. The thought of people hating him simply because of the office he held spiked her anxiety. She forced herself to push those worries to the back burner to focus on the job at hand with the secondary goal of keeping him right where he was—in the number two job. "If you can think of anyone specifically, we'd like to know."

"I'll think about that."

"What's the theory on where the story about the affair came from?"

"We think it came from her."

"Seriously?"

"That's the theory. She was pissed that he'd cut things off with her, wasn't returning her calls, etc. So she found a way to get his attention by leaking the story about the affair and the baby."

"Well, that's a bombshell," Sam said.

"No kidding," Freddie said.

"So she blew the lid off her own affair with the president, as well as the child that possibly resulted from the affair, and was dead forty-eight hours after the story went live." Sam tried to wrap her head around the victim's motivation for outing her own scandal. "What did she have to gain?"

"The attention of the man who fathered her child?" Freddie asked.

"Maybe."

"Had she been trying to reach the president before her death?"

"Relentlessly," Derek said. "We received more than two hundred calls from her in the two weeks before her death, and who knows how many more to his personal phone."

"We can find that out with a warrant to her carrier," Sam said. "What's the president's personal phone number?"

Derek recited it from memory. "Can I tell you something off-the-record?"

"Sure."

"The entire West Wing staff wants to quit over this. People are furious that he did this to Gloria while she was sick."

"Will they quit?"

"Probably not. Like me, they have families to support and people counting on them. But they want to."

"This has been really helpful, Derek. If you think of anything else that might be useful in the investigation, please call me."

"I will. I hope you get whoever did this to her. I didn't approve of her relationship with the president, but she certainly didn't deserve to be murdered."

"No, she didn't, and I'm sure this strikes too close to home for you."

"It really does."

"I wanted to tell you that I'm working on a group for victims of violent crime to come together in support of each other. I thought it might be of interest to you."

"Maybe."

"Having walked this journey, your experiences might be helpful to someone just beginning it."

"Keep me in the loop."

"I will."

"Did you know Pat Connolly?" Derek asked.

"No, I didn't, but I met his wife after he was killed. Such a tragedy."

"It really is. I played in a softball league with him years ago, before we were married. He was a good guy and, by all accounts, an IT genius."

"That's what I've been told. His wife, Roni, is just the kind of victim I'm hoping to help with the new group."

"It's a good idea. Those first few weeks and months after Vic was killed were just dreadful." He stood, as if he needed to move to keep the painful memories at bay.

Sam's heart ached for him, his beautiful daughter and his late wife, who'd been a friend. "Thanks again for your help."

"Whatever I can do. Should I send Tom in?"

"If you wouldn't mind."

"Will do."

When they were alone, Sam turned to Freddie. "Thoughts?"

"I can't believe she would out her affair with the president."

"That shocked me too, although we don't know anything for sure yet. As Derek said, that's the theory."

"Still, who brings that kind of attention on themselves willingly?"

"Someone who wants the attention of a man who's stonewalling her?"

"And the part about them getting busy in the Oval Office… Ew."

"I know! That makes for one hell of a midlife crisis."

"Except he's a little past midlife. I remember the press saying Nick was twenty-five years younger than Nelson, so that'd put him at sixty-two or -three."

A knock sounded on the door.

Sam got up to admit Tom Hanigan.

The gray-haired man seemed rushed and stressed as usual. Sam didn't know him well, but he always struck her as an intense sort of guy. He'd been Nelson's closest aide throughout his career, coming with him to Washington from South Dakota.

"Thanks for your time."

"No problem." He took the seat recently vacated by Derek. "I assume this is about Tara."

"You assume correctly."

"This whole thing is just…" His angry expression indicated his feelings on the matter.

"How well did you know her?"

"I hired her. She came highly recommended and did a fantastic job with the polling and market research. She was instrumental in our strategy in several of the swing states."

"Your interactions with her were described by others as contentious. Is that fair?"

"We often didn't agree about the polling results. Any contention was strictly professional."

"When did you realize her relationship with the president had become personal?"

"Almost as soon as it happened."

"Which was when?"

"Right after the convention. He and I had words over it, more than once. He assured me there was nothing to worry about, that they were just friends and she was helping him with his messaging."

"Did you believe him?"

"No, I didn't."

"Had that happened before?"

"Not once in all the years I've worked for him. It was like he'd taken leave of his senses at the worst possible time." Hanigan seemed to catch himself, sitting up straighter. "This is just between us, right?"

"For now. I can't promise that whatever you tell us won't be part of building a case against whomever killed Tara."

"I want the person who killed her to be found and brought to justice. She didn't deserve to be murdered. But it doesn't break my heart that she's out of his life. She'd become a serious liability with the nonstop phone calls and the histrionics."

"Mr. Kavanaugh told us that the president had been refusing her calls?"

"Yes, he had."

"Had he no concern for the mother of his child?"

"The child isn't his, and he can prove that."

Sam glanced at Freddie, who seemed equally surprised. "How's that?" She wasn't sure she wanted to know.

"He had a vasectomy after his youngest son was born, and is willing to provide proof of the procedure should that become necessary."

"Whoa."

Freddie said what Sam was thinking, even as relief coursed through her system. The baby wasn't his. Okay, so the affair was bad, but the baby wasn't his. *Thank you, Jesus.*

"It might be a good idea for him to produce the proof."

"Tell me you aren't seriously looking at him for this."

"We're not seeing a motive for him to kill her, since the affair had already become public. What would be the reason to silence her after that?"

"He didn't silence her. He froze her out when she became too big of a liability, but he didn't kill her."

"Since vasectomies can be reversed or even fail, we're going to need to rule him out as the child's father. I'd like to send someone over to take a DNA sample."

Hanigan made no effort to hide his shock and revulsion. "I just can't believe we're having this conversation."

"I understand, but you'll see to it that he cooperates with the DNA test?"

"Yes, of course. I can also provide proof that he had the vasectomy."

"That'd be good. Do you have any idea who might've wanted her dead?"

"Everyone who loves Gloria, and those numbers are in the millions. Her approval rating is double his, and I'm sure it'll go even higher in the wake of this crap."

"Did you know she was sick during the campaign?"

"I was one of the few who knew, which was why I had so many arguments with him over what was happening with Tara. I told him if it got out, it would be devastating in more ways than one. I hate to say I told you so, but… Now it feels like we're bailing the *Titanic*, and right after we cleaned up the last mess."

"Derek said the West Wing morale is low."

"As low as it's ever been. People are infuriated. Gloria is very well liked around here, and that he would cheat on her at all is astonishing, but while she was *sick*? Revolting."

"It is rather hard to fathom. I assume Tara had a clearance and other background checks done before she joined the campaign."

"She was thoroughly vetted."

"Would it be possible to see the vetting documents?"

"I could make that happen."

Sam handed him her card. "My email is on there."

"I'll have someone send the reports today."

"If there's anything else you can think of that might be relevant, I hope you'll let me know."

"Have you spoken to her former business partner? We hired them both, but something happened right before they started. I never did hear what went down there."

"We haven't spoken to her yet, but she's on my list. Was there anyone else from the campaign that she was particularly close to?"

"Not particularly. She tended to keep to herself when she wasn't with the president."

"We appreciate the help."

"No problem. And I'll see about getting that proof of the vasectomy…"

"Thanks. We'll let you know when someone from the ME's office will be by for DNA."

He nodded, got up and left the room.

"This gets nastier and nastier," Freddie said.

"No kidding. Never thought I'd need proof of a president's vasectomy and DNA to get him off the hook in a murder case."

"We need to figure out who else she was seeing who might've fathered her baby."

"Yes, we do. Call the mom and find out which carrier she was with. Also ask the mom if she has any other info about men her daughter was seeing. If Nelson wasn't the baby's father, I want to know who was. But don't tell the mother what we found out about Nelson. Not yet." Sam didn't want that info getting out until she had the proof in hand that there was no way Nelson could be the baby's father.

"Got it. I'm on it."

While he did that, Sam called Lindsey to ask her to take care of getting a sample of the president's DNA.

CHAPTER EIGHTEEN

AFTER THE SURREAL conversation with Lindsey, Sam wandered into Lilia's office.

Her chief of staff smiled in welcome.

"I thought about the NAPO speech, and I guess I'll do it."

"They'll be thrilled."

Sam rolled her eyes. "Whatever."

Lilia laughed. "How's it going with the investigation?"

"It's going. Hearing things about the commander in chief that make my skin crawl a little, but other than that…"

"The whole thing is hard to fathom."

"Not to mention that it happened during his reelection campaign when he was once again casting himself as a family kind of guy."

"That too."

Lilia lost some of her usual sparkle as she discussed the president's behavior. "I know that politics is so much smoke and mirrors, but I still like to think the best of people. It's painful to be so disillusioned." She looked up at Sam. "You have to promise me that you and your husband will never disappoint me this way. I don't think I could handle it from you two."

The thought of Nick cheating on her was impossible

to wrap her head around. "I can promise you we won't let you down in this way."

"I'm honestly not worried about that. The two of you are what the rest of us aspire to be. When I first knew you, I wondered if your public persona was too good to be true. But after spending time with you and getting to know you both, I tell everyone who asks that you guys are every bit the real deal that you appear to be."

"That's nice of you to say. He's my real deal."

"And she's mine," her husband said as he slipped an arm around her from behind.

Sam smiled as the scent of home filled her senses. "Aren't you supposed to be tending to world domination or something equally important?"

"It's hard to focus on world domination when my best girl is in the building."

Lilia fanned her face. "See what I mean? Hashtag couple goals."

In a past life, before him, she would've been embarrassed to be part of a couple that inspired a hashtag. Now she didn't care because being part of that couple meant she got to spend her life with him.

"How's it going?" he asked.

"We're done here. Getting ready to head back to HQ."

"Were Derek and Tom able to help?"

"They were great and gave us a few threads to pull."

"I know how you love your threads."

From behind Nick, Freddie said, "Hate to interrupt the White House snuggle session, but I wanted to tell you that Malone is requesting the warrant from Tara's cell carrier."

"Thank you. Wait for me in the car."

"Yes, Mom. Will do."

"Young Freddie is a brat," Sam said. "We need to do something about that."

"We've got our hands full with our other three and a half kids." They had taken to referring to the twins' older brother Elijah as their half kid, as he was technically an adult but now very much a part of their family.

"That we do. Let me go so I can get back to work and home to you and the crew that much sooner."

"If I must." He kissed her neck and let her go. "Tell me this… Are you any closer to making it so he won't have to resign?"

She turned to face him, noticing once again how tired and stressed he looked. "I hope so, and trust me, that's my number two goal right after getting justice for Tara."

"Excellent."

"Try not to worry."

"What? Me, worry? I'll walk you out."

"See you soon, Lilia," Sam said, "and thanks again for such a great time the other night."

"It was my pleasure. We'll do it again soon."

Nick put his arm around Sam and kept it there as they walked toward the exit with Brant keeping a respectful distance as he followed them. Though they passed several people who looked familiar on the way out, Nick kept his attention entirely on her.

"What were you and Lilia talking about when I found you?"

"She was saying that if we ever turned out to be like the Nelsons, she wouldn't be able to handle the disillusion."

"There's no need to worry about that with us."

"That's what I told her."

He looked down at her. "You know that for one thousand percent certain, right?"

"Of course I do."

"With all the things we both have to worry about, that should never be one of them."

"Agreed. You keep me so entertained, why would I need anyone else?"

"My evil plan is working then."

"You're all I need."

"Likewise."

"I feel so badly for Gloria in all of this. Have you heard anything about how she's holding up?"

"Not really, but he wants to see me this afternoon."

"Ugh." Sam stopped and crooked her finger to bring him close enough to whisper. "Hanigan told me Nelson had a vasectomy. The baby isn't his."

"Is that right?"

She nodded. "I also heard that their theory is Tara leaked the story about the affair and baby."

"Wow."

"I don't want to say too much more here. I'll fill you in at home."

"I'll look forward to being debriefed by you."

"Why do I suspect we're talking about a different kind of briefs?"

He laughed—hard, which pleased her greatly. She loved to make him laugh and when his gorgeous hazel eyes sparkled the way they were now.

"Love you best of all," he whispered as he kissed her.

"Love you best of all."

"Take care of my wife out there."

"Always do. See you soon."

"Can't wait."

As she left him at the doorway, she felt his gaze on her as she walked to the car where Freddie waited for her. "Let's get at this," she said to her partner. "Nick is about to buckle from the stress." She recalled her plan to check in with Harry and tossed the keys to Freddie. "You drive. I have a call to make."

Harry answered on the second ring. "To what do I owe the honor of a phone call from the second lady?"

"I'm worried about the VP."

"Ah, yes, nothing like another presidential scandal to have the vice president sweating out his future."

"Exactly. Did you really check his blood pressure today?"

Harry laughed. "I did, and everything is normal."

"Thank you for keeping an eye on him. The insomnia is *bad*. There's got to be something you can do about that."

"I would, but the meds leave him groggy the next day, so he won't take them."

"Ugh. I'll talk to him again. Groggy is better than being a zombie."

"You're preaching to the choir, my friend."

"Text me if you see anything to worry about?"

"I will, but try not to worry. He's rock solid. You know that."

"Not this time. He's putting on a good front, but he's freaking out on the inside."

"I'll talk to him again."

"Thanks, Harry. Appreciate it."

"Anything for you guys. Hang in there and find the person who killed Tara Weber. That'll help."

"We're on it. Talk to you later." Sam ended the call and took a deep breath, needing to clear her mind of worries about her husband so she could refocus on the case. "What did Tara's mom say about other guys?"

"She said her daughter was circumspect about her personal life, and that Bryce is the only guy she dated for any amount of time. He's the only one they met."

"So that's a dead end. Let's go back to HQ and see if the warrant came through for the phone data and the dating app. I also want to check in with Archie."

The street leading to HQ was now completely lined with satellite trucks.

"What do they think they're going to get here?"

"An exclusive from you? Because that's how you roll."

"Right? Are they expecting me to suddenly get the urge to share my innermost thoughts with them?"

"Hope springs eternal."

"That's very poetic, young Freddie."

"Wait till they hear the baby isn't Nelson's. That's gonna be huge."

"Yep, but I want proof before we go public with that detail. I can't believe I'm actually awaiting a report about the president's sperm count and DNA. How is this my life?"

Freddie snorted with laughter. "Right?" He drove around to the morgue entrance.

"I can't wait to be able to say the baby isn't Nelson's. Maybe that will make some of this insanity go away."

"The baby might not be his, but he still had the affair. I don't think that part of the story is going away."

"Let me have my illusions, will you, please?"

"My apologies. Of course the whole thing will go away as soon as it's revealed that the baby isn't his."

"Better. Thank you."

"I live to serve you, Lieutenant."

"You're an expert suck-up, I'll give you that."

"That might just be one of the best compliments I've ever received."

Inside, they found the rest of the squad working the computers and phones.

"Conference room in ten." Sam ducked into her office to check her email. The autopsy report from Lindsey had arrived, confirming what they already knew—that Tara had died by manual strangulation with no sign of sexual assault. Sam wanted to know how Tara had ended up naked in her bed if she'd gone to her condo to retrieve clothing and other necessities. At what point in a quick errand did she suddenly decide to remove her clothes and get into bed? She didn't decide that. Someone else had made her do that, and when they figured out who, they'd know who killed her.

Captain Malone appeared at the door. "Two things. Conklin says he has info that we're going to want—and he's hoping we'll make a case for leniency in exchange."

"Like that's going to happen. What's the other thing?"

"Final arguments are being delivered in Stahl's trial. It's expected to go to the jury by the end of the day."

Sam's stomach dropped. Soon enough that nightmare would be over, but would she get the verdict she deserved?

"When he's convicted, they're going to want you to do a victim impact statement."

"I already did that when I testified, and besides, I'm not giving him the satisfaction of hearing what impact he had on me. No way."

"I understand, but you know how this works. The judge wants to hear from the people most impacted by the crime. In this case, that's you."

"They've already heard from me." There was no way in hell she was going back to that courtroom. "Let's see Conklin after I meet with my squad. Thirty minutes?"

"Yeah, okay. Sam, I know you have a lot on your plate, and your heart is broken over the loss of your dad, but you have to do whatever it takes to make sure that son of a bitch never again sees the light of day. After that, you can forget he exists."

Sam nodded to acknowledge she'd heard him as she left the office. "Let's go, people." She led the way to the conference room and waited until everyone was settled.

The captain came in and took the last seat at the table.

"Cruz, go ahead and brief on what we learned at the White House this morning."

As he went through the details of their conversations with the Secret Service agents, Derek and Tom, Sam tried not to think about Stahl or the trial or having to make a statement at his sentencing. Under no circumstances could she picture herself doing that. If she had her druthers, she'd never see that rat bastard again.

"Holy crap," Jeannie McBride said. *"The baby's not his?"*

"That's what his aides are saying. He allegedly had a vasectomy after his last son was born, so there's no way he could've fathered Tara's child."

"Is it okay to say that I can't believe we're sitting here talking about the president's vasectomy?" Matt O'Brien asked.

"Detective Cruz and I said the same thing earlier. The challenge now is to figure out who *did* father the child and whether he might've been annoyed enough by the news of Tara's affair with the president to kill her. We've gotten DNA from the baby and we're getting Nelson's. We'll put a rush on the results, but it's going to take a few days." To Malone, she said, "When will we have the warrant for the cell phone carrier?"

"I'm hoping we'll hear in the next hour or two."

"That's going to be key."

"I'll stay on it."

"What else do we have?" Sam asked.

"I did some more digging into Tara's financials and her background," Jeannie said. "Her best year in business was when she worked for the Nelson campaign. In total, she earned more than seven hundred thousand dollars that year."

"Whoa," Sam said. "That's five hundred thousand more the figure we were previously given. If the media got ahold of the fact she made seven hundred grand while she was sleeping with the president, that'd make the story even more insane than it already is."

"That info is publicly available," Jeannie said. "It's only a matter of time before they have it."

"Great." Sam released her hair from the clip and ran her fingers through it. "I feel like we're getting nowhere fast here. What're we hearing from Archie?"

"They're going through security tape from other locations in Tara's neighborhood, but they don't have anything yet," Cameron said.

"And no sign of her cell phone?"

Cameron shook his head. "We've got Patrol checking the trash in an eight-block radius around her building, but nothing so far."

Sam glanced at the murder board that Jeannie, Cameron and Matt had started on one of the large dry-erase boards. She studied the photo of Tara in life and the one from the crime scene in which the dark bruises on her neck were the primary difference. "What do we think of the theory that she leaked the story of her affair with Nelson?"

"What would she have to gain?" Cameron asked.

"Getting the attention of the man who'd stopped returning her calls?" Freddie said.

"She was trying to stick him with the baby," Sam said. "What was her motivation in doing that when she had to know there were at least two men who could've been the father? And did Nelson tell her that he'd had a vasectomy? Did she know that?" Sam dropped her head into her hands. "God, am I going to have to ask him these questions?"

"I think you might," Malone said. "I want to know if *she* knew he'd had the vasectomy."

"I can't even…"

Malone laughed. "You can do it, Lieutenant."

"Not until I get the report Hanigan promised me that will prove he had the vasectomy in the first place. In the meantime, I want to know who else she was talking to. We need those phone records."

Malone got up. "I'll go see what I can do to move that along." Speaking directly to Sam, he added, "Come find me when you're ready to do the other thing."

"Okay."

After he left the room, Freddie glanced at her. "What other thing?"

"Conklin wants to talk to us again."

"I thought you already talked to him and he stone-walled you?"

"We did and he did, but apparently he's had a come-to-Jesus in the meantime and wants to talk."

"Are you sure it wouldn't be better to let one of us do that?" His concern for her was etched into the furrow of his brows.

"I'm fine. After I see Conklin, I want to double back with Delany, the assistant who found her. If anyone knew who her boss was dating, it would be her."

"Sounds like a plan."

"Keep me posted on any developments." Sam got up to leave the conference room, putting her hair back up as she walked toward the lobby to find Malone. She wanted to get this chat with Conklin over with so she could get back to the case. Who should be coming the other way but her nemesis, Sergeant Ramsey, the last freaking person in the universe she wanted to see.

She kept her head down so there'd be no chance of making eye contact with the son of a bitch.

"Heard some interesting rumors about your good friend Gonzales floating around. Apparently, he was a bad, bad boy, scoring shit on the street." He made a weird sound as he brushed by her. "Heard he's in rehab and not out sick like everyone was told. Lies, lies and more lies."

Sam kept walking, but her heart skipped a beat at what she'd heard. She already knew what Gonzo had done in the throes of his addiction, but how in the fuck did Ramsey know about it, and what did he plan to do with the information?

This was not good. If Ramsey had dirt on Gonzo, he'd do whatever he could to discredit him *and* her. Damn it. This was the last fucking thing she needed right now.

CHAPTER NINETEEN

"WHAT'S WRONG?" Malone asked when she reached his office.

"Nothing." She wasn't telling him or anyone what Ramsey had said until she had a chance to talk to Gonzo about it. "Let's get this done with Conklin. I've got far more important things that need my attention." Only because she wanted to know who else had known the details of her father's shooting would she give Conklin even five more minutes of her precious time.

"I had him brought up to interview two."

"Let's go."

Sam wondered how many times she would have to see her former deputy chief in an orange jumpsuit before it would sink in that he'd actually known who'd shot her father—and why—the whole time Sam had been on a desperate search for answers. How did he live with himself and the guilt of pretending to be Skip's friend while hiding the truth?

She decided to ask him that before giving him the chance to speak when she and Malone entered the room where Conklin and his attorney waited for them.

Conklin sat up a little straighter when they came in, but otherwise didn't react.

Sam stared him down. "I want to know how you can live with yourself. How did you sleep at night for *four years* sitting on information that would've led to justice for a man who'd been your friend for *thirty years*? How do you live with the guilt of knowing he died without ever getting that closure?"

His eyes narrowed and his jaw tightened with displeasure while his eyes filled with tears.

Too fucking bad if he was uncomfortable. She wanted to know. "Well?"

"It made me sick, all the time, for four years."

"Well, that's good, because it makes me sick to know that you pretended to be his friend while withholding information that would've brought his shooters to justice."

"I didn't have any choice!"

Sam laughed. "Sure, you did. You chose to protect your own ass rather than do the right thing, and now the whole world knows what a fucking coward you are."

The lawyer cleared his throat. "While I understand the lieutenant's frustrations—"

"Shut the fuck up. You don't have the first clue about my frustrations."

"I'm sorry, Sam," Conklin said, slumping with defeat. "I don't know what else to say besides that."

Sam remained standing, arms crossed, her expression hard. She would never forgive him for what he'd done. "You called this meeting. What do you want?"

He sat up a little and leaned forward on the table. "You wanted to know about that note you received."

She remained silent.

"This is a big department, a lot of people... Not everyone was a fan of your father's, as much as that might hurt you to hear. Officers start out together, they come up together and some just do better than others. That's the way it goes. But not everyone understands that, and people's feelings get hurt when someone gets pushed ahead of them in the ranks."

As she listened to him, her mind raced with possibilities. Had they considered everyone who came up in the ranks with her dad? Not just in his academy class, but the ones immediately before and after his.

"Do you have specific information on who else knew or are you speculating?"

"I'm speculating. If someone else in the department knew, that'd be news to me."

"Anything else?"

"I want to try to make this right."

"You can't."

"Sam, please. Try to understand. They would've killed me and my wife. I was backed into a corner."

"Do you honestly expect me to feel sorry for you? We could've protected you both, as you well know."

"I couldn't ask her to live like that."

"So you subjected my dad to four years in hell instead?"

Dunning cleared his throat again. "Deputy Chief Conklin has cooperated with the investigation. His cooperation should be noted to the prosecutors."

"Is that what you think is going to happen here?" Sam asked, incredulous. "You basically signed my dad's death certificate by telling Gallagher that he was taking another look at Coyne's murder. You knew they'd go after him, and you told them anyway."

"Because if I didn't and they found out I knew, they'd come for *me*! What was I supposed to do?"

"Tell someone. Come clean about what you knew before another good cop could be murdered at their hands."

"I couldn't." Conklin dropped his head into his hands,

his body shaking with sobs. "I was too afraid of them. I tried to support Skip every way I could after…"

"I suppose you want some sort of reward for being a good friend to him after he was nearly murdered, but sorry to say that being responsible for putting him in that chair to start with makes you the worst 'friend' he ever had." She glanced at Malone. "I think I've heard enough."

Malone glared at Conklin. "Me too."

"Will you tell the prosecutors that I cooperated?"

"Fuck you." Sam turned and walked out of the room, sucking in greedy deep breaths of the fresh air outside the small room. Aware of Malone following her, she didn't slow down until she reached her office and ducked inside, needing a minute to get it together before she faced her squad. They probably thought she was a lunatic, but it wouldn't be the first time she'd given them reason to think that.

Malone came in after her and shut the door. To his credit he said nothing for several minutes, giving her the time she needed to collect herself.

When she felt ready, she looked at the captain. "Imagine that he wants to be rewarded for doing the right thing *now*."

"His audacity knows no limits."

"He did give us a thread though. The others that came up with Dad, not just in your class but above and below."

"I have a few thoughts on that, but I'd like to discuss it with the chief first."

Sam shrugged. "Whatever you want to do is fine with me." The adrenaline that had surged during the confrontation with Conklin subsided, leaving her wrung out in the aftermath. "Will this ever stop being shocking?"

"No, never. It'll never make sense to those of us who try to do the right thing on and off the job."

"Are there more like him than like us?"

"I can't allow myself to believe that or the job will stop making sense to me."

"I worry that it's already stopped making sense to me."

"That's not true. You're grieving the loss of your dad and the betrayal of a man you and your dad had considered a friend and ally. That's a lot to process, but you *will* wrap your head around it. Eventually. In the meantime, you continue to do the job, which is exactly what Skip would want you to do. He was so damned proud of you."

For the first time in days, Sam's eyes stung with the start of tears that she could not give in to while on the job. She hated people who cried at work and tried to never be that person. But sometimes... Sometimes, it was all too much.

"There's something else." She recalled her dad's advice from her first day on the job—if you know something that your chain of command needs to be made aware of, disclose it immediately. Do not hesitate to report it or you, too, are culpable.

"What?" Malone took on a guarded stance.

"Ramsey said something about Gonzo scoring pills on the street."

Malone's eyes went wide for a second. "What'd he say?"

"Something about Gonzo being a bad, bad boy scoring shit on the street and how word is he's in rehab and not out sick like people were told."

The captain's shock was palpable. "Is there any chance he could be telling the truth?"

"Yes."

"Sam... Are you kidding me right now?"

"I wish I was."

Malone's expression was unreadable as he processed the information. "I have to take this to the chief."

"I understand. In the meantime, can you do something about Ramsey and his big mouth?"

"I'll do what I can, but if this gets out..."

He didn't have to tell her that Gonzo's career could be ruined right as he seemed to be turning the corner in battling his addiction and the grief that had nearly ruined him after Arnold's murder. The timing couldn't be worse.

"Keep me posted."

"I will."

Malone left, closing the door behind him.

Sam fired up her computer and looked up the rehab in Baltimore where Gonzo was being treated. She placed a call to the number listed on the website and cycled through an automatic greeting in an effort to reach an actual person. When she finally got through to an operator, ten minutes had gone by.

"I need to leave a message for one of your patients. It's urgent that I speak with Thomas Gonzales as soon as possible."

"May I please have your name?"

"Sam Holland with the Metro PD in Washington."

"You... You're..."

"Yes, I am. Will you give him the message and ask him to call my cell as soon as possible? Tell him nothing is wrong with his fiancée or son so he won't panic."

"I'll let him know."

"Thanks." Sam ended the call before the woman could

go on about her being the second lady or ask why she didn't have Secret Service protection or how she could continue to do her job while her husband was the vice president. She was sick of answering those questions.

She took a minute to check her email, which included one from Hanigan containing Tara's vetting documents. Sam forwarded the email to Green with instructions to review it.

Grabbing her coat, keys and portable radio, she got up to leave the office. "Cruz, let's go."

Not bothering to wait for him to get his shit together, she headed for the morgue, needing to get out of the building where she'd been so profoundly disappointed.

Freddie caught up to her. "Where're we going?"

"To talk to Delany again. And to City Hall."

"Everything okay?"

"Yeah, it's just dandy."

"You talked to Conklin? How'd that go?"

"He wants us to put in a good word for him with the prosecutors because he's trying to help. Now."

"Seriously? I hope you told him to eff off."

Sam glanced at her partner, feigning shock. It was a big deal for him to say "damn," let alone "eff off."

"Don't look at me that way! Tell me you told him where to go."

"I did. But he gave us a thread, mentioning the petty jealousy that goes on inside departments when one person gets promoted over another. We should look at the academy classes above and below Dad's to see who would've been put out by his success. Maybe someone else had stumbled upon the truth of Dad's shooting but kept it to themselves because they didn't like him for whatever reason."

"It's not a bad idea."

"Definitely worth considering. Conklin said he was sick over what he knew the whole time Dad was in that wheelchair and that he tried to be as good of a friend to him as he could be after the shooting."

"With friends like that…"

"Right?" They got into Sam's car and headed for Georgetown, where Delany lived in an off-campus apartment that was within walking distance of Tara's place. "I honestly couldn't believe his lawyer was actually suggesting we put in a word for him."

"The whole thing is beyond disgusting."

"There's something else." She told him what Ramsey had said about Gonzo and watched as Freddie's expression flattened with shock.

"No way. He'd never do that."

"He did do it."

"Sam, there's no way he would've risked his career that way."

"He told me he did. He hasn't been himself since Arnold was killed. We'd all like to believe he never would have crossed the line, but we've seen the lengths other addicts go to in order to score. Why should he be any different?"

"I just… I can't…"

Sam sighed. "I know. Believe me." If this came to light, she would have one hell of a time protecting her friend and sergeant from the ramifications. "I left a message for him at the rehab. I'm waiting for him to call me."

"The fact that Ramsey has this…"

"I'm going to talk to Erica Lucas and see if she can find out what he knows and how he knows." Detective

Lucas worked with Ramsey in Special Victims and disliked him nearly as much as Sam did.

"That's a good idea."

Making use of the GPS app on Freddie's phone, they found Delany's apartment building. "No idea how these kids can afford tuition at Georgetown and an apartment in this city."

"Right? They must have loans up the wazoo."

"I had loans up the wazoo, and I lived at home while I was in school. I worked extra details for years to pay off my student loans. I don't miss that grind."

"No kidding. Details were the worst."

Hours in the broiling sun or frigid wind, directing traffic around construction sites, among other things cops did for extra money, had helped Sam pay down the staggering debt she'd accumulated while getting her bachelor's and master's degrees. It'd been worth it, as her education had helped to move her through the department ranks more quickly.

"You know, Ramsey hates me for making lieutenant ahead of him, but did he bust his ass with dyslexia to get a graduate degree? I think not."

"No one ever wants to hear that there're good reasons why someone else was promoted ahead of them."

"They think advancement is their God-given right if they show up and punch the clock every day."

"Right?"

"I hate to say that Conklin might be right about anything, but there probably were people above and below my dad who felt he'd gotten promotions that should've been theirs. People can be so fucking petty. And if this person blabbed about it, then maybe someone clued them in on how Skip Holland was going to get what was coming to him."

"It's a thread." His lack of enthusiasm had her glancing at him after she had found a parking space three blocks from Delany's building.

"You don't like it?"

He shrugged. "I just think it's far-fetched to think that multiple people in the department would've known that one of their own was putting himself in mortal danger and done nothing to stop it. Or that they would hear about it after the fact and not say something."

"That's because you're the kind of cop who'd do the right thing. Sadly, not all our colleagues think the way you do."

They got out of the car and backtracked to Delany's place. As they walked, Sam kept her gaze down so as not to attract attention she didn't want from people they passed on the sidewalk.

In the vestibule, Freddie found Delany's name on the list of tenants and pushed the button.

"Yes?"

"Lieutenant Holland and Detective Cruz."

After a long pause, she buzzed them in.

"Is it my imagination or is Ms. Delany not happy we're here?" Sam asked in the elevator.

"She was a little hesitant to buzz us in. Maybe she's not dressed or her boyfriend is there or…"

Sam rolled her eyes.

"We're both a little too jaded to believe it's anything that simple."

"Very true. I love that you're as jaded as I am now. You were so annoying back in the rose-colored glasses days."

"When did I have rose-colored glasses?"

"Like the first two years we worked together when you still wanted to believe that people were inherently good? I believe I've shown you otherwise since then."

"Aren't you the one who preaches that I shouldn't judge all people by the crap we see on the job?"

"Don't use my own words against me. It's annoying."

His bark of laughter followed her off the elevator.

Outside her door, Sam and Freddie showed their badges to the officer who'd been assigned to provide security at Delany's home. Though the officer clearly recognized her, he went through the motions of examining their badges. After he granted approval, Sam knocked on the door at apartment 6C.

Once again, Delany made them wait, which was also annoying.

Sam was about to knock again when the door swung open.

"Hey." Delany stepped aside to admit them into a small but neatly kept space. "Have you figured out who killed Tara?"

"Not yet, but we have more questions for you."

"Sure, whatever I can do to help."

Sam helped herself to a seat on Delany's sofa. "Besides the president, who else could be the father of her child?"

"It was Nelson's kid."

"He says otherwise."

"Well, of course he does."

"The thing is, it's possible that he can prove it's not his." Sam waited a moment to see if Delany would connect the dots on her own.

"Oh, so he had a vasectomy, then?"

"We're awaiting conclusive proof of that, but that's what we're hearing. What I'd like to know is who else was she seeing who could've fathered her child?"

"I don't know."

"You had access to her schedule?"

"Yes."

"Do you still have access to her calendar from that time?"

Delany bit her lip and nodded.

"We'd like to see it."

"I...I'm not sure I should do that. It's her private business."

"She was murdered, Delany. That means her private business is now *our* business." Seeing that the woman wasn't entirely convinced, Sam added, "We can get a warrant and take you into custody until it comes through."

That got her attention. "Why would you have to take me in?"

"So you can't fuck with the calendar while we wait for the warrant."

"I...I wouldn't do that."

"Maybe not, but I don't know you well enough to be sure of that, so you can either give us the info we want now or we'll head downtown to get a warrant. It's up to you."

Delany appeared to give her options significant thought before getting up to retrieve an iPad from her desk. She returned to her seat on the sofa and started poking at the screen. When she had the info they needed, she handed it over to Sam, who passed it to Freddie.

"Who else besides Nelson was significant at that time?"

"There were a couple," Delany said hesitantly. "I don't want people to think she was a slut or anything. She was heartbroken after Bryce ended things. She went a little nuts with guys and dating and stuff…"

"I'm not out to slut-shame her, Delany. All I want to know is who killed her. The rest is her business."

"So you won't say anything about how many different guys she was with?"

Was it Sam's imagination, or was Delany the one who had a problem with the number of men her boss had seen? "I'm only interested in whoever killed her. The rest is her business." Sam glanced at Freddie, who was seated at Delany's desk taking notes from the calendar.

"Did you know any of the guys whose names we're going to find in the calendar?"

"Just one. Ben Wilton."

The name hit Sam like a shock from a live wire. "The *congressman*?"

Delany nodded.

Sam had to take a second to fully absorb this information and the implications that came with it. "How long was she seeing him?"

"On and off for a couple of months. Until she started traveling with the Nelson campaign, and then they didn't see as much of each other, but I know she still saw him after the campaign."

"Was she still seeing him while she was with Nelson?"

"I think so. It was hard to keep track of what she was doing during that time. Not all of it made it onto the calendar that I kept for her." Delany leaned forward, her expression earnest. "You have to understand. She wanted to marry Bryce. She thought she had it all figured out, and when he broke up with her… Well, she went a little crazy. And not just in her dating life. Everything was crazy. That was right around the time that her partner left the business."

They needed to talk to the partner. "Can you hook me up with her contact info?"

"Sure." Delany used her cell phone to find the number and wrote Paige Thompson's number on a piece of paper that she handed to Sam.

"Talk to me about what precipitated their split?"

"Tara never talked about it with me, but I think Paige was pissed that Tara was neglecting the business after she broke up with Bryce. I overheard them fighting a few days before Paige decided to leave. She said that she understood Tara was disappointed and heartbroken, but they still had a business to run and that Tara couldn't be out all night every night and still carry her weight."

"What did Tara say to that?"

"That it was easy for Paige to criticize her as an engaged woman with her whole life figured out."

"Stay available," Sam said to Delany when she got up to leave.

"What does that mean?"

"That means if I call you, answer the phone. If I come by to talk to you again, let me in. Don't leave town without telling me. Got it?"

Seeming rattled, Delany nodded. "O-okay."

In the elevator, Sam made a decision based on the gut that had never let her down yet. "I want to dig deeper into her."

"Delany?"

"Yeah. She's too nervous for my liking. I feel like she knows something else that she's not telling us."

"Could she be nervous after having found her boss strangled?"

"Sure, but I sense this is something more. She's too skittish."

"I'll call Green and tell him to get everyone on it."

"Tell him the lieutenant is having one of her feelings."

CHAPTER TWENTY

As THEY WALKED OUTSIDE, Sam's phone rang with a number she didn't recognize. But she did recognize the Baltimore area code. "It's Gonzo. Make that call to Green." She flipped open her phone and walked away from Freddie. "Hey, thanks for getting back to me."

"What's up?"

"Well, I'm not quite sure how to say this, but I had another encounter with Ramsey this morning."

"That guy needs to get a life."

"Agreed, but he said something I couldn't ignore, as much as I'd like to."

"What's that?"

"It was about you scoring on the street."

Dead silence.

"Gonzo." Sam closed her eyes and took a deep breath.

"How does he know?"

"He didn't say."

"Fuck, Sam. This is bad."

"Yep. I had no choice but to mention it to Malone. I'm not sure how this will go, but we're all aware of your illness and how it can manifest itself."

"I'm sorry, Sam. All I can tell you is I wasn't myself then. The addiction had me by the throat, and there was nothing I wouldn't do to feed it. I'll take full responsibility."

"Don't say anything to anyone about this until we figure out what he's got and what he plans to do with it."

"If he's got it, others probably do too."

"I don't have to tell you that this could end your career."

"No, you don't have to tell me that."

"I'm sorry to hit you with this while you're working so hard to get back on track."

"I don't expect you to stick your neck out for me, Sam. I fucked up. I have to own that."

"I appreciate you taking responsibility, but in light of the circumstances that led to your addiction, I'm not going to sit by and let your career get ruined without at least trying to see if there's anything I can do. Give me a couple of days to figure things out on my end."

"Will you let me know what you find out?"

"As soon as I can. In the meantime, keep doing what you're doing there and don't let this sidetrack you."

"I'll do my best not to let it get in my head. If I lose my job, I'll figure something out."

"Let's hope it doesn't come to that." Neither of them mentioned it could get a whole lot worse than losing his job if he was charged with a crime. "I'll be in touch." She slapped the phone closed and turned to walk back to where Freddie waited for her.

He could tell just by looking at her that the news wasn't good.

"He said the addiction had him by the throat, and he did things he's not proud of to feed it."

"And freaking Ramsey, of all people, knows that."

"Yep."

"This isn't good, Sam."

"No, it isn't. With the shit already flying over Stahl

and Conklin, this will be a bigger deal than it would be otherwise. And it has me wondering if Ramsey and his minions are going out of their way to look for dirt on me and my squad due to his intense dislike for me."

"Wouldn't put it past him."

They got into the car and headed for the Capitol. "Find out which building Wilton's office is in." While Freddie got busy on his phone, Sam placed a call to Erica Lucas.

"Hey," Lucas said, sounding rushed. "What's up?"

"You got a minute?"

"Just one. Sexual assault reported at American University. I'm at the ER waiting to talk to the victim."

"You want to call me back?"

"Nah, go ahead."

"It's about Ramsey."

"How did I know you were going to say that?"

"Sorry to put you in the middle of our feud, but he's got something on one of my people."

"Gonzales, right?"

"How'd you know?"

"When Ramsey has something, he spews."

Sam had been afraid of just that. "What's he saying?"

"That Gonzales was scoring pills on the street and he's in rehab, not out sick like everyone thinks. Is he in rehab?"

"Yeah, he is."

"Oh crap. Well, I hope he's getting the help he needs. Most of us understand that he's been through a horrific ordeal since Arnold was killed and would cut him a break for anything he did in the throes of grief and addiction. But Ramsey isn't most people."

"Do you know how he got ahold of this info?"

"He's got a lot of eyes and ears on the ground. His team of informants is impressive, considering he's such a douchebag. It must've come from one of them. Is it possible that Gonzo scored on the street?"

"It's more than possible."

"Oh shit."

"Is Ramsey going out of his way to look for dirt on me and my people?"

"I wouldn't be surprised if he was. He was enraged that you weren't indicted for assaulting him. After that, I'd say anything is possible."

It killed her to think that her feud with the sergeant was spilling onto the officers who reported to her. Not that she blamed herself for what Gonzo had done, but no one would know about it were it not for her ongoing beef with Ramsey—and his with her. "If you hear anything else, will you let me know?"

"Absolutely. I've got to run."

"Thanks for taking the time."

"No problem."

Sam closed the phone and tucked it into her pocket.

"What'd she say?" Freddie asked.

Sam conveyed the gist of the conversation to him. "I need to warn the others that there's never been a better time to keep their noses clean on and off the job. If Ramsey's got eyes on us, we're not going to give him anything else."

"Agreed. Wilton is in Longworth. He's a Democrat representing Seattle, known for being a supporter of business and technology."

Sam directed the car toward Independence Avenue,

while her brain spun with the potential implications for Gonzo. Would he be charged or would the U.S. Attorney cut him a break due to the circumstances surrounding his addiction? And if they did go easy on him, what would Ramsey do then? He'd nearly lost his mind when the grand jury had chosen not to indict her for assaulting him, and since then, he'd been more unhinged than usual.

Her job was hard enough as it was without her own colleagues turning on her. She'd assaulted Ramsey after he'd said she'd gotten what she deserved when Stahl wrapped her in razor wire and dumped gasoline on her in preparation for setting her on fire. When she'd punched Ramsey in the face, she hadn't expected him to fall backward down a flight of stairs and break bones. That'd been the least of what he'd deserved for saying such a hateful thing to her.

Sam had always thought that jealousy was the most ridiculous of emotions, especially on a job like theirs. Not everyone could rise to the upper echelons of command, and those who did, usually did so because of a dedicated effort that spanned their entire career. Her dad, for example, had set out to be chief or deputy chief, never deviating from that goal. And when his best friend had been chosen over him for the top job, he'd swallowed his own disappointment and supported Joe as his faithful deputy. He'd understood that they couldn't both have the top job, and if it couldn't be him, then he wanted it to be Joe.

Someone like Ramsey expected promotions and awards to come his way just for showing up and doing the bare minimum each day. It infuriated him that Sam had made lieutenant over him when he'd had more years on the job, but he hadn't used those years as productively as she had. She'd taken full advantage of every opportunity that had come her way and had busted her ass for the rank she now held. To hear him tell it, the only reason she still had a job, let alone the rank of lieutenant overseeing one of the most critical divisions in the department, was because her dad was the chief's best friend.

Whatever.

"I can hear you fuming over there."

Freddie's comment interrupted her musings. "I am fuming. His beef is with me. Why's he going after my team?"

"Because he knows that going after us would upset you more than if he comes for you."

"That's a fact. What I don't get is if he's so disillusioned, why doesn't he just retire and move on with his life?"

"He's the type that'd want to see you crippled before he goes."

"Yeah, he would because he's sick that way. I'll never understand how people have the emotional energy to do this kind of shit."

"It's probably because they have nowhere else to expend it. If he's unhappy in his professional life, that probably extends to his personal life."

"Maybe we should do a little digging of our own and see if we can find dirt on him."

"Hmmm, that's not the worst idea you ever had."

"It probably is one of the worst ideas I ever had, but that's not going to stop me from acting on it. When we get back, I'll bring Jeannie and Cam in on the plan, but not O'Brien."

"He's too new and untested. We're not sure yet if we can completely trust him."

"Exactly. I want to trust him, but until I'm a hundred percent sure…"

"Say no more. The four of us will be enough." He grinned at her. "I really, *really* like this terrible idea of yours. If we can find something on him, that might save Gonzo."

Sam wasn't convinced that Gonzo could be saved since he'd admitted to having committed a crime. However, the fact that he was battling addiction and PTSD over the loss of his partner would go a long way toward leniency, or so she hoped.

"Before we see Wilton, we need to get a rough date on when conception of the baby would've occurred."

"Let me consult the Google." He did some tapping on his phone. "So there's this reverse calculator site where we can put in the baby's birth date and figure out when conception would've occurred."

"He's two weeks old, right?"

"Yes." He typed in the baby's birth date. "It gives a weeklong range of implantation dates. January 31 to February 6."

"Is there anything we can't find out online these days?"

"Hardly anything."

"It's downright handy at times like this."

"No kidding. If you had a smart phone, you'd know how much you can find out."

"Why do I need a smart phone when you have one?"

At the Longworth office building, they were once again forced to turn over their firearms and submit to security checks to gain entrance.

Wilton's office was on the second floor, tucked into a corner at the end of a long hallway. Inside, they encountered one of Sam's favorite things, this time in triplicate—three receptionists. Awesome. Could this day get any better?

She showed her badge while Freddie did the same. "Lieutenant Holland, Detective Cruz, Metro PD, here to see Congressman Wilton?"

"Do you have an appointment?" one of them asked. She was blonde, blue-eyed, perky and efficient.

Sam could tell that just by looking at her. "No, we don't have an appointment, but then again, we don't need one when we're investigating a homicide. Please tell the congressman we're here, and that it would be better for him if he doesn't waste our time with unnecessary delays."

The woman started to say something but wisely thought better of it and picked up the phone. With the mood Sam was in, it would give her great pleasure to arrest the woman for interfering in her investigation.

"Don't even think about it," Freddie said under his breath. "I'm not doing all that paperwork."

"Stop being a killjoy." She absolutely loved how well he knew her, but it was a little disconcerting that they'd reached the point where he was actually reading her mind. That could become a problem if she wasn't careful. Her mind was a scary place to be, and no one needed to know the full extent of what went on there.

The door behind the row of receptionists opened and out strode a tall, handsome, dark-haired man who Sam recognized as the congressman.

"Come in," he said.

Now that was the kind of cooperation she expected

but rarely received on the job. He scored five points right off the bat for cutting through the bullshit and ushering them into his small but elegant office and offering them seats in his visitor chairs.

"How can I help you?"

"We're investigating the homicide of Tara Weber." Sam watched him carefully, looking for any sign of emotional reaction to hearing the late woman's name.

"It's a terrible tragedy. Tara was a great person."

"We understand that you were involved with her?"

"A long time ago."

"How long ago exactly?"

"Almost a year maybe."

"Can you be more specific? When was the last time you were romantically involved with her?" Sam didn't want to come right out and ask the guy when he last slept with her, but she would if he didn't take the hint.

He picked up his phone. "May I?"

"Of course."

While he poked at the screen, she cooled her heels, waiting for him to determine the actual date of their last get-together.

"February 1. We had dinner, spent the night together, and I never heard from her again after that, despite repeated efforts on my part to see her again. I know now that was because she was also involved with Nelson." This last part was said with a tinge of bitterness.

"Congressman, is there any chance her son is yours?"

The question clearly shocked him. "I thought the baby was Nelson's?"

"We have reason to believe that's not the case."

"I…I have no idea what to say. She told me she was on birth control. We talked about how we both were clean.

I told her I could prove it. She said that wasn't necessary. I thought… I thought we were starting something, you know? It never occurred to me that I'd never see her again after that last night together."

"Would you be willing to submit to a DNA test to determine the baby's paternity?"

"Um, yes, of course. If he's mine, I want to know that."

"We'll set that up. Can you confirm that you had no further contact with her after February 1 of this year?"

"Yes, I can confirm that, and you're welcome to check my phone if you don't believe me." He handed it over to Freddie, who looked at the text message history.

"Do you mind if I look at your emails too?"

"Be my guest. I have nothing to hide where she's concerned. I was interested in more with her, but apparently that didn't work both ways."

Sam appreciated the man's forthrightness, another thing that was rare in her line of work. People tended to hedge, even when they had nothing to hide, which only made them seem guilty even when they weren't. People were stupid that way.

"I hope you understand that we have to ask where you were the day Tara was killed."

"I was right here, in committee hearings all day. My assistant can give you my schedule for that day and any other day in question."

"That day would be great."

He picked up the desktop extension and requested the information while Sam watched him, looking for cracks in his armor and seeing none. After he ended the call, he glanced at her. "How soon can I find out if the baby is mine?"

Sam gave him Lindsey McNamara's number and asked him to get in touch with her about giving a sample of his DNA. "It can take a couple of weeks to run DNA, but we'll see what we can do to expedite it."

"This is… It's crazy. I'm in a new relationship, and it's going really well. This…" He seemed at a loss for words.

"Would be something that happened before you met the new person in your life."

"True, but a baby…" He took a shaky deep breath and released it. "That's… Well…"

"It's only natural you'd be shocked, Congressman. Most people have nine months to prepare for a child." The scenario reminded her of how Gonzo found out about his son, Alex, months after the child was born.

"Yes, exactly." Running his hands through his hair, he seemed to be trying to wrap his mind around the possibility.

"I should mention that our investigation has revealed that Ms. Weber dated a number of men during the months that followed the end of a long-term relationship."

"So you're saying there's also a good possibility the baby isn't mine?" His expression was a mixture of relief and sadness, as if he couldn't decide which he preferred—being the baby's father or not.

"I'm saying nothing is definite until it is." In other words, she wanted to say, don't get your hopes up in case the baby isn't yours.

"I understand."

Sam stood to leave. "We'll be in touch about the DNA test."

He stood to walk them out. "The sooner the better."

"I understand."

When he opened the office door, the assistant appeared with a printout of his schedule from the day Tara was murdered.

Sam took it from her. "Thank you. We appreciate the cooperation."

"Whatever we can do." Wilton handed her a business card. "Will you keep me posted? My cell number is on there."

Sam reciprocated, giving him one of hers. "Will do. If you think of anything else that might be relevant, call me. No detail is too small."

He nodded. "I will."

Sam and Freddie left the congressman's suite and headed for the main security checkpoint to retrieve their weapons.

"Call Lindsey and tell her she'll be hearing from Wilton."

While Freddie made the call, Sam let her mind wander from one detail of this case to the other, looking for new threads to pull. They were almost back to the car when her phone rang with a call from Cameron Green. "What's up?"

"I wanted to let you know I talked to Archie about the dump of Tara's phone, and we're still waiting for the phone company to respond."

"I'm going to call Malone and have him put some pressure there."

"He's already taking care of that, and Agent Hill has been exerting pressure as well with the phone company and the dating app."

"It's good of him to help. Sometimes the FBI gets faster results than we do." A fact that rankled her.

"The dating app is pushing back hard, due to member privacy concerns."

"Isn't that rich? A woman is dead, possibly because of someone she met on their app, and they're worried about protecting the privacy of a potential killer?"

"I know, but we're looking for one person out of a pool of men she dated, so I can sort of see their point."

"You can't see their point and be on my side too."

Green laughed. "My apologies."

"Don't let it happen again."

"I'll see that it doesn't. Are you guys getting anywhere?"

"Not really. We met with another of the guys she was involved with around the time the baby would've been conceived. We gave Congressman Wilton of Seattle the shock of his life when we indicated that her baby could be his."

"I can only imagine how shocking that would be."

"Anything in the vetting documents?"

"Nothing we don't already know."

"Ugh!" Sam recalled her plan to dig for dirt on Ramsey. "In the morning, report to my office fifteen minutes before your tour begins. Tell McBride too, but only the two of you."

"Okay…"

"I'll tell you why in the morning. You guys can call it a day."

"All right. I'll be there early."

"See you then."

Sam glanced at the clock, which was inching closer to seven thirty. If she didn't head home soon, she wouldn't get to see the twins before they were tucked in for the night. She looked at Freddie. "Go home. We'll pick it up in the morning."

"I'll see you then." Freddie took off toward the Metro, eager as usual to get home to his new wife.

CHAPTER TWENTY-ONE

SAM DROVE HOME, thinking about each of the three things that had her attention—the Weber case, the hunt for the author of the anonymous note about her dad's shooting and the situation with Gonzo and Ramsey.

At times like this, she wondered if it was possible for a head to explode. If so, hers was going to blow at any moment. The Gonzo situation was the last freaking thing she needed, and part of her was seriously pissed with her sergeant for putting himself—and her, by extension—in such a difficult position. On the one hand, she believed addiction was a disease that made sane people do things they'd never ordinarily do. On the other hand, he was a freaking cop who knew better than to go looking for drugs on the street.

Her stomach twisted with nerves and disappointment and fear for what was ahead for him. She'd do anything she could for him, but if word got out that he'd committed a crime, there wouldn't be much she could do to protect him from the consequences.

She blamed the man who'd gunned down Arnold for all the troubles Gonzo had suffered through since that fateful night last January. Soon it would be a year since the young detective's tragic death, which was hard to believe. So much had changed since then. Gonzo had been lost to the deepest kind of grief and self-recrimination for much of the last year, while Arnold's close friend, Detective Will Tyrone, had decided to leave the department rather than continue to face the risks of the job on a daily basis. It had become too much for him.

Sam understood how that could happen. On many a day, it was too much for her, but she pressed on because the job was in her blood. She couldn't imagine walking away, no matter how bad it got. Sometimes she allowed herself to entertain the idea of leaving, but she always came up short when trying to figure out what the hell she'd do with herself without the job that had defined her entire adult life.

She was waved through the Ninth Street checkpoint and parked in her designated spot. As she got out of her car, Celia drove through the checkpoint, waving to Sam as she went past. Sam waited for her stepmother to join her on the sidewalk and gave the other woman a quick hug. "How's it going?"

"Oh, you know. It's going."

"Are you doing all right?"

"One minute I am. The next minute, I'm not."

"What can I do?"

"I'm told it'll take time." Celia shrugged. "I'm thinking about finding a job so I don't have so much time to kill. Taking care of your dad was a full-time job, and now that I don't have that, I'm sort of lost."

"That sounds like a good idea, but maybe go part-time at first. Ease into it."

"I've put out some feelers with former nursing colleagues. We'll see what comes up."

"Why don't you come have dinner with me? I'm sure everyone else has already eaten."

"Sure, that sounds good. I'd love to see the kids."

As they went up the ramp together, Sam was glad that Celia had agreed to come. She couldn't bear to see the woman who had so lovingly cared for her father looking so sad.

"I suppose we should get rid of the ramps now that we don't need them anymore," Celia said.

"We can do it when we're ready."

"Will we ever be ready?"

"I think we will be eventually, but I'm not there yet." Celia offered a small smile. "Neither am I."

"Then that's not something we need to worry about now."

"One day at a time."

Nate, the agent working the door, greeted them with a warm smile. "Good evening, Lieutenant, Mrs. Holland."

"Evening, Nate."

Per usual around this time, they walked into bedlam, with Nick overseeing two five-year-olds in pajamas, their hair wet from a recent bath, as they pounced on thirteen-year-old Scotty, who was on the floor.

Celia laughed at the "ooph" that came from Scotty when Alden landed on his midsection.

Aubrey let out a shriek of excitement when she saw Sam and came running toward her, screaming Sam's name.

Sam scooped up the little girl and wrapped her up in a tight hug, breathing in the fresh, clean scent of her. Over the child's shoulder, she caught Nick watching her with a contented look on his face that made her heart lurch with happiness.

"How was your day, sweet girl?" Sam asked Aubrey.

"I miss Mommy and Daddy."

"I know, baby." Sam's heart broke for her, as it did

every time one of the twins mentioned their late parents. She couldn't imagine absorbing such a blow at the tender age of five. In some ways, they were lucky because they wouldn't remember much about the horror of losing their parents. But that also meant they wouldn't remember much about the two people who'd loved them more than anyone. "Do you want to talk about Mommy and Daddy?"

She shook her head.

"You know you can, right? Anytime you want to talk about them, you can."

"Uh-huh."

"Do you want to call Elijah?"

"Can I?"

"Of course. You know he always wants to hear from you."

"I'll call him," Nick said.

Elijah was good about taking their calls and being available to his siblings whenever they needed him. Now was no different.

"Aubrey wanted to say good-night," Nick said. "Here she is."

Sam put the child down on the sofa so she could talk to her brother.

Nick slipped an arm around her and kissed the top of her head. "Long day, huh?"

"Yep. Is there food?"

"Of course there is. Shelby never disappoints. Chicken and stuffing keeping warm in the oven."

"Yummy. I brought home a hungry friend."

"I see that." Nick hugged and kissed Celia. "How're you doing?"

She leaned into his embrace. "Eh, okay. It helps to be here surrounded by kids and activity."

"Our home is your home. Anytime you need kids or chaos, we've got you covered."

"Thank you, Nick. It means a lot to me to have so much support."

"Keep an eye on Aubrey and send her in if she needs me when she gets off the phone." Sam took Celia by the hand to lead her into the kitchen. "Wine?"

"Yes, please."

Sam poured chardonnay for both of them and served up the dinner Shelby had made. "Thank God for Shelby."

"You must say that every day."

"I do. We'd be lost without her. She's the glue that keeps this whole operation from spinning out of control."

"You don't give yourself enough credit. You're part of the glue too."

"No, I'm not. She's the one who makes it all happen."

"I beg to differ, but I'll let you give her all the credit."

"We're very lucky to be able to have a family and two demanding careers. I'm under no illusions that we could do it without our village, which includes you and Tracy and Angela." Sam's sisters were a critical part of the glue that held her together.

"I'm happy to be part of your village." Celia's eyes filled with tears that she dabbed at with a napkin. "It's good of you girls to keep me around now that your dad is gone."

Sam stared at her. "Keep you around? We're not doing that because we have to, Celia. We're doing that because we *love* you. And not just because you took such marvelous care of Dad when he needed you, but we love you for *you*."

Tears rolled down Celia's cheeks. "Thank you. I love all of you so much. I never had children of my own, but if I had, I'd hope they'd be just like you and your sisters."

"We're all yours. There's no getting rid of us."

"I'm sorry to be such a waterworks. I'll be totally fine one minute and a blithering mess the next."

"I cry in the car when there's no one around to see me."

"I cry in the shower."

"That's a good place too." Sam placed a hand over Celia's. "From what I'm told, all of this is perfectly normal. We miss him."

"I miss him so much. Even when he was unable to do anything, we still talked about everything, and that's what I miss the most. His company."

"He was always very good company."

"Yes, he was." Celia smiled softly. "He was my favorite person to talk to."

"He was tied for first with Nick for me." Sam took a sip of her wine. "Whenever you need someone to talk to who knows exactly what Skip would say in just about any situation, call me."

"That's very kind of you, Sam, but you're so busy—"

"I'm never too busy for you."

While they finished their dinner, Sam steered the conversation in a lighter direction. They talked about Angela's third child, who was due next summer, her niece Brooke's internship at the Smithsonian and the Alaskan cruise that Celia planned to take with her sisters in the spring.

They worked together to clean up the kitchen before Sam walked her stepmother home, hugging her at the foot of the ramp that led to her front door.

"Thank you for this, Sam. It was just what I needed."

"We're three doors up the street anytime you need us. Just come over whenever you want. No need to call or text or knock. My home is your home."

Celia hugged her again. "Thank you."

"Sleep tight." Sam waited until Celia was inside with the door locked before she returned to her own home, slowly walking up the ramp, filled with grief that her dad would never again come buzzing up that ramp in his chair. He'd loved being able to visit them.

Sam would never forget the day that Nick had the ramp installed as a surprise for her. Of course she'd thought someone had blown up the stairs to their house and had nearly called in the cavalry, but fortunately she'd been set straight before she did that. That still ranked right up there as the nicest thing anyone had ever done for her.

Nate admitted her just as Nick was coming down the stairs.

"How's Celia?" he asked.

"She'll be okay. Eventually."

"And you?"

"Same." She put her arms around her husband and held on tight, appreciating that Nate stepped outside to give them some privacy. "I miss him like crazy."

"I know you do. I do too."

"How do you think Scotty is doing with it all?"

"He misses him, but he seems to be rolling with it in his own way. They're reading in the twins' room if you want to tuck them in."

"I want to. Let's go."

They went upstairs and stood in the doorway, watching Scotty read to the rapt little ones who hung on his every word.

"My heart," Sam whispered to Nick.

"I know. I can't take it."

"Get a picture, will you?"

He subtly removed his smart phone from his pocket and took the photo, earning a scowl from Scotty even as he never missed a beat in the story. When the book was finished, Alden wanted another.

"You already had two, and that's enough for tonight," Scotty told him. "You have to get up early for school and so do I." He kissed each of them on the tops of their heads and scooted out from between them. "All yours," he said to his amused parents as he cut between them to exit the room.

Sam and Nick went in to tuck in the twins and kiss them good-night.

"Sweet dreams," Sam said, caressing Aubrey's soft hair.

The children's eyes were heavy with sleep so they tiptoed out of the room, leaving the door cracked open the way the kids liked it.

Next, they popped into Scotty's room, where he was finishing up some homework while listening to a Capitals game on the TV.

"Yes, I took a shower. Yes, my homework is almost done. Yes, my alarm is set and my backpack is ready for the morning. Anything else?"

Sam bit her lip so she wouldn't laugh out loud at his sauciness. "Am I allowed to ask how your day was?"

"It was fantastic. My algebra teacher was out sick and we had a sub who had no clue what we were supposed to be doing. Best day of eighth grade I've had yet."

Sam couldn't stop the laughter that exploded out of her at that.

Nick glared at her. "It's not funny."

"Yes, it really is."

Scotty offered her a fist bump. "Mom for the win."

Sam bumped her fist with his. "Thanks for reading to the Littles."

"I love to read to them. They're so fun to have around."

Sam sat on the edge of his bed. "I'm so glad you think so. A lot of thirteen-year-olds would be annoyed by the sudden appearance of two five-year-olds."

"I'm not most thirteen-year-olds." There wasn't an ounce of arrogance in the statement. Only truth.

"No, you're not, and we're incredibly thankful for you."

He flashed a crooked grin. "You guys are okay too."

"Gee, thanks, pal."

"Where are we with the dog discussion?"

"It's still in the consideration stages. We'll get back to you when our team makes a decision."

As he rolled his eyes, Sam leaned in to kiss his cheek, and he allowed it. "Love you."

"Love you too."

"Lights out at ten," Nick said as he followed Sam from the room.

"Yeah, yeah. Let's hope there's no overtime in the Caps game."

"Ten." Nick closed Scotty's door and followed Sam into their room, where he released a deep breath. "Another long-ass day in the books."

"How're you holding up?" Sam locked her service

weapon and cuffs into the bedside table drawer and turned to him.

"I'm okay, but the press attention is unprecedented. The GOP leadership is demanding Nelson's resignation, but he's not planning to resign. He told me that in our meeting earlier, said I don't need to worry. If they want him out, they're going to have to force him out. The matter is personal, between him and his wife, and has no bearing on his job. The White House press office released a statement to that effect earlier."

"And how was that received?"

"As you might expect. Some people agree that it's a personal matter between the first couple. Of course the opposition thinks he has a moral obligation to resign. Yada, yada, yada. It was good to hear right from him that he has no plans to resign though."

"I'm sure it was. I, too, am relieved to hear that news."

"What's the latest on the case?"

"We informed Congressman Wilton today that he might be the father of Tara's child."

Nick's mouth dropped open. "Seriously?"

"Yep. He was one of several guys Tara was seeing around the time the baby was conceived. We're working on locating the others." Sam went into the bathroom, stripping off clothes as she went. "What's your take on Wilton?"

"He's a good guy."

"That was my sense as well. He was genuinely shocked to hear that the baby might be his."

"Anyone would be, especially if the relationship ended."

"I get the feeling that having a relationship wasn't a priority for her after the guy she planned to marry broke up with her. I think she did want a baby more than anything, and was possibly determined to make that happen. We're still trying to get the full list of the men she dated around that time. We'll get DNA from all of them to determine who fathered the baby." A thought occurred to her that had her reaching for the phone to call Freddie.

He answered on the fourth ring. "Hmmm?" He'd better answer or she'd have to remind him once again how Homicide detectives are *always* on duty. She thought he'd learned that lesson after Elin shut off his phone when they were first together.

"You're not already asleep."

"How do you know?"

"Wake up and listen to me. It's entirely possible that Delany really didn't know about all the guys Tara dated. I mean, if you're Tara, do you tell your assistant that you're going out with several different guys at the same time? I wouldn't tell you that."

"I'm extremely glad to hear that."

"I'm calling Malone to see where we stand with the dating app and the dump of her phone."

"Do you want me to call him?"

"Nah, go back to bed or whatever you were doing."

"You really don't want to know."

"I'm out." She heard him laughing as she ended the call. "I don't know why I put up with his nonsense."

"Because you love him like a brother?" Nick said.

"Ugh, whatever." She put through the call to Malone, who answered on the first ring. "Thank you for not being a newlywed."

"Huh?"

"Took Cruz four rings to pick up the damned phone."

Malone laughed. "You're spreading the joy around evenly tonight, I see."

"That's me. A good time had by all."

Nick cracked up in the bathroom.

"What can I do for you this evening?"

"You can tell me what the hell is happening with the warrants for Tara's phone company and the dating app."

"We're getting major pushback from both. The phone company says we need to find her phone and then they can help us. The dating app is screaming about the privacy of its users and how it'll put them out of business if cops start showing up on the doorsteps of the men she dated."

Frustration boiled up inside her, threatening to spill over into a tirade of epic proportions. A woman was dead. In Sam's world, nothing was more important than getting justice for her. "Tell me we're fighting back."

"Of course we are. There's a hearing in the morning on both matters. Faith is going to bat for us," he said of Assistant U.S. Attorney Faith Miller.

"Okay. Keep me posted."

"You'll know when I do."

"I'm meeting with my squad in the morning."

"You need me there?"

"Nope." She most definitely did not need her captain there when she asked her squad to start subtly digging into Sergeant Ramsey.

"Why don't you take a Skip Holland half day and get some sleep."

Though meant as a joke, the reminder of one of her dad's favorite sayings hit Sam like a knife to the heart. "Yeah." She forced herself to reply for the captain's sake. "I'll do that."

"You okay?"

"Yep. Talk to you tomorrow." She closed the phone and plugged it in to charge. For a few minutes, she sat on the edge of the bed, thinking about all the times Skip had teased her about taking a "half day" after a twelve-hour shift. It had been one of his favorite things to say, and hearing it now from Malone was a reminder that she'd never again hear it from her dad.

Nick sat next to her on the bed and put an arm around her. "What's up?"

"Nothing."

"Don't say nothing when it's obviously something."

"I can't get away with anything when you're around."

"No, you can't, so quit trying."

"Malone said something just now… One of my dad's things. It just hit me that I'll never hear him say it again."

"I'm sure it's like a fresh wound every time you remember something."

"It is."

"What was it this time?"

"No matter how late I worked or how many hours I'd put in, if I told him I was leaving, he'd say, 'Taking another half day, I see.' No matter how many times he said it, it was always funny. And no one laughed harder at his own joke than he did."

"I can picture it." He caressed her back and arm, offering the kind of comfort she could only get from him. "I know it's small solace right now, but you're lucky to have so many amazing memories of him."

"I know, and I also know you don't have that with your dad."

"It was just different between us."

What he meant but didn't say was that he didn't see

enough of his dad for most of his life to have the kind of inside jokes Sam had with Skip. "I'm very lucky to have had him, and I know it."

"But that also makes losing him so much harder."

She nodded and leaned her head on his shoulder. "Even after he was injured so gravely, he never lost his sense of humor or his ability to laugh at his own jokes."

"What can I do for you?"

"Some power snuggling would be nice."

"Lucky for you, I'm all charged and ready."

Sam laughed and nudged him. "You're always charged and ready."

"For you? Absolutely. Come on." He stood and helped her up, turning her toward the bathroom so she could get ready for bed. "I'll be waiting for you in the snuggling capsule when you're ready."

He always made her feel better, no matter what madness had overtaken her life and even in the throes of the most profound grief she'd ever experienced. She got undressed and while she brushed her teeth, she studied her face in the mirror. To look at her, you'd never guess that her heart was broken. But inside… Inside, she ached all the time knowing he was gone forever, especially now that she knew more about why he'd been taken from them too soon.

It was all so pointless. Like most things, it had been about greed and people protecting themselves and their source of wealth at the expense of two great police officers.

The wrongness of that was something it would take her years to accept, if she ever actually accepted it.

"Samantha… I'm waiting for you."

She wiped the toothpaste from her lips, ran a brush through her hair and shut off the bathroom light.

Propped up on an elbow, Nick watched her walk from the bathroom, around the bed to her side. "Best thing I've seen all day."

She got in bed. "That can't possibly be true."

He reached for her and pulled her across the mattress until she was snug against him. "It's absolutely true."

"Don't haul me around like a side of beef."

"You're my side of beef, and I'll haul you around if I feel like it."

She would've argued with him, but he kissed her and fried all the brain cells that objected to being called his side of beef.

"I hate to see you sad." He cupped her face and ran his thumb over her cheek. "Even though I know you're going to be for a while."

"People say time helps. I want to feel better, but I don't want to 'get over' losing him, you know?"

"You'll never get over losing him. You'll just go forward from here and take him with you."

"Yes," she said, her eyes filling. "I will. I love that." She looked up at him. "You always know what to say to me."

"That's because I'm the only one in the whole world who speaks fluent Samantha."

"Yes, you do, and the rest of the world is thankful to you for that."

"The rest of the world can eff off. You and our kids are the only ones who matter."

"You looked so happy when I came in tonight."

"I am happy. We have it all, babe. Best thing you

ever did was bring home our Littles and make our family complete."

"I'm glad you love them so much and that you finally have the family you always wanted."

"I do, but everything begins and ends with you. You're the sun." He wrapped his arms around her, snuggled her in close to him and made everything better just by being there. "Close your eyes, let it all go and get some sleep."

"I will if you will."

"I'll try."

She hated that he struggled so much with sleep. "You're going through this ordeal with Nelson, and here I am making it all about me."

"Hush. I'm fine. You're fine. We're fine. Go to sleep."

She would've thought she was too wound up to sleep, but with the steady beat of his heart echoing under her ear, she was able to drift off into peaceful slumber.

CHAPTER TWENTY-TWO

THEY WOKE TO banner headlines in the city's premier newspapers. Nelson Defiant, Refuses Calls to Resign in the *Post* and Nelson Says Affair is "Private" Matter in the *Star*.

Nick's head ached as he absorbed the nonstop coverage that showed no signs of waning, days after the scandal first broke.

In yesterday's meeting with the president, he'd seen the same defiance the papers were reporting this morning. "This is between my wife and me," he'd said. "It's being handled."

Nick wanted to ask him why he felt the need to meet with his vice president about it if he had no plans to resign, but he kept his mouth shut.

"I know you're probably disgusted that it happened, but so am I. I made a mistake and I'm paying for it, believe me."

He was disgusted. Gloria Nelson was beloved around the world. After standing by his side through the political career that had taken them from South Dakota to the Senate and then the White House, she'd endured two national campaigns and had been a model first lady, advocating for children's health initiatives.

She deserved better than what she'd gotten from her husband, and the country deserved better than what they'd gotten from their president. But Nick would never say as much to the man's face. He hoped his silence spoke for him. Sometimes he wished he had a time machine, so he could go back to being a senator.

Though he was honored to serve his country as vice president, at times like this, he wished he had it to do over again so he could say no to the president's offer.

Especially when he saw the strain weighing on the ones he loved.

Scotty noted the headlines when he sat down for his usual breakfast of cold cereal and chocolate milk. "The kids at school are saying you're going to be president."

"How do they know?"

He shrugged. "This one kid said I should pick out my bedroom at the White House, like that'd be up to me. They're so stupid."

Nick tried not to smile and knew he should tell him not to call the other kids stupid, but sometimes that was the best word for the way people behaved. He pointed to the papers. "Nelson is saying he's not going to resign. I think we're safe."

"But the Congress can impeach him, right?"

"They can, but I don't think they will. As bad as it is that he had an affair, that doesn't rise to an impeachable offense."

"Why do they call it that? An affair? That's an awfully nice way of saying the guy cheated on his wife."

"Uhhh…"

Sam came in, fully dressed for work. "Yes, Nick, do tell. Why do they call it an affair?"

"I, uh, I'm not sure where that term came from."

Sam poured herself a cup of coffee.

"You would never have an affair, Dad, would you?"

Nick choked on a mouthful of coffee. "Hell, no. First of all, I'm madly in love with your mother."

"I know." Scotty rolled his eyes. "It's *so* gross."

Sam nudged him with her hip and then sat with them at the table. "No, it's not."

Scotty made fake vomiting noises that cracked up his parents.

"Second of all, I took vows to love and honor my wife for the rest of my life, and I would never disrespect her by being unfaithful. And third of all, she would stab me through the heart with the rustiest of steak knives."

"No, I wouldn't. I'd be too heartbroken to bother."

"As you well know, you never have to worry about that, my love."

"Neither do you."

Scotty cleared his throat, probably to remind them he was still in the room. "Is there gonna be kissing? Because if so, I am out of here."

Sam leaned in toward Nick. "You might want to beat feet."

"Hurry," Nick said, leaning into her. "It could get messy."

Scotty let out a scream and bolted from the table while his parents laughed themselves silly.

"Are we scarring him for life?" Nick asked after a very sweet kiss.

"On a daily basis. But we also feed, clothe, house and love him as well as provide Wi-Fi. Hopefully, those things will override the gross stuff he's forced to witness."

"I'm living for the day when he gets a girlfriend. I plan to be merciless."

"It'll be the least of what he deserves." Sam got up

to make herself some peanut butter toast and returned to the table with the toast and a second cup of coffee. "What fresh hell is in the papers this morning?"

"They're reporting on Nelson's defiance. He's calling it a personal matter between him and his wife."

"Which it really is until my thirteen-year-old asks why they call it an affair over breakfast. That's when it becomes a personal matter in my family and families all over the country who're having to explain this to their kids."

"I know. It's very disappointing, to say the least. But like I said to Scotty, it doesn't meet the threshold for impeachment."

"Unless he orchestrated some sort of illegal cover-up to keep it quiet."

Nick hadn't considered that possibility. "Which we all hope he didn't. How close are you to figuring out what happened to Tara?"

"Not as close as we'd like to be. Hopefully, we'll know more after today." She got up to put her dishes in the dishwasher and downed the last of her coffee.

"Time to get the Littles up."

"I'll give you a hand before I go."

They spent the next half hour rousing, washing and dressing sleepy five-year-olds, who were most definitely not morning people. Nick could hardly wait to see what they'd be like as teenagers. He looked forward to every stage with them. They'd all been relieved to decide with Elijah that the kids would remain with them until they came of age.

Seeing Scotty in big brother mode had been one of the best parts of having the Littles join their family. He'd been so good with them, and had an understanding of what the kids were going through that no one else had. Nick had never been prouder of his son than he'd been watching him step up for two kids who needed all the support they could get.

When the kids were ready for the day, he knocked on Scotty's door to let him know it was time to go and then took the Littles downstairs for breakfast as Scotty left with his detail.

Sam came down a minute later, kissed the kids goodbye and then turned to him. "Call me if anything comes up on your end."

He hooked an arm around her waist. "I might just call you anyway, even if nothing comes up."

Her smile was one of his favorite things in life. "I'm always happy to hear from my favorite VP."

He kissed her. "Be careful with my wife. She's everything to me."

"Will do."

After seeing her off, Nick rejoined the twins in the kitchen, keeping watch over them until Shelby arrived to relieve him. He kissed both kids and wished them a good day before running upstairs to get in a workout and shower before he had to leave. He was knotting his tie when his cell phone rang with a call from Terry.

"What's up?"

"Good morning. I got a call from Hanigan that the president would like to see you at nine-thirty."

"I just saw him yesterday afternoon. Did Hanigan say what's going on?"

"Nothing more than he wants to see you."

What now? "All right." Nick dreaded whatever he would hear from Nelson.

He arrived at the White House thirty minutes later,

surrounded as always by the Secret Service detail that kept him safe. While he appreciated their diligence and attention to detail, he chafed against the restrictions they imposed on him. He couldn't walk outside his own front door without their involvement, something he was still getting used to all these months later.

Nothing could prepare you for the ways your life would change when constantly surrounded by world-class security.

Terry met him in the reception area of his suite and followed him into his office.

Nancy, one of the administrative assistants, brought him a cup of coffee, fixed just how he liked it, as she did every morning.

He'd told her he could get his own coffee, but she insisted on taking care of that for him.

"Thank you, Nancy."

"You're welcome, Mr. Vice President." She left the room, closing the door behind her.

"Nancy loves you," Terry said when they were alone.

"Shut up."

"What? She does. They all do."

Nick rolled his eyes. "Whatever." He took a sip of the piping hot coffee. "What's the word on the street?"

"Derek came by earlier and mentioned that Gloria is planning to move home to Pierre."

"Whoa. Seriously?"

"That's what he heard from the first lady's chief of staff, but let Nelson tell you himself. I assume that's what he wants to see you about."

"I'm so afraid he's going to buckle to the calls for him to resign."

"He won't."

"What makes you so sure?"

"He doesn't want that asterisk next to his name, or to be lumped into the same boat as Nixon, who committed actual crimes while in office."

"True." Nick released a deep breath. "All this drama… Not what I signed on for, even if I knew to expect there'd be some."

"No one could've seen all this coming. I don't blame you for being pissed." With the time they had remaining before Nick's meeting with the president, they went over his schedule for the next few days, including several upcoming events at local schools. That was part of his initiative to meet with young people to share his passion for public service and to hopefully encourage them to consider it as a career path. Of course, the president having an affair didn't do much to help his efforts, which was just another reason to resent the man for thrusting the entire administration into damage control mode.

A few minutes before nine thirty, Nick walked to the Oval Office for his meeting with Brant accompanying him.

The West Wing was unusually quiet this morning, which only added to the stress boiling in Nick's gut. Sometimes he thought it would be better if Nelson left office and he took over, just so he could stop worrying about that happening. But those thoughts were fleeting. The closer he got to the top job, the less he wanted it.

Nick was shown right into the Oval Office.

The president stood at the window, looking at the world outside his gilded cage.

"You wanted to see me, Mr. President?"

Nelson turned to him, his face bearing the signs of sleepless nights. He had puffy bags under his eyes and deep dark circles. "Thanks for coming in, Nick." He gestured to the sitting area. "Can I offer you anything?"

"I'm good, thank you, sir."

Nelson sat across from him, elbows on knees, shoulders hunched, deeply troubled.

Nick's heart would've gone out to him if he hadn't been mired in a mess of his own making.

"I wanted you to hear from me that Gloria has decided to move home to Pierre for the remainder of my term."

Nick kept the fact that he already knew to himself. He wasn't sure what he should say in response either.

"In fact, she's planning to file for divorce, so things could get nasty."

Nastier than they already were? He knew he was expected to express his condolences on the demise of the man's marriage, but he really wanted to send up a cheer for Gloria for dumping the cheating asshole. Good for her for not "standing by her man" after he humiliated her.

"Anyway, I just wanted you to know what's going on."

"I appreciate the courtesy."

"I'm still not planning to resign, in case you were wondering."

"Okay." That was good news.

"Although, I expect the calls for my resignation to get louder when the news hits that Gloria is planning to divorce me." Nelson raised his head and looked directly at Nick. "I regret that I've hurt my wife, my children, my grandchildren and the country this way."

"Maybe you should say that publicly. It might help."

"Maybe I will." He sat up straighter. "Your wife is working on Tara's case, right?"

"She is."

"Do you know if she's figured out who killed her?"

It was interesting to note that the man seemed more grief-stricken when he spoke of Tara than he did when discussing his wife of forty years and her plan to divorce him. "I'm not sure where the case stands." And even if he did know, he wasn't at liberty to share that information with anyone, even the president.

"I understand. Of course I'm praying for justice for her. She certainly didn't deserve what happened to her, and it pains me to think it might've happened because of me."

Now Nick sat up straighter. "Why would you worry about that?"

"Because of the timing. The news broke of our affair, and she was dead soon after. How can that be a coincidence?"

"Mr. President, if you know anything about what happened to Tara, I urge you to share it with Sam as soon as possible. If you hold back information that could be relevant, you can be implicated in a crime."

"I don't know anything that would be relevant."

"Are you sure?"

He looked Nick dead in the eye. "I am."

"Was there anything else you wanted to discuss?"

"No, not now."

Nick stood and buttoned his suit coat. "Very good. Then I'll let you get back to your day."

"Nick…"

He turned back to face the president, brow raised in inquiry. "I know you don't approve of my behavior—"

"Whether or not I approve is hardly relevant, sir."

"Still…I'm sorry that I disappointed you along with

everyone else. It was never my intention to cause so much hurt to the people around me."

"If I might ask… What was your intention when you began the relationship with Tara?"

"I know it may sound silly to you. Hell, it sounds silly to me when I say it out loud. But I fell in love with her. She was young and beautiful and exciting and…I'm the worst sort of cliché, but that's just what happened."

"Did you know she was expecting a child?"

"I didn't." He looked down at the floor. "I ended things with Tara in January. After the inauguration, I came clean to Gloria. I confessed my indiscretion and begged for her forgiveness." Nelson glanced at Nick. "She agreed to work on putting things back together, as long as the affair remained private. Needless to say, after the news went public, all bets were off as far as Gloria was concerned. I hate that she was humiliated in this way."

What did you think would happen? Nick wanted to ask him, but held his tongue. He had no desire to pile on at this point.

"Do you have any idea how the story became public?"

"It certainly didn't come from me. My staff is speculating that Tara released it, hoping to put pressure on me to acknowledge the child. What she didn't know, however, is that there's no way I could be the baby's father. I, um, had a vasectomy years ago, after our youngest was born. I've provided documentation to that effect to the police."

Nick couldn't believe he was actually standing in the Oval Office discussing the president's affair and his vasectomy. It was just too sordid to be believed.

"I just want to thank you for your support and your loyalty," Nelson said.

"I want to be clear about something. I do not support or approve of what you did to your wife, who is a decent, wonderful, lovely woman. She certainly didn't deserve this, especially when she was dealing with a life-threatening illness. This whole thing makes me sick, frankly."

"I understand. All I can do is apologize for my behavior and try to do better in the future."

"You don't have to apologize to me."

"And yet I feel the need to anyway. Your tenure as vice president has been far more dramatic than you ever could've anticipated, and that's due to me and my son."

Nick couldn't deny that, so he didn't say anything.

"At any rate, I've taken enough of your time. Thanks for coming in."

"No problem." Nick left the Oval Office and headed back to his own office with Brant in tow. He felt like he needed a shower after that conversation. "I need a minute," he told Terry as he ducked into his office and shut the door. He withdrew his phone and called Sam.

"Hey." She sounded rushed and maybe a little breathless. "What's up?"

"I just met with Nelson again. He told me he fell in love with Tara but ended it after the inauguration. He said he didn't know Tara was expecting and was as shocked as everyone else when the news broke about the child. He confirmed that Tara didn't know about the vasectomy. He told Gloria about the affair, and they were working on putting things back together. Her only stipulation was that the affair remain private. When the news leaked, that blew the lid off their marriage. She's moving back to Pierre and planning to divorce him."

"Whoa. You did good work, deputy. This is all very helpful."

He laughed at the title she'd given him. "It was so surreal being in the Oval Office talking about his affair and his vasectomy."

"Indeed. I never imagined the day would come when the president's vasectomy would figure into one of my cases."

"They didn't cover presidential vasectomies at the academy?"

"Believe it or not, that never came up." She winced audibly. "Bad pun."

"Stop," he said, laughing. "I don't need that visual in my head."

"You said head."

He choked on a laugh. "Sam! Knock it off."

"Your behavior is not very vice presidential."

"No, it isn't, and that's because my wife has the sense of humor of a junior high school boy."

"Aw, thanks. That might be the nicest thing you've ever said to me."

"In other news, are you making any progress on the case?"

"I'm digging in hard on where the story about the affair came from and tracing it back to its origins. We're hobbled without her phone and the dating app is still stonewalling. A woman is dead and all they care about is protecting their bottom line."

"Along with the privacy of their millions of users."

"To hell with privacy. A woman is *dead*!"

"She's very lucky to have you working on her behalf, babe."

"You know what I'm most afraid of with this one?"

"What's that?"

"That the media will slut-shame her for playing the field after her breakup. I'm trying to finesse it so no one knows about anyone other than the baby's father and Nelson, but it's like trying to keep a lid on a pressure cooker. Everyone and their brother is digging into her background and looking for dirt. When there's dirt to be found, they'll find it."

"Hopefully, you can solve the case before they get too far."

"That's the goal. I've got to get back to it. Thanks for the help."

"Anytime. Call me if you need me."

"I will. Love you."

"Love you too." As he ended the call, he glanced at the clock and tried not to groan at the idea of another eight hours before they'd be together again. Even after all this time, he still counted the hours until he could see her. He would never understand men like Nelson or why they hurt the women they loved. He'd rather be dead than do anything to hurt Sam. She was the most important thing in his life, along with their kids. All he wanted was as much time as he could get with her and their family.

This had been a tough time for her, and watching her soldier on the way she had made him so proud of her. He sat behind his desk and fired up his computer. Opening the browser, he did a search for local florists, found one that could deliver that day and placed an order for flowers to be delivered to her at work.

It was corny and clichéd and she'd probably be pissed for the public display of affection, but as he composed the message and placed the order, he couldn't find it in him to care if she was pissed. He loved her, and he wanted the whole damned world to know it.

CHAPTER TWENTY-THREE

SAM HELD A brief closed-door meeting in her office with Freddie, Jeannie and Cameron before their shift officially began. "Ramsey is coming for us. It's time for us to fight fire with fire."

"What do you have in mind, LT?" Green asked.

"He's looking for dirt on us, so we're going to return the favor. Let's take a nice, quiet look at what he's got going on behind the scenes." She made eye contact with each of them. "That said, no one is required to participate in this. If I had my druthers, none of us would be doing something like this to a colleague."

"I'm in," Cruz said.

"Me too," McBride said.

Green hesitated, but only for a second. "Me three."

Sam met the gaze of the earnest detective who'd replaced Arnold, the most by-the-book member of her team. "You're sure?"

"Yes, ma'am."

"No one outside the four of us is to know about this, and you report anything you find directly to me in person. No paper trails or emails or texts. Everything is verbal. Understood?"

They nodded in agreement.

"The priority is the Weber case and finishing the paperwork on Conklin. This takes a backseat to the regular stuff." Which meant it would take a while. That was fine. She'd rather they do it right than fast.

With everyone on the same page, she released them to start their shift, hoping she was doing the right thing by fighting Ramsey with some of his own tactics. If it went bad, she'd take the heat for all of them.

Malone had gotten the warrants for Tara's phone and her account on the dating app, but neither company had yet complied with the order to turn over the information they'd requested. In truth, she wasn't holding out any hope for the dating app. If word got out that they were disclosing private information about their clients to the police, their business would be ruined. She fully expected them to fight the order in court, which would tie things up long enough for the investigation to play out without them.

The cell phone data, however, she expected to receive anytime now, and once they had that, they could find out who Tara had been talking to around the time her child was conceived as well as her recent communications. In other words, they could get what they needed from the dating app without the dating app ponying up. However, it gave her great pleasure to know the app's management was probably sweating the warrant and having to pay for lawyers to figure out how to fight it.

She found the report she'd been promised detailing the president's vasectomy in her email and checked that box.

Her phone rang with a call from Faith Miller. "Hey, what's up?"

"After the hearing about the warrant yesterday, I got a call from the attorney for the dating app company who told me unofficially that the 'person in question' hadn't been active on the app in more than fifteen months."

"Well, that's info we didn't have before. Thank you for that."

"No problem. Wish it could've been more."

"It's just enough. Thanks, Faith."

"Sure thing."

After ending the call and notifying her team of the development with the dating app, Sam turned her attention toward tracing the origins of the story that had broken about Tara's affair with the president. She placed a call to Darren Tabor at the *Washington Star*.

"This is an unexpected surprise. By any chance, are you calling to tell me how you feel about the possibility of moving to 1600 Pennsylvania Avenue?"

"Shockingly, that's not why I'm calling."

"Oh damn. And here I thought I was going to get the exclusive of the year."

"Sorry to disappoint."

His huff of laughter came through loud and clear. "No, you're not."

"No, I'm not, but I'm wondering if you've gotten anywhere on figuring out the origins of the Nelson affair story. I'm trying to figure out who knew what and when."

"I was going to call you this morning. I've done some digging, and from what I can tell, the first place to have the story was a small website called DailyPolitic. Have you heard of it?"

"I haven't."

"It's relatively new and made its mark during the last election cycle with some rather revolutionary reporting about the various candidates."

Sam was ashamed to admit that she'd paid very little attention to the relentless coverage of the campaign. She often wondered why it was allowed to drag on for years, rather than just being confined to the election year. The resources expended to elect people to office made her crazy when she thought of all the causes that could benefit from the obscene amounts of money that went toward the business of politics.

Other than Nick's involvement, she kept her distance, mostly because there was so much about the process that irritated her.

"The person you need to speak with there is a guy named Tim Finley. He's the CEO and editor in chief. If anyone would know where that story came from, it's him. Their offices are on Connecticut Avenue."

"This is very helpful, Darren. This earns you some points in your column."

"How can I cash in these points toward an exclusive about how you and the VP are handling the latest Nelson scandal?"

"The points are blacked out on that topic, but feel free to use them toward a different topic."

"That's funny, but I refuse to laugh because it might encourage you to continue stonewalling your favorite reporter."

"When did I *ever* say you were my favorite reporter?"

"It's so obvious to me and everyone else that I'm your favorite."

"You're giving yourself an awful lot of credit."

"It's okay. I know the truth."

"Whatever. How's Roni holding up?"

"Not well from what I'm hearing. Someone else on

our team had to write the obit. She couldn't bring herself to do it."

Sam grimaced, recalling how important it had been to Roni, an obituary reporter at the *Star*, to get her husband's story just right. "I feel so badly for her. She had her whole life figured out and then it's just over." And what'd happened to Roni struck at Sam's deepest fears about something happening to Nick. She shuddered from the sick feeling that went through her at the very thought of having to face the rest of her life without him. She wasn't at all sure she could do it.

"It's so hard to believe," Darren said. "We were just dancing at their wedding not that long ago, and now we have to go to his funeral. Hard to wrap your head around something like this."

"I know. Well, thanks for the info."

"I'm available at any time for an exclusive."

"Bye, Darren." He was tenacious. She'd give him that, and he actually was her favorite reporter, due to his inherent fairness and ability to portray victims of violent crime in a thoughtful, caring manner. But she couldn't ever tell him that.

"Cruz!"

Freddie came to the door of her office. "You bellowed?"

"I've got a thread to pull."

"What's that?"

She told him about DailyPolitic and the CEO/editor they needed to see. "A guy by the name of Tim Finley. Do a run on him and get me the lowdown. When you're done with that, we'll pay him a visit."

"Got it."

Freddie no sooner walked away than Malone ap-

peared at her door. He had an odd look to him as he came
in and shut the door, taking a seat in her visitor chair.

"What's up?"

"Sometimes I hate this job."

Sam had never heard him say anything like that and
it had her sitting up straighter in her chair as her stomach dropped with dread. "Why?" She almost didn't want
to know.

"Hernandez."

The captain in charge of Patrol. "What about him?"

"He's up to his eyeballs in debt."

"Okay…"

"Because he has a gambling problem."

Sam didn't need Malone to connect the dots for her.
If Hernandez had known about the gambling ring, he
probably also knew the lengths the organizers had gone
to in order to protect their cash cow.

"We had the FBI's lab analyze handwriting samples
from Hernandez's reports against the card you received
after your dad died."

"Let me guess. A perfect match."

Malone nodded. "There were also texts between Hernandez and Gallagher, and if that's not enough, the deep
dive on the Conklins' phones uncovered cryptic texts between Hernandez and Conklin over the last few months
that show a connection between the two of them. Taken
in context, it's clear that Hernandez knew about your
dad's shooting, and Conklin knew he knew. So today, I
have to arrest yet another high-ranking member of our
own department, as well as file new charges against
Conklin for holding out on us on Hernandez's involvement. Thus, I hate my life."

"I'm sorry." Sam felt sick hearing another high-ranking

officer had sat on the info for years. The betrayal cut her to the quick.

"Not your fault."

"Everyone will make it my fault, I'm sure." Any time a fellow officer was accused of wrongdoing as part of one of her investigations, they tried to make her the problem.

Malone's brows narrowed with displeasure. "Let them try. This is on Hernandez and his guilty conscience that had him sending that anonymous note during the investigation. He made his own bed, and now he can sleep in it."

"At least he wasn't one of my dad's good friends."

"There is that."

"What's this going to mean for the chief?"

"He's making a statement expressing his profound disappointment in Captain Hernandez's choices as well as his culpability in the Holland/Coyne murder investigation. He's got a line in there that perfectly sums up how we both feel about the latest goings-on. He says he'll go to any lengths necessary to ensure the officers working under his command are doing so with the highest ethical and moral values."

Sam's stomach soured when she thought of Gonzo committing a crime to feed his addiction, and her orders to her team to dig for dirt on Ramsey.

"Hopefully, that'll keep the jackals off his ass after word about Hernandez gets out." Malone took a deep breath and released it. "Where are we with the Weber investigation?"

"I've got a lead on the site that first posted the news of the affair. Cruz and I are headed there to talk to the CEO-slash-editor in a few."

"Glad to hear the dating app came through with some useful info."

"They did, but we still need the phone data."

He stood to leave. "I'm working on that."

"Hey, Cap?"

Turning back to her, he raised a brow.

"What's the thought on Gonzales?"

"The chief and I discussed it and after he completes rehab, we'll talk to him. Ramsey has been warned that spreading rumors about fellow officers won't reflect well on him."

"So there's a lid on it for now, then. That's good."

"We might be able to spin it as an effect of the illness. I'm working that angle."

"I'm concerned that Ramsey is looking for dirt on my squad to get back at me for the real and perceived slights."

"I wouldn't put it past him. This would be a great time to let your squad know that it's never been more important to keep their noses clean, on and off the job."

"Will do. Keep me posted on what you hear about Gonzo's situation?"

"As much as I can."

"Thanks."

"Before you head out, can you please update the media about the Weber investigation?"

"If I must."

"You must."

"All right." Sam watched him go, noting the weight of his responsibilities in the rounding of his shoulders. He would want to protect his friend the chief from any more disasters, but he couldn't protect him from the shit other officers stepped into on and off the job.

In preparation for the media briefing, she went through the updates from the other detectives on her squad that had come in overnight and first thing this morning. They didn't have much of anything new, so she'd have to wing it.

When she was as ready as she ever got to face off with the press, she ran a brush through her hair, put on some lipstick and went to leave her office.

She was blocked by a massive arrangement of multi-colored roses. "Um, what the hell?"

"For you, LT," Jeannie McBride said from the other side of the roses.

Sam's annoyance was immediately replaced with giddiness. She stepped aside so Jeannie could put them on her desk. "I really hope those are from my husband."

Jeannie handed her a card. "This fell out of them."

Sam opened it and read the message.

No matter what happens, we've got this. Don't ever forget that. Love you. —N.

She sighed with pleasure and happiness and love for him, a love so big it was too much for one heart to hold.

Then she realized Jeannie was still there and felt slightly embarrassed.

"They're gorgeous," Jeannie said. "Tell Nick I said well done."

"I will." Sam tucked the card into her pocket and gestured for Jeannie to lead the way out of the office.

Cameron Green looked up from his monitor. "Are they making you brief the press?"

"What was the giveaway?"

"Um, the lipstick?"

Sam laughed. "I can't look like a total troll. I've got an image to uphold. Anyone got anything new before I head out?"

They didn't, so she went on her way to the lobby where the chief and captain waited for her.

"You don't have to come out with me," Sam said to the chief. "I've got it covered."

"I'm coming." He gestured for her to lead the way, his expression closed off and seemingly resigned to whatever shit would be thrown his way.

When they walked out together, the larger-than-usual group of reporters snapped to attention.

Sam didn't see Darren's usually friendly face in the mix. "I don't have a lot to say about the Weber investigation other than we're continuing to follow the leads and work the case the way we always do. While we understand the greater-than-usual interest in this one due to her relationship with the president, we're doing everything we always do for homicide victims. Our tip line is open and we urge the public to report anything they know that might be relevant." She recited the number twice. "I can inform you at this time that President Nelson has most likely been ruled out as the father of Tara Weber's newborn son. We're trying to determine who else might've fathered her child, and anyone with information pertaining to the paternity of her child should reach out to us." She again recited the phone number. "At this time, I'll take a few questions."

They came at her in a barrage of shouted words that she ignored until they realized she wasn't going to play that way. Hands shot up in the air.

She pointed to one of the female TV reporters.

"How do you know the baby isn't Nelson's?"

"He had a vasectomy after the birth of his last child and has provided documentation to that effect."

Sam pointed to a male reporter from the *Post*.

"The president is under tremendous pressure to resign in the wake of his affair with Tara Weber. Are you and the vice president prepared for that possibility?"

"Next." Sam pointed to a male TV reporter. It always amused her that the TV reporters were much better groomed than the print reporters, who tended to look like a bunch of hobos with notebooks.

"We're hearing that the first lady is moving back home to South Dakota. Can you confirm that?"

"You'd have to check with the White House about anything having to do with the Nelsons and the vice president. If that's it?"

"Lieutenant, our viewers would like to know if you and the vice president are still planning to have children of your own."

The question came from a dark-haired TV reporter, a woman Sam didn't recognize, not that it mattered. It took everything she had to hold back the urge to walk around the podium and throttle the woman. "We already have children of our own."

"You know what I mean," the woman said, digging a deeper hole for herself.

"No, I'm afraid I don't." The implication was so big, so overwhelmingly offensive, she could barely process it.

"*Biological* children."

"Ah, I see. *Real* children, you mean."

Sam couldn't believe when the woman actually nodded. "I hope you know how incredibly offensive and ignorant that question is. We have *real* children. Three of them, whom we love the same way you love your *real* children." She shook her head in utter disgust. "I'm done."

Turning, she walked away, fueled by outrage.

"That was so far out of line as to be unreal," the chief said when they were inside. "I'm sorry you were subjected to that."

"People are stupid." She looked up at him, noting the exhaustion etched into his face. "How're you holding up?"

"I'm fine. You heard about Hernandez, I understand?"

"I did."

"I'm sorry, Sam. I hate that you were let down by colleagues who should've done better."

"It's not your fault."

"Isn't it? They worked for me."

"I understand that the buck stops with you, but you can't control what other people do. You set the best possible example for all of us to follow. People will make their own decisions when it comes to crossing lines. That's not on you."

"I appreciate your support and Celia's, but you know as well as I do that not everyone thinks the way you do."

"It's a blip. This too shall pass. Something else will happen that'll have everyone scrambling for the next big story. People are focused on the president at the moment."

"Plenty of reporters and city administrators are focused on this department too. I've even heard talk of an independent investigation by the FBI."

That shocked her to the core. "Seriously?"

"Nothing definite, but the mayor has to do something in light of the scandals that've been revealed in recent months. The city council is after her to find out if it's a symptom of a larger problem."

"Like the city council should talk! They had a *murderer* in their ranks for almost *thirty years*."

"Right? But you can't tell them that. The way I see it, I have nothing to hide. If she wants to send the FBI in to investigate us, I'm not going to fight it."

"I really hope it doesn't come to that."

"You and me both. I'll let you get back to work. An arrest in the Weber case would be helpful."

"I'm on it." She took a heavy heart with her back to the pit. "Cruz, let's go. Everyone else—stay on the Weber case. Leave no stone unturned."

She headed for the door, still fuming over the obscene question she'd been asked.

"We were watching the briefing," Freddie said as they navigated the winding corridors that led to the morgue exit. "I'm sorry that you were asked such a horrible question."

"People suck."

"Yes, they certainly do." Her phone rang and she took a call from Nick. "Assume you saw the press briefing."

"I'm fucking furious."

"You and me both."

"I'm planning to issue a statement letting that reporter and anyone else know that our three *real* children are off-limits and that neither you nor I will ever answer questions about our plans or lack thereof in regard to our family."

"It's very sexy when you use words like *thereof*."

"Sam! I'm serious. I'm bullshit pissed right now."

"I know," she said, sighing. "I am too. How could anyone ask something like that?"

"I have no idea, but I also plan to address it with the management at her network. She shouldn't be allowed out until she gets some decorum."

"That's a good idea. Thanks for taking care of it and thank you for the gorgeous flowers."

"Of course I'm taking care of it, and you're welcome. No one is going to get away with coming at my family like that. Not while I've got a breath left in me."

"And you will have breath left in you for another sixty years."

"At least that long. If not longer."

"Longer would be good."

"Are you okay, babe?"

"I'm better now. Thanks for calling and going to war for us."

"I'd say I'm happy to, but the fact that I have to even address something like this is infuriating, to say the least."

"Yes, it really is." She got into the driver's side of her car and tried to find the inner calm she needed to focus on her work. "I'm off to see the head of Daily-Politic about the origins of the Nelson affair story. Do you know Tim Finley?"

"I know the name. He gained a reputation for hard-hitting coverage of the last campaign."

"Was he fair?"

"For the most part."

"Well, that's something. I'll let you get back to work."

"Are you working late today?"

"I don't know yet, but I'll hit you with a text when I do."

"Sounds good. Be careful out there."

"Always am." She ended the call, and when she

snapped the phone closed it came apart in her hand.
"Oh shit!"

"What?" Freddie asked.

Sam showed him the two halves of her phone.

"Uh-oh."

CHAPTER TWENTY-FOUR

"WHAT DO I DO?" Sam tried not to panic over the demise of her beloved flip phone.

"Get a new phone?"

"I don't want a new phone. I want *this* phone. I bet they can fix it."

"Um…"

She could tell he was trying not to laugh. If he laughed, she'd stab him. "When am I going to deal with this?"

"After we talk to Finley?"

"This isn't funny."

"I'm not laughing."

"You are too! I can hear it trying to come out of you."

"You're insane."

"And this is news to you? Text Nick and tell him my phone broke and if he needs me, to text you."

"Anything else I can do for you, madame?"

"Just that and hurry up about it." Being without her phone only added to the edgy, anxious feeling she'd been contending with all day. The kids' schools had Nick's number and Shelby's, so there was no chance of them being left sick or stranded or anything else, but being out of touch made her feel a little crazier than usual. And then it occurred to her—the number one reason why she'd needed to be reachable at all times was gone now that her dad had passed away.

They'd lived in restless uncertainty for four long years after his near-fatal injury, always waiting for the next disaster to strike. It was, she realized, a relief to no longer have to fear the endgame for him. She no sooner had that thought than she felt guilty for being relieved that he was gone. It wasn't that so much as she was glad his dreadful injury was out of her life. This grief business was complicated. The next time she saw Dr. Trulo, she'd ask him about the dueling emotions of relief and sorrow.

Two blocks from the offices of DailyPolitic, Sam found a parking space and parallel parked.

"You're very good at that," Freddie said.

"Skip wouldn't let us drive away in a car of his until we could parallel park." She hadn't thought of that in a long time. "We thought he was so mean making us learn that until we figured out how much we would need it living here."

"He was a smart man in more ways than one."

"Yeah." It would take a lifetime to fully catalog all the lessons he'd taught her and how almost all of them played into her daily life.

"Nick texted back and said he hopes you can get another flip phone, and if you can't he's moving out." Freddie lost it laughing. "And I'm asking for a reassignment."

"You two have your laughs. I *will* get another flip phone, and I *will* be slapping it shut with satisfaction before the end of the day."

"God, I hope so."

"What'd you find out about Finley?"

"He's a graduate of the Columbia School of Journalism and worked for most of his career as a DC-based reporter for the *New York Times*. He left the *Times* four years ago and started DailyPolitic three years ago. The site made its mark during the last presidential campaign and has been growing in influence and revenue ever since. I found an article that had it listed as one of the top five political news sites of the last year. He's married with two kids in college and lives in Potomac."

"Good work." The info painted a picture of a man who'd had a successful career in journalism that he'd parlayed into a new business that had found its niche during the campaign.

They got out of the car and walked toward their destination, heads down against the bracing chill.

"I hate the cold."

"Ugh, me too. Sucks."

The crappy weather made everything harder than it was the rest of the year, not to mention the DC area was paralyzed by the slightest bit of snow or ice. They approached the information desk, where a receptionist asked where they were heading.

"DailyPolitic," Sam said after showing her badge.

The woman handed them visitor passes. "Third floor."

"Thank you. And may I say how much I appreciate your quick cooperation."

"No problem, Mrs. Cappuano."

Normally, Sam would correct her and say she was Lieutenant Holland on the job, but in light of the woman's outstanding cooperation, she let it slide. "Maybe we can hire her to do a training for all city receptionists on the proper way to greet and handle cops when they show up at your place of business."

"That's an excellent idea."

"Get on that, will you?"

"No, I won't, but it's nice to dream."

"I could make you."

"But you won't."

Sam bit her lip so she wouldn't laugh. The last thing she ever wanted to do was encourage his insubordination. They strolled through glass double doors into the DailyPolitic offices, where they were met by a receptionist.

Sam showed her badge. "Lieutenant Holland, Detective Cruz, MPD. We'd like to see Mr. Finley, please."

"He's in a meeting. Could you leave your number so he can give you a call?"

Sam glanced at Freddie, who made a visible effort not to laugh as she leaned an elbow on the reception counter. "Let me tell you how this is going to work." She leaned in closer to the woman's workstation. "Debbie. You're going to go tell Mr. Finley there're cops here to see him. And then you're going to come back, get us and take us to him. Or, we can go back there, find him, take him into custody and have this conversation at our place. Are we clear on how this is gonna go?"

"Y-yes. I'll…" She got up and her chair toppled over. "I'll be right back."

The falling chair gave Sam tremendous satisfaction. "Excellent. Thank you."

Debbie took off toward the back part of the office.

"Mean and scary," Freddie muttered.

"Sign her up for the receptionist cooperation workshop."

"I'll get right on that."

They waited five full minutes, which stretched the outer limit of Sam's patience. She was about to go back there and find the guy herself when Debbie returned with a man in his fifties, who looked seriously irked. He was tall and handsome, with silvery hair and sharp eyes that looked at her with disdain that immediately put her on alert.

"What's this about?" he asked.

"Are we doing this here or in the privacy of your office?"

He didn't like that.

Ask her if she cared.

"Come on back."

Sam and Freddie followed him past the wide-eyed Debbie to his office in the far corner at the end of a long corridor of cubicles. The people they needed to see usually occupied the corner offices, the place of importance in any company.

Freddie shut the door.

"What do you want?"

"Why so hostile, Mr. Finley?"

"You come into my place of business, intimidate my employee and demand to see me when I'm in a very important meeting and then you ask me why I'm hostile?"

"In my experience, people who have nothing to hide are often cooperative when we ask for their assistance in a Homicide investigation."

That took some of the starch out of his dress shirt. "What in the world would I have to do with a Homicide investigation?"

"Your site broke the story of Tara Weber's affair with the president."

"So?"

"We'd like to know where that story came from."

"I can't tell you that. If I reveal my sources, I won't have any sources, and without them, I have no business."

"I understand the position you are in, Mr. Finley—"

"Do you really? Do you understand that if I tell you where that story came from, it'll put me out of business? That all the people I employ will be out of jobs?"

"Did you know Tara Weber?"

"I've met her." As he said the words, he shifted his weight from his right leg to the left and crossed his arms.

The defensive pose, coupled with the shifting movement, put her on alert. She'd learned to pay attention to body language. "Where and how did you meet her?"

"I met her while I was covering the Nelson campaign."

"What, specifically, was your interaction with her?"

"I interviewed her a number of times about the polling data and research she was overseeing for the campaign."

"Were your interactions with her strictly professional?"

His posture went rigid. "What does that mean?"

"It means I want to know if you had a personal relationship with her in addition to the professional one."

"We were friendly, if that's what you mean. The campaign is a grind. We might've had a drink together once or twice, usually in a group with others."

"Mr. Finley, I'm sure you understand that our goal is to figure out who killed Tara Weber. We aren't here to bust your balls or ruin your business. So if there's anything more that you need to tell us about your relationship with her, now is the time. If we find out later that you held out on us in any way, that could go bad for you."

For the longest time, he didn't move or speak or even seem to breathe. "We had a one-night stand after the inauguration. It was the only time I've ever been unfaithful to my wife. I'm not proud of it, but it happened and it was only once."

"And when did this occur?"

"You want like a date?"

"That'd help."

He went to his desk and fired up his laptop, making a show out of figuring out when it happened.

Sam would bet everything she had that he knew exactly when it had happened, but she let him play it out his way.

"February 2."

Sam glanced at Freddie, whose brows went up. "It's possible that you're the father of her child."

He came back around the desk to face off with them. *"What?"*

"I understand that this might come as a shock to you, but—"

"That's not possible. She was on birth control. She told me she couldn't get pregnant."

"I'm sorry to say she may have misled you. We have targeted the week of January 31 to February 6 as the dates during which she likely became pregnant. We're going to need your DNA, sir."

"No way. You're not going to pin this on me. It was *one night*. A moment of madness that was over before it began. There's no way that baby is mine."

Sam held her tongue, letting him get it all out and waiting for him to realize that what she had told him was the truth.

He sat back against the edge of his desk, his shoulders slumping. "You've got to be kidding me."

"I know this comes as a shock to you—"

His head shot up, his eyes flashing with rage. "This is

going to ruin me. My wife… She's the best. She doesn't deserve this."

There was so much Sam could say to that, but hopefully he'd figure out—eventually—that *he* was the one who'd ruined his marriage, not Tara and not Sam. *Him.* People were always looking for someone else to blame for their fuckups.

"Are we going to need a warrant for your DNA?"

He ran a trembling hand over his mouth. After a long, charged moment, he shook his head.

"I'll have someone come by shortly to take the sample. Make sure your receptionist lets them right in and they receive your full cooperation. We don't appreciate people who waste our time."

"I understand."

"I'm going to ask you one more time to tell me how you got the story of Tara's affair with the president."

She expected him to fight back, the way he had before. But it seemed the fight had gone out of him after he learned he could be the father of her child.

"She told me."

Sam found it interesting that Tara had believed Nelson was the father, even though she knew it was possible the father could be someone else. "So you kept in touch with her after your one-night stand?"

He grimaced at the term. "Not regularly. I saw her a couple of times and about two weeks ago, she contacted me, asking if I wanted the scoop of the century. Of course I said I did. And when she told me about her affair with Nelson, I couldn't believe what I was hearing at first. But she had details that gave her story credibility."

"Such as?"

"She told me his wife had been going through cancer treatment during the campaign, and he had turned to her for support, but that part was off-the-record. One thing had led to another... In speaking with some of the other campaign staffers, I ascertained that there had been *concern* about the president's seemingly cozy relationship with Tara. That was enough for me to verify that her story was accurate. We went with it." Once again he rubbed his face with a shaking hand. "It never once occurred to me that the baby she tried to pass off as his could be mine." His gaze connected with Sam's. "How can you be *sure* it's not his?"

"We have documentation to prove he had the vasectomy."

Finley sagged into himself. "I can't believe this is happening. I swear to God, I've never done anything like this in the thirty years I've been married. There was just something about her..." He shook his head. "If you'd met her, you'd know what I mean. She was dynamic and beautiful and smart. So fucking smart. Everyone wanted to be around her, and I was no different. Once you met Tara, you never forgot her."

It was plainly obvious that he'd developed tender feelings for Tara, despite his claims that theirs was a one-night affair.

"Is there any chance the baby isn't mine?"

"Yes."

He brightened considerably at that news. "Really?"

"We'll know more after we have a chance to run the DNA."

"And you'll let me know? As soon as you do?"

"I will."

"Is this going to make the news? That I slept with her?"

"Not unless it turns out to be relevant to our investigation."

"It won't be relevant. I would've had no reason to kill her. The last thing in the world I'd ever want to do is draw attention to what was a onetime indiscretion."

Sam handed him her notebook and a pen. "Please write down your contact info."

He did as she directed and handed both items back to her.

"Stay available."

"What does that mean?"

"Just what I said. If we need more information from you, we'll expect you to take our calls."

"Of course. I will."

"And Mr. Finley? I can't promise we'll be able to keep a lid on this. It might be a good idea to tell your wife what happened."

CHAPTER TWENTY-FIVE

"WHY DO PEOPLE hurt the ones they're supposed to love the most?" Freddie asked when they were back outside.

His feelings on the matter were no surprise to her, especially as a newlywed completely besotted with his wife.

"I don't know, but the way his face went totally pale there at the end tells me this won't go over well with Mrs. Finley."

"I feel sorry for her. She's been married thirty years and thinks they've somehow managed to survive when lots of others didn't… And now he's going to drop this bomb in the middle of her life."

"I know. It's not going to be a good day for either of them."

"The sad part is that it was all so completely avoidable."

"Right? What was it about Tara that had these guys losing their minds over her and risking so much?"

"I was wondering that too."

"It seems to me that after she'd failed to get pregnant with Nelson, she decided she wanted a baby and didn't much care who the father was as long as he was someone professional like her."

"It's as good of a theory as I've heard yet for her actions after the affair ended."

"I want to better understand this woman and what motivated her. We need to talk to the former business partner."

He consulted his notes. "Cam sent her number."

"Let's give her a call from the car."

When they were in the car with the engine running and the heat cranked up, Freddie placed the call to Paige Thompson.

"This is Paige."

"This is Lieutenant Sam Holland from the Metro DC Police Department. I'm with my partner, Detective Cruz, and we're investigating the murder of Tara Weber."

"You're the vice president's wife."

"I am." Sam rolled her eyes at Freddie. Why did people feel the need to state the obvious?

"I'm so sad about Tara. I can't believe she's gone."

"So you were still in touch with her?"

"I was. Our business breakup was difficult, but when the dust settled, we were able to resume our personal friendship."

"We're looking for some better insight into her personal and professional life and were hoping you might be able to help us."

"Whatever I can do. The last couple years had been difficult for her. After Bryce ended their relationship, she sort of went a little nuts when it came to guys and dating and all of that."

"Did you know that she'd been involved with the president?"

After a long pause, she said, "I did. She told me about it after it was over."

"Can you give us any specifics about what she said?"

"Just that she'd become very close to him on the campaign, and their professional association became something more."

"I find myself wondering how they pulled off an affair while surrounded by other campaign staff and Secret Service."

"I wondered that too, and when I asked her about it, she said Nelson was fanatical about time to himself every night. By nine o'clock, the campaign staffers had retreated to their own rooms and the Secret Service had been told he was in for the night. Other than the agent assigned to the hallway, no one would have known she was in his room after nine o'clock."

"Did she know that his wife was sick during the campaign?"

"She did. She told me he was so upset that he couldn't be with Gloria while she was undergoing treatment, and that he'd toyed with dropping his bid for reelection so he could go home to be with her."

Sam glanced at Freddie, eyes wide with shock. That was a bombshell. "So let me get this straight—he felt so badly about his wife having cancer that he was willing to abandon his reelection campaign but not so badly that he refrained from having an affair?"

"According to Tara, it started off as her providing him with someone to talk to about it. The affair just swept them both up. Neither of them intended for it to happen."

Sam rolled her eyes at Freddie. Somehow, two consenting adults ended up naked in bed together, but neither of them intended for that to happen? *Whatever.*

"I know you may not believe me, but Tara was a good person. She tried to do the right thing. She felt awful about being involved in this situation, but I think she had genuine feelings for him."

"Were you aware that she was seeing other men toward the end of her affair with Nelson?"

"What? No, she wasn't."

"Yes, she was. We've identified several others."

"She didn't tell me that."

"How often did you speak with her after you left the company?"

"At least weekly. More often during the campaign when I consulted on a freelance basis on a few of the projects she had going for the Nelson team." She sighed loudly enough for them to hear it through the phone. "She was wrecked after Bryce broke up with her. Things were kind of a mess for her. She made a lot of choices that were out of character for her, especially the affair with Nelson. Before Bryce, Tara never would've slept with a married man. After Bryce, Tara was more jaded, less concerned about playing by the rules."

"Was that true only in her personal life?"

"It was across the board. She threw a lot of effort into the business, and it had its best year ever during the last campaign cycle. She'd become a highly sought-out pollster and market researcher. Her business was booming."

"Can you think of anyone who might've wanted her dead, Ms. Thompson?"

"God, no. Everyone loved Tara. She somehow managed to work in one of the most competitive, dog-eat-dog environments without alienating people. She was known as a straight shooter, who told it like it was and never fudged the data to get a client the results they wanted the way some pollsters will do. That wasn't her style at all."

"This has been very helpful. If you think of anything else that might be relevant to the investigation, please let me know. You can call this number anytime."

"I will. I really hope you find the person who did this to her. She made some mistakes, but she didn't deserve to be murdered, especially now when she finally had the child she'd always wanted."

"Thanks for your time."

Freddie ended the call and they sat in silence for a few minutes, reflecting on what they'd learned.

"It doesn't add up," Freddie finally said.

"What doesn't?"

"She's a straight shooter in her business, never fudges the numbers and stays inside the lines, but she goes and has an affair with the president, knowing the man is married and that his wife is undergoing cancer treatment? Those two descriptions of her don't jell."

Pondering that, Sam pulled out into traffic. "So where do I go to get my phone fixed?"

"Um, the phone store?"

"No kidding, wiseass. Where is this phone store of which you speak?"

Freddie rolled his eyes. "There's one at Union Station. Let's go there so I can get some food too."

"It's almost dinnertime."

"So?"

"So don't you want to eat with your wife?"

"I will eat with her. *Too.*"

"It's completely unfair that you can eat eight full meals a day and never gain a freaking pound."

"That's just one of my many special gifts."

"No one will celebrate harder than me when you finally have to start watching what you eat."

"Don't be a mean cow, Sam. It's not a good look on you."

She cracked up. "It's a good look on me when it's directed at receptionists."

"That's different. They deserve it. I don't. I'm the only thing standing between you and complete disaster with this cell phone situation."

"My heartfelt apologies. I hope you can eat eight meals a day for life and never gain a pound. Better?"

"Much. Park over there."

"Finding an open spot on the street around here is like spotting a unicorn on the National Mall."

"Seriously."

They hoofed it inside the majestic train station that also housed shopping and a wide array of restaurants. The place brought back a lot of memories for Sam.

"I used to hang out here with my friends in high school."

"I've always loved this building." He consulted the directory and led her to the phone store where her appearance had the salesclerks falling over themselves to assist her.

For fuck's sake. Sam picked a young woman who wasn't making a total fool of herself. She held up two pieces of her beloved flip phone. "How do I get a new one of these."

The other salesclerks took a step back, suddenly not as interested in her business as they'd been before they saw her phone.

The woman named Michelle took the phone from her, examined it closely and then handed the pieces back to Sam. "They don't make these anymore. In fact, the network that runs these phones is due to shut down at the end of the year. We're moving everyone to the new network when they upgrade."

"I don't want the new network or a different phone. I want a new version of what I already have."

"I'm sorry that we don't carry those phones anymore. It wouldn't be right for us to sell them to our customers when they won't be able to use them in a couple of months."

Beside her, Freddie cleared his throat, which meant he was trying not to laugh.

Sam's head felt like it could explode at any second.

"The good news is we carry other flip phones that might work for you."

Sam sent a smug smile Freddie's way. "Take me to them."

Thirty minutes later, she had a brand-new cherry-red phone that made a satisfying smacking sound when she slapped the two ends together. "You hear that?" She slapped it closed in front of Freddie's face.

"You might want to ease up on the slapping. That's probably what got you into this predicament in the first place."

"The slapping is the best part of the flip phone. I need to make a call on my *new phone*." She found Nick first on her list of contacts that the lovely Michelle had copied over for her and put through the call.

"Hey, babe."

"MPD to White House, come in White House. I'm calling you on my brand-new phone."

"You got a new phone?"

"I did."

"And it must be a flip phone or you'd be snarling and snapping."

"You are correct, sir. It makes a very satisfying smacking sound when I slap it closed."

"Then all is right in our world."

"You know it. Young Freddie tried to freak me out and tell me I wouldn't be able to get another flip phone, but he was *wrong*. Do you know how much I *love* it when he's wrong?"

"Almost as much as you love it when I'm wrong?"

"He's wrong way more than you are, so it's more fun with him."

That earned her a glare from her partner, who was leading her toward the food court where she'd gain three pounds breathing the air while he shoveled crap into his face and retained his zero body fat ratio.

Nick laughed, and the sexy sound made her shiver in anticipation of seeing him soon. "How close to done are you?"

"Very. I need to hit HQ, dump off Freddie, do a couple of things and then I'll be home."

"Let's go out tonight. Just you and me."

"Like on a date?"

"Yeah."

"Can we do that?"

"Hell, yes, we can do that."

"Poor Brant. You can't just throw this at him at the last minute."

"He won't mind."

"Sure he won't."

"Where do you want to go?"

"I'll let you surprise me."

"All right. I'm on it."

"Hey, Nick?"

"Yeah, babe?"

"This is the best call I'll ever make on my new phone."

"Aww, thanks. Love you."

"Love you too. See you soon." She slapped the phone closed with gusto. "Hurry up. I gotta get home. Hot date with my hot husband to get ready for."

"It's cool that you guys are going out."

"We don't get to do it enough anymore. The gilded cage gets old after a while."

"I'm sure it does. I'd go mad being surrounded by security all the time and not being able to do whatever I wanted."

"I know. Me too. My greatest fear is that I'll one day have to put up with that, and I'm not sure I'll be able to handle it."

"Does he say anything about whether he plans to run?"

Sam knew she could trust Freddie not to repeat anything she said on the topic. "Not much. I don't think he really wants to, to be honest, but the pressure from all sides is so immense, I'm not sure how he'd ever get out of it."

"He shouldn't do it unless he *really* wants to."

"I agree. He says he doesn't have the fire in the belly to be president, and I'd imagine that's a key component. Of course, you can't repeat that to anyone, even Elin."

"I never would."

"He's told Graham that he doesn't think he wants to do it." No one wanted Nick to be president more than Graham did. "But of course Graham doesn't want to hear that. He's got his heart set on seeing Nick in the Oval Office, and you can't tell him that it's not going to happen."

"I get that Graham is super important to him, but it's Nick's life—and yours. If it's not what you both want, you shouldn't be pressured into doing it. We all know he'd be great at it, so you can't think of it in terms of four years. You have to look at it as eight years."

"And then a lifetime of Secret Service protection afterward. I have hives just thinking about that."

"Hey!" A teenage girl screamed in Sam's direction. "It's the second lady! Oh my God. You guys! *Look!*"

The girl's announcement led to a mob of teens swarming around Sam, who was instantly on alert for trouble.

"Back up," Freddie said with unusual force. "Right now."

The teens did as he asked.

"I'm happy to say hi to you guys," Sam said. "But you've got to give me a little room."

"I think you're *so* cool, and your husband is *hot.*"

Sam tried to hide the grimace. "Thank you." She shook hands with each of them, signed a few autographs and then made her escape. "Stay in school and out of trouble." They beat feet away from the teen mob. "That was intense."

"That, right there, is why you should have a detail."

"Shut your face. And don't tell my husband that happened, you got me?"

"I got you."

"I can take care of myself."

"So you say."

"Hurry up and get some food. I need to be done with this day."

Freddie bought six tacos, which he ate in the car on the way back to HQ.

"If you get one shred of lettuce in my car, you're having the whole thing detailed."

"Got it," he said over a mouthful.

The smell was making her mouth water. He'd polished off all six tacos and a large cola by the time they got back to the house.

"You're disgusting."

"I'm a growing boy. Leave me alone."

"I'm going to tell your wife you already had dinner."

"Why would you do that to me, Sam? I thought we were friends."

They bickered their way into the morgue entrance and through the corridors that led to the pit, while he sucked on the last of his drink, intentionally making obnoxious noises to irritate her.

In the pit, she found the day shift handing things off to Carlucci and Dominguez, who were working until midnight.

"Meeting in five, everyone."

"Lieutenant, the phone company came through with Tara's calls and text log," Green said. "We're going through it now."

While she was thrilled to hear they had the vital info they'd been waiting for, she hoped she'd still be able to get out of there in time to enjoy the night out with Nick.

"Focus first on the dates of January 31 to February 6," Sam said. "We believe that's when her child was most likely conceived. And then cover the most recent two weeks."

"On it," Green said.

The team assembled in the conference room, where Sam and Freddie briefed them on the meeting with Finley.

"I want a full run on him," Sam said to Carlucci.

"We'll get on that tonight."

"Check his wife too," Sam said on a hunch.

Freddie shot her a questioning look.

"Who's to say she didn't know?" Sam asked.

"We'll work on the Finleys tonight," Carlucci said.

"I'll take the phone records home with me and keep going on that," Green said.

"Make sure you record the time on your sheet. I'll authorize the OT."

"Will do, thanks."

"One more thing we need to talk about." This needed to be said while everyone was there. "Ramsey is digging for shit on us. Everyone needs to make sure they're dotting the i's and crossing the t's—all the time, but right now, in particular. If there's anything to be found on us, he's coming for it. Let's not give him anything to find."

"I wish they could get rid of scum like him," O'Brien said. "He makes us all look bad."

"Agreed," Sam said, "but it's not that simple. He made me his enemy long before shit got real between the two of us, and I'm sorry that my shit with him is raining down on you guys. Watch your backs. That's all I can say. Day shift, go home. Night shift, call me if anything pops on the phone log."

"Will do, Lieutenant," Carlucci said.

They filed out of the conference room, and Sam headed straight for her office, determined to get the hell out of there while the getting was good. She was on her way to a clean getaway when she ran into Dr. Trulo in the hallway.

CHAPTER TWENTY-SIX

"JUST THE LIEUTENANT I was coming to see."

"What's up, Doc?"

"I received official word that we're good to go with the grief group."

"That's great news."

"We'll need to talk about who we want to reach out to in order to get it started."

"I'll give that some thought tonight and let you know after I wrap the Weber case?"

"Perfect." He gave her what she'd come to think of as his probing look. "How're you holding up?"

"I'm doing okay."

"I hear there's been another in-house arrest in your father's case."

"Yes."

"I'm sorry. It has to be so incredibly disappointing to you."

"I feel like I shouldn't be surprised, and yet…"

"It's a stunning betrayal of your father and you."

Sam nodded because she didn't trust herself to speak. She cleared the emotion from her throat. "In a way, it's a blessing that he never knew. Especially with Conklin, who was his so-called friend."

"Indeed it is." He gave her arm an affectionate

squeeze. "Find me when you have time to talk about our grief group."

"I'll do that. Thanks, Doc." She continued on her way, thinking about the group she'd suggested for victims of the crimes they investigated. She'd met so many people in the course of her work who would benefit from added support. It would be nice, in the future, to be able to refer devastated family members to the group, rather than sending them on their way never to be seen again until the trial.

She used the drive home to stew over the case, to start from the beginning and think it through every which way while wishing she could stop by her dad's to bounce it off him. He'd always had good ideas and suggestions. Since it was still fairly early, she made an impromptu decision to swing by the cemetery before she went home.

Located a few blocks from her home on Ninth Street, she had the cemetery to herself, which wasn't necessarily a good thing. Cemeteries had always creeped her out, but she was determined to get past her aversion so she could visit her dad's final resting place without it being an ordeal every time. His headstone hadn't been placed yet, but she found the mound of dirt that covered him with no problem. By spring, grass would cover the dirt and the headstone they'd chosen would be in place. But for now, the site was lonely, desolate. A wave of profound sadness came over her.

She squatted to get closer to him. "Hey, Skippy. It's me, Sam. I'm not sure if you can hear me but I wanted to stop by to say hello. I've caught a new case. Tara Weber was murdered after her affair with the president came to light. I know, right? What was he thinking? And get this—it happened when his wife was undergoing treatment for ovarian cancer. Nick is trying not to freak out about Nelson being forced to resign. People are so disgusted with him. Gloria is moving home to South Dakota and divorcing his cheating ass. Can't say I blame her. That whole stand-by-your-man thing doesn't count when your man cheats on you when you have freaking cancer.

"The woman, Tara… I'm having trouble figuring her out. She broke up with her longtime boyfriend—or I should say, he broke up with her—and she went a little wild, dating all kinds of guys, some of them married like Nelson. Her friends say that wasn't like her, but after the breakup she was different. I'm trying to figure out who would've wanted her dead while still maintaining her privacy. It's no one's business if she dated around, and I don't want people to judge her. I'm not sure where this one is leading, but I sure could use your input. I also wanted to tell you that your good buddy Conklin is pond scum. He knew all along who was behind your shooting. Can you believe it? And it turns out that freaking Hernandez knew too. It's disappointing, to say the least. I'm kind of glad you're not around to hear how we were let down by people we should've been able to count on to have our backs. Feel free to haunt Conklin if you can. Go after Stahl and Ramsey too, especially Ramsey. He's making trouble for me—and Gonzo. Not that you'll be surprised to hear that.

"Anyway, I just wanted to come by and tell you I miss you. Nothing feels right without you around to tell me what to do and act like you're the boss of me." She stood and stared down at the barren ground for several minutes. "I got a hot date with my husband tonight, so I ought to get going, but I'll be back soon. See ya, Skippy."

She returned to the car and sat for a few minutes in

contemplative silence, getting her emotions in check before she went home to her family. Oddly enough, she felt a little better after having aired the case and the latest news to her dad. She had to believe he was close by and could hear her all the time, not just when she came to see him there.

She called her sister Tracy.

"Hey, I'm with Ang, and we were just talking about you."

"Hi, Sam," Angela said.

"What were you guys talking about?"

"Just wondering how you and Nick are holding up with all this Nelson nonsense," Tracy said. "We can't believe he cheated on Gloria. She's awesome."

"I know. She really is."

"He didn't kill the mistress, did he?" Ang asked.

"I don't think so, but I really hope not."

"Ugh, what a mess," Tracy said.

"Yep. Hey, I just went to see Dad at the cemetery. Did we order the headstone?"

"I did it two weeks ago," Tracy said. "They said it could take a month or two."

"Thanks for doing that. How you feeling, Ang?"

"Sick as a dog."

"That sucks. Sorry to hear it."

"Eh, no biggie. I hear the kid will be worth the all-day morning sickness."

Sam laughed. "If he or she is anything like Jack and Ella, they'll definitely be worth it. I gotta jet, ladies, but let's do something as soon as I close this case."

"You got it," Tracy said. "Call if you need us."

"Will do."

When Sam arrived home a few minutes later and was

waved through the Secret Service checkpoint, she was happy to see black SUVs lining the street, which meant Nick was already there. She was surprised to see FBI Agent Avery Hill getting out of his car, toting numerous bags.

Sam took two of the bags from him.

"Thanks."

"What's all this?"

"I was tasked with picking up takeout because, as I was told, 'Mom and Dad are going out to dinner.'"

Sam laughed. "So you're babysitting for me tonight, I take it?"

"Apparently."

"That's awesome." The agent who'd once been such a thorn in her side had become a friend, especially now that he was engaged to Shelby and raising her son, Noah, as his own.

"I'm glad I ran into you. I was going to stop by tomorrow to invite you and the vice president to a little gathering at our place for Shelby's birthday next Saturday."

"We'd love to come."

"The kids are invited too, of course. She'd never forgive me if I left them out."

"We'll all be there. What can we bring?"

"Nothing. I'm having it catered."

"Look at you stepping up to the plate."

"I figured it was the least I could do. She handles everything all the time. She deserves a night off."

"Yes, she does. I'll have to think of some fabulous pink present I can get her."

"Jesus, more pink. I can't take any more."

They walked up the ramp together.

"You're engaged to the woman. Your whole life is going to be pink."

"Ugh, don't remind me. I suppose the pink is a small price to pay for the rest of what comes with the amazing Shelby Faircloth."

"Indeed. She's the best."

Inside, they were greeted by the usual mayhem of the twins running around, shrieking with laughter as Scotty chased them in a circle around Noah, who sat on a blanket in the middle of it all, clapping his chubby hands and laughing at everything the other kids were doing.

Shelby was close by, ready to intervene if needed. She lit up at the sight of her handsome fiancé and came over to kiss him. "Thank you so much for picking up takeout. It's such a pain to get anything delivered here."

"No problem."

The twins came running over to jump into Sam's outstretched arms. She hugged and kissed them, asked them about their day and got a full rundown of another day in kindergarten. "How was the algebra test?" she asked Scotty, planting a kiss on his forehead after the little ones squirmed out of her embrace to return to their game.

"We're not discussing that."

"Uh-oh."

"I don't think it was a total disaster." He looked into one of the brown bags. "What's for dinner, Avery?"

"Spaghetti and meatballs."

Scotty pumped his fist into the air. "*Yes*. Let's eat, you guys." The twins ran after him when he took the bags into the kitchen.

Sam loved the way they followed him around like two adoring puppies and how he tolerated them with patience, love and understanding that only someone who'd once been where they were now could understand.

"He's so good with them," Shelby said. "They worship him."

"I'm so glad he's getting to be a big brother."

"Me too." Shelby squeezed Sam's arm. "Go get ready for a night out with your man. We've got things covered here."

"Thank you for giving up your evening for us."

"It's no problem. We'd be doing the same thing at home."

"You're very good to us, and we appreciate everything you do."

"I love my job and all four of my kids."

Sam smiled and gave her a quick hug before heading upstairs to find Nick. She found him in their bedroom, fresh from the shower, a towel wrapped around his waist.

"Hey, babe."

She leaned back against the closed door and gawked at his bare chest and the defined abs he worked hard to maintain.

"What's up?"

"Nothing much. Just checking out the magnificent scenery." She dropped her coat on the floor, kicked off her shoes and pulled the sweater over her head. "What time is our reservation?"

"Not for an hour."

"Perfect." She pushed her jeans and panties down, added them to the pile on the floor and locked the door.

"Um, what is happening?"

She sauntered across the room to him, gratified when his erection turned the towel into a tent. "A little date night warm-up round and a very sincere thank you for the flowers you sent that made me go all gooey and girlie." Reaching him, she flattened her hands over his pecs and then slid them up to draw him into a hot, tongue-twisting kiss. "Is that okay?"

"Ah, *yeah?*"

Sam laughed at his reaction and walked him backward until his back was pressed against a wall. "Remember the first time we ever did it?"

His lips attacked her neck, making her shiver. "I'll never forget it."

"As I recall, there was a wall involved."

"Mmm, yes, there was. Are you up for a little trip down memory lane?"

She unknotted his towel, pushed it out of the way and wrapped her hand around his hard cock. "I'm up for it if you are."

"I'm most definitely *up* for it." He turned them so her back was to the wall, and with his hands cupping her ass, lifted her. "Did my fierce Samantha really get gooey and girlie over flowers?"

"She really did, but only because they were from her favorite husband." Sam wrapped her legs around his waist and breathed in the rich, appealing scent of him. "I came home expecting dessert, not appetizers."

He laughed and tightened his hold on her. "Maybe if you're a very good girl, you'll get both."

"Oh yummy. I'm feeling particularly hungry tonight."

The gorgeous hazel eyes that always looked at her with love and affection heated with blatant desire. "This is going to be fast."

"I can handle fast."

True to his word, they were gasping with completion ten minutes later, clinging to each other as they cooled off and came down from the incredible high they found together.

She nuzzled his neck, breathing in the familiar scent of home. "I *love* date night."

His laughter rumbled through them both. "Me too. I've been negligent on that front since the Secret Service took over my life, but we're going to get back to regular nights out."

"I'm perfectly content to watch TV in bed with you. I hope you know that."

"I do, but we still need to go out by ourselves every now and then."

"We got to go to Harry and Lilia's last weekend."

"I didn't get to have you to myself, so that doesn't count."

She pushed the hair back from his forehead. "I got you all dirty. You're going to need another shower."

Without breaking their intimate connection, he carried her into the bathroom and stepped into the shower before he put her down, holding on until he was sure she had legs under her.

"That was hot, Mr. Vice President."

"I do what I can for the people."

"That's my line, and it's trademarked."

They laughed and teased their way through a shower, sliding soapy hands over each other until they had to call time-out or miss their reservations. While Sam got ready, Nick went to check on the kids.

As she dried her hair, she thought about how different things were since she'd married Nick. In the past, she would've brought work home, spent all night poring over the reports and notes, stayed up too late stewing over the case of the moment, and generally had no quality of life. Nick had brought quality to her life—in more ways than one. The cases still got closed, and if it took a day or two longer than it used to, well, she wasn't about to apologize to anyone for only working ten hours a day.

That made her laugh, thinking of the Skip Holland Half Day.

And then she was sobbing, missing him so badly that she wondered how she could still manage to breathe without him right down the street, there for her anytime she needed him. The pain ran so deep as to touch the very heart of her. How could he just be *gone*?

She finished drying her hair and mopped up the tears, determined to pull herself together to enjoy the rare evening out with her love. Thank God for him and their family to prop her up during these difficult days.

A touch of makeup helped to cover the blotchiness on her face, and when she was satisfied that she'd done what she could to hide the redness in her eyes, she went across the hall to get dressed in a clingy black wrap dress and the black Louboutins that Nick had bought her. She put on her engagement ring and the diamond key necklace he'd given her on their wedding day. With a quick visual inspection, she decided she looked as good as she possibly could under the circumstances.

She went downstairs to spend some time with the kids before they were due to leave. Shelby had ordered their favorite dinner, which Scotty would eat every night if he had his druthers. The twins loved it too, even more so because Scotty did. Their little faces were stained red with sauce, their smiles happy and their plates nearly clean.

"Looks like everyone is getting dessert tonight, Shelby."

"I know!" Shelby wiped little faces and refilled glasses of milk while tending to Noah in the high chair. She made taking care of four kids look effortless, and from what Sam could tell, she loved every minute she spent with them.

"Scotty had thirds!"

"It's so good," Scotty said over a mouthful of meatball. "And Shelby made brownies for dessert. Life is good."

Amused by him as always, Sam took comfort in seeing him rebounding from the difficult loss of his grandfather as well as could be expected.

"And no math homework tonight. Best night ever!"

Nick came into the kitchen, dressed in gray pants, a dress shirt and the navy cashmere V-neck sweater she'd bought him for Christmas. Her heart still gave a happy lurch at the sight of him, almost two years after they were married. She'd long ago accepted that she'd always react that way to him.

"Whoa." Nick let out a low whistle when he saw what she was wearing. "Check out my date. Is she hot or what?"

Scotty scowled. *"Ew."*

Shelby gave his hair a playful tug. "Be nice. Your mother is gorgeous."

"Yes, she is, but does he have to talk about how *hot* she is in front of the children?"

The three adults cracked up laughing.

"Well, does he?"

"My apologies, son. I'll try to refrain from discussing your mother's hotness in front of you in the future."

"Thank you. I don't have to remind you there're actual children in the house these days, do I?"

Nick's lips quivered with suppressed laughter. "No, son, you don't."

"Let's break out the brownies, Shelby!"

The twins clapped in support of Scotty's declaration.

"What's the magic word, sport?"

Scotty grinned from ear to ear. *"Please."*

"You got it."

Nick took hold of Sam's hand. "Let's make our escape while the brownies have everyone's full attention."

"Call us if you need anything, Shelby," Sam said.

"We'll be fine. Avery is finishing up a conference call in his car and then he'll be in."

"He could've used the office for that."

"No worries. He doesn't mind."

They kissed the kids good-night, donned coats and headed for the front door, where Brant waited for them.

With his hand on the small of her back, Nick ushered Sam out ahead of him. They were whisked into the back of one of the always-ready black SUVs that waited at the curb. When they were buckled in, Sam turned to him.

"Where're we going?"

"You'll see."

CHAPTER TWENTY-SEVEN

"YOU'RE NOT TAKING me to some White House thing you weren't going to tell me about until we were there, are you?"

"Would I do that to you?"

"Um, hello? The night we got engaged? Ring any bells?"

He took her left hand and kissed the ring he'd placed on her finger in the Rose Garden. "I remember every second of that unforgettable night, especially the part where you said yes to forever with me."

"As if there was ever any doubt I'd say yes."

"You were so mad that I took you to the White House with no warning that I was a little afraid you might turn me down."

"You knew I wouldn't because you knew by then I couldn't live without you."

"And thank goodness for that because I can't live without you." He leaned his forehead against hers. "You've been crying."

"The downside of being known so well by someone is being known so well by someone."

He smiled, which made his eyes twinkle. "What's up?"

"A rough dad moment. I got through it."

"I'm sorry, babe. I hate that you're hurting this way."

"I know, but I read somewhere that the pain of losing someone you love is the price you pay for getting to love them in the first place."

"I like that."

"I went to see him on the way home."

"You don't have to go there alone, Samantha. I would've gone with you."

"I know. It was spur-of-the-moment."

"Did you feel better after you went?"

"Sorta. I'm not sure how to feel about that place yet. It's not like he's actually there or anything."

"Maybe you can imagine him listening to whatever you want to tell him when you're there."

"Maybe. I suppose I'll figure it out in time."

"You will. It won't happen overnight, but you'll find a way to keep him present that works for you."

"That's all I want—to keep him present."

"You will. He's so much a part of you that he'll always be with you."

"That's true. I really worry about how Scotty is doing with it."

"He has his moments when he's really sad. Shelby says it's tough for him after school when he used to go see your dad."

"I wish I was home at that time."

"He's very well loved by Shelby and Celia."

"Yeah, I know, but I still wish it could be me."

"And I wish it could be me, but he understands that we have to work."

"What're we going to do about this dog he wants?" Sam asked.

"I suppose at some point we need to consider the possibility."

"Maybe for Christmas?"

Nick's smile lit up his handsome face. "That'd be one hell of a great surprise."

"It really would."

"Let's talk more about it and figure out how to make that happen."

"If we give him everything he wants, will we mess him up?"

"He doesn't want much."

"True. Hopefully, we're not doing everything wrong with him and the Littles."

"We love them. We make sure they're cared for by people who love them when we can't be there to care for them ourselves. They know there's nothing we wouldn't do for them. Those are the things that matter to kids. Trust me on that as someone who didn't have any of that growing up."

"Ugh, it makes me bleed inside when you talk about your childhood."

"It was a long time ago, and now I have everything I didn't have then. And that's all because of you, because you said yes to me from the very beginning."

"I was rather easy that first night."

He laughed as she'd hoped he would. "We were both easy that night. It was meant to be from the very beginning."

"With a significant detour."

"We found each other again because we were meant to be."

Sam leaned her head on his shoulder. "Sometimes I think about who I was when I first met you, and I'm pretty sure I would've messed it up if things had worked out back then."

"Nah, I wouldn't have let you mess it up."

"Even you and your superpowers might not have been enough to save me from myself back then. I needed to grow up a little so I'd be ready for you. I also needed to experience the bad to appreciate the good."

"No, you didn't. You would've been able to appreciate this and us without having to go through what you did with *him*."

It still saddened her to think about the violent end to her ex-husband's life. Even though he'd put her through hell, he hadn't deserved what'd happened to him. No one did.

The car came to a stop outside a building Sam recognized. They'd held their wedding reception at the iconic Hay-Adams Hotel.

Brant opened the passenger side door and helped Sam out of the car, his eagle eyes scanning the surrounding area as he waited for Nick to alight.

They were taken inside and straight to elevators that whisked them to the top-floor ballroom where their reception had been held. The vast room was empty now, except for one table set for two.

Sam whirled around to face him. "*How* did you do this?"

He shrugged. "I made a phone call. They weren't using the room tonight, so they were happy to let us borrow it."

"I love it. It's perfect."

"I'm glad you approve." Nick turned to his lead agent. "Thanks, Brant. We're good for now."

"Very well, Mr. Vice President, Mrs. Cappuano. Enjoy your dinner." Brant turned and left the room.

Sam had no doubt he'd be right outside the door the

whole time should he be needed. She worried about Nick a little less than she would have otherwise with Brant leading his detail.

Nick took her hand to lead her to the table, where he held a chair for her. After she sat, he bent to place a kiss on her neck that electrified her entire body.

When he was seated across from her, a middle-aged waiter appeared with a bottle of champagne. "Welcome, Mr. Vice President, Mrs. Cappuano. It's an honor to have you back at the Hay-Adams. I'm Daniel, and I'll be taking care of you tonight."

"Thank you, Daniel," Nick said. "We're thrilled to be back at the scene of the crime."

Sam laughed. "That's how he sees our marriage."

Daniel laughed and then went through the dinner specials for the evening before handing them each a menu.

"I thought about ordering ahead, but then I thought better of that."

"Good thinking." Sam scanned the menu and settled on salmon. "What're you getting?"

"The filet. You?"

"Salmon."

"We can share."

She sent him a saucy look. "Maybe."

After they ordered, they enjoyed the champagne while taking in the expansive view of the National Mall and the Washington Monument in the distance.

"How did Nelson seem when you saw him earlier?"

"Not good at all. He's wrecked that Gloria is leaving him."

"Did he expect her to stand by her man? And why, exactly, do women do that when their high-profile husbands humiliate them so publicly?"

"I'll never understand why they do it."

"Just so we're clear—I'd never stick around after something like that." Not that she worried about such a thing with him.

He smiled. "Just so we're clear—you'll never be in that position." Nick buttered one of the hot rolls that Daniel brought while Sam looked on in envy. She'd cut back on bread a while ago in deference to her expanding backside. "Tell me you know that."

"Of course I do. I was joking."

"There's nothing funny about fidelity, Samantha."

"Sure there is. For example, if I were to remind you of my rusty steak knife, you'd be well aware of what you'd be facing should you ever stray. See? That's funny."

"It's not funny that you think I'd ever stray. Where would I go to get something better than what I have at home?"

"I've never realized how sexy fidelity is until you just said that. And PS, I don't actually think you'd ever stray. That's not something I worry about—and it's not something you should worry about either."

"Now that we have that settled, tell me what's up with the case. Unless you'd rather not talk about it."

"I don't mind talking about it." She sipped champagne and sampled the cheese board Daniel had brought. "After I talked to you earlier, we interviewed Tim Finley of DailyPolitic."

"What'd you want with him?"

"He got to know Tara on the campaign trail and had a one-night stand with her around the time we believe her child was conceived."

"Oh wow."

"He was rather shocked, to say the least. Apparently,

it was a one-off, he's married, never done anything like that, etc. Tara had a very active social life after Bryce Massey broke up with her. It seems like she was looking for something that couldn't be replaced, at least in her mind. I know that feeling. I felt that way after I met you and then didn't hear from you."

He cringed. "I can't even think about that without wanting to scream."

"Me too, and that's why I get how she felt when Bryce broke up with her. She thought she had things figured out until he pulled the rug out from under her."

"How hard have you looked at him?"

Sam thought of the way he'd creeped her out on the street after the first time they met. "He has an airtight alibi."

"That doesn't mean he wasn't involved."

"What would be his motive though?"

"He found out how 'busy' she'd been after they broke up and was enraged by it?"

"What right would he have to be enraged when he was the one who ended it with her?"

"Who knows? Maybe he retained some sense of 'ownership' where she was concerned, even after he ended it."

"That's a possibility." Sam pulled her new phone out of her clutch and placed a call to HQ. "Can you put me through to the pit, please?"

"The what?"

Sam wanted to scream. "Homicide."

"Oh yes, of course. One moment, please."

"These damned operators need to learn to speak the lingo," she said to Nick while she waited.

"Carlucci."

"Hey, it's me. I was thinking some more about the ex-boyfriend, Bryce Massey, and whether he was still feeling possessive of Tara even after he ended it with her. We kind of wrote him off because he had a rock-solid alibi, but I want to take another look at him." The creepy feeling he'd given her on the street had stayed with her in the aftermath, but the alibi had kept her from digging deeper there.

"It's a good thought."

"I have to give Nick credit for it."

He smiled widely at her across the table.

"We'll do some digging on that angle."

Sam felt a tingle in the vicinity of her backbone, which tended to happen when she had a new thread to pull or felt like she was onto something that could break a case wide-open. She wasn't sure yet if this was one of those moments, but she'd know soon enough. "Thanks a lot. Anything else popping?"

"Not yet."

"I'll let you get back to it. Call me if anything comes up."

"Will do."

Sam closed the phone with a satisfying slap and held it up for Nick to see. "Isn't she pretty?"

"Gorgeous. Thank God and all the saints in heaven that you were able to get another one."

"I know! I'm not made for phones that're smarter than me."

They ate the delicious meal that Daniel served, taking bites from each other's plates, drank more champagne and enjoyed chocolate mousse for dessert. When the table had been cleared, Nick stood and held out his hand to her.

She took his hand and let him help her up. "What's going on?"

"Come with me and I'll show you."

Because she'd follow him anywhere he chose to lead her, she went with him to the dance floor and smiled when she heard the opening notes to the Bon Jovi song they'd danced to on their wedding day.

He drew her into his arms and gazed down at her. "Thank you for loving me. In case you didn't already know, you've made my life."

Sam curled her arms around his neck and drew him into a kiss. "Thank *you* for loving me. I know it's not always easy."

"Samantha… Loving you is the easiest thing I've ever done. It's easy like breathing."

What had she ever done to deserve the love of this extraordinary man? Whatever it was, she was thankful every day for the divine intervention that had brought him to her not once but twice in this lifetime.

When the song ended, he kissed her neck and whispered in her ear. "Let's go home."

"Yes, please."

Nick slipped Daniel a tip before they left the room to find Brant waiting right outside the door.

He spoke into a microphone to alert the other agents that Hot Shot and Fuzz were on the move.

"Who can I talk to about getting a better nickname?" Sam asked when they were in the elevator.

"I'm not sure," Brant said. "No one has ever objected to one of our code names before."

"Never?"

"Not that I'm aware of."

"Figures I'd be the first."

Nick snorted with laughter. "Of course you are."

"Why don't you like Fuzz?" Brant asked.

"It makes me think of frizzy hair."

"You do know that's an old slang word for police, right?"

"Yes, Brant, I know that, but I don't *like* it."

"Duly noted."

"He's not going to do anything about it, is he?" she asked Nick.

"I don't believe so. I think he has more important things to do than to worry about your nickname, such as keeping me alive."

Brant pointed to Nick with his thumb. "What he said."

"I'd like my objections to be formally entered into the Secret Service objection book."

"I'll be sure to take care of that as soon as possible, ma'am."

"He's not going to do it."

"Nope."

"I'll be happy to address that concern when I'm finished keeping your husband alive."

"Now he's just being fresh."

Brant cracked a rare grin. "My grandmother used to say that."

"Are you equating me to your grandmother?"

"Not at all, ma'am. I would never make that mistake."

"He's good. I've got to give him that. He actually reminds me a lot of Freddie before I ruined him."

"I can see that, and I can see that the ruining is happening because the nice agent who first took us on wasn't quite as cheeky as he is now."

"True. He was much more reserved and respectful."

"I beg your pardon?" Brant tapped on his earpiece. "I couldn't quite hear you."

Sam and Nick laughed as they followed him off the elevator and back into the waiting vehicle.

"Thank you for an awesome date," she said when they were alone in the backseat.

"Entirely my pleasure."

"You got it just right with the walk down memory lane. That was the best day of my entire life."

"Mine too."

Sam leaned her head on his shoulder and curled her hand around his. "What was your favorite part of that day?"

"It had to be when I found out you told off my mother and sent her packing."

"That was one of my finest moments. There was no way I was letting her ruin that day for you when she'd already ruined so many other days."

"And for that I shall be forever grateful."

"She's been quiet lately."

"I know. That's never a good thing."

"Eh, we don't need to worry about her tonight."

"No, we don't. What was your favorite moment from our big day?"

"You might think it was when you got Jon Bon Jovi to sing our wedding song live or when we discovered we'd had the same thing engraved inside our wedding rings."

"You're my home," he said, giving her hand a squeeze.

"That was pretty incredible, but for me, the very best moment of that day was when we arrived at the Hay and got a minute to ourselves to simply marvel at the fact that we were finally, finally married, all those years after our first night together."

"Best day ever. Followed very, *very* closely by the day I met Scotty."

"And the day I met the twins."

"All good days that brought us an amazing family."

"It hasn't happened exactly the way we'd planned, but I wouldn't trade them for anything, even 'one of our own.'" She made quote marks around the last four words.

Nick frowned. "I had a good talk with one of the honchos at that reporter's network and suggested she teach the reporter some manners before she sends her out to question people."

"What'd she say to that?"

"She agreed and apologized profusely. Apparently, the producer has adopted children and was equally horrified."

"Good, she should be. I wouldn't trade our kids for anything, even 'one of our own.'"

"Me either," Nick said.

"I'm glad you were able to do something about her. It's amazing how my thinking has changed on the baby topic. I used to believe I could only be fulfilled if I had a baby of my own, and now…"

"Now you have what you need, even if it didn't happen the way we thought it would."

Sam nodded. "We both went through so much before we had this. All of it made us who we are today, and who you are today works for me on every level."

"I feel the same way about you."

"If I hadn't gone through hell before I found you the second time, I might not have been ready for this life we live. I never imagined I'd actually be thankful for the bad times, but in a weird way I really am."

"Me too, babe."

CHAPTER TWENTY-EIGHT

THEY ARRIVED HOME and went inside to find Shelby curled up on the sofa watching a movie. She got up when they came in and folded the sofa blanket. "Did you have a nice time?"

"It was great. My lovely husband took me back to the scene of the crime at the Hay-Adams."

"Oh, well played, Nick."

"It was great. We had the ballroom all to ourselves, so no one was gawking at us."

Nick glanced at Sam, looking sheepish. "This would probably be a good time to tell you that Shelby is the one who made it happen when I called to ask if she still knew people there."

Shelby gasped. "You didn't have to tell her that!"

"I can't take credit that belongs to you. Thank you again for making it happen."

"It was my pleasure."

"Thank you, Shelby," Sam said. "For helping Nick to arrange the perfect night and for staying late with the kids."

"No problem at all."

"Where's Avery?" Sam asked.

"He took Noah home to bed a while ago. He told you he's having people in to celebrate my birthday next weekend even if I'd rather skip it?"

"You're not skipping your birthday. We'll be there."
Sam gave her a hug. "Thank you so much. We really
needed this."

"Anytime."

After she left, Nick put his arm around Sam and
guided her to the stairs. "Loft. Five minutes. Don't make
me wait."

He set her on fire with seven words.

Upstairs, they looked in on the kids. They tucked in
the twins, kissed their foreheads and tiptoed from the
room. In Scotty's room, they shut off his TV and bedside lamp, kissed the top of his head and stepped out,
closing the door behind them.

As Sam went into the room she used as a closet, she
heard Nick telling the agent on duty in the hallway to
take a break.

She moved quickly to change into a nightgown and
matching robe, before crossing the hallway to their room,
where she brushed her hair and teeth. With seconds to
spare, she scooted up the stairs. While he waited for
her, he'd lit the coconut-scented candles and turned off
the lights.

He was on the double lounge chair waiting for her.

Sam dropped the robe onto the floor and crawled into
his outstretched arms.

They were kissing wildly before she'd even fully
landed. Hours of buildup and anticipation only made
the desire hotter and sharper than usual. They held on
tight to each other as the kiss became more desperate
by the second. Without breaking the kiss, he rolled her
under him, pushed up her nightgown and joined their
bodies in one deep thrust of his cock into her.

Sam broke the kiss, sucked in a deep breath and held

on to him as he took them on a wild ride. She had nearly reached the summit when he slowed down all of a sudden, leaving her hanging.

"Nick!"

"Yes, love?"

"Ugh. You did that on purpose."

"Of course I did. I'm not looking for a wham, bam, thank you, ma'am."

"Because you had that earlier."

"Exactly." His lips skimmed over her neck and the outer shell of her ear as he continued to move in her, albeit slowly. "This time, I want to take my time."

She sagged into the mattress, resigned to doing this at his pace and not hers.

"Don't glare at me. It ruins the mood."

"Nothing ruins your mood."

"You're right—any time I get to make love to my beautiful, funny, smart, sexy, adorable, grumpy wife, nothing can ruin my mood, even my adorable, grumpy wife."

She stabbed him in the ribs with her index fingers, drawing a grunt of surprise and laughter from him.

"I suppose I ought to be glad you don't have your rusty steak knife with you."

"Yes, you should. I was on the verge of an epic orgasm and you took it away from me."

"Aww, baby, don't you know? Whatever I take away, I give back in spades."

He was too cute for words, and she loved him madly, which was why she'd forgive him for teasing and tormenting her. Besides, no matter how they got there, he always made the grand finale worth the wait. This time was no different as he moved in her while gazing down at her, forcing her to look at him, to dwell in the intimate bubble they lived in together, where there was only them and only this.

"I love you, Samantha. More than you'll ever know."

"Love you too. Just as much. Maybe more."

"Not possible."

"Yes."

He smiled. "No way."

"Yes way."

Shaking his head, he kissed her while holding perfectly still inside her, adding to the torment. He had her completely pinned and at his mercy, just the way he loved her best.

Sam had learned to surrender to him, to let him take the lead. Giving up control didn't come naturally to her in the rest of her life, but it was effortless with him.

Grasping her hands and pinning them over her head, he picked up the pace while holding her gaze.

The orgasm that had started earlier broke over her in a tidal wave of pleasure that seemed to come from the very heart of her.

"Samantha." Her name was a whisper on his lips as he thrust into her one last time and found his own release.

They held each other tight for a long time afterward. Sam liked this part almost as much as the main event. No one did snuggling the way he did. No one did anything the way he did. She dozed and drifted, her mind and body settling the way they did only at times like this with him.

In the blissful aftermath, warm and cozy in the arms of her love, she closed her eyes, letting her mind wander over the parts and pieces of the case, thinking it through from every angle, each angle leading her in the same direction—back to the odd encounter she'd had on the street with Massey. Her eyes snapped open. "Bryce."

"Um, babe? Saying another man's name while your husband is still inside you isn't the best idea you ever had."

"It's him. I should've known he had something to do with this from the first second he tried to intimidate me on the street."

Nick raised his head to look down at her, brows furrowed. "Wait. *What?*"

"I told you that."

"No, you didn't." He withdrew from her and moved to his side. Propped up on an elbow, he raised a brow. "Start talking."

Sam told him about the interview with Tara's ex and the encounter she'd had with him on the sidewalk after.

"So you were there by yourself after Freddie left, and he came at you? This is the stuff that gives me nightmares."

"Don't forget I'm armed at all times and know how to take care of myself."

"Samantha… Your former boss is on trial for wrapping you in razor wire. We both know that no one can take care of themselves all the time."

"That was a onetime mistake in judgment on my part."

"You're in no way responsible for what happened to you that day, but the thought of some random dude attacking you when there's no one there to help you…" A shudder went through his big body. "Unbearable."

"I'm sorry. I hate that you worry the way you do. I swear that ninety-nine percent of the time, I never feel unsafe or in any kind of actual danger."

"The one percent is all it takes."

"I fended him off, but we need to make sure his alibi holds up." She reached for her phone, which she kept close at hand ever since the night Arnold was killed while she was off the grid. Every part of her buzzed with the certainty that she'd missed something with Bryce.

She found the text from Isabel, the intern, and put through a call to her.

"This is Sam Holland."

"I never thought I'd hear from you."

"Sorry to call so late, but I have a question regarding the World Bank."

"Oh, um, sure. Happy to help if I can."

"Bryce Massey's assistant, Janice. She said he was in meetings all day and that neither of them left the building. What I want to know is if she'd be with him at his meetings, or if there were times she wouldn't know for *sure* he was in the meetings."

"I'm not sure if she goes or not, but I have a friend who works on their floor. I can call her to ask. She'd know."

"Do it and call me back?"

"I will. Right away."

"Thank you." Sam closed her phone and tried to be patient in the two minutes it took for Isabel to call her back.

"She said Janice never attends meetings with him."

Sam wanted to shout hallelujah. "This was extremely helpful, and I won't forget it. Let's have coffee in the next few weeks."

"I'd love that."

"Shoot me a text, and we'll set it up." Sam ended the call and put through another to Carlucci.

She answered on the first ring. "Hi, LT, what's up?"

"What's the latest with Bryce Massey?"

"Funny you should ask. We're preparing a report for you now in which he's the star."

"Give me the highlights."

"We found a connection between him and Delany Russo."

Sam's backbone buzzed with sensation. "I'm on my way in." She slapped the phone closed and started to get out of bed when an arm around her waist stopped her.

"Where do you think you're going at midnight, my love?"

"To get justice for Tara and to save us a move to 1600 Pennsylvania Avenue."

"As much as I don't want to make that move, you need rest."

"I need this more." She kissed him. "Please?"

He let her go, albeit reluctantly. "Be careful with my wife. I love her madly."

"I will. I promise. Thank you for an amazing night."

"My pleasure."

Sam flew out of bed, grabbed her robe, put it on and tied it as she went down the stairs. She hated leaving him but this was the best lead they'd had yet, and she would never sleep wondering what was happening at work. Besides, she didn't get to work with her two third-shift detectives very often, and this was a good opportunity to give them some attention—and some overtime.

She nodded to the agent in the hallway and ducked into her closet to get clothes and then crossed the hall to her room, making a beeline for the shower.

Fifteen minutes later, she was on the way to HQ, zipping through the Secret Service checkpoint and across town in record time. Maybe she ought to start working overnights again to avoid the traffic. She'd done third shift early in her career, and it'd been a bitch. Her body's internal clock had never fully made the adjustment, meaning she'd walked around in zombie mode for two full years before she'd been mercifully moved to days.

The other benefit of showing up to work in the middle of the night was no press staked outside the front door. She parked in the main parking lot and walked into the building, enjoying the freedom to come to work without being stalked by reporters. The first person she encountered inside was the last person she expected to see there at that hour.

"What's up, Chief?"

"Vice did a big sweep on the gambling ring tonight. A lot of unhappy people in lockup, all of them claiming to be innocent bystanders, of course."

"Of course. Did Public Affairs get the word out about the arrests?"

"They're working on it now."

"Good. We need all the positive publicity we can get."

"You mean *I* need all the positive publicity." Though he looked tired, he seemed measurably better than he had the last time she saw him. "Celia's statement has really helped to calm things."

"That's great. I'm glad to hear it."

"I really appreciate it, and I'll tell her so when I see her. We're having lunch the day after tomorrow."

"It's good of you to do that."

"She's my friend as much as he was."

Because there was no one else around, Sam hugged

him. "You're the best." She let go of him before she could lose her composure and headed for the pit.

"What're you doing here?" he called after her.

"Pulling a thread," she said over her shoulder.

In the pit, she found Dani Carlucci and Giselle "Gigi" Dominguez working in their side-by-side cubicles. While Dominguez was a petite, curvy Latina, Carlucci was tall, blonde and stacked. "Ladies, what've we got?"

"Let's go in the conference room, and we'll draw you a picture," Carlucci said. With two more years on the job, she was the senior partner.

Sam clapped her hands. "Oh, I love pictures!"

In the conference room, Sam noticed the large dry-erase board that'd recently held the details of her father's case had been wiped clean.

Case closed.

She took a deep breath and fought through the wave of grief that came over her when she hadn't been expecting it. That's how grief worked, or so she'd been told. Always there, waiting to surge to the surface to remind you that your loved one is gone forever, even when you're in the middle of something else.

Dominguez dragged the empty dry-erase board closer to the table and wrote Bryce Massey's name at the top. She drew a line to Tara Weber and another line to Delany Russo and then connected the two women to each other.

"We believe that Bryce paid Delany to keep tabs on Tara for him," Carlucci said after Dominguez had completed the drawing.

"Holy bombshell, Batman," Sam said. "Do tell."

Dominguez produced financials for both parties with various transactions highlighted. "Note that the dates of the withdrawals from his account match the dates of deposit for the same amounts in hers."

Sam's spine buzzed with sensation, which is what happened when they closed in on murdering scumbags. "Tell me more."

Dominguez placed text message records on the table in front of Sam. "This came from Detective Green's review of the phone data. The first set of messages is between Tara and Bryce. We went back to the week in early February when the baby was most likely conceived and found that Tara was in close touch with Bryce and they spent time together."

Sam scanned the text exchanges that showed Bryce pleading with Tara to see him so they could talk.

At first, Tara put him off, claiming she was busy and only in town for the week before traveling for work again.

After some more back-and-forth, she agreed to let him come over for a short visit on January 31.

"Do we have any way of knowing how long he stayed?"

"Until noon the next day," Carlucci said, handing another page to Sam.

I've just left you and I already miss you. I can't tell you how much it meant to me to have this time with you, babe. I still think we can put things back together.

The message had been sent at 12:12 p.m.

"What was her reply?"

"She didn't reply. As far as we can tell, she never again replied to a message from him. We've gone through her emails and calls as well. While he reached out to her repeatedly, it appears she never replied. Shortly after that, he starts texting Delany, reminding her they have a deal. So we went back to when he and Tara first broke up and found that he'd started paying Delany around that time. We found multiple exchanges between them about Tara and a few that indicate there might be more to their 'friendship' than just spying."

Sam mulled over the information, spinning it around in her mind every which way.

"Any clue about how the building video might've gotten wiped? The two of them don't seem capable of thinking it through to that extent."

"We didn't see anything about that," Carlucci said.

"Let's pick him up."

"Now?" Carlucci asked.

"Right now." Sam told them what she'd learned from Isabel about Bryce's so-called alibi. "And while we're at it, I want to bring Delany in too." Adrenaline rushed through her system the way it did when they were close to closing a case.

She called for backup from Patrol, asked them to pick up Delany and to keep her separate from Massey at HQ so they didn't know the other was there. Sam drove Carlucci and Dominguez to Massey's house near Rock Creek Park. As they drove, she talked out the case with her detectives.

"Here's what I'm thinking. Massey broke up with Tara because she wanted to get married and he didn't. But he never expected her to really move on from him. He expected her to stay in close touch, to continue the dance they'd done for the previous six years while she held out hoping for more, which he never intended to give her. Then they reunite for a night, things are like they used to be, and he believes he's got her back where he wants her—taking the scraps he's willing to give her, filled with hope that he might change his mind about a future together. Except this time, she's wise to him. Maybe she feels weak for letting him back in her bed for that one night, but she's upset that things didn't work out with Nelson. After spending that time with Bryce, she's more resolved than ever to move on without him. Maybe she decided after being with Massey again and realizing he was never going to change that she wanted a baby more than a relationship. She has the nights with Wilton and Finley. And when she gave the story to Finley, she was sending a huge 'fuck you' to Massey, letting him know that she was done with him and had moved on to much bigger fish, and she was sending a massive 'fuck you' to the president, for whom she may have developed an emotional attachment until he blew her off after the affair and refused to acknowledge her child could be his."

"Why would someone so media savvy bring this firestorm down on herself though?", Carlucci asked.

"Because she was sick of being dicked around by men and wanted them all to suffer."

"I like it," Dominguez said in her usual low-key way.

"I freaking *love* it," Sam said. "Well, except for the part about Tara being dead."

"My question is still who killed Tara though," Carlucci said. "Massey has an airtight alibi. He was at work all day."

"I'm going to bet that he left for a time, perhaps when his airtight alibi was at lunch." The more she delved into this line of reasoning, the more she liked it. "And I'm going to bet that Delany let him in, perhaps not knowing that he intended to kill Tara, but we're going to use her to get to him." Sam pounded her hand on the steering wheel. "Sometimes I *fucking love* this job."

The other two detectives laughed.

"You're a weirdo, Lieutenant," Carlucci said.

"That's a compliment to me, as you know. The thing that makes me mad is that I should've looked harder at him after he tried to intimidate me on the street."

Dominguez looked at her with surprise. "What? When did that happen?"

Sam filled them in on the incident with Massey. "I just thought he was being a typical tool, trying to show me how big his dick was. After his assistant put him at work all day, I sort of wrote him off. The thing on the street should've been a heads-up to me, but I didn't take it that way."

"You needed more info before it made sense to you," Dominguez said. "Nothing wrong with that. In the end, that and the phone data helped to lead us to him."

As they pulled onto his street, Sam zeroed in on his townhouse, which is how she saw him coming down the stairs carrying a box. She stopped the car in the middle of the street. "He's running. Let's go." After taking one minute to contact Patrol to tell them they were moving in, Sam got out of the car and left the door open, so as not to alert him to their presence.

Because Carlucci and Dominguez had connected the dots that led to him, Sam gestured for them to go ahead and make the arrest.

He was so focused on what he was doing, the detectives were able to walk right up behind him.

Carlucci pressed her weapon into his back. "Freeze."

CHAPTER TWENTY-NINE

MASSEY'S BODY WENT rigid and then sagged against the back of his car.

"Going somewhere, Mr. Massey?" Dominguez asked.

"I'm getting ready to move."

Carlucci looked around him into the back of the SUV, which was packed full of stuff. "Mr. Massey, you're under arrest for the murder of Tara Weber. You have the right to remain silent—"

"I didn't kill her! *I loved her!* I'd never hurt her."

"You have the right to an attorney." As she recited his rights, Carlucci cuffed him and turned him over to the Patrol officers. "Take him in and get him booked."

He blanched when he saw Sam.

"We meet again, Mr. Massey."

"I want my lawyer!"

"Call his lawyer and have the ME on duty get a DNA sample," Sam said to the Patrol officers who hauled him away, while hoping he wasn't the baby's father. She checked to make sure Massey's car and townhouse were locked before returning to her car. "That was awesome. Very well done, ladies."

"Sometimes this job really is fun," Carlucci said.

"The Patrol officers told me they've got the assistant and they're bringing her in," Dominguez said.

"Outstanding. Totally worth losing a night of sleep to watch this go down."

"You're a little giddy, Lieutenant," Carlucci said.

"Yes, I am. We needed a win, and these arrests take care of a rather massive problem for me at home too."

"Ah yes, a pesky little problem called the potential resignation of the president."

Had she ever noticed before that Carlucci shared her snarky sense of humor? "Exactly. With these arrests, we'll hopefully be able to show that while Nelson committed adultery at the worst possible time, that was as far as it went."

"What's the plan for interrogation?" Dominguez asked.

"We're going to get Delany to tell us how it went down in exchange for the possibility of leniency." Sam put through a call to Malone. "Wake up."

"I'm awake." He sounded anything but.

"We've made arrests in the Weber case."

"Talk to me."

Sam ran through the connections Green, Carlucci and Dominguez had made between Bryce and Delany. "They put all the pieces together and did some fine work tonight."

"That's excellent."

"Put in a call to Faith Miller, if you would, and let her know we'll have them in interrogation within the hour."

"I'll make the call and be in shortly."

"Thanks, Cap."

"Tell the ladies I said great job."

"Will do." Sam slapped her new phone closed, loving the extra loud cracking sound it made when the two halves came together. It was even better than the old one. That, too, made her giddy. "The Captain says job well done."

"We share the credit with the day team," Dominguez said. "We picked up where they left off."

"Take the credit where you can get it. You did good work."

"Thank you, LT," Dominguez said. "It feels good to get justice for her—and her son."

"Justice is always a good feeling."

"Have you heard anything new about Stahl's trial?" Carlucci asked.

"Just that it's with the jury." Sam shrugged. "Out of my hands." It rankled her that the jury was taking so long to arrive at what should be a slam dunk conviction.

"There's no way they won't convict him," Dominguez said. "He was caught red-handed."

"That's my feeling as well, but you never know." She thought about Dr. Trulo warning her to be prepared to not get the outcome she deserved and expected, but she couldn't go there. She just couldn't conceive of that possibility.

At HQ, they were forced to cool their heels for more than an hour waiting for Massey and Russo to be processed and delivered to interrogation rooms. Then they had to wait for Massey's attorney to arrive.

Once all the players were in place, Sam briefed Assistant U.S. Attorney Faith Miller, who wore yoga pants and running shoes for the middle-of-the-night mission, as well as Captain Malone and Chief Farnsworth, who'd never gone home.

"What's the plan?" Malone asked.

"We're going to talk to Delany first. If we're right about this theory, she'll be the one to tell us."

"Agreed," Faith said. "I heard she's been hysterical since the cops showed up to arrest her."

Sam was glad to hear that. If the woman was hysterical, Sam could only hope it was because Delany knew she was fucked. "Let's get this done. Dominguez, Carlucci, you're with me."

She loved that the two detectives exchanged glances, seeming shocked to be invited to join her in the room. In the future, she vowed to spend more time with them so they'd know how much she valued their contributions.

Outside interrogation room two, Sam took a moment to summon her mojo and prepare to sew this thing up for Tara and her family.

She burst into the room, enjoying the way Delany jolted and looked at her with startled doe eyes gone wide with fright. Good. She ought to be afraid. Sam didn't recognize the young female attorney sitting with Delany.

"Detective Carlucci, please record this interview."

Carlucci recited the date, time and the names of the people present.

"My client hasn't done anything wrong," the lawyer said.

Sam ignored the attorney and spoke directly to Delany. "Are you willing to answer our questions?"

"Yes!"

"How long have you been communicating with Mr. Massey separate of Ms. Weber?"

Clearly, she hadn't been expecting that. She glanced at the attorney and then at Sam. "I, um, for a while now."

"Please describe your relationship with him."

"We… He… He paid me to tell him what she was doing."

"Did you tell him she was pregnant?"

Delany shook her head. "She said it was very, very important that no one know about the baby. She wouldn't tell me why, but she wore larger clothes and kept it hidden from everyone. I didn't tell Bryce about the baby."

"But you told him everything else?"

Delany nodded.

"Use your words."

"Yes."

"And what would Tara have said if she'd known this?"

"She would've murdered *me*. The last thing she wanted was for him to know what she was doing. She was very bitter about him after she saw him last winter. She never would say what happened between them, but she was through with him."

"If that was the case, why'd you betray her?"

"I needed the money, and I was worried about her. She went a little nuts after they broke up, and I was afraid something would happen to her."

"On the day she was murdered, did you let Bryce into her home?"

"You don't have to answer that, Delany," the attorney said.

"I...I want to. Yes, I let him in, but he made me swear I wouldn't tell anyone. He said he needed to talk to her about the baby, because he thought it might be his, and he needed to know. She wasn't returning his calls or texts, and he said if the baby was his, he had a right to know that."

"Had you told him that she planned to come home that day?"

Delany looked down at the table, seeming ashamed.

Good, she should be. Sam felt sick over the way Tara had been betrayed by someone she'd trusted.

"Yes, I'd told him that."

"So you let him in and then what?"

"I left like he asked me to."

"I'm trying to understand, as a woman, how another woman sets up her female employer to be ambushed by an ex in her own home. How does that happen?"

"I'm sorry!" Delany broke down into sobs. "I had no idea he'd hurt her! He told me he loved her and wanted to keep her safe always. If I'd known he was going to do this…" She shook her head.

"How long after you left did you return to her place?"

"A couple of hours. Her mother called me and asked me to check on her when they couldn't reach her. The baby, he was due to be fed and they were wondering when she'd be back to their house." Delany wiped away tears.

"Did you know right away what was wrong?"

"No! I told you! It never occurred to me that he'd hurt her. He said he just wanted to talk to her."

"Tell me again what happened when you returned."

"I let myself in and called for her. When she didn't answer, I went into her room and found her on the bed."

"And did you immediately know that Mr. Massey had killed her?"

"Yes," she whispered.

"Why didn't you tell us that the first time we talked?" Sam wanted to throttle her for wasting so much of their time. That was also a crime, in her opinion.

"Because I was afraid of what would happen to me!"

"You understand that you subjected Tara to a nightmare before he killed her, right? He forced her to remove her clothing and lie on the bed where he attacked her."

"I'm so sorry." Delany's sobs sounded like hiccups. "I loved Tara. I never would've hurt her."

"Yet you *betrayed* her by working for Bryce and then by letting him into her home, where he was able to ambush her."

"It wasn't like that."

"Wasn't it?" As another possibility occurred to her, Sam leaned in. "Were you sleeping with him?"

The attorney pounced. "Don't answer that, Delany."

Sam stared down the younger woman until she broke. "Yes," she whispered.

"For how long?"

"More than a year."

"Did he tell you he was also fucking one of the receptionists he works with? A woman named Ashley?"

Delany's face went blank with shock.

"Didn't think so." Sam pushed a yellow pad and pen across the table to her. "Write it down. Every detail, from the second he first made contact with you until you let him into her place the day she was murdered. Don't leave anything out. I want to know every time you saw him, banged him, reported to him about her."

With shaking hands, Delany took the pen from Sam.

"Wh-what's going to happen to me?"

"You'll be charged with accessory to murder."

Her face went blank with shock. "I didn't kill anyone! I had no idea he was going to do that to her!"

"You let him in and didn't warn her he was there. This is on you."

"No!"

"If you help them nail him, they might go easier on you." The attorney glanced at Sam for confirmation.

"That depends entirely on what kind of help your client gives us." Sam got up and left the room with Dominguez and Carlucci in tow.

"You were awesome in there, LT," Carlucci said when the door closed behind them.

"What she said," Malone commented when he came out of the observation room with Miller and Farnsworth.

Sam sagged against the cinder block wall. "I feel sick as a woman for what she allowed to happen to Tara."

"Unimaginable," Dominguez said.

"What's the plan with Massey?" the chief asked.

"I'm going to let him stew for a bit while I wait to see what Delany gives me. We need the DNA results. I'd like to know ASAP if he's the baby's father."

"I'll see what I can do to exert some additional pressure," Farnsworth said. Requests from him tended to get top priority with the lab.

"You ought to go home and get some sleep," Malone said. "We can pick it up at seven."

Sam checked her watch. That would give her five hours. She'd take it. To her detectives, she said, "Excellent work tonight. Feel free to come back for the fireworks in the morning."

"Wouldn't miss it," Carlucci said.

"Before you leave, ask Patrol to take Mr. Massey to a cell downstairs until we're ready to talk to him, and stay on Delany."

"Will do."

While pumped about closing the case, Sam was horrified by what'd happened to Tara. In the morning, she'd report the outcome to Tara's parents.

"And with that, I'm out for now."

SAM WAS BACK at HQ at six forty-five, having slept fitfully for a couple of hours. With adrenaline and dread pumping through her system, it'd been hard to sleep. The adrenaline came from nailing a killer, the dread from having to detail their daughter's death to Tara's parents.

"Massey is raising a ruckus downstairs," Malone said. "He's demanding to be told why he's in custody."

"Have we gotten a report back on whether his prints match the ones on Tara's neck yet?"

"Not yet."

"Until we have that, he's on ice. I want this locked and loaded before we square off with him."

"Does it matter if he's the baby's father?" Carlucci asked.

"It may go to motive, that she withheld that information from him and he found out about the baby at the same time everyone else did," Sam said. "But that's a detail we can confirm later. I want the prints to be his before we confront him."

"They're his," Freddie said when he joined them holding a printout he handed to Sam.

Sam scanned the report. "Got you, you motherfucker. Have him brought upstairs, please."

Freddie turned to see to her order. "I'm on it."

Sam went into her office to review the reports on the case, going through the details methodically, preparing to nail the son of a bitch who'd taken Tara's life.

Freddie returned twenty minutes later. "He's in interrogation one. A real pleasant sort of guy."

"I missed this at the beginning of this case."

"No, you didn't. He had an airtight alibi and had been broken up with her for more than a year. It never occurred to me either that it was him."

"Still, I feel like I missed it."

"If you did, I did too."

Sam rose, grabbed the file with everything about the case and headed for the door. "Carlucci, Dominguez, let's sew this up." She lowered her voice so only Freddie could hear her. "They've earned this."

"No worries."

She appreciated that he understood there were times when she had to give others a chance to shine. It was never lost on her that being her partner wasn't the easiest job, but he always rose to the challenge and for that she was eternally grateful to him.

With the two detectives in tow, she headed for the interrogation room where a uniformed Patrol officer stood watch outside the door.

These were the moments she lived for, confronting murderers with the irrefutable proof of their guilt. She thought of Tara, of the baby she'd yearned for and finally had, only to be taken from him two short weeks after his birth. The only thing she could do for Tara—and her son—was to make sure that the man who'd killed her never again walked free. With that goal in mind, she burst into the room, taking the two men inside by surprise.

CHAPTER THIRTY

SAM WAS SURPRISED herself to see Devon Sinclair sitting next to Massey. She'd met Devon during the investigation into his uncle Julian Sinclair's murder, during which Devon himself had nearly died after being shot. His presence threw her momentarily off her game until she recovered herself and proceeded into the room. She wanted to know how Devon knew Massey, but she could ask him later. For now, her job was to nail his client to the wall.

Massey glared at her. His hair stood on end, and Sam noted with satisfaction that orange wasn't his color.

Sam kept her unblinking gaze fixed on him. "Detective Dominguez, please record this interview."

While Dominguez noted the date, time and who was in the room, Sam continued to stare at Massey. Then she took her time sitting and opening the folder. "When did you decide it would be a good idea to fuck Tara Weber's assistant and then hire her to spy on Tara for you?"

Judging by his shocked expression, Massey hadn't expected that question. He glanced at Devon, as if to ask him what he should do.

"Answer the question, Bryce."

A defense attorney who encouraged cooperation was indeed a rare species in her world. "Do you need me to ask the question again, Mr. Massey?"

"No, I don't need you to ask it again. Delany and I were friends, separate of Tara."

"So you knew her before she worked for Ms. Weber?"

"No, but—"

"Then you knew her *because* of Ms. Weber. Because you were keeping tabs on her?"

"It wasn't like that."

"What was it like, then?"

"Tara went wild after our breakup. She was out with different guys every night, sleeping with some of them."

"What did that have to do with you? As I recall, you told us you ended the relationship because you and Ms. Weber wanted different things."

"That's the truth."

"I guess I don't understand, then, what business it was of yours what she was doing after you broke up."

"Just because we weren't together anymore didn't mean I stopped loving her."

Sam raised a brow that she hoped conveyed skepticism. "You loved her so much you hired her assistant to spy on her while you were also banging the assistant?"

A fleeting look of panic crossed his face.

That's right, asshole, we know all about Delany.

"That's not what happened."

"Isn't it? Detective Carlucci, can you please read to us the part from Delany's statement where she talks about how Mr. Massey hired her to keep him informed of Ms. Weber's activities?"

Bryce's wide eyes conveyed his complete shock that Delany had turned on him.

Watching his stunned reaction to the words that Delany had written brought the sort of satisfaction that made this job so rewarding at times like this.

"I'm sure you thought you had Delany thoroughly brainwashed, but alas, when faced with felony accessory to murder charges, she sang like a canary. Would you like to hear the rest of what she had to say?"

"No." His fierce expression had become less so as it seemed to settle on him that he was screwed, glued and tattooed.

Time to drop the bomb. "Your prints were on Tara's neck. We're charging you with her murder."

His mouth flopped open in disbelief as if it had never occurred to him that fingerprints could be taken from skin or that he would be caught.

Sam propped her elbows on the table, keeping her gaze fixed on him. "I have to give you credit. You gave us a run for our money with the airtight alibi that turned out to be not-so-airtight. Did you sneak out when your assistant was at lunch?"

"This interview is over," Devon said, seeming shocked and maybe appalled by what he'd heard.

Bryce started to object.

Devon tried to stop him with a hand on his arm.

"I want a deal!"

"What I really want to know is how an idiot like you managed to wipe the security video."

"If I tell you, will you give me a deal?"

Sam stood, leaned in so she was a foot from him. "You've got nothing to deal. We already got the whole story from Delany. Since you were good enough to leave your fingerprints on Tara's neck, we don't need anything more from you." She turned and left the room, ignoring Bryce's shouts that she let him explain. She'd heard more than enough. They might never know how he'd managed to mess with the security video, but they could pursue that at trial.

Faith met her in the hallway.

"He's all yours."

Faith's normally rosy complexion had gone pale. "All these cases make me sick, but this one…"

Sam put her hand on the other woman's arm. "I know. It's obscene. What'll you charge Delany with?"

"I need to talk to Tom." Faith referred to U.S. Attorney Tom Forrester. "Without her cooperation, we have a flimsy case against Massey, but what she did…" Faith gave Sam a fierce look. "There's no way she's getting away with that."

"Agreed. Without her involvement, Tara's still alive and raising the child she yearned for." Sam shook her head. Sometimes the depravity she saw on the job was almost too much to bear. "And now I have to go see her parents and explain this to them."

"I don't envy you that."

Worst part of the job, hands down, was dealing with the family members of homicide victims. That was why she wanted the grief group to further support those left behind.

Malone came around the corner from the lobby area.

Sam had thought he was in the observation room.

"The jury's back."

SAM TOLD HERSELF it didn't matter. She had work to do and would focus on that rather than obsessing about whether the jury had done the right thing and convicted Stahl. She'd know soon enough. Malone had asked if she wanted to be there when the verdict was read.

"Hell no," she'd replied. That son of a bitch had gotten as much time from her as he was ever going to get.

Rather than go to court, she picked up the phone and called Tara's mother, asking if she could come see them to update them on the case.

"Yes, of course. We'll be here."

"I'll be there shortly." She gathered her keys, phone and handheld radio before donning her coat. "Cruz! Let's go to Herndon."

He popped up from his cubicle and came trotting after her, working his way into a down parka as he went. "You heard the jury's in?"

"Yep."

Thankfully, he got the message that she didn't wish to talk about it and didn't mention it again on the torturous ride to Herndon. How anyone could stand to live so far from the action in the District was beyond her. They were almost there when Nick called.

Sam took the call while juggling the steering wheel and earning a glare from her passenger as the car swerved. "Hey."

"Samantha."

"Uh-oh. Why am I getting the full title?"

"Did you forget to tell me the jury is in?"

"Oh. That."

"Yeah, that. How're you doing?"

"Fine. I'm on my way to tell Tara's parents that her ex-boyfriend murdered her with the help of her assistant. Other than that, I'm great."

"Ugh. I'm sorry you have to do that."

"Someone's gotta do it."

"Listen, no matter what happens, I've got you covered. Okay?"

"That helps, thanks. If he's convicted, they say I have to do one of those victim impact things."

"I'll do it."

"What?"

"I. Will. *Do. It.* You don't have to go anywhere near him. I'll take care of it."

Sam's chest seemed to expand, allowing in more oxygen than she'd been able to handle since she'd been told she'd have to speak at the sentencing. "In case I forget to tell you later, you're the best husband I ever had."

He laughed as he always did when she said that. "As we both know, the bar was set exceptionally low."

"But you… You just take it to a whole other level every single day, and I'm so, so thankful for you."

"Right back atcha, babe. Don't worry about a thing. He's going to be convicted, and then I'll make sure he's sent away forever. You'll never have to see him again."

"That'd be really nice. How are things over there?"

"Still tense. It'll be better when you've announced the arrest of someone who is not the president."

Sam laughed at the way he said that. "We'll be announcing arrests soon and the whole world will be glad to hear it's not the president."

"Well, thank goodness for that. Jeez, that's such a huge relief."

"I know. Wait until you hear the whole story. You won't believe it."

"I'll look forward to hearing all about it. Let me know what you hear from the courthouse?"

"I will. I'm sorry I didn't call you when I heard the jury was back. I can't bear to even think about it."

"I get it. Believe me."

"I'll call as soon as I hear anything."

"Okay, babe. Hang in there. Love you."

"Love you too." Sam closed the phone quietly, taking a deep breath and giving thanks once again for whatever she'd done right in her life that had made her deserving of him.

"He's the best," Freddie said.

"He really is."

"You've got a whole lot of support behind you no matter what happens in court. I hope you know that."

Sam sent him a small smile. "I do. Thanks."

Freddie's phone chimed with a text. "Crime Scene found Tara's phone in one of the boxes in Bryce's car."

"That's awesome. Just another nail in Massey's coffin."

They arrived at the Weber's home a few minutes later and were met at the door by Mr. Weber.

"Come in." He led them to the kitchen, where Mrs. Weber held a bottle for the baby. Tara's parents looked exhausted and stressed. The last thing they'd probably expected at this point in their lives was to be raising their grandchild.

Sam's heart went out to them as she and Freddie sat with them at the table.

"Can I offer you coffee or something else to drink?" Mr. Weber asked.

"Thank you, but we're fine. And we have news for you. We've arrested Bryce and Delany in Tara's murder."

They both gasped with shock.

"What?" he asked. "That's not possible."

"I'm afraid it is." Sam took them through the whole thing, from Tara's breakup with Bryce to his hiring of

Delany to her confession and the charges that would soon be filed against them both.

"Delany let him in," Mr. Weber said, his face blank with shock. "She knew from the start it was him."

"I'm afraid so."

Mrs. Weber wept as she tended to the baby, who had big wise eyes and a sprinkling of dark hair. "He didn't want her, but he didn't want anyone else to have her either."

"I believe that's the case. I also think it's possible that your daughter had genuine feelings for President Nelson and thus her effort to get his attention by leaking the story of their affair."

"Which ultimately led to her death," Mr. Weber said.

"Yes. When Bryce found out she'd had the affair with Nelson and possibly borne him a child, he was outraged."

"She could've had anyone," Mr. Weber said in disbelief. "Anyone at all. Why in the world would she set her sights on the married president?"

"Only Tara could answer that question, and perhaps in her things you might find something that provides closure."

Her mother shook her head. "We won't. She didn't believe in journals or diaries or anything that could be found and used against her. She didn't trust easily, and for her to know that Delany had betrayed her would've been as bad for her as knowing Bryce was there to harm her."

"We're so sorry for her and for you and her son. We've taken DNA from Bryce and two other men, and as soon as we know who fathered him, we'll let you know."

"I don't want to know," Mrs. Weber said. "What difference will it make to us?"

"None, I suppose, but someday it might matter to him."

"That's true," Mr. Weber said.

"We're also obligated to inform the child's father, regardless of who that turns out to be."

"When you do, let him know we want nothing from him but the opportunity to raise the child our daughter loved with all her heart."

"I'll pass that along." Sam gazed at the adorable baby, who would someday have to learn the sordid tale of his mother's murder. "What's his name?"

"Jackson Henry," Mr. Weber said. "He's named for both his great-grandfathers."

"He's beautiful."

"He looks just like Tara did as a baby," Mrs. Weber said. "I'm so sad—and mad—that she won't get to see him grow up. She wanted him so badly." Her voice faltered and broke on a sob. "I'm sorry."

Sam reached over to put her hand on the other woman's shoulder. "There's no need to apologize. We will keep you informed as the case proceeds."

"Please do," Mr. Weber said. "We'll be there to represent our daughter." He got up to walk them out.

Sam handed him her card. "If there's anything I can do for you, don't hesitate to reach out."

"We appreciate what you've already done. Your reputation for being very good at your job is well deserved."

"In this case, the credit goes to the outstanding team I have working with me. They put the pieces together that led to the arrests."

"However it happened, we're thankful."

"I'll be in touch."

Sam and Freddie rode back to the city in silence until their phones chimed with a text.

"Convicted on all counts," Freddie said.

Sam took a deep breath and blinked back tears she refused to give in to.

Thank God.

Justice had been served—this time, for her.

EPILOGUE

"My name is Nick Cappuano, and I'm the proud husband of Metro Police Lieutenant Sam Holland. I want to tell you about the day that Leonard Stahl took my wife hostage, wrapped her in razor wire and threatened to set her on fire." He said the words in a matter-of-fact tone, but they still gave him chills even after all this time.

Because he was vice president, the networks were providing live coverage of the sentencing portion of Stahl's trial. It'd been one week since the conviction, during which Sam had barely spoken of it other than to express relief that it was over.

However, it wouldn't be over for her—or for them—until Stahl was sentenced to life in prison with no possibility of parole. That had been Nick's only goal as he'd prepared his remarks.

In the last week, they'd learned that Congressman Ben Wilton had fathered Tara's son, and that headline had pushed the Nelson affair news out of the headlines—for now anyway. Tara's reputation had taken a beating, but Sam had issued a statement supporting Tara's right to live her life however she wished to, and to judge her choices when she wasn't there to defend herself was unfair and disgusting.

Minute by minute, Nick took the jury through the horrifying details of the day Stahl had taken Sam hostage, telling the story from his point of view, starting with the reception he'd been attending in honor of his first day as vice president. "I was with our son Scotty, and we were waiting for Sam to join us at the White House. My chief of staff took a phone call from my former staffer, Christina Billings, who is engaged to Sam's colleague Sergeant Thomas Gonzales. That's how we heard that Sam was possibly being held hostage at the Springer home on MacArthur Boulevard. They weren't a hundred percent sure yet, because Sam had gone there alone, doubling back to close a loop with Mrs. Springer. I had to beg my new Secret Service detail to take me to what might've been an active crime scene. Needless to say, that took some doing. If I'd had to run there on foot, I would've done it because nothing in this world is more important to me than my wife and our children. Nothing.

"Much later, I read the report of what Sam's colleagues went through that day, tracking her down, figuring out what was going on and trying to get to her before it was too late. You've read the report and heard the testimony so you know that when they burst into that basement they found Sam wrapped in razor wire and Leonard Stahl about to ignite the gasoline he'd spread all around her.

"Imagine, if you will, what that must've been like for Sam, to know her body would be ripped to shreds if she so much as moved and a madman was about to set her on fire. I don't know about you, but to me, that's the sort of crime that life imprisonment was invented to deter. As it was, her colleagues got to her seconds before he would've set her on fire."

With his composure wavering, Nick took a deep breath, determined to get through this without becoming emotional. He refused to give that to Stahl, who'd probably relish it. He'd also refused to so much as glance in the direction of the disgraced lieutenant. "She was cut all over, from her neck to her feet and everywhere in between. She smelled of gasoline for a week. Do you know what my amazing wife did throughout Stahl's prolonged attack? She ignored him. She gave him *nothing*, not even when he wrapped her in razor wire and prepared to set her on fire. She gave him *nothing*.

"Do you have any idea what kind of courage she displayed that day while at the mercy of a man who hated her simply because her name was Holland? That's right. He was jealous of her father's successes and retaliated against Skip by making his daughter's life a living hell for every minute that she reported to him—and long after she replaced him as the lieutenant in charge of the department's Homicide Division. And he hated her for *her* successes. While he was in command of Homicide, the division closed seventy-five percent of its cases. Since Sam has led the division, their success rate is one hundred percent. A short time after she was nearly murdered by Leonard Stahl, she was back at work, fighting for justice on behalf of those who can't advocate for themselves. Because that's who she is.

"I'm in awe of her courage and tenacity every day, but on that day, on the day Leonard Stahl held her hostage, planning to murder her in the most gruesome way he could think of, my wife displayed the kind of courage few of us would have under the same circumstances. I'm always proud of her and how hard she works for justice on behalf of the victims of violent crime in our city, but I've never been prouder of her than I was the day she didn't let Leonard Stahl break her. She showed him he was *nothing* compared to her, he *is* nothing compared to her. He belongs in a jail cell for the rest of his life so he can never harm anyone again."

Having said his piece, Nick got up and left the room, aware of his Secret Service detail trailing him as they always did. Eager to get out of there and get home to his wife, he kept moving until he reached the curb where another agent waited with the door to his vehicle open and ready for him.

"Hey, sailor. Give a girl a ride home?"

Samantha.

He slid across the seat to her and took her into his arms, holding on tight to the love of his life. "This is a nice surprise."

"I figured it was the least I could do after you took one for the team." She drew back so she could see his face. "And PS, you were awesome."

"You saw it?"

She pointed to the dark screen on the back of the seat in front of her.

He curled a strand of her hair around his finger. "I thought you weren't going to watch."

"My hot, sexy husband was making a rather public declaration of how much he loves me. I couldn't bear to miss it. In fact, watching you just now sort of made the entire ordeal worthwhile."

"That can't possibly be true."

"You made it better. You make everything better."

"Thanks for surviving that day. I really appreciate it."

She shrugged. "I do what I can for the people." Curling her hand around his neck, she brought him in close enough to kiss. "Thank you for what you did today."

"I'd say it was a pleasure, but…"

"I love you madly."

"I love you more madly."

"No way."

"Yes way."

Smiling, he kissed her.

"Guess what else?"

He nuzzled her neck. "What's that?"

"The mayor was back to talking about parking and garbage issues today, which means she's *not* talking about how Joe Farnsworth needs to go. Instead, she's focused on helping him choose a new deputy chief."

"Well, that's a relief."

"Yeah. I just hope we can keep a lid on this situation with Gonzo. The last thing he or the chief need is for that to blow up into something."

"If anyone can protect them both, babe, it's you."

"I hope so." Sam smoothed the hair back from his forehead. "Did I tell you I took the whole day off?"

"That's funny because I did too."

"Does that mean we've got hours and hours and *hours* to kill before our kids come home from school?"

"It does." She ran a finger down the length of his navy blue tie. "You wanna hook up?"

"Yes, please."

With her lips close to his ear, she said, "Tell Brant to take us home."

* * * * *

Turn the page for a bonus epilogue...

BONUS EPILOGUE

THEY'D BILLED IT as a birthday party, but it was much more than that.

Shelby Faircloth stood in front of the full-length mirror in her bedroom, examining the blush gown that shimmered in the palest shade of pink when she moved. She smiled, pleased with the presence of her favorite color on the most important day of her life—a day she'd once thought would never happen.

She placed a hand over her belly, where she harbored another secret—the baby she and Avery would welcome in seven months.

Her heart was full to overflowing. She had everything she'd ever dreamed of, and today, on her forty-fourth birthday, she'd marry the love of her life.

Shelby's sister Ginger came into the room, her eyes bright with excitement. She carried three bouquets of flowers, one with white roses, gardenias and hydrangeas for Shelby, and two with colorful blooms for Ginger and their other sister, Monica. They were the only other two who knew what today was about.

Avery planned to ask his brother Josh to be his best man—at the last minute.

It was all so exciting. After a career planning other people's weddings, the last thing she wanted for herself was an elaborate, over-the-top production that would've taken time she didn't have to plan. A small, intimate gathering at home was her idea of the perfect way to make things official between them.

They'd traveled a winding, difficult route to get to this day, and with the hard times now far behind them, she looked forward to everything they'd have together.

Ginger handed Shelby her bouquet that was held together with pink ribbon and fussed over Shelby's dress until she was satisfied that everything was where it belonged. As the oldest of the three, Ginger had always mothered Shelby and Monica, and they let her because Ginger loved them so much.

"You're stunning. The dress is perfect. The man is perfect. Everyone is here and looking for the birthday girl. Are you ready?"

"I just need to get Noah up from his nap, and then I will be." The festivities had been planned around his nap time.

"I'll get him."

"He'll need to be changed."

Ginger laughed. "Yes, I know." She had her own kids, who were now nearly grown, but she hadn't forgotten the basics.

"Will you tell Dad to come up?"

"Yep. He's gonna cry."

"I know."

"Don't mess up your makeup."

"I won't."

God forbid, Shelby thought. They'd been taught from an early age to always be presentable and put together. Today, she wanted to be beautiful for the man who'd changed her life so completely. By the time she met him, she'd given up on ever finding her Mr. Right, and then there he was, so beautifully handsome he took her breath away and when he spoke to her in that South Carolinian accent, well… He could have just about anything he wanted.

A knock sounded on the door before her dad, Davis, walked in. "Ginger said you wanted to see me."

Shelby turned to him, and he stopped dead in his tracks.

His face softened into a sweet smile. "What're you up to, Shelby Lynne?"

"It seems I'm getting married on my birthday, and I wondered if you might be willing to give away one more daughter."

He placed his hand over his heart. "You sure do know how to take your daddy's breath away."

"Is that a yes?"

Davis closed the distance between them, placed his hands on her shoulders and leaned in to kiss her forehead. "It'd be my honor, honey."

Ginger came in with Noah, who'd been changed into the light blue dress shirt and tiny khaki pants Shelby had laid out for him to wear to his parents' wedding. He let out a happy squeak at the sight of his mother.

Shelby took him from her sister and kissed his chubby cheek. "Are you ready, buddy?"

He replied with the baby chatter she loved so much.

She handed Noah back to her sister and tucked her hand into her father's arm. "Shall we?"

"By all means," Davis said.

AVERY HAD BEEN on pins and needles all day, hoping their surprise wedding would go off without a hitch so Shelby would have the best birthday ever. All he needed to be happy was for her and Noah to be happy. And to know their little threesome would soon become a foursome was like the sweetest pink frosting on his beloved's birthday cake. He'd ordered two cakes—one for her birthday and one for their wedding—both done in tasteful shades of pink.

He'd like to think he could be trained, and by now, he understood that the color pink would play a big role in his life with Shelby.

That was fine with him. In her he'd found a woman who loved with all her heart and soul, who gave everything she had to the people she cared about, and he knew he was so damned lucky that she loved him— that she still loved him, even after everything he'd put her through.

She'd made him a better man. She'd made him *want to be* a better man. She'd made him a father by allowing him to play such an important role in her son's life, and he'd never again take her or what they'd found together for granted.

As he watched her start down the stairs on the arm of her father, heading toward the living room where their families and closest friends had gathered, he switched the music from the classic rock he'd had playing to the traditional wedding march that let everyone in the room know this wasn't going to be your average birthday party.

Avery tuned out everyone who wasn't his Shelby so he wouldn't miss a second of this life-changing moment in which she came toward him, her gaze fixed on his. Around them, he could hear the startled gasps of their guests and their excited whispers. Cell phone camera flashes flickered all around them, but he didn't so much as blink while she took the final steps to join him.

When she smiled, his heart gave a happy lurch.

Her sister Ginger handed Noah to him, as they'd planned ahead of time.

He and Shelby wanted their son with them when they pledged their hearts and lives to each other.

The judge he'd asked to perform the ceremony came into the room from Avery's home office where he'd asked the man to wait until they were ready. With everyone else in position, he tipped his head toward his brother Josh, asking him to come to the front of the room.

Josh smiled and moved to stand beside Avery and Noah.

In the group, he found his onetime crush, Sam Holland Cappuano, standing next to her husband the vice president, both of them now his close friends. The madness of his attraction to Sam seemed like a lifetime ago since he'd put it behind him to focus exclusively on the woman who would soon be his wife.

He would be forever thankful to Sam and Nick for bringing Shelby into his life.

Davis escorted his daughter to the spot they'd chosen in front of the fireplace that cast a warm, cozy glow over the room full of the people they loved the best. Davis hugged and kissed his daughter and shook Avery's hand.

"Take good care of my little girl."

"Always."

Davis nodded and turned to join his wife and the rest of their family.

Avery's parents were close by too, and with all the

most important people in place, Avery turned his full attention to Shelby.

"You're exquisite," he whispered.

"You're not so bad yourself."

Noah tried to grab his mother's hair, and Avery averted disaster by shifting the little guy to the opposite hip. Then he offered his free hand to Shelby and nodded for the justice of the peace to do his thing.

They'd decided on simple, traditional vows that were exchanged efficiently. When it came time for the rings, Avery handed Noah to his uncle Josh and found the rings in his pocket. He handed his to Shelby and then slid the one they'd chosen for her onto her finger. "With this ring, I thee wed."

Her hand trembled ever so slightly as she put his ring on. She looked up at him. "With this ring, I thee wed."

"I now pronounce you husband and wife. Avery, you may kiss your bride."

Since there was nothing he'd rather do than kiss his bride, he wrapped his arms around her and kissed her until Noah squeaked in protest at being ignored by his parents.

They broke apart laughing, and Avery took Noah from his brother.

As planned, the judge once again asked for everyone's attention. "It is also my honor today to certify the adoption of Noah Faircloth Hill by his daddy, Avery. I declare Shelby, Avery and Noah an official family. May the Hill family live together in peace and love for the rest of their lives."

Everyone in the room was in tears as they cheered for the family he and Shelby had created together.

And as she smiled up at him with tears in her eyes,

he had everything he'd ever dreamed of and more than he'd ever dared to wish for.

* * * * *

Do you want MORE Sam and Nick?
Go to Marie's website at marieforce.com/fatal
to read a bonus short story and some frequently asked
questions and answers about the series!

ACKNOWLEDGMENTS

THANK YOU FOR reading *Fatal Accusation*! I hope you enjoyed being back with Sam, Nick and their crew for book 15. I want to also thank you for the amazing comments, posts and messages about *Fatal Reckoning*. I was so touched by the outpouring of love for Skip, Sam and me after that book, which touched so close to home. I never imagined Sam and I would go through losing our dads together, but that's what happened and my lovely readers were there for me—and for Sam. Thanks for that.

Join the Fatal Accusation Reader Group at www.facebook.com/groups/FatalAccusation/ to discuss this new book with spoilers allowed and encouraged. And join the Fatal Series Reader Group (no spoilers please) at www.facebook.com/groups/FatalSeries/ to be among the first to hear the latest series news.

A huge thank-you to all the people who make it possible for me to do what I love: my husband, Dan, and my HTJB team: Julie Cupp, Lisa Cafferty, Holly Sullivan and Nikki Colquhoun, as well as my amazing publicist, Jessica Estep. Thank you to my HQN editors Allison Carroll and Alissa Davis, and my longtime beta readers Anne Woodall and Kara Conrad. As always, my appreciation goes to Newport Police Captain Russell Hayes (retired), for his input into each of the Fatal books. Special thanks to my fantastic "last line of defense" Fatal beta readers: Jennifer, Sarah, Julianne, Betty, Gina, Sheri, Marianne, Jenny, Viki, Mona, Maricar, Irene, Tiffany, Kelley, Martha, Isabel, Karina and Phuong.

And to the readers who love Sam and Nick so much... My profound gratitude for embracing this series over the last nine and a half years and making it so fun to write. Much more to come!

xoxo

Marie